Philip First is the author of the novel *The Great Pervader* and a collection of short stories entitled *Paper Thin*. He lives in London.

GW00507544

By the same author

The Great Pervader
Paper Thin (short stories)

PHILIP FIRST

Dark Night

*The Gospel According to the
Late Adam Shatt*

PALADIN
GRAFTON BOOKS

A Division of the Collins Publishing Group

LONDON GLASGOW
TORONTO SYDNEY AUCKLAND

Paladin
Grafton Books
A Division of the Collins Publishing Group
8 Grafton Street, London W1X 3LA

A Paladin Paperback Original 1989

Copyright © Philip First 1989

ISBN 0-586-08671-4

Printed and bound in Great Britain by
Collins, Glasgow

Set in Korrina

All rights reserved. No part of this publication may
be reproduced, stored in a retrieval system, or
transmitted, in any form, or by any means, electronic,
mechanical, photocopying, recording or otherwise,
without the prior permission of the publishers.

This book is sold subject to the condition that it
shall not, by way of trade or otherwise, be lent,
re-sold, hired out or otherwise circulated
without the publisher's prior consent in any
form of binding or cover other than that in
which it is published and without a similar
condition including this condition being imposed
on the subsequent purchaser.

The Appendix, *The Simile of the Cave*, is taken from PLATO: THE
REPUBLIC translated by Desmond Lee (Penguin Classics, 1955, 1974,
1987). Copyright © H. D. P. Lee 1955, 1974, 1987. Reproduced by
permission of Penguin Books Ltd.

For
Elizabeth

Part One

'A man came to me recently saying, Master, what must I do to be truly a success in this life? I told him, Keep breathing.'

Iddio E. Scompiglio.

Red snow falls silently at night. Lies like sleep's conjuring over mountain, city and plain.
All is mystery. Enter a plaything.

Adam's nightmare, which was really only just beginning, had taken on its own life and was giving no indication of ever letting up. It kept him forever on the edge, meaning he had not slept easily in months.

It gave him infrequent minimal variations, a detail slipping in here seemingly at random, slipping out again, maybe unnoticed. But the basic elements were unchanging: he was running from something, always running, and he was frightened for his life.

Night ran into night and it would bring him from sleep like a cat with a banger on its tail. And on his feet in darkness he would know the beast was close at hand. It swept his trail with its snout to the ground, snarling, snuffling, moving towards him through the undergrowth. And he was blind.

Seeing nothing he was afraid to move, so one hand would stretch forward trembling, then two. Perspiration gathered and ran down his spine. He leaned forward, everything gone silent now, and his fingertips made contact.

They brushed, patted, and he found confidence as somewhere, vanquishing the expectation of snapping, tearing, furied jaws and the impulse to flee, came a disorienting thought. Something recognizable, something familiar. *This has happened before.*

His hands explored further and he edged a step forward, his fear now beginning to recede. The beast was no longer present. There was nothing there. But where, then, could it have gone?

A voice spoke and he froze. He could not tell from which

direction it had originated, but there had been other times like this.

'Adam!'

His hands moved agitatedly. 'It's gone under the covers!'

'Adam!'

'Ssshh!'

He waited, bewildered, half-knowing what would happen next. The sudden dazzling light. It came out of the dream, making him screw up his eyes, and as they adjusted the room took form around him.

'Adam, it's all right.' Judith sat up in bed. 'You're dreaming again.'

Again.

He stared, at her then at his hands spread wide on the duvet.

'Come on, get back into bed.'

When he climbed in beside her, terribly cold, she held him and stroked his hair. After a little while she asked, 'All right now?'

He nodded and she rolled away for a moment to return the room to blackness. She snuggled against him and he lay on his back, thinking, stealing her body's heat, still very ill at ease in the residue of his terror. Judith's breathing grew deeper and more even and her warmth began to relax his limbs. He was slowly sinking and wondering whether this was a break in the nightmare or a subtle protraction of it, because the red snow was starting to fall.

He watched and it drifted hazily across his vision, falling on a landscape he could not place. He grew gradually conscious of his merging with it, finding no passion to resist, until the cold prickle of snowflakes on his skin, the taste of them on his tongue, were the only messages his senses conveyed. He floated downwards in the gently swirling, drifting snowclouds, unafraid now as he was drawn into the calming dispersion of sleep.

Doctor Geld, the consultant psychiatrist whom the late Adam Shatt had long since ceased to consult, had assured him countless times that his was a relatively normal reaction to a 'really not-so-normal occurrence in a person's life'.

Not enough is known, he had emphasized, still, in this day and age, for a clear-cut prognosis to be possible on my – or anybody's – part. But as Adam was certainly aware, dreams, nightmares, hallucinatory fantasies ... experiences of this province are far from uncommon in an average person's life. Everyone has nightmares from time to time and they can be disturbing. But they are not to be unduly worried about. And if in Adam's case they were a little more, ah, vivid, a little more frequent, a little more disruptive than for others, well, it was to be expected, wasn't it? After all, he had suffered extreme trauma. His mind had been affected at least as much as his body. It would take time for everything to settle down.

But settle down it would. He believed that.

And in the meantime – affecting an inspirited air of buoyancy more suited to a youthful cleric than a supposedly dignified middle-aged mental health practitioner – in the meantime, *do not be too distressed.*

This was during Adam's days as a hospital out-patient, visiting Doctor Geld on a twice-weekly basis at his Marylebone clinic. It was not his personal choice, nor with foreknowledge would it have been, but it was accepted that he had to see somebody, and Geld, appointed through circumstances beyond the control of either of them, was that somebody.

Troubles other than nightmares had brought the late Adam Shatt to the psychiatrist's consulting-room. The nightmares, or more precisely, night*mare* – for this was still the period during which everything focussed on the one recurring theme – was only an indication amongst indications of something far more encompassing. But Doctor Geld, with the zeal of an experimental biologist contemplating a fluffy white rabbit and a gleaming scalpel, was at this stage drawn to the constituent parts.

The condition of Adam presented something of a mystery to professional and layperson alike. Established beyond doubt was the fact that it was progressive; a process of psychological degeneration was underway which was causing the patient to part company by degrees with all recognizable forms of spatial, temporal and causal awareness. But beyond that lay a diagnostic void, a forbidding series of questions yielding a paucity of answers.

For Adam himself the greater part of his day-to-day existence had been reduced to psychotic chaos. Periods of lucidity began to lose their identity in a reality that changed face without warning. His attention turned increasingly inwards and his nightmare became his obsession, for somewhere within it, he had come to believe, must lie the clues that would deliver him to an understanding of his condition.

He sensed his withdrawal from the world, and his growing inability to communicate effectively with others. Nevertheless, though anxious to get to the root of his problems, he began deliberately to turn less and less to others for advice and opinions. Others, demonstrably, could not know what he was experiencing. Their help, he reasoned, could therefore be of only limited value.

To make matters worse he had been subject from the outset to a lack of affinity for his psychiatrist.

Adam fostered doubts about certain aspects of the doctor's methodology. Hearing only the whispers of his over-sensitive inner world, for example, he was led to question the good doctor's objectivity. Geld's objective approach, his unswerving dedication to the cause, his undisguised fascination with the effect, suggested itself to Adam's mind as an obstacle to progress. Concerning himself with the clinical symptoms, the observable details and minutiae of his patient's case, encouraged, Adam felt, a waning empathy with Adam himself, serving only to nourish an already prospering sense of alienation.

This in turn made him wonder about the doctor's integrity. He could never fully rid himself of the notion that Geld's efforts were not being directed solely for the benefit of his patient. Where his motives might lie Adam could not begin to imagine, and was careful not to dwell too deeply on it, being fully aware of the places that kind of thinking might lead him.

Outside of Adam's world Doctor Geld was a brilliant man. A skilled surgeon in his younger years, he had turned his talents to the mental sciences, a lifelong interest, in which he rose rapidly to a position of eminence. He was known professionally across nations, his inspirational and sometimes controversial ideas having excited the imaginations of his contemporaries in many lands. He had his share of detractors, too, inevitably, but they were in the minority. On the whole he enjoyed a growing and glowing reputation as a man who had contributed immensely, and had much yet to give, to the fields of mental health.

In general he preferred to shun the limelight his accomplishments might have placed within his grasp, claiming little time outside of his work in its varied aspects. He spoke of his work almost as a personal crusade demanding paramountcy over other forms of diversion in his life.

He was recognized as a versatile man, to date the author of nine seminal volumes. His subject matter took in the pathology of memory phenomena and the nature of electrical activity in the brain, studies in cerebro-cranial microsurgery, hysteria and auto- and hypnotic suggestion, the future of psychiatry and more. He had produced books dealing with micro-chip technology and artificial intelligence, and he had also published two novels and critiques on the lives and works of George Cantor and John Milton.

Physically he cut a wholly unremarkable figure, slight in stature, angular, narrow-skulled and bald. His baldness was accentuated to the observer's eye by a dense, dark mass of hair that ran hedge-like around the back and sides of his head. This hedge was prevented from uniting with his eyebrows to form a complete circle around his crown by a break of about an inch or so at each temple. And the eyebrows were in fact normally one, a thick, dull, black, ragged-edged bar shading small, penetrating brown eyes.

He was an archetype, a caricature. A parchy, unmarried professorial figure in his mid-forties who wore heavy, black-rimmed bifocals which rested uneasily on the bridge of his nose. He favoured ill-fitting, ill-pressed suits: worsted or tweed, in sober shades with perhaps an unexpressive check or stripe. Shoes, shirts and ties followed a similar trend, or lack of it, and his only concessions to ostentation were a gold monogrammed signet ring and, sometimes, a brightly patterned handkerchief poking from the breast pocket of his jacket. Of central European lineage, years of living in London had not erased his accent, which did nothing to improve his standing in Adam's eyes.

In truth Doctor Geld was a sincere believer in the correctness of the course he was pursuing in Adam's case. It was tried, and inasmuch as matters of mental healing can ever be, trusted. It was the way he knew best.

He was genuine too in his desire to aid Adam on the long road to complete recovery. He maintained a personal interest in the case, and in the late Adam Shatt himself.

The doctor's method when alone with his patient had always been to lend an avuncular ear, inviting, lucidity permitting, the kind of intimate disclosures that might have remained tight-sealed to a more immediate relative. An orthodox enough approach, but to Adam's mind, said disclosures being success-fully elicited, he did his utmost to disregard them. He evinced an almost extraordinary talent for evading or dismissing a particular point Adam was struggling to put across. And his sense of humour, nervous and often inappropriate, at times verged close on derision.

Doctor Geld: More than a dream? What do you mean when you say it is *more* than a dream?

Adam: I don't know. That's why I'm discussing it. I'd hoped you would tell me.

But you are convinced that it has some kind of significance to something in your past? And, you say, even to your future. Can you tell me what it is that makes you so certain of this?

Adam couldn't. It was a feeling, that was all. *It was instinct.*

Doctor Geld had crooked one index finger pensively beneath his nose at that. He had leaned back in his big, winged and studded, burgundy leather-upholstered chair. After a moment or two the hand had dropped. It had taken up a position in his lap and he had grinned. His grin was an adornment that could appear at any time, punctuating conversation with little respect for congruity. It was a wide, polyodontal, open rictus grin which could spread at its widest across a face that seemed too narrow to contain it.

With the grin fully manifest the doctor's rear fillings became evident. And in the adumbrous area between them a glistening purplish tongue would move, to Adam's eyes like a fat slug peering myopically from the interior of a cave.

In instances of genuine amusement the doctor would augment his grin with bursts of staccato laughter: Ah! Ah-ha! Ah-ha-ha! The effect, as if Doctor Geld were taken in the throes of sudden spasm, could disconcert the uninitiated. It no longer disconcerted Adam, it merely made him look away.

The doctor had brought his upper torso forward again. His arms slid across the top of his walnut desk to form a baggy loop, fingers linked. Grin still intact, he had adopted a faintly conspiratorial air: Tell me again about the dream.

But telling was one on a long list of things Adam could not do. That dream which so dominated his conscious and unconscious lives left him with so few details of its nature. It brought him from sleep then vanished into the sealed vaults of his memory, leaving little more than a chaos of emotion and a lingering dread of . . . past? Present? Future? He knew not what.

Try to put a finger on some part of it, the doctor had urged. Try to get to the root of this feeling you have about it. Try to *recall*.

Adam tried. All the time, in therapy and out. But like every other aspect of his personal history it resisted him.

Tabula rasa.

Carte blanche?

'Then tell me again about the red snow.'

The red snow was a more recent element. He could not recall having encountered it in the earliest days. Though independent of the original sequence he had now come to accept the two as inseparable. And it was one certainty that remained available to him after sleep.

He could say that the original sequence involved a hunt, himself pursued by something monstrous. Real-world circumstances had lately half-convinced him it was a huge dog, but he saw nothing, was always in darkness and awoke at the moment of attack.

With the red snow came a particular, focusless emotion. Drawn back towards sleep he was made aware of what, for want of a readily applicable term, he described to his psychiatrist as 'a kind of prescient sorrow'. By this he said he meant that he was filled with a sense of loss, of grieving without knowing why. He said there was a feeling of something pervasive and tragic, of moving towards something, of something impending, inevitable, even necessary. It was as if the sorrow had to be experienced before something else might be understood.

Trying to explain more clearly Adam compared it to the

emotion felt by two people deeply in love who are forced to part for an unknown length of time. A painful separation made necessary in order to benefit others as well as themselves, with the consoling knowledge that their eventual reunion, whenever it might be, must be the more joyful and fulfilling because of it. Precisely why he should make such associations he was at a loss to say. In more objective moments he would dismiss it for its sentimentality. Nevertheless, the recalling of it, even in session, was enough to evoke an echo of the same haunting emotion.

'There's nothing more I can tell you,' he had said. 'That's really all there is to it. It's a vision. Red snow falling. I feel it has a meaning. I don't know what.'

Doctor Geld was taking notes. He waited, and his silence asked, 'And that is it?'

Adam had nodded dispiritedly. That day had brought him to the consulting-room with a feeling of anticipation and optimism. Since his last visit his mind had created for him a delusion, no rare thing, conjuring an image of Doctor Geld as a worker of miracles. It had presented the doctor as The Man With The Answers, a man gifted with a clarity of vision and a natural expertise that would enable him to penetrate to the source of Adam's dilemma. He would reach into Adam's mind, reassemble the fragments of his personality and return him whole to an ordered, harmonious, comprehensible universe.

As on previous occasions the big world had delivered its numbing blow halfway up the stairs. At the sound of Doctor Geld's voice, muted through the half-closed reception-room door, and the faint aroma-aura of naphthalene and furniture wax, he had remembered how low the esteem in which he actually held the man.

'It is not very much to build a house on,' Doctor Geld had remarked. 'These details ... these, ah, lack of details. They are the sum total of what you are basing your conviction on?'

The doctor, it seemed, had not heard what Adam was saying.

Amongst his colleagues, amongst Adam's family, and even with Adam himself, Doctor Geld had been persuasive in his opinion that occlusion was the key to Adam's illness. His mind was not irretrievably lost. His personality remained intact, so to speak, *in potentia*, but buried by a sudden uncontrolled influx of distorted, unsifted information and vivid hallucinatory impressions erupting from his subconscious. If this could be checked, he maintained, and a way cleared through the existing material, then it should be possible to return Adam to the surface functioning normally.

He had once sought to lighten his patient's darkness by way of a simile. Adam's mind he had likened to an attic room now filled to overflowing with unwanted junk.

'We don't really know how it got there, or why,' he had said, 'and its origins can only really be guessed at. But the fact is that it has piled up inside this beautiful, spacious room and is preventing the room from being utilized to its best advantage. And what is more, it is continuing to accumulate. It clutters up the landing outside and has even begun to creep down the stairs!'

Doctor Geld had laughed sharply to himself – 'ah-ha!' – his eyes on Adam, alert to his response, before going on: 'So what should we do? I shall tell you what I think we must do. We should find the most efficient way of removing it all. Throw it all out. And at the same time we should take care to examine every item to see if it might be of any value. And we should take careful measures too, to ensure that no more is brought in. Once we have achieved this – and I believe it can be done – the room will be as new. Pristine and sparkling again. Perhaps even better than before.' He chuckled. 'No longer merely an attic room but a veritable penthouse studio! Ha-ha!'

The doctor had settled back between his wide leather wings. Adam was puzzled. Was this not what he was trying to do by giving Doctor Geld the details, however sketchy, of his nightmare? Was this not what he had tried to do in hospital, describing his mental impressions, his confusion?

He had mentioned his growing disaffection to Judith that evening. As on other occasions she had tried to reassure him. She had reminded him of the doctor's past record, his successes, the position he held amongst his colleagues. Later she had given him a couple of Doctor Geld's books to browse through, and with patience and tact had confronted him with the irrationality of his feelings, helped him to see them as simply an additional symptom of his overall condition. Adam could not deny the logic of her argument, and for a time had been partially mollified.

But now the doctor was telling him again in almost accusatory tones that the details of the dream upon which he laid such store were so meagre as to be virtually worthless. He was belittling, it seemed, his attempts to understand and rationalize the chaos that afflicted him, implying that he was misguided in his approach. Further feelings of animosity began to arise.

Doctor Geld was watching him intently. 'But you know what happened,' he reminded him. 'You have been given all the details relating to your accident.'

He favoured the term 'accident', though whether it was a euphemism couched with regard for Adam's sensibilities or his own it was difficult to say.

'You have spoken to a great many people. You have all the newspaper clippings, video recordings . . .'

All incontrovertible facts. Judith had dutifully cut out and saved the news reports. Three British squaddies had been shot dead that night, two others taking serious injuries. Out of the blood and darkness had come a hero: ENGLISH JOURNALIST SUR-VIVES IRA MASSACRE. The press had made Adam, still coma-tose in an army hospital bed, a very popular human being.

He had read those reports time and again throughout his convalescence. He had studied the television news coverage that Judith had saved on tape, read his own shorthand notes on the events leading up to the 'accident'. He had grilled numerous persons in the hope of stimulating some inner response. To no avail.

'I can't explain it. I'm aware of how unsound it must appear to you, but to me it's important. I'm bound up in all this and I can't extricate myself from it. I *have* to investigate it because it demands that I do. All of that . . . I don't remember it. It doesn't mean a thing to me.'

'Of course, I understand this.' The doctor put down the gold Parker with which he'd been writing and began lightly probing his bald crown with the pad of a bony second finger. He looked shrewdly at Adam over the rim of his spectacles, but in his eyes there was a definite twinkle. The finger descended to push the spectacles back to the bridge of his nose.

'Let me put something to you – and I hope you will accept this in the spirit in which it is intended. Let me ask you a question. Is it your suspicion then, that your wife, your family, your friends and former colleagues, the newspapers, television and – ha-ha! Heaven forbid! – even your psychiatrist are not being honest with you? Are you of the opinion that everything is fabrication?'

Doctor Geld paused for a moment for effect. Then his thick black eyebrow revealed itself in its true glory. It shot skywards with startling mobility and divided in two high up on his wrinkling forehead. At the same time he threw his body back into his chair. His laughter came out in sharp, dry spurts like the sound of automatic gunfire.

His eyes had filled suddenly with water. His grin filled the lower half of his face and his limbs had stiffened. His entire being seemed convulsed with mirth.

Adam had been caught unawares. He stared at him in confusion then looked away.

'No. No. You must not take me seriously,' the doctor had wheezed. One hand clutched his belly, the other waved weakly towards his patient. 'Forgive me. Ha-ha! It was a little joke – ha-ha-ah! – I could not pass by. Please. Don't be alarmed.'

He collected himself, fumbling in his breast pocket for a violently scarlet-spotted yellow handkerchief with which he dabbed his eyes. Then he re-folded it fastidiously and returned it. He picked up his Parker.

In the brief silence that followed Adam grew conscious that the doctor was actually waiting for an answer. He was aware, too, that behind Doctor Geld's show of jocularity a shrewd and calculating intellect was at work. The question had been loaded, the laughter a screen. He found himself prompted into uneasy laughter, far too late. It sounded hollow and obsequious.

'No, I don't think that. Of course I don't.'

'No. Of course you don't.' The doctor was scribbling notes again. His grin had shrunk to half its previous size.

'Let me be at pains to point out,' he said at length, laying the pen carefully on the desk in front of him, 'that I am by no means discounting the possibility, even the likelihood, that there is indeed something of significance in your dream – to yourself if not – ha-ha! – exactly the world at large! You have raised it enough times for me to be inclined towards that view. But even if this is the case it seems quite evident from what you have been able to tell me, and from what you have not – equally important – that your conscious mind, that is, the everyday, thinking, perceiving, analytical part of you, is not yet sufficiently, ah, restored, shall we say, to fully reopen its portals and allow that information to enter. The chamber of consciousness, for the time being, is not the place for such information to be.'

He had smiled reassuringly. But Adam's mind was shifting and he had barely heard. The smile, he thought, was intended for someone else.

'It will come, I'm confident of that. But only at its own time, and that's not something that can be predicted or decided by you, me, or anyone else. We like to speak of "your" mind or "my" mind, but the fact is that the human mind reveals itself to be a curiously autonomous phenomenon. It defies rationalization and to a frustrating degree, investigation. It is the possessor rather than the possessed. It is a mystery, covering itself with every turn and twist. Each time we discover some new facet of its nature we discover too that there is a vast' – he spread his arms – 'vast, *vast* territory still hidden from us. The Law of Diminishing Advances I call it. Ha-ha! For every yard gained another square mile of unexplored terrain becomes apparent. And if you want my honest opinion, the mind's true nature is such that it will always remain a mystery to us. As we explore it expands. I personally consider it the *tremendum mysterium*, the greatest mystery of all, known intimately only to God.'

For a second the doctor looked uncertain, then his brow cleared. He chuckled briefly as if at some private joke.

'So you must be patient. You must be a patient patient! and not try to force it. That will not help at all. The worst thing you can do is get yourself all worked up into a tizzy over it.'

'I'd just like to know what's happening to me,' Adam said. 'I'd just like a little peace of mind.'

'Ah, peace of mind . . .' Unbeknown to Adam he was facing a man who had devoted most of his life to a search for the very same thing, who had arrived, with the first finger of middle age beckoning from an encroaching horizon, at the hard-won conclusion that, in this world at least, no such condition was attainable.

The doctor's inevitable acceptance of this had at the time sent tremors through the very bedrock of his religious conviction. A devout Christian, he had found himself pitched headlong into a prolonged period of tortured introspection. In the final analysis his faith had proved too deeply rooted to be seriously undermined in such a manner, but it took a sound hammering. When he re-emerged he was shaken, still a God-fearing Christian citizen, but now his thoughts were darkly tinged by an evolving cynicism.

Doctor Geld's prime dilemma from that day, dealing as he was with persons of unsound mind, was one of duty. Was his new belief – correction, *knowledge* – something to be imparted to those unfortunates who came to him seeking release from life's problems? Was his therapy best effected with this at its core? He might conceivably spare his patients years of fruitless soul-searching, a lifetime of wasted endeavour, but at what cost? Better, perhaps, to leave them intent upon their quest, hopefully never to reach its end.

When Doctor Geld knelt and bowed his head in prayer this was a question he put most often to his Creator.

In Adam's case, though, he had skirted the issue. Evincing his profession's customary mistrust of specifics and combining it with a fondness for technical imperspicuity, he had applied himself to a lengthy monologue. His intention, ostensibly, was to enlighten Adam, to provide him with valuable insight into his condition. But his speech was peppered with such myriad psychiatric vaguenesses as to leave Adam with the impression once more that he was speaking rather for his own benefit, or for the benefit of some person or persons unseen.

Adam had therefore listened with largely uncomprehending ears as his doctor touched upon such arcane factors as experience-association, compensation and repression, primary and secondary elaboration and post-traumatic shock-syndrome. He heard him from a distance, loving tones dwelling on intra-cortical conflict, selective mechanisms, neuro-psychic organization and more. At the close he was left with a sensation of utter estrangement. The doctor seemed to be treating him as a colleague, or one of his own students, assuming connections between them that did not exist.

Done expounding, Doctor Geld had linked his fingers around one knee, rocking gently back and forth. His grin was so wide and yellow-toothed and final now as to suggest that the problem was virtually solved. Adam had terms now. A variety of terms: some in another language. He could apply them to his nightmares as and when he was disturbed. Day, night, any time. And they, by their very application, would serve to resolve his conflict.

And he had the doctor's reassurance that, when the time was most favourable, all was going to work out to its best advantage.

On top of that he had his medication.

Ergo, it seemed the doctor was saying from behind those shining lenses, ergo, why not just run along now and leave me to get on with my work. Until our next session.

In Adam's eyes Doctor Geld was an anachronism, a representative of an old school too proud to acknowledge what might lie beyond its own walls, and too stiff to lie down graciously, and too afraid to keep silence. Which was one reason why he left the consulting-room that day believing he had dispensed with the doctor's services. One reason too for his rarely bothering any more with his medication. On more than one occasion since he had come close, though not quite close enough, to taking the phial and flushing its contents down the lavatory.

The late Adam Shatt, disillusioned and three-parts deranged, was opting for an alternative to proffered assistance. Deciding that there never would be a next session he left his psychiatrist delving and discarding in an attic filled with useless junk, driven personally to pursue another course of enquiry. He was lurching forward blindly, all sails unfurled, into the storm-filled night of his senses. He felt he had no choice now but to do it alone.

Flesh

It was five A.M. and he had gone out to the wall. His gloved hands lay on the damp cold brick and his knees were half-bent as he listened tensely and peered into the darkness on the other side. A heavy mist lay over the world, further obscuring his vision, and the still air held the silence and suspension of a tomb.

Minutes earlier his phantoms had invaded his sleep to leave him like wreckage in their flight. He'd crawled into Judith's arms

23

and lain for long minutes listening to the sound of her breathing, the laboured tick of the battery alarm and the urgent beating of his own heart.

He didn't hear the sound outside. The first flakes of red snow had begun their slow drift across his vision, frozen mountains forming in the darkness behind. He was at the borderline of sleep, but he sensed rather than felt Judith's body stiffen, and was immediately awake, knowing the dog had whined.

And he had fought back the desire not to respond. Sleep now was so tempting but he knew that to succumb would bring him no peace. The process, already in motion, demanded his participation. Gently disengaging himself from his wife's arms he'd switched on the bedside lamp and left the bed. Judith's eyes half-opened for a second then she turned over, pulling the duvet up to cover her shoulders without protest.

He put on trousers, thick socks, shirt and a woollen jumper and went upstairs. From a hall cupboard he got a scarf and gloves, and boots and a flak jacket for protection from wet grass and dripping leaves and branches, for it had rained quite heavily during the night. Then he went out through the kitchen onto the balcony that overlooked the back garden.

It was cold, October dwindling into November, and there was not a breath of wind. At the end of the garden he could make out the shapes of trees through the murk, standing like patient giants. Two limes, one ancient leaning horse chestnut, their topmost branches, breaking free of the mist, more easily defined against the dark sky.

Adam paused there to listen, and waited. Above him, above the mist, a yellowish rectangle of light flicked on in an attic window. Sleep-slurred voices, their words indistinct, reached him. From some distance away he heard the deadened rumble of a heavy goods lorry as it travelled north on empty roads. A sparrow chirruped briefly in one of the trees, then fell silent again. He caught the subdued clatter of early morning breakfast preparations in a neighbour's house.

A movement below him and to his left drew his eye. A sleek, smoke-grey cat padding along the top of the garden wall. It seemed to grow aware that it was being observed for it stopped, one paw suspended, and glanced back at him over its shoulder.

Then it moved on and vanished beneath a tangle of elder branches.

Adam breathed in deeply and nervously. These moments had an eerie, ethereal quality. Not for the first time he had the sensation of being sole witness to a slowly awakening world.

He descended the dozen steps to the garden. The maisonette he and Judith owned was an example of the self-consciously iconoclastic conversions that were virtually *de rigueur* in the late sixties and early seventies: the kitchen and living quarters were upstairs, bedrooms and bathrooms below − so he stepped carefully past the window to avoid disturbing his wife further.

The garden was a twenty-five-yard long rectangle, the width of the five-storey terrace house. It was bounded by a brick wall five feet or so high. On either side gardens of similar dimensions ran the length of the terrace. And beyond the dividing wall at the end, behind the natural screen of the trees, other gardens led up to the backs of the houses of the neighbouring terrace.

Adam stood at the edge of the unmown lawn. Here he could smell the damp earth and grass, the fallen leaves decomposing back into the soil. He was anxious to get on but his eyes fell back on a patch of earth at the end of the lawn. He found himself thinking back to a time some months earlier, in March. He had been taken then with the idea of growing crops for food, and had dug and weeded that patch, despite his physical frailty. He had brought seeds and roots to plant in the soil, feeling, for the first time since leaving hospital, a sense of oneness with himself. Working, having a purpose, even one as simple as cultivating a few vegetables, helped him feel that he was coming alive again after such a long period of enforced inactivity.

But waiting at a physiotherapy session one morning an article in a Sunday supplement had caught his eye. It covered a major survey conducted by a university professor working on behalf of an environmental group researching the effects of inner city pollution. Concentrating on most major cities, but the Greater London area in particular, his findings suggested that food grown in such regions could represent a threat to health. Roots and leaves were found to contain more lead, even after peeling and washing, than the 1 $\mu g/g$ limit prescribed by Food Regulations.

This information was sufficient to dissuade Adam from continuing with his project, and he had fallen to sitting in his back window staring out at the garden and brooding for hours at a time. Until one afternoon a new possibility dawned on him. He saw, in the garden with its contaminated soil and inedible plants, a perfect allegory. He immediately began furiously composing a book, a modern-day parable in which a fertile garden became gradually reduced to infertility owing to the negligence of those who were supposed to be its caretakers.

Adam saw in the garden a mirror reflecting the minds of men who were its gardeners. Their greed and ignorance, clouded thinking, had led them to create an environment that could not support them. Each man and woman, therefore, every single one of them, had to be made to understand that he or she shared the responsibility. Only by a universal change of attitudes and actions might their dying Eden, and thus themselves, be rescued.

Adam had made copious notes, absorbed to total distraction. For a time he had believed he was going to save the world.

But his euphoria could not last; his mind soon regressed to earlier jungles from where the whole thing took on a crass and naïve aspect. He could see, with hindsight, how it bore further testimony to his increasing loss of contact with reality. And how, in the wrong hands, and in combination with his case records, it might be deemed evidence enough to warrant his compulsory admission and detention under the provisions of Part Two, Sections Two, Three or Four, of the Mental Health Act. So he let the idea drop, caching all his notes, thankful he had never discussed it with anyone.

His vegetable patch was now a proving ground for weeds. Nettles, thistles, dandelions, bindweed, brambles, all vied for dominance over his failing earth, and their success discomfited him, making him more aware of his fecklessness. He pulled himself out of his reverie and moved on towards the wall.

Beneath the first low branches of the chestnut he stopped, listening again. He heard nothing so moved forward, keeping his body low like a criminal. At the wall the mist and darkness prevented him seeing more than a few feet into his neighbour's garden. The closeness of the silence unnerved him and he realized he was trembling.

With his hands flat on the top course he breathed in deeply, tensed his muscles and carefully raised himself until he was able to lift one foot and hook it over the brick. He clenched his teeth and hauled himself laboriously onto the wall, hard put not to cry out: the 'accident' and subsequent surgery had left him with a body that protested harshly at exertion.

He lay for some moments panting, sick and afraid to stir. Then, as he shifted his position slightly, something moved in the murk ahead, and his nightmare came to life.

There was a rapid rustling noise. An indistinct chinking as something rushed towards him through long grass. With a sudden infuriated snarling sound a dark moving shape formed before him in the mist.

Adam instinctively recoiled. The creature sprang and he almost toppled from the wall. In an instant of suspended time he gazed at the great, scab-infested head only inches from his own. The teeth were bared, foam flying from loose-fleshed chops. Small pendant ears were flattened against the broad skull. The short, wide, coarse-haired muzzle was drawn back into deep wrinkles. The beast hung there in the air before him, and he stared at his own reflection in its crazed and blood-rimmed eyes.

Then the sound that spewed from its throat was cut short. An indescribable, anguished expression suddenly filled its features, and in the space of a millisecond Adam was witness to the beast's entire miserable existence. It was a revelation that shook and numbed him, but it didn't end there. Intuitively, in the same moment, he received a most awful, thrilling shock of raw knowledge. He knew he was witnessing the world in the eyes of a mad dog.

But the moment was gone. The beast's head flew to one side. Its hindquarters were catapulted upwards, flipping over awkwardly as the hind legs kicked the air. A long steel chain attached to the collar at its neck had been jerked tight under the animal's forward flight. Now the chain wrenched it roughly back to earth.

The dog fell clumsily but was swiftly on its feet, leaping again. The chain tightened and it fell back, but landed evenly this time and was poised to spring again.

Adam, shuddering, clung to the top of the wall. These exquisitely horrifying moments had the effect on him of a drug. Despite the danger he was drawn back for more again and again. He could not prevent himself. He knew there was always the chance that the chain would snap, or that it might have been lengthened – or even that the animal would not be tethered at all – but he came back. The physical peril was immaterial in the face of the mesmeric terror the creature's materialization out of the mist drew from him. It stirred some intangible, mystical or primordial connection within him. His nightmare was alive. That which his dreams would never reveal was here, transposed into the physical world. If the two states of dream and reality had merged then he, somehow, stood at the point of their conjunction.

Below him the animal ran back and forth and made threatening lunges. Though its quarry was out of reach it could not resist attacking.

It was an ugly hybrid of a dog. It had the height of a wolfhound, but the strong, compact body, broad chest and shoulders, and foreshortened head and snout of a Rottweiler. Its coarse coat was a lustreless black with patches of tan. Around its throat and neck the hair had been rubbed away in places and the skin was raw, bleeding from the constant chafing of its collar and chain. The marks of frequent beatings scored its back and flanks. Adam did not know if it had a name.

Adam knew the dog's owner only by sight, a brutish Slav who occupied the dingy rear basement of the house backing onto his own. He was a solitary man, a drinker who spent much of his life behind closed curtains, nursing, Adam guessed, murderous hangovers.

The Slav would emerge from time to time to throw meat to his pet, but the animal was not well fed. He would come out, too, when its whining, howling dirges grew intolerable, and beat it into silence. He kept a length of rubber hose by the back door for the purpose. Sometimes he would beat it for no perceivable reason at all.

The Slav was morose and uncommunicative. He and Adam had passed on the street now and again, but without greeting or acknowledgement of any kind. Like Adam, presumably, he had his reasons for maintaining a distance, though Adam was sure he must be aware that they were neighbours.

BARBARA RAINE-ALLEN

EDITOR

RAP PUBLISHING LTD

120 WILTON ROAD
LONDON SW1V 1JZ
TEL: 071-834 8534
FAX: 071-828 6297

...tted him in the distance, walking
...lav's powerful stocky frame would
...ain wrapped around his waist and
...ed to hold back the animal that
... The dog was far too dangerous
...could see little point in walking it.
...ome where at least it had the run
...ut on reflection it had struck him
...lav who really needed to get out,
...s merely his excuse.

...self carefully into a more secure
...From here he was able to edge
...which angled out from the bole
...t away. It snaked some metres
...fingers above a shadowy corner
...e eased himself onto the bough.
...trembling uncontrollably as he

...neath him the dog slavered and growled. It made half-
hearted attempts to reach the bough and spun around in
frustration on the dark, leaf-littered earth, entangling itself in its
chain.

Some way out the bough arched, dipped, then rose again,
forming an uneven dish shape. Adam manoeuvred himself into
a sitting position in the dip, his feet hanging in the air.

This provoked the dog even further. It launched itself at him
with renewed ferocity, the chain, now slack, no longer preventing
it from leaping as high or as far as its muscles could propel it.
But Adam's position was precisely calculated, and the jaws
snapped shut each time just short of his dangling feet.

After a minute or so the dog began to tire. Panting, it paused
to stare malevolently up at its tormentor. Adam could only stare
back.

He had wondered, on this and other occasions, whether it was
possible that what he was experiencing was still part of a dream.
This took over at the very point at which he invariably awoke.
Could he have dreamt he had woken and in fact have still to
wake?

'I dreamed I was a butterfly, fluttering and contented, not

knowing I was a man,' wrote the philosopher Chuang Tzu. 'Then I woke and realized I was a man. Now how can I know if I was then a man dreaming he was a butterfly, or if I am now a butterfly dreaming I am a man?'

There was no way he could know, but his mind was clear on one thing. No matter the paradox, no matter its origin or cause, it was his own, real, experience. The mystery, the madness, devoid of logic or reason, urged him to enter, in fact gave him no choice. It was his to investigate, to observe, participate in, and above all to learn from. What its lesson, if any, might be, he could not even begin to imagine, but inside him a small voice whispered that his one hope was to pursue it.

So without knowing why, he stayed in the tree and antagonized the animal beneath him. He was aware that he was consciously fuelling its madness, that should it ever break free he would have to share the blame for the consequences. The animal was a killer, he couldn't doubt it. And in the garden next door young children often played. His only excuse was that he could not help himself.

In some warped, half-sentient way, that might have been the brutish Slav's reasoning too. Adam could see that. The man lived under some kind of compulsion to mistreat his pet. Beating it, withholding affection, deliberately restricting its food. And he left it alone outside in all weathers, all hours. The garden gave no shelter, other than the insufficient windbreak of the walls and the paltry cover of brambles and trees. The miserable creature spent its days and nights huddled to the wall, or paced whimpering up and down outside the Slav's door, head low, tail tight between its legs, shivering in driving winter snow and rain. But perhaps the Slav, too, was not wholly devoid of compassion. Perhaps he, too, could act in this world in no other way.

Despite his treatment the dog retained a fawning affection for its master. When he appeared it would wag its tail nervously and sink to a crawl. To appease him it would roll submissively onto its back and expose its underparts. It accepted his thrashings in virtual silence, and when he was done would creep forward and try to lick his hand.

To Adam it seemed that in this unexplainable dream-situation they were all three somehow irrationally linked. Each was experiencing with a differing perspective something none of them understood or desired. But in the fog of it all he was becoming convinced they each had a definite part to play.

He had spoken of none of this, other than to Judith, from whom it could hardly be kept secret. He allowed her, though, to accept it as part of his madness, knowing he could not effectively communicate his deeper feelings to her. Judith quietly tolerated his actions; Doctor Geld, whom he had once considered confiding in, would certainly not have encouraged them.

Some weeks had passed since he'd last spoken to Geld. Time had tempered his hostility a little but he could still not believe that Geld would have a satisfactory explanation for what was happening. In fact the doctor was as likely to disturb him further as he was to ease his mind on the matter.

Once, for example, being aware of the progressive nature of his condition Adam had asked the doctor about his prospects for a future. Deeply distressed at the time he had needed some kind of reassurance that he *had* a future, that he was not losing his mind for good.

Doctor Geld had considered the question, folding his arms across his narrow chest as his gaze drifted to the ceiling.

'Terms such as "losing one's mind",' he had said, 'are, strictly speaking, anathema to a man in my profession. A discriminating practician will do his utmost to avoid them. Of course, they continue to be bandied about quite freely. I'm as guilty as the next man at times, I have to confess. One cannot keep one's guard up every second of the day, can one? But really, "losing your mind" . . . It's a misleading and ultimately meaningless term, wouldn't you agree?'

He had revolved in his winged chair to scan a shelf of reference books to his left. He swung back without selection, his eyes suddenly bright with amusement.

'We must be alert to misapplications. Language is a wonderful invention, but used inappropriately or without thought it will ensnare us. Drag us into a pit of confusion. How often misused words generate misleading thoughts, as Spencer so astutely observed. And yours is a perfect example. "Losing your mind", as if to suggest that it is going somewhere minus yourself. As if to suggest — ha-ha! — the existence of some timeless location where perhaps lost and departed senses might meet — conceivably to compare impressions! Ha-ha-*ha*! No. It is too ludicrous! Don't dwell on it. We are not dealing with your mind "going" anywhere, we are dealing with your impaired ability to interact with the world, to carry on normal human relations and live a normal life, whatever that might entail.'

'But — '

'But, semantics apart, what is actually happening to you? Correct? Well, I've explained before, and as you are quite aware anyway, you are suffering the effects of extreme trauma. Your entire system has been badly shaken up and will take time to regain its equilibrium. Our tests show no lesions, no organic irregularities of any kind. So we can work on the premise that the problem is of the mind rather than the brain. Given time, then, and the right approach, the healing process will prevail. We can only try to aid that process.'

Adam had left that session in a worse mental state than when he'd arrived. Doctor Geld seemed incapable of giving him a straight answer; did he actually know anything more about Adam's condition than Adam himself? At home, in an effort to escape his clamouring thoughts he had grabbed a bottle of Glenmorangie and a spade and rushed into the front garden. When Judith found him on her return from work he was stretched out in the shrubbery. He was delirious and weeping and had dug up the front lawn.

He was also crippled. In his weakened condition the sudden exertion had proven too much and the following week was spent flat on a board in a hospital bed.

So he held fast to his resolve to tell Doctor Geld nothing of this. Despite his years of experience, Geld was not the man to turn to with such confidences. Even so, Adam could never quite rest easily with his decision, for he could not rid himself of the suspicion that Doctor Geld knew what he was doing anyway, and always had done.

He looked down. The animal had settled restlessly on its haunches on the ground.

'I don't know,' he whispered. The dog cocked its ears, tipping its head slightly to one side. Its upper lip curled and it let out a low growl.

'I mean you no harm,' he said. 'I can't explain anything. Forgive me.'

He closed his eyes.

When he opened them again the morning had grown stronger. The mist had still to disperse but the darkness was yielding to the push of inevitable day. Beneath him the dog half-lay, half-crouched on the damp earth, its head resting on its paws, casting surly glances in his direction.

Adam was cold, he could barely move, but his mind felt clearer. He had lost all sense of time but had to some extent succeeded in concentrating and focussing his milling thoughts. He shifted his weight, preparing to climb back along the bough, and the dog, snarling, sprang to its feet. As he lifted his frozen feet it made a futile leap into the air.

The improving visibility made him keen to get back. He did not want to risk discovery by any near-neighbour curious enough to investigate the dog's commotion from a window.

He reached the wall and paused to lean against the bole of the tree, breathless. The brutish Slav's pet had reared onto its hind legs, gagging on its steel-studded collar as it strove to reach him before he moved away.

He lowered his body stiffly to the ground and looked back over the wall at the crazed animal.

'I'm looking,' he said quietly, 'and I keep looking. And when I find the answers I need I know I'll be able to set you free.'

The animal lunged, and deep in the mist he heard the steel post to which its chain was fastened shaking under the tension. He turned and made his way back down the garden to the house.

At Helm's Place

'That poor creature,' Judith said.

With those words Adam's thoughts were brought up sharply. His activities on the brutish Slav's side of the wall were exposed without ceremony as something truly shameful.

She was in her usual calculated morning rush. Spreading

33

butter and marmalade on Hovis toast, pouring Earl Grey, checking herself in the mirror as she prepared to leave. At this time of day everything had to be just so, automatic. She poured tea for Adam.

He shed his gloves, scarf, jacket and boots and sat down at the kitchen table.

'Anything happen?' she asked brightly. 'Any conclusions?'

He shook his head. It was pointless trying to explain. He had tried, they both had, but he could not expect her to visualize his world. In general he preferred to play things down; she had enough to deal with. He was more than appreciative of the fact that she loved him virtually unconditionally and had stuck with him through all the difficulties. Living with a madman was no soft option. She could have spared herself much anguish by simply having him committed to care of some kind where she might visit him regularly. He marvelled that she hadn't. She had never faltered and he owed it to her to keep her troubles to a minimum.

'You made a lot of noise.'

He looked up. 'I did?'

'The dog did.'

'Do you think anyone noticed?'

'Doubtful.' She took a tortoiseshell comb from her bag and began to hurriedly comb her shoulder-length light brown hair. 'Any plans for today?'

'I thought about checking Helmut out.'

'Helmut?' She paused for a moment, then, 'It will probably do you good to get out. Be careful, though. And don't get lost.'

'I'm all right.'

'Do you want to come with me now and wait at the office? I could make sure you got the right bus.' From experience they both knew the lack of ease with which Adam crossed town. Judith was based in a Westminster government office, which was more or less en route for their friend Helmut's place. Though she had her own car, a blue Metro, she used it mainly outside of working hours. Weekdays she chose the rush-hour crush of public transport over the costly crawl of her own.

'I'm all right,' he repeated a little tetchily. 'I wasn't planning on leaving yet.'

She finished her tea while slipping into a smart blue wool jacket that matched her skirt.

'You know,' Adam said, 'I did come up with something out there.'

As soon as he'd said it he regretted it. A surge of emotion left him in little doubt that he'd tapped into something he would probably not be able to control. The moment was not made for it. Judith was about to leave, he was going to delay her. He grew agitated.

'What was that?'

He spoke quickly, unconvincingly offhand. 'Well, I was thinking about Doctor Geld and those other specialists at the hospital. Their methods, dealing with me. I was thinking about the way everyone has approached all this.'

Judith rested her slim fingers lightly on the table top. 'And?'

'And it struck me that there is something fundamentally wrong in their approach. In *our* approach. We're doing it, too. You and even me. I think I've always known it. It's only just come to me consciously.'

It rose up inside him and he clenched his jaw, angry with himself. Judith lowered herself onto the edge of the chair beside his. Puzzled, and seeing that he was upset, she took his hands which were bunched into fists in his lap.

'Go on.'

His eyes were fixed on an area of the floor in front of him and he was beginning to tremble. He looked up suddenly into her face.

'Nobody wants to know!'

He half-shouted it, and it wasn't what he'd intended at all. His mouth contorted as he struggled to contain his feelings. The tears welled then flowed and Judith took him in her arms and soothed him like a child.

Sometime, perhaps, given a space for his overwhelming self-pity to pass, she would touch on the subject again. Doctor Geld had stressed the importance of encouraging Adam to talk about his feelings, but the time had to be selected carefully. For now she could only try to calm him.

Presently his sobs subsided and he drew away. 'You'll be late.'

'It's all right.' She stood, fetched a light overcoat from the hall, and returned. 'Do you want me to stay for a while? Talk?'

He shook his head. 'I'm fine now. It slipped out, but no more tears. I'm a man, you know.'

She smiled and bent to kiss him. Adam averted his eyes, unwilling to see in her face any sign of the strain he was putting her under.

He followed her with his gaze as she left the house. He went to the front room window and watched her make her way up the street, a slim, smart, attractive professional young woman. She could be so patient, understanding, loving; she could be brisk, cool, efficient, enterprising; always reliable. On rare occasions she could break and be a little girl. Adam loved her.

Back in the kitchen he poured himself more tea and sat at the table, lost in thought. Later he made toast, and about mid-morning recalled his resolve to call on Helmut. He washed and changed, put on shoes and a warm jacket and was about to open the front door when he hesitated. He stood where he was in the hallway, immobile, from time to time muttering to himself beneath his breath.

When he came dazedly back to consciousness he removed his jacket and shoes and put on slippers. He shuffled into the lounge and sat down on the carpet, picked up a notepad and pen and began to write.

A further two hours passed before he put aside his writing materials and remembered Helmut.

Helmut Wasser, self-styled Nuclear-Age thinker, psychic philosopher, man of letters, and the world's first radioactive poet, was Adam's closest friend.

He was the son of an ambitious expatriate Austro-Hungarian merchant seaman of dubious background who had married above his station, and a wealthy, rebellious English former debutante who had married below hers. The bond had been fated from the beginning. Her family disowned her because of it and he, unable to adapt to the apron strings, fathered a son and ran. He'd last been heard of when Helmut was two, having jumped ship somewhere in America, never to show his face again.

Helmut's mother, defiantly independent of her upper-class forebears, had bravely struggled single-handedly to provide a decent upbringing for her son. She had never been a strong woman, though, and at the age of thirty-four the cancer which some two years later was to rob her of life, was first diagnosed.

Helmut, then nine, was sent to live with Aunt Kate, a doting middle-aged spinster who languished alone in a crumbling mansion in Finchley, and was in fact no blood relation. Under Aunt Kate's over-protective wing he remained for a further nine years, until the beginning of his Oxford days prepared him for his subsequent independence.

He had reached adulthood an amiably eccentric Anglophile, content to base himself solo in a one-bedroomed tenement flat on the seedier side of Victoria. This he occupied rent-free under the aegis of a socialist housing association, of which he was nominal Secretary, and which never quite seemed to get around to enforcing its own conditions of tenancy and membership.

Though litigation was ever pending to grant him the inheritance he had always been denied Helmut showed little concern for the outcome one way or the other. His ambitions did not stretch to riches, which experience had taught him led to endless painful and unnecessary problems. In his mind, however, he rather fancied himself as a carefree, well-heeled, somewhat dandified English gentleman, and in his own inimitable manner liked to act out that role.

The world Helmut had created for himself was orderless and unpredictable. Unlike Adam's it remained just about manageable. A cosy kind of chaos with shadowy corners, held back from mindless havoc by an almost mystical ability Helmut had of being ever unfazed by, and even largely inattentive to, events and surroundings. Like a ghost in a combat zone he maintained a blithesomely unconventional lifestyle where others would have imperilled life and limb and probably lost their wits trying to restore sanity, system and order.

In his little flat he composed and from time to time published his poems, wrote social commentaries for low-circulation alternative publications, and drafted and re-drafted unfinished philosophical treatises.

Helmut, the Nuclear Age Thinker, was the man who had

formulated the philosophy of 'Anything Goes'. This disturbing comment on our times received mention in various literary and offbeat political magazines, and had lately gained him a handful of doggedly aimless followers.

Put briefly 'Anything Goes' states the following:

In this, the Nuclear Age, mankind is faced with the growing knowledge that it cannot hope to survive as a species beyond a few generations. It has created for itself and other life-forms on the planet an environment that is so severely disrupted as to be past salvation, and even hostile to those organisms it has previously supported.

Beauty has gone. Love has gone. Life has become so devalued as to make a mockery of any kind of moral virtue. Existence has been reduced to an essentially meaningless morass of fear, suspicion and hopeless bewilderment. Under such conditions nothing can be held to be of any real value.

Faced with this knowledge the individual is forced to try to survive by any means, assuming an attitude of *carte blanche*, taking whatever he or she needs and doing whatever he or she desires, knowing that others will be doing likewise. Any other course can only be seen as non pro-survival.

It is a lamentable condition arrived at through our failure to take heed of past mistakes. It is nevertheless a reality, and one has to strive to make the most of it if one is to live.

Desperation rules. We are witnessing the death of Conscience. With Conscience gone the only Law is No-Law. It is the Time of the Psychopath, an Age of Unreason. In short, 'Anything Goes'.

Pessimistic it might sound, but 'Anything Goes' is not the product of an overtly glum mind. Helmut was developing a number of concepts and this one, having attracted attention, albeit limited, was currently top of the pile.

In Helmut's company Adam felt able to relax, free of the pressure he often felt to be explaining or apologizing for himself. Their friendship went back some years to Oxford where they had graduated together. From Adam's point of view, of course, it was a relatively new one.

Helmut frequently regaled him with reminiscences of their pre- and post-graduation exploits, hoping to stimulate in his memory details of his former life. But his tales were never more than good entertainment. A gifted raconteur, he had yet failed to inspire a genuine recollection of the old Adam.

In Adam's imagination the 'accident' in Northern Ireland, favoured in the press as 'the incident', had assumed capitals. It had become The Incident, synonymous with The Birth. An existence had ended with that dark night, and a new one had begun. When told stories of his former life he might be carried along, and could enter into them with some enthusiasm, but it was with nothing more than his imagination.

Helmut had a knack for bringing laughter out of Adam where others had turned him in upon himself. He was never slow to highlight the humorous side of Adam's condition, and in contrast to Doctor Geld could do it without giving offence. He it was who had given Adam his nickname after a particularly bloody free-form martial arts competition in which Adam, an expert in those days, had fallen heavily with a cracked skull. He, Adam, had claimed later that whilst unconscious he had found himself floating in a haze of brilliant white light, looking down upon his own body and experiencing himself to be separate from it and from the world. He had been moving away, he said, the scene growing hazier and a sense of profound peace filling his being, until a sudden overwhelming impulse brought him back. He felt he should not go yet, that he had too many things still to accomplish.

When Helmut heard that story he had promptly christened him 'the late' Adam Shatt, and the title had held since.

In philosophical terms Adam gave Helmut much to think about. Life after death, and particularly reincarnation, were concepts he had still to reach acceptable conclusions on. In his own essentially bleak philosophy they did not find a comfortable niche, though he remained open-minded on the subject. But the paradox inherent in Adam's situation was not lost on him, and kept him delighted and intrigued.

His concern over his friend was always apparent. He was anxious for him to regain the whole of his past, and though he probed and searched it was never in a way that caused distress.

Daylight was moving away from the city when Adam, exhausted, entered the tenement warren where Helmut had his home. He crossed two cheerless courtyards, flanked on all sides by high brown brick walls crowded with dark windows, and arrived at the foot of a flight of smoothworn stone steps in one corner. He ascended and rattled the knocker on Helmut's green front door. When Helmut answered, his round, flushed, sleepy face crinkled into a smile.

'My friend!' He held the door wide with evident pleasure. 'Come in!'

He was a man of average height, broad-shouldered, wearing a red and grey paisley patterned dressing-gown and fleece-lined slippers. In one hand he held a chipped yellow mug of tea. He threw his free arm around Adam's shoulder and guided him into his living room.

The room, like the flat, was small and untidy, cheaply and sparsely furnished and subject to damp. It had a faint odour of gas, past fry-ups and mouldering laundry. Its main focus, on one corner, was Helmut's writing table and bookshelves. Books stacked in irregular piles also ran the length of one wall. Clamped to the table was an angle-poise lamp, the only modern fixture visible, other than a telephone, and this was poised to illuminate an open exercise book. The book's pages were covered in lines of verse written in Helmut's uneven and threadlike script.

Above the table Helmut had pinned to the wall a poster-sized sheet of white card. On this, in a downward curving crescent, was proclaimed, in brash red Letraset, the legend: 'We are witnessing the Death of Conscience'. And in the centre, in capitals: 'ANY-THING GOES'.

Sheets of paper, some written on, some screwed up and discarded, littered the area around the table.

Adam dropped gratefully into one of two scrawny old arm-chairs in front of a moderately glowing gas-fire.

'You are pale and haggard,' Helmut said with a solicitous grin. 'Have you by any chance just stepped out of an Edgar Allan Poe?'

'I had an experience coming here,' Adam said without smiling.

'An experience?'

'A bad one. It shook me up. I've taken a long time getting here.'

'What happened? Wait, I'll get you some tea.'

He brought a second mug from the kitchen and took the chair alongside Adam, stretching his bare white legs in front of the fire. The legs, like most of his body, were covered in a fine fuzz of soft, light, downy hair. They were rather stubby, in contrast to a long torso and arms. The hair on his head was fair and fell to below his shoulders. Wispy-thin on top it revealed an extraordinarily broad and bumpy cranium. He had a wide, heavy, thoughtful brow and grey-blue eyes which peered without focussing at the fire as he waited quietly for his friend to begin.

'It started as a vision, for want of another word,' Adam said. He sipped from his mug and let the hot liquid roll down to his centre. 'I decided to leave the bus at Victoria Street and walk the rest of the way for some exercise. I'd only gone a few yards when this image suddenly flashed on inside my skull. Now that's not such an unusual thing in itself, as you know. But this one was vivid. It had an emotional effect on me that I can't account for. It stopped me dead in the street. I think I must have stood there for a couple of minutes at least.

'I was seeing a man playing dice on a big office desk. The building he was in wasn't modern, I think the walls were stone. There was a map hanging up and a couple of paintings, I don't know of what. The windows were arched and mullioned, with fine lead or iron tracery, like an old manor or church annexe.

'He was touching fifty, I'd guess, but he looked in good shape. He was standing and was tall and athletically built. No flab or stoop or anything. He had on a dark blue suit, well cut, maybe with a pinstripe, and was immaculately groomed, quite striking in appearance. His hair was silver-grey and he had glittering blue eyes. There was a definite air of authority about him.

'He kept throwing dice onto his desktop, over and over. Up to six at a throw, concentrating very intently. And each time he would note down their values on a pad at his side. From time to time I'd see his eyes light up, presumably at a particular combination which he would jot down and encircle.

'Then he suddenly looked up, directly at me as though he could see me. He looked ... angry, at being intruded upon, but also surprised. Then it faded. That's all there was.'

Helmut said nothing. His eyes were half-closed and his face

wore an almost Buddha-like expression of inscrutability. He could have been dozing, but Adam knew better.

'I was left feeling very disturbed. I don't know why. It was some time before I moved on.'

Helmut raised one eyelid. 'Interesting,' he said. 'Interesting that this one should stand out to you. You are so regularly subject to perceptual disturbances. Do you have any idea why it – '

'That's not the end of it, Helm,' Adam cut in. 'Listen. I'd only gone a few yards when I caught sight of someone about twenty yards ahead. A man, he had his back to me, in a blue pinstriped suit. Tall and well-built, straight-backed with silver-grey hair and a very purposeful stride. He was carrying an attaché case and a rolled up newspaper. It could have been anyone, I know. A man of that description hardly stands out down there. The Yard just down the road, and Parliament and St James's. But it gave me a turn all the same, and I couldn't just leave it. I had to find out.

'So I moved up on him until I was a yard or two behind. It wasn't easy, he was walking at a healthy pace and I could feel my nerve going. I kept telling myself, Don't do it. You're going to make a fool of yourself again. You don't know.

'It's a long time since I've done that, Helm. You know, after leaving hospital I used to walk up to people all the time thinking I recognized them. Remember? You were with me once.'

Helmut nodded slowly.

'I used to be so certain sometimes. "Are you sure?" I'd say. "Look more closely. Don't we know each other?" I gave up in the end. People don't like it. Their eyes began to warn me off even if they said nothing. I didn't once get a hit, anyway.

'But this character had the hooks in me. I couldn't walk away without seeing his face.

'I had to half-run to get past him, and as I went by I gave him a sidelong glance.'

Adam was sitting forward in his chair, turning to face Helmut, his hands fiercely gripping the arms. Two tiny red spots had bloomed high up on his cheekbones, standing out against the almost ghostly paleness of his face.

'It was him, Helm,' he said. His voice was shaking slightly. 'It was the man with the dice.'

* * *

Helmut looked closely at his friend for a second, then shifted his gaze back to the glowing firebrick grid of the gas-fire. He kept silence and his expression still failed to disclose his thoughts.

Adam drew a long unsteady breath. 'It was a shock. When I saw him I didn't know what to do. I kept on moving, but there was only one thing to do, of course. I had to ask him. So I turned around, and as he came up I said, "Excuse me."

'He didn't stop, He didn't adjust his gait, so I had to go with him. "Yes?" he said. Very abrupt, hardly glancing at me. Cold. There wasn't a flicker of recognition in his eyes. I felt that old familiar feeling. I was nothing to him. I just felt bloody small.

'"Well, what is it?" he wanted to know. He was obviously a man with little time for dalliance. I apologized. I said I thought he was someone I knew. He just grunted and strode away up the street.

'But I couldn't let it drop like that, Helm. My head was spinning. He was the man. The man I'd seen playing dice. I couldn't just let it go and walk away, could I? So I followed him.'

'You followed him? Where to?'

Adam shook his head. 'He went off left down Strutton Ground. I had to see where he was going, just to try and satisfy myself somehow. So I kept a distance and followed him. He went through three or four sidestreets, and I came around a corner just in time to catch him disappearing into a doorway halfway along an alley. I crossed to the opposite pavement and carried on up until I had a clear view of the building.'

Adam paused for a moment and some of the tension slid visibly from his body. He picked up his tea and sat back in his chair, staring ruefully into the mug.

A few seconds passed, then Helmut gently prompted him. 'And?'

'There was nothing remarkable about it,' he said. 'Five or six storeys. The upper ones were bare brick and the ground floor had a large tinted fascia window. The lower half was opaque, decorated in black and gold, with red velvet drapes behind. The door was varnished oak. There was nothing to indicate what went on inside until you stepped up to the door. On the wall was a small brass plaque, with the words engraved: "SOCIETY. Club Amour For Gentlemen".'

Neither said anything for some seconds, then Helmut let out a throaty chuckle. Adam sighed.

'I was lost by then, of course,' he went on. 'Completely lost my bearings. I wandered around for a while in a daze until I found a landmark that put me back on the map. By that time of course I'd reasoned it all out, too. Everything fell neatly into place, no sinister overtones at all.'

'What is your explanation?' Helmut enquired.

'It seems to me that I must have passed that character when I was still on the bus, probably just before I alighted would be my guess. For some reason he made an impression on me subconsciously, although I wasn't aware of him in the crowd. After I got down his image was thrown up front. I don't know why, but it isn't wholly untypical. So I stood there in the street hallucinating and in the meantime he caught up and passed me. I came out of it, spotted him up ahead, and *whap*! Disruption on the beta waves!'

Helmut nodded and smiled to himself. 'And does that explanation truly put your mind at rest?'

Adam shrugged. 'It has to, doesn't it. Do you have a better one?'

'It sounds feasible. More than likely.'

'It doesn't explain the dice, though. I haven't accounted for that.'

'Perhaps they were symbols? Indicative of the randomness of it all?'

Adam nodded. He closed his eyes and began to massage his temples with the tips of his fingers. He'd brought on a blinding headache. 'Christ, I'm tired.' He turned wearily to Helmut. 'I'm chasing tonto, Helm. At a hell of a gallop. I could be there already, how can I tell? But I'm scared. I don't know what I'm doing. I can't seem to help myself.'

'I disagree.' Helmut reached over and squeezed his arm. 'You are looking at the negative aspects rather than concentrating on the positive. The very fact that you have been able to reason sense out of what was obviously a very bewildering experience shows that you have not lost your analytical powers. The fact that you can sit here and discuss with me what happened is further evidence.'

Adam grimaced and arched his back.

'The war wounds?'

'I overdid it, I think.'

'A little each day,' Helmut said sympathetically. He rose to his feet. 'Build up slowly. Erratic bursts will do more harm than good.'

'I'm not disturbing you, am I, Helm? I didn't think to phone before I came over. Did you have any plans?'

'Not at all. I'm pleased to see you. It's far too long since we've talked. I've nothing planned for this evening.' He bent to pick up Adam's mug. 'Make yourself at home, my friend. I'll make a fresh brew and see if I can find something for your headache.'

He left the living room to clatter around in his kitchen. When, five minutes later, he returned bearing fresh tea and paracetamol, he found his friend lost to the world in a deep and weary sleep in front of the fire.

Opening his eyes Adam looked around him blearily, uncertain at first of his whereabouts. A mug of hot tea steamed on the floor beside his chair and the gas-fire still glowed moderately. All was as before – barring one thing. He was covered in teddy bears.

Six of them. They nestled in his armpits and on his stomach and thighs. He was hugging one to his chest.

He was familiar with all of them, they made up Helmut's crew, although the full complement was not present. Under his chin lay Pinky, alongside Ted – two small, tatty old bears with their stuffing poking out. Rupe, on the other hand, was a dapper young bear resting on his chest, and Matilda, his companion, was not in truth a bear at all.

The two remaining members were Gripper, an ill-tempered looking fellow with a hoarse squeak, and Wilfred, the biggest, softest, floppiest old bear of all. Absent were Bismarck, the one-eyed panda, and Bruno, a pocket-sized furry chap who was Helmut's personal favourite. Adam guessed these two had been kept back to man the bed.

He had made the acquaintance of Helmut's crew earlier, on the first visit of his new life to Helmut's place. They were lined up neatly side by side and tucked securely into Helmut's single bed. 'They help keep the old ship afloat,' thirty-four-year-old Helmut had remarked by way of explanation. In the light of everything else it had not struck Adam as strange.

He craned his neck over the back of the chair. Behind him Helmut sat at his table, sucking pensively at the blunt end of a fibre-tip, his eyes on a half-filled page. He still wore his dressing-gown and slippers. He looked up, sensing Adam had woken, and smiled. 'I thought you might like some company.'

'Thanks,' Adam said, rearranging the bears so that he might pick up his tea. His head felt like a mangrove swamp but at least it no longer ached. 'I'm sorry. I didn't mean to crash on you like that.'

'No problem. I shall make us something to eat in a moment. I'm sure you must be very hungry. Then I had better get some clothes on. I'm calling on a friend a little later on to discuss some of my work . . . and some of his. Would you like to come along? I think you will find him interesting company, and I know he'd like to meet you. You are very welcome.'

Adam stared at him for a moment without replying, aware that something was amiss but unable, at first, to put a finger on it. At length he said, 'Helm, I asked you if you were going out. You told me you had nothing planned.'

Helmut replaced his pen on the table top. Smiling gently he said, 'Ah.' He said, 'My friend, when exactly did you ask me that question?'

Adam frowned. 'Just a little while ago, before I fell asleep.' It came to him then as he spoke. 'Oh Christ. I don't believe it. How long?'

Helmut checked his wristwatch. 'You arrived here at about six-ish in the evening. It is now three-twenty-five in the afternoon.'

He nodded towards the window. Adam followed his direction. Outside, through grimy panes, rain was falling in a fine drizzle. Two pigeons huddled together on a windowsill across the court, unaware that some yards off along the walkway a ginger tomcat was creeping up on them. The daylight was a leaden silver-grey and had not yet begun to fade.

'They must have been interesting dreams,' Helmut said. He came over and began to gather his teddies from Adam's arms. 'If you have no objection now that you're conscious I'll return them to their regular duties. Don't worry, my friend, you have not been in the way. I did wonder about waking you but you looked so washed out I thought it better to let you rest. I called Judith, by the way, to put her mind at ease. She agreed.'

Adam muttered thanks. He had done full blank-outs before, but never in someone else's home. And never for a whole day.

'She tells me you've been writing.'

Across the way the two pigeons lifted off in a flurry of wings and air, the tom gazed at its empty paws and slunk off.

'Writing?'

'She found several sheets. From her description it sounded quite interesting. I would like to read it. You have not shown me anything for a long time.'

Adam had no recollection of the things he'd written before leaving for Helmut's, but it wasn't unusual for him to discover pages filled with his handwriting around the house. Gobbledygook, most of it. Psychotic ramblings, confused epigrams and essays, with construction and subject matter sometimes hardly figuring, all thrown up through an inner impulse, a compulsive emptying out. For reasons he was unsure of he kept them, in folders in the same drawer that contained his original notes for the abandoned Poisoned Garden allegory.

He had in the past shown samples of his writings to Helmut, as he had Doctor Geld. More recently, not solely out of modesty, he had preferred keeping them private. On occasions not so long gone he'd been present at recitals Helmut gave of his poetry, and as his friend's gently lilting voice showered chosen words on attendant ears he thought he had detected a ring of familiarity in certain phrases, certain terms and ideas.

With closer listening he was certain. Subtly incorporated into Helmut's works, altered, even improved upon, were ideas and word combinations that Adam himself had been the originator of.

The discovery that his best friend was a skilled and indiscriminate plagiarist might have come as an uncomfortable shock to someone of Adam's sensibilities, but instead he found it rather amusing. It somehow placed Helmut in a more favourable light, accenting his vulnerability as an artist rather than any unscrupulousness. For it was questionable whether he was even aware that he was doing it. He soaked up influences from innumerable sources, read reams, had scores of acquaintances. He was like a radio receiver, taking signals out of the air and transforming them into something others might appreciate. And it could hardly be said that he lacked originality of his own.

So viewing it in that way Adam had never bothered to raise the issue. It was too trivial to give time to; but he kept his work to himself now all the same.

'I'm afraid I can't tell you much about it,' he told him. 'I don't remember writing anything.'

Helmut nodded to himself. 'Pity.' He transported his teddies back to the bedroom, then went into the kitchen.

They ate frankfurters, baked beans and French bread prepared by Helmut. Not surprisingly Adam discovered a ravening appetite, so his friend rooted out and heated up a tin of rice pudding, then left him to it and went to the bedroom to change. He re-emerged freshly shaven and scenting the air about him with his distinctive masculine French perfume.

He was wearing a sharp, light grey woollen suit, yellow jersey and shining cream and grey brogues. He wrapped a long yellow and blue banded scarf around his neck, donned a grey trilby, grabbed a sheaf of selected writings which he pushed into a manila folder, and ushered Adam through the door.

Outside the drizzle had ceased and a mild breeze was chasing down the passages and walkways of the tenements. Helmut led the way across the courtyard and out through a passage onto the street, to a beat-up, once white, baby Fiat 500, circa sixty-nine or seventy, parked at the roadside.

'New wheels,' he announced with pride.

But Adam didn't hear him. He had looked up to a first floor window across the road to see a young woman standing looking down at the two of them. She was wan and sad and rather beautiful, with pale blonde hair that fringed her face and brow and fell almost to her shoulders. As he watched she backed away from her window and was engulfed in darkness inside her room.

'I said, "new wheels",' Helmut repeated.

Adam ran his eyes over the tiny vehicle.

'I'm so pleased. I traded in the Beetle. This one is much more me, don't you think? A new paint job – I'm thinking cherry red or electric blue at the moment – and she'll be perfect.'

Adam looked up at the window again but the girl did not reappear. He bent forward to peer inside the car. 'Have you had her long?'

'No. A couple of weeks.'

'You won't have her for another two if you neglect her like this.' He nodded to the passenger window which was wound partially open.

Helmut stepped around to look.

'Oh, my Lord!' he started to say, then Adam, reaching inside to open his door, suddenly let out a scream and leapt backwards into the air. His hands shot out and grabbed Helmut's arm involuntarily.

Inside the Fiat there was a movement. A dark shape materialized suddenly on the passenger seat. As Adam fell back it sprang up onto the window frame. It hovered there, alternating its weight rapidly from side to side. Then it leapt out as Adam screamed again. It landed on the pavement, darted between the legs of the two petrified men, and shot off up the street, a terrified black cat emitting a squeal like a sick ambulance.

Adam collapsed against Helmut. 'Oh my God! Oh my God!'

'My friend,' Helmut protested, trying to prise loose Adam's grip on his biceps. 'My friend, you are hurting me!'

With difficulty Adam released him. 'It nearly killed me,' he stammered. 'What was it?'

Helmut told him as his face began to crinkle into mirth. 'I don't know who was frightened most. You or the cat. Look!'

Some yards away the road ended in a cul-de-sac. The cat, now voiceless, had come up against the brick wall of a neighbouring schoolyard. In panic it was trying to scale the wall, which was some ten feet high. It ran up, fell back after a few feet, ran up again, fell back. Crazed with fright it shot from one side of the road to the other, then went for the wall again.

Helmut's face had turned red as tears began to spill from his eyes. He sat back against the wing of his little car; his whole body began shaking and the car shook with him.

'So funny!' he wheezed when he was able to get a word out. He stretched a hand towards Adam. 'So funny!'

Adam tried to smile but found himself closer to weeping. He was trembling violently. The incident had shocked him through.

He leaned on the car and hung his head between his outstretched arms.

Helmut rolled against the wing, helpless with laughter. Eventually he recovered himself enough to enquire, 'Is a black cat meant to signify good luck or bad? I can never remember.'

Adam shook his head. 'Ask the cat.'

He opened the passenger door and warily checked the car's interior before lowering himself into the front seat. His day was not yet three hours old but he already felt as weak as an abandoned babe.

En Route To A Room At The Top

The first thing Adam noticed as he pulled the car door shut and belted himself in was the lack of space. The second was that the interior of the little Fiat had been substantially reinforced with steel strutting. Thick, tubular bars, bolted or welded together, ran along the sides and across the front and rear at floor and roof level. Additional cross-struts reinforced the ceiling and chassis. The whole formed a strong protective cage-structure within which the vehicle's passengers were contained.

He took it in dazedly at first as Helmut, still red-faced with laughter, squeezed himself into the driver's seat and turned to face him. His expression now resembled that of a schoolboy who had just won a bag of prize marbles.

'What do you think?'

Adam didn't know. 'What's it for?'

'Ah.' Helmut grinned and lifted one finger, admonishing him to be patient as he sparked the engine into life. And here was Adam's next surprise. Rather than the timid splutter and Noddy-car put-put he was expecting the engine announced its awakening with a triumphal roar, dropping to a no-nonsense purr of confidence and power wholly unsuspected in a tiny car of such advanced years.

Helmut's eyes shone with pure pleasure. He pushed his hands into black leather driving gloves then reached across to the glove compartment and slotted a cassette into a cunningly secreted deck. He played on the accelerator a few times for emphasis, then shifted the gear-stick and, with a glance into the rear-view mirror, pulled away. The little car darted into the street, U-turned on a sixpence and glided happily down the road to the corner.

'I told you!' Helmut cried, hunched over the wheel. 'Like a dream!'

'I'm suitably impressed,' Adam said as they pulled out onto a local shopping thoroughfare to the opening strains of Dvorak's 'New World' Symphony. 'But what's with the hot-up job and the armour plating?'

He sat with his knees squashed against the dash. His head, retracted between his shoulders, still brushed the sun-roof. He was feeling sick after the encounter with the cat, and though anxious not to dampen Helmut's spirits, was hard-pressed to summon up much enthusiasm over his friend's new toy.

Helmut laughed. 'A minute!'

The car swerved into the kerbside and halted on double yellow lines. Helmut climbed out and crossed to an off-licence nearby. When he returned he was carrying a can of Yorkshire Bitter in one hand. For an all-but-total abstainer this was somewhat out of character but Adam was too preoccupied to question him.

'It belonged to an acquaintance of mine,' Helmut explained, referring to the car. They were pulling out onto the Vauxhall Bridge Road when a green Granada approaching at speed suddenly veered into the bus-lane to overtake a slow van on the inside. Helmut was forced to hit his brake pedal hard. The Granada flashed past, almost clipping the front of the little Fiat. Helmut cursed and pulled out quickly.

'What was I saying? Yes, an acquaintance of mine. He works in the motor trade. A very nice fellow, providing you don't cross him. Has a penchant for rallying and stock-car racing.

'So he came up with the idea that a car like this, suitably customized, would make an excellent racer. Highly manoeuvrable and zippy enough to avoid most clashes, take advantage of openings a larger model would have to ignore. You know. Etcetera. So he put in some time on this one. This strutting you see before you runs right along the chassis, under the bonnet, everywhere. It will take a lot of punishment.'

'And the engine?'

'Ah. The engine is a miracle.' Helmut was close on the tail of the offending Granada now. He dropped a gear, pulled out and flew past with a roar. 'Feel that thrust?'

He accelerated quickly as an oncoming number thirty-six bus flashed its headlamps, and as Adam held his breath in horror the little car darted diagonally into a near-impossible gap between the Granada and a black cab up front.

The bus roared past with blaring horn, the Granada braked with a screech of tyres and flashed its lamps. Helmut laughed and slapped the wheel, his nose almost pressed to the windscreen. 'Don't be afraid, my friend! I'm in control! Don't you love her? Don't you think she's wonderful? All she needs is a name, eh?'

'I like her,' Adam said, swallowing hard. Tiny beads of sweat had formed on his forehead and upper lip.

'Any suggestions?'

'For what?'

'A name for my beauty. Boadicea is the current favourite, but I haven't settled on anything definite yet.'

'I'll think on it,' Adam said. As they slowed to a halt for a red light up ahead he asked, 'How is it, if someone else spent so much time and money on the car, that you come away the proud new owner?'

'Ah, that's the sad part of the story. And though as you know I am not one who would seek to profit from the misfortunes of another, I'm afraid in this case I may, in a manner of speaking, just stand accused. You see, it seems he was involved in some kind of shady dealings – people in the motor trade often are. And a few weeks ago he was shot at his local. A spot of inter-gang rivalry, I would think. They do tend to live on such short fuses. Three men burst in and let go at him and his partner with a shotgun. Very nasty business. I visited him in hospital. He's not gravely wounded but he took it in the knees. Won't be driving for a long time. And, well, knowing how attached I'd become to his little beauty he agreed to a trade off, at a price, my friend, that has left me somewhat out of pocket.'

'But money well spent . . .'

'Oh yes.' Helmut caressed the dash with a gloved hand. 'Without – '

He was interrupted by an abrupt tapping at his offside window.

A face had appeared there, a man, bent almost double to peer through. From where Adam sat he looked none too friendly. He made motions indicating that Helmut should wind down his window, which he did.

'Is there a problem, my friend?'

'Are you crazy?' the man demanded.

'I don't believe so,' Helmut replied, his tone slightly affronted, then added with a smile, 'But then, I'm hardly in the best position to judge. My companion here is, though.' He nodded towards Adam. 'Quite stark staring.'

'You think it's funny? You could've killed me back there!'

'What on earth are you talking about?'

'What am I talking about? I'm talking about your driving! You almost had me off the road!'

Helmut glanced back through the rear window. Behind the little Fiat the green Granada ticked over, the driver's door hanging open like a petrified gill. 'Ah,' he said.

'Well? Is that all you've got to say?'

'If my memory is not playing tricks on me,' Helmut said, 'you yourself came much closer to causing an accident a little distance back.'

'What?'

'Yes. And I can see from your expression that you haven't the faintest idea what I'm talking about. Which I think rather adds power to my cause. You see, I did what I did quite consciously, purposefully and with a consummate degree of vehicle control. You, on the other hand, are guilty of driving with the skill and cognitive abilities of a narcoleptic badger. I have been thoughtful enough to give you a lesson, so kindly have the grace to learn from it.'

The man, his hands squeezing the window frame of Helmut's car door, was changing colour. 'Now you listen,' he said, his voice rising to a near shout on the last word, 'If you'd like to step out of this little sardine-can we'll see who's giving out the lessons round here!'

'Good day, sir!' The lights up ahead were changing to green. Helmut depressed the clutch and slipped into gear, ready to move away.

'No you don't!' The man reached angrily inside. He seemed to be aiming to grab the ignition key but Helmut neatly deflected his arm with a side-hand chop to the wrist. Easing his foot off the clutch he put a hand out through the window.

'Hey!' the man shouted as the Fiat rolled away. 'Hey!'

Helmut accelerated steadily, and the man trotted, then ran, and finally sprinted alongside, unable to do anything else for Helmut had him firmly by the belt of his trousers.

He cruised along for a hundred yards or so, keeping his antagonist at full sprint before releasing him to take a left turn to avoid the Victoria bottleneck. Out of the rear window Adam watched the man totter to the roadside and drape himself over the crash barrier.

'Boorish fellow,' Helmut muttered as he wound the window up. 'Do you think I overreacted a little? Perhaps I did, but I do believe he had violence in mind. And after all, I was in the right in pointing out that his was the original offence. My initial gesture was merely one of response to his oafish use of the road. And yet he had the gall to leave his car and accuse *me* of dangerous driving!

'I did not intend humiliating him like that, but when he stooped to insulting Boadicea and then tried to take my keys I felt he had gone just a little too far. I think that man was well overdue for a lesson in social etiquette, don't you?' He began to rotate his right shoulder slowly. 'That was quite an effort, you know. I hope I haven't strained a ligament. Oh, look, he's scratched the back of my hand!'

Adam kept his eyes on the road ahead and wondered whether the journey was going to be a very long one. They wound through Belgravia sidestreets, neither speaking for some time, until they came to Exhibition Road, heading towards Notting Hill and Helmut's destination.

'My friend,' Helmut said when they had entered the park and were gliding along The Ring, 'you are very quiet.'

'Thinking,' Adam replied.

'Is there something you want to talk about?'

'I don't think I can tell you anything you don't know, Helm. There's nothing new.'

'It seems to me, though, that you are keeping things very much inside yourself these days. More than previously. You no longer talk to anyone, do you? Have you still not felt inclined towards resuming relations with your psychiatrist?'

'To what end? He was no help.'

'Can you be so sure of that?'

'The man is manifestly unsuited to his job, Helm. He has no idea how to deal with people. He thinks his patients are objects for study and experiment, not human beings. He never really listened to anything I was trying to tell him, never answered my questions, just shot off on tangents, intent on his own predetermined course.'

'But don't you think it's possible he has a better overall view than you, a fuller perspective? His experience must count for something, after all. Maybe he sees things that you, being so entangled in it all, cannot. He has so many successes behind him.'

'I know about his successes,' Adam said shortly. He lapsed into silence, then added, 'I don't trust him.'

They left the park and Helmut accelerated suddenly. He weaved his little car deftly between rows of larger, more sluggish vehicles in a series of manoeuvres that made Adam shut his eyes tight.

'I ask only because Judith mentioned on the phone that you'd had something on your mind,' he said, nodding in satisfaction at the sight of the clear road ahead. 'And I sense a tenseness in you. More so than usual.'

Adam recalled his emotional outburst in the kitchen at home. It seemed a long time ago. Under Helmut's solicitous prompting something was coming back to him. That which had first come to mind when he was sitting in the cold over the brutish Slav's back garden, which at the time had been too emotionally charged to effectively convey to Judith, felt clearer and less volatile now. And there was not the earlier restriction on time.

'Listen, Helm,' he said. 'I've been giving a lot of thought to the way I've been handled through all this. Something always felt wrong but until now I haven't been able to pinpoint it. Now I see. It's our attitudes, our preconceived ideas. More than anything else they have been responsible for alienating me from therapy, and from Doctor Geld especially. He of all people has been most guilty of promoting it.'

'Hold on, my friend,' Helmut admonished him. 'Promoting what? I don't think I'm quite with you yet.'

'Helmut, we are all so intent on one object: returning me to the person I used to be. That is *all* Doctor Geld concerned himself with. And you too, and Judith. And myself, even.'

'Well, is that a bad thing? You want to regain your memory, don't you?'

'Of course. But that is only a part of it. We seem to be ignoring something. It strikes me that this overriding devotion to me as I was generates a disregard for what I am now. Therapy has had the sole aim of returning me to my original state, something I have no knowledge of. And what I pick up all the time is that nobody has any interest in what I have become. Everyone operates along the lines of how they would prefer me to be.'

They had pulled up outside a tall, detached Notting Hill mansion that had seen a lot of better days. Helmut cut the engine and lights but made no move to get out of the car. He sat back, removing his gloves with delicate tugs and pursing his lips thoughtfully.

'It is not very pleasant to be the object of that kind of reasoning, Helm. Do you see? I'm asking, what about what I am now? Is that of no importance? And more importantly, perhaps, something is happening to me. We aren't capable of analysing it or comprehending it, but we are at least able to see it is an ongoing process. Or we ought to be. But we seem to be missing the point that it *is* ongoing. There is motion, Helm. Where is it leading? It's an avenue that no one has even thought of exploring. We are all trying to go back. Why not forward? What is really happening, Helm? What am I *becoming*?'

Helmut reached over to eject the cassette from the player, then turned to face him. 'I don't wish to sound unsupportive or unsympathetic, my friend, because I'm not. Indeed I am most sympathetic, as you know. What you are saying is very interesting and I certainly see your point.

'But in answer to your questions, what springs immediately to my mind is this: What you are at present is a piece of flotsam in the grip of a mighty storm. What you are going to become if we fail to haul you back onto dry land is a piece of flotsam that has been dashed to smithereens on jagged rocks.'

'But why, to further the analogy, is it necessary to bring me back to the same shore?' Adam took hold of Helmut's wrist. 'What happens if I ride the storm?'

'You will be dashed to smithereens on another distant shore. Believe me, I am not being cynical, my friend. I do not want to invalidate your feelings. I feel simply that trying to ride the storm alone is a surefire recipe for disaster.'

'But all these feelings, hunches, hallucinations, dreams, impulses ... They can't be totally without value. I feel too deeply that they have a direction.'

'I would not necessarily dispute that. My argument is simply that alone you run a far greater risk of losing your way. And my friend ...'

'Yes?'

'You are hurting my arm again.'

'Oh, sorry.' He relinquished his grip on Helmut and stared out through the windscreen at the darkening street. It was deserted but for one man a little way up on the other side, who stood in a pale suit between two truncated brick pillars at the entrance to a house. It was difficult to tell in this light but he seemed to be looking in their direction, possibly even observing them in the car.

'I do understand your feelings,' Helmut said. 'I know how disconnected you feel.'

'But Helm, you're crazy too, aren't you? Your way of life would be considered way over the line by most people. The only difference as far as I can see between you and me is that you're in control of your craziness and I'm not. And you're not allowing anybody to try to change you.'

Helmut laughed. 'Perhaps you're right. Look, I would like to discuss this further, and my friend Dennis is also very interested in these kind of topics. Would you have any objection if we went in now and continued the conversation indoors? I'm sure he will have much to contribute.'

Adam shrugged indifferently and they got out of the car. As Helmut gathered his folder from the back seat Adam turned to inspect the exterior of the house they were about to enter.

It was set back from the road behind a low brick wall, an austere, joyless edifice several storeys high. The mortar on its external walls was cracked and falling, the paintwork flaking on the front door and window surrounds. The curtains were closed on all visible windows, bar that of the basement, and behind two of them dim lights glowed.

Steep steps ran up to an imposing forest green double door which stood like a portal to some unwelcoming land. As Helmut took his arm and they mounted the steps Adam shivered without knowing why, a distinct feeling of unease beginning to creep through his bones.

The front door had been left off the catch. As Helmut pushed it open Adam turned his head and glanced back over his shoulder at the road. The solitary figure in the pale suit still rested between the two brick columns, leaning on one, his hands in the pockets of his trousers. The focus of his gaze remained indiscernible. Apart from him there was no sign of life.

They entered the house and the big door swung shut behind them.

They were in a hallway, partially lit by a single naked lightbulb which hung from the ceiling at the far end. Beneath it two closed doors faced them, and nearby a staircase led up to the first level. The floor and stairs were covered in red carpeting, blotched and worn and flattened with age. The walls bore a tracery of hairline cracks and the faded green paint was blistered and peeling like diseased skin.

The place had an odour of staleness, fusty and slightly scented, redolent of unwashed flesh, airless rooms and neglected pensioners languishing in their final days. From deep within the building came vague thumps and creaks, and somewhere overhead the sound of snoring.

Helmut began to climb the stairs and Adam followed, his apprehension mounting with every step. On the first floor landing there was no light. They felt their way past several more closed doors until they reached the foot of a second flight of stairs, also carpeted in red. A dull light glowed from the landing above, and revealed a big man asleep on the stairs about two thirds of the way up. His body blocked their path. He was snoring loudly and erratically, his head supported by the banister rails, and around him lay a dozen or so discarded beer bottles.

Helmut turned to Adam and raised a finger to his lips. 'We might just be in luck.'

With Adam close behind he began to move silently up the stairs.

Pressing himself close to the inside wall Helmut was successful in stepping carefully past the sleeping giant without disturbing him. Adam followed his example, stretching to pass up through the narrow space between the wall and the man's great bulk.

He had almost made it, was almost past and about to lift his back leg through onto the stair above when his foot caught a bottle and tipped it with a loud chink against another. The man stirred and his eyes opened. Adam froze, caught red-handed doing he knew not what.

The man belched, blinking his heavy eyelids as his bleary eyes rolled, seeking a focus somewhere. His head swivelled slowly until he was looking up at Adam askance.

He frowned and a meaty hand shifted and clamped itself around Adam's ankle, securing the foot firmly to the carpet. He stared unsteadily into Adam's face then brought the other arm around. The hand battened onto Adam's thigh, a little above the knee, making him grimace in pain.

'T' fokk'n whooorrre!' he swore in a loud Scottish drawl. Into his eyes came a look of suppressed rage. He squeezed Adam's thigh harder. 'T' fokk'n wwwhhhhooooorrrre, 'll kuller!'

Adam blanched under the combined assault of pain, fear and the foul reek of sweat and alcoholic breath. He had no hope of struggling free of the man's grip.

'Excuse me,' he said weakly. 'Would you mind letting go?'

The big man cocked his head with a puzzled look. 'Ih?'

Adam was suddenly angry. 'Let go!'

The man moved in an attempt to bring himself into a more upright position, and Adam groaned as his full weight bore down on one foot. Then Helmut interceded.

He tapped the drunk on the shoulder. 'Excuse me, my friend. How are you?'

The giant sat back and twisted his bulk until he could take in Helmut seated on a stair above and behind him.

'I have something for you,' Helmut said. He produced the can of Yorkshire Bitter he'd mysteriously purchased earlier, and let it hang loosely between finger and thumb. Aside to Adam he said, 'Be ready to move.'

The giant's features melted. 'F' me?'

'For you.'

'Och, yerra paal.' He released Adam, who moved swiftly to the top of the stairs, and reached up for the beer.

'You're most welcome,' Helmut replied, rising as the ring-pull was flipped back and the golden liquid began to flow down the Scotsman's throat. 'Can't stop to chat, though. Pressing business. Good day.'

He was chuckling to himself as they continued along another landing, up three stairs and into a narrow passageway leading off to their right. 'The Guardian of the Stairwell,' he told Adam. 'He means no harm. It's just his way.'

Adam kneaded his thigh. He carried several scars on that leg and the giant's mauling had caused him a deal of discomfort. 'Will he follow us?' he said.

'Oh no. We're forgotten.'

'Who is he?'

'He lives here. Or rather, he lives there. He rents a room somewhere in this rambling domicile but spends most of his life these days on the stairs. He's waiting for his wife to come back.'

'Where's she gone?'

'Away. Wherever. She took French leave a little over a year ago and hasn't been heard of since. One of the other tenants went with her. Our friend back there remains convinced that one day she will come back on bended knees. He plans to take her back for as long as it takes her to complete her apology.'

'And then what?'

'Oh, he will kill her, I should imagine. And/or her lover, should he be so foolish as to show his face. In fact it's the lover he really wants to wreak his revenge upon. The wife, he feels, is not half as guilty, being only a woman.'

'But he'd still kill her?'

'Oh yes. I believe he might. The lover he'd probably kill twice. Dennis seems to think he keeps a gun hidden somewhere about his person. I can't imagine he'd ever find himself in an able enough condition to use it with the desired effect, though. Not within the limited time he would have available. But anyway, I'd personally wager that there's not a chance in heaven or hell of the object of his disaffection ever returning to his open arms, wouldn't you?'

They mounted two more steps and turned into another passage, this one inadequately lit by two wall-mounted frosted pink glass globes.

'Does he do that to everyone?' Adam asked.

'Yes, most people, I believe. If he's awake. You know, when I first had occasion to call here he had me for a good ten minutes pinned to the wall by the collar of my jacket. He gave me his life story, or what he could remember of it. I thought I was never going to get away. Nowadays I always come prepared. He isn't difficult to appease, as you just witnessed.'

'How did you get away?'

'Ah.' Helmut paused at the foot of a flight of narrow stairs which wound upwards to the attic. He looked down at his shoes as if inspecting them for scuff marks, then raised his head and took off his hat and examined its lining. Then he looked at Adam. 'I discovered the common bond, my friend. I discovered the common bond.'

Adam said nothing.

'It cost me a further ten minutes of self-pitying exchange,' Helmut went on, 'but at length I was permitted to make my escape unhindered. I tried to tell him it was best not to drink, that it only stirs up the memories. I thought at the time that I had made a new friend, but the next time we met he failed to recognize me. My advice had gone unheeded.'

Adam did not probe further. He knew that some seven years past Helmut had loved a woman for whom he would have given his life. She had jilted him, almost at the altar, in circumstances which were still unclear to Adam but which involved another man. By all accounts Helmut had been shattered. He had immersed himself in work and in the years since had not been near another woman other than in the course of his day to day business. He rarely mentioned it, in fact it had been Judith, not Helmut, who had passed on most of the details, for it had happened towards the end of their Oxford days. Adam wondered that his friend alluded to it now, and knew better than to press the matter.

Helmut replaced his hat. 'The Upper Levels!' he announced with a grin, clearing the memory from his thoughts.

For some reason the uneasiness Adam had been experiencing since they stepped through the front door intensified now. 'Helm,' he said, 'is everything all right here?'

'My friend, what do you mean? Everything is fine. Is something bothering you? You are very pale again.'

'I don't know. It's just a feeling.'

'Don't worry, we're almost there. You can sit down and have a nice hot cup of tea. And if you still want to we can continue the discussion we began in the car. You will probably feel better then. But if you don't, just say. I can always drive you home if you feel you don't want to stay. It's no trouble. Now if you will just excuse me for one minute, nature calls.'

He left Adam's side and stepped through a door a little further down the passage, closing it behind him. Some seconds later another door opened almost alongside it and a figure emerged. Adam said hello, but the man just grunted and pushed quickly by, head down. Adam watched as he hurried along the dingy corridor and disappeared around a corner.

He turned back and was gazing absent-mindedly at the door Helmut had gone through when something caught his eye. The floor here was uncarpeted, and underneath the door he could see a pool of dark liquid forming. He stepped forward for a closer examination. Blood was dribbling out beneath the lavatory door and advancing amoeboid fashion across the floorboards.

'Helm,' he said. 'Helmut!'

There was no answer. He called Helmut's name again and raised his fist to bang the door when he heard the toilet flush on the other side. A moment later the door opened.

'Yes, my friend?' Helmut said.

'Are you all right?'

'Yes, of course. What is the matter?'

Adam looked at his feet. There was no blood. He looked up in confusion at Helmut then back at the floor. He shook his head.

'Nothing. It's all right. I felt a bit faint, that's all.'

'Come along, my friend,' Helmut said. 'Let's get you upstairs where you can sit down and rest.'

Once again Helmut led the way, up the steep winding staircase to the attic. And as they climbed, Adam, clinging to the banister for the support he was beginning to feel he needed, began to grow aware of something. On the stairs, impeding his progress in places, were objects, discarded household items, pieces of junk.

First he noticed an empty cedar cigar box, then a dead Swiss cheeseplant in a broken earthenware pot. Then there was a pair of black polythene bin-liners stuffed with rags and scraps of material; and an old bike frame leaning against the wall.

Closer to the top was the neck of a cheap classical guitar, broken, its pink nylon strings coiling over the steps. A coffee table, two of its legs absent, crowned the staircase, and as he arrived at the top, breathing heavily and unevenly, he saw that the small area of the landing was strewn with miscellaneous junk.

The space he and Helmut stood in was directly beneath the roof, and through a skylight overhead dark clouds were visible scudding across an unsettled evening sky. There were two doors here, one on the right, one on the left, both painted a sickly pale yellow.

Helmut knocked twice on the right-hand door. There was a thud and a scuffling on the other side, then the sound of someone approaching. Adam, too weak to do anything but lean on the banister and wait, looked up at the noise of bolts and security chains sliding free. Then the lock turned and the door of the attic room was opened a few inches.

A waft of warm, cloying air blew out. It carried with it the smell of cheap incense, poached fish and hash smoke. Then, in the crack of the door, against a background of muddy reddish light, a face appeared.

Dennis

It was a face that belonged on the bottom of a pond.

The skin was an unhealthy grey. It gave the impression of unnatural moistness, seemed to be covered in some thin, filmy sheen. The eyes were small and hidden, sunken in dark sockets like pebbles. The nose was bulbous, unlike the rest of the face, and pocked and palely purple. A small, fleshy-lipped mouth was almost concealed behind a dense shaggy beard. And the thick tangled hair was long and unkempt, dark fronds and tendrils falling over the forehead and wreathing the face like matted black weeds.

The body, those parts that were visible to Adam, was thin and slightly hunched, clothed in loose brown heavy duty cords, socks, and a black sweatshirt bearing a Hunt Saboteurs logo.

'Hi, man.' A voice came out, seemingly with difficulty as it navigated a route from the vocal cords up through the oral cavity, between lips which made no effort to part, through strands of muffling beard and into the big world. Here it had to funnel its way through the door crack whilst contending with the atmospheric draughts doing battle around the doorway as the sluggish air of the attic room butted up against the weightier coolness of the landing and stairs.

So when it reached Adam's ears the voice was tired, with a laden, doleful quality, and might easily have been missed had he not been anticipating its arrival.

Helmut beamed and bobbed lightly on the balls of his feet. 'Dennis, my friend! How are you?'

'Come on in,' Dennis said. 'Glad you made it. Any problems getting here?'

'No problems,' Helmut said. The incidents with the cat, the Granada and the drunk on the stairs had found no lodging place in his memory.

'I'm sorry, man, you'll have to squeeze through. I'm a bit cluttered up in here.' Dennis was trying to open the door more fully but something seemed to be preventing him.

'Of course.' Helmut stepped forward, and as Dennis pulled on the door from the inside, prised his body through the narrow opening. Adam, who was less well padded, found the going a little easier.

When the two of them were inside the room and the door had been closed behind them, Dennis turned to Helmut and took hold of him by the throat. In his free hand a long knife had materialized. He brought it up to slash viciously across Helmut's larynx and up towards one ear. A dark red line appeared and spilled unevenly down Helmut's neck.

Dennis released him. He turned wild-eyed towards Adam and

yanked up the front of his Hunt Sab's sweatshirt, exposing his belly and chest.

'Yeah?' he said. 'Yeah?'

From arm's length he plunged the knife with a yell deep into his stomach, below the sternum. Adam gaped in horror as the blood gushed around the hilt.

Dennis stared at him, glassy-eyed. 'Anything Goes,' he said blankly, and Adam sighed inwardly, realizing he was in the presence of one of Helmut's most ardent devotees.

Helmut smiled. 'Anything Goes,' he agreed.

'You weren't ready for that, were you?' Dennis said.

'I wasn't. It was most effective. Might I examine the knife?'

Dennis handed it over. 'Theatrical and Joke shop. It's the best I've ever seen. Retracting blade and gallons of blood. Brilliant!'

'Very fine craftsmanship,' Helmut commented, then, 'Oh, forgive me. I haven't introduced you. Dennis, this is my very good friend the late Adam Shatt.'

Dennis gave Adam a penetrating look then shook hands.

'Adam is experiencing a certain difficulty of being,' Helmut explained when Adam remained silent.

'Aren't we all?'

'Ah, but I think you'll find this one poses some rather intriguing questions. If you've the time and the inclination I thought we might discuss it for a while.'

'Suits me. I'll make tea.' He turned to Adam. 'Do you take sugar?'

But Adam was not listening. His attention instead was on the room. It was piled to the ceiling and crammed to every nook, crack and cranny with junk. It was quite a small room with a ceiling that sloped on one side along the angle of the roof. Under the most favourable conditions living space would have been limited, as it was now it was hard to accept that so much could take occupation in such a confined area. The room seemed to contain more junk than it could conceivably accommodate.

There were three wardrobes, one of them lying on its side beneath the sloping roof. There were tea chests and wooden and cardboard boxes by the dozen. They were filled with books, bric-a-brac, old toys and market-stall antiques, crockery, metal brackets and fittings, and things that were presumably designed for particular purposes which could only be guessed at now they were seen outside their customary locations.

There were clocks, some ticking, some not, all over the place. There were radios and four televisions, one of which, a big monochrome, was switched on but flickering picturelessly.

There were chairs stacked up here and there amongst the debris. One stack of nineteen-fifties diners touched the ceiling. There were icons and lamps, cigarette lighters, Buddhas and goldfish bowls, old guitars, bags of nails, lampshades and chipped porcelain figurines, a haversack, some old green bottles, a box full of rocks, a cruddy Dansette player, records, tapes, several briar and meerschaum pipes, oriental masks, pictures without frames, frames without pictures, washers, screws, old clothes bulging from the wardrobes, a tarnished Bullworker, some bicycle tyres, a set of handlebars, wood carvings, a lawnmower, two toilet seats, some brass bathtaps, folders, files, ledgers, three typewriters and a collection of teapots.

There were some fat jute sacks tied up tightly at their necks. There were housebricks and mirrors, an up-ended rabbit's coop, some dolls, some board games, some chess sets, some Airfix models. There was a box filled with brass, copper and pottery items, some of which looked as though they might be of some value. There were lots of things wrapped in newspaper. There was a bed in there somewhere, where at night Dennis laid his weary head to sleep, though that too was laden down with assorted items of hardware.

The floor was layered unevenly with sundry old rugs and mats, to a depth in places of more than an inch. Three old gas meters occupied one lightless corner alongside a polythene sack of fertilizer.

Heaps of greetings cards, rolls of wallpaper, boxes of tubes of household adhesive, collections of Beatles monthlies and pop annuals, soft-porn and computer monthlies and *New Scientist* were stuffed into available spaces. There were pots of paint and a sheaf of brand new broom handles tied up with wire.

There were lengths of rusting chain. There were cricket bats, plastic sausages, trousers and handcuffs. And crouched on the top of one of the wardrobes, wearing a permanently bemused expression, its bald head wedged against the ceiling, was an incredibly ugly, virtually hairless female orang-utan. Around its feet were perched several bedraggled birds, stuffed long ago, some protected in bell-jars.

There was a ship in a bottle. And there were quite a lot of wooden puppets hopelessly entangled in their strings. There was a car radiator. A metal detector. A rake, some plastic fruit. Some fan heaters. A gilt-framed photograph of the Queen. Some swords. Bags of marbles. A small box of gleaming dentist's mirrors. Planks of wood. Silver Christmas trees. And a kitchen sink.

A Sinclair Spectrum was connected to the aerial socket of the flickering television set. Various other leads ran off it and disappeared under the bed.

All of this Adam took in at first long glance. He transferred his gaze slowly to Dennis, who was still waiting to hear whether he took sugar in his tea.

'That's quite a collection,' he said dazedly. 'What do you do for a living?'

'I'm a gardener,' Dennis replied.

Helmut, stepping judiciously, made his way towards a half-buried dining chair which stood beneath a small, high slatted window cut into the roof. He dropped his scarf, which he was holding in one hand, over the back, took off his hat and sat down, linking his fingers loosely in his lap and smiling amiably. He said to Dennis, 'My friend Adam does not know who he is.'

'Does anyone?' Dennis asked. He had moved away and was busying himself in a tiny kitchen area squeezed into a corner of the room.

Helmut leaned forward to shift a heap of cardboard, books and clothing and reveal a low armchair which he indicated Adam should take if he wished.

'Ah, but this is rather a special case,' he said. 'Apart from the fact that Adam is a very dear friend, I find that his psychological disposition and concomitant problems raise some fascinating philosophical questions. For instance, lacking memory he finds himself totally reliant upon the memories of others for details of his past. Think about that for a moment. And additionally he is beset by dreams and visions which he is convinced contain some kind of meaning which at present he is unable to decipher, and I know that is a topic which interests you. And further, his problem – your problem, my friend,' he inserted, squeezing Adam's knee warmly, 'please don't feel I am talking around you – presents itself, it has struck me, as a quest. A quest for self. Something we are all faced with but which most of us prefer not to enter upon too deeply. It seems to me, my friend, looking on the positive side, that you may have been given a head start over the rest of us. You are being forced to take on the quest, and indolence, fear, apathy, all the usual excuses we are prone to, cannot deter you. You are not being offered that choice and it is merely a matter of finding the right road. Is that how you view it?'

Adam shrugged. He wasn't feeling like discussing anything just then. Thoughts were skittering around in his head without order, he was nervous and confused, the flickering black and white tv screen irritated him and the heady, smoky, drugged atmosphere of the room was already exerting a powerfully disorienting effect on him.

Dennis delivered tea, then negotiated a path to his bed, cleared a space and sat down. On the way he gave the tv a sharp tap on its top. The flickering ceased and a picture appeared, a computer representation of two figures clad in martial arts gear.

Dennis depressed a key on the computer. The two fighters bowed and advanced circumspectly towards each other to engage in unarmed combat. Adam's attention was immediately captured. His eyes narrowed and he stared intently at the action on screen.

'Did you bring any poems, man?' Dennis asked as if he had failed to hear a word Helmut had spoken.

'I did. I did.'

'I've fixed up a reading for you, if you want to go. Some friends are having a party. I thought we could stir their brain cells a little.'

'Capital,' said Helmut. He took a small diary from his jacket pocket. 'When?'

'Any time, really. But I doubt if things will liven up much before closing time.'

'You mean this evening?'

'Yeah.'

'Oh. Yes. Capital.'

'I've told them about you,' Dennis said. 'They're really looking forward to meeting you. If they haven't forgotten. They're pretty weird on the whole.'

He reclined his thin body across the bed, his head supported by the wall at an angle that caused his thick beard to cover most of his chest. 'You know, I thought that name tinkled a little ding-dong. You were in the papers, weren't you?'

He was looking at Adam, but Adam was watching the television.

'Oi! Adam!'

Adam looked up.

'You were famous, weren't you?'

'Famous?'

'In the papers?'

'Oh.' Adam expelled air tiredly. 'Not exactly famous. I just happened to be in the wrong place at the wrong time.'

'Nah. You were famous. I remember. You were a hero.' On his belly he began to gather the ingredients to construct a joint. 'I remember you told me about him,' he said to Helmut.

'Yes. And now here is your opportunity to rub noses with the man himself,' Helmut said.

'Far out,' Dennis intoned without enthusiasm. 'So what happened? What were you doing? Northern Ireland, wasn't it?'

Adam nodded. 'I don't know. I was on a story and went out one night with an army patrol. We were ambushed.'

'Yeah, that's right. A rocket attack.'

'The Landrover I was in was hit. I managed to get out but was hit by rifle fire as I ran. Then it knocked me down as it was trying to reverse out of the firing line. I was lucky, I guess. Three other guys were killed.'

'You dragged a man free, though,' Dennis said. 'A soldier. Saved his life.'

Adam nodded and fell silent. His eyes returned to the screen.

Presently Dennis said, 'But you don't actually remember any of that?'

He sighed. 'No. None of it.'

Dennis sprinkled some dry black resin along the length of his joint. 'Great,' he said. 'What do you remember?' he said.

Adam thought for a moment. 'My first memory is of waking up

in intensive care. All wired and tubed up to drips and monitors and things, and hurting everywhere. I couldn't see. The pain in my head blinded me, and I didn't know anything. Not a single thing.'

Dennis licked his joint and sealed it, exchanging a look with Helmut. 'What happened?'

'I kept passing out and waking up. At some point I was able to open my eyes without so much pain. And after a while I realized that there had been someone sitting beside the bed every time I came to. A woman.' He hesitated, watching the television. 'I couldn't ask her who she was because I couldn't remember how to form sentences, and it was too much of an effort to turn my head to look at her. But she was always there, and eventually, when I learned to speak again, I asked her who she was. She told me she was my wife. That's when it really struck home. I really did have no knowledge about myself. So then I asked her who I was, and little by little she began to fill me in.'

'Nice one,' Dennis said, and lit up.

As he had been speaking the television that Adam was watching had been tipping by infinitesimal degrees sideways on its central pedestal. Half-consciously he had moved with it to stay with the action on screen. This meant that he was now leaning at an awkward angle over the side of his chair.

The two computerized combatants had done battle several times. Each time, one or the other being k.o.'d, they would return smartly to the edge of the playing area, bow, and begin a new contest.

'This is very accurate,' Adam observed.

Helmut adjusted his position for a better view. He watched in silence for a while, then said, 'Memories?'

'No, not memories. I don't think so. Just recognition.'

'Memories?' Dennis enquired curiously.

Helmut explained. 'Adam was adept in several oriental fighting forms. He had quite a name for himself around Oxford at one time. This was in the days before such practices had achieved the popularity they enjoy today. He was taught by the army.' He chuckled. 'Would you believe it? This shambling wreck of a man?'

'Look out!' Adam cried. The television had finally tipped to its limit, and as gravity took the upper hand it was toppling in a smooth arc towards the floor. But Dennis, unexpectedly agile, slid across the bed, extending a foot. Catching the tv with his toes he nudged it back to an upright position.

'Reflex,' he said. 'It comes with time. I've got it judged to the last millimetre now.' He offered his joint to Adam, who declined, as did Helmut, then suggested shifting from demo-mode and playing a bout against Adam.

Adam shook his head, feeling overwhelmingly tired. His heart was beating fast and the claustrophobic atmosphere of Dennis's room made him more and more unhappy.

He had noticed that everything he touched seemed to be covered in a layer of light grit or dust; his hands had acquired a faint covering of grime. He experienced an unwillingness to breathe, afraid of what he might be drawing into his body. Already the fumes from Dennis's joint were making him feel a bit wild. He closed his eyes.

He opened them again and allowed them to wander over the contents of the tiny room. It was hard to imagine the purpose of so much junk. Almost all of it was worthless, much of it damaged or broken, or simply clogged and ruined by dust. He wondered how it was possible to live with it all.

He was being stared out by the orang-utan on the wardrobe; he shifted his gaze.

'Why do you keep all this stuff here?' he asked Dennis, realizing even as he spoke that the other two were deep in conversation.

Dennis was glazed-eyed. 'What?' His shaggy head swayed unsteadily on his shoulders. The television was no longer on.

'Sorry. I didn't mean to interrupt. I just couldn't help wondering about all this.'

'Oh, yeah. It's just a sideline, you know. I keep meaning to get a stall on the Portobello or somewhere. I reckon I could make a bit of money, don't you?

'I just haven't got round to it, you know. When I get home at night I'm too knackered to get anything together. Keep getting more in somehow, but never get round to getting shot of any. Just don't have the time.'

'But where does it all come from?'

'Outside. Skips and things. Sometimes I do door-to-door, or check out house renovations. They're a major source.' He giggled. 'Hah! I could have the Holy Grail hidden in here and no one would ever know!

'A little shop would be nice though.'

Adam calculated that a period of years must have passed to allow this much material to accumulate. By degrees it would have placed greater and greater restrictions on Dennis's activities. It was astonishing that no real attempt had been made to clear any out.

'I hope you have no objection, my friend, but while you were asleep we discussed certain aspects of the dreams and hallucinations you have told me about,' Helmut said.

'Asleep?' Adam queried. He was not aware that he had lost consciousness again.

'Yes. You fell asleep.'

'We tried talking to you, man, but you didn't say anything,' Dennis said. 'We figured that meant sleep. *Hup!*' He shot horizontally across the bed again to right the television.

'Don't worry, my friend,' Helmut added with a smile. 'It was less than two hours this time. Dennis has made some interesting comments on your dreams.'

'Powerful images, man,' Dennis said, resettling himself. 'Very symbolic. That red snow falling across the land. Beautiful.'

He stroked the corner of his mouth. The ends of two nicotine-stained fingers, between which protruded another long smouldering joint, disappeared into the thicket of his beard. His gaze seemed to focus on his upturned toes in their woolly socks. 'Beautiful,' he repeated.

'In what way symbolic?' Adam asked.

'Jung talks about something that happened to him. Have you read him? He wrote about the power of the unconscious to communicate with us via symbols and archetypes. He considered such symbols to be universal, you know, common to all rather than unique to the individual. If we learned to interpret its messages he said we could become more whole, more in touch with our deeper selves.

'Individuation. That's what he called the process. He said there is no knowledge we can't have. I think he said that. The psychic is as natural a sense as sight, or hearing. We just haven't developed the ability to use it properly, man. He said that because of its power the unconscious was as likely to destroy us, because we try to rely solely on our objective senses instead of looking to the inner world.'

Dennis paused. He took a long drag and watched the hash smoke as it billowed in a fat cloud towards the ceiling. His eyes were half-closed and his voice as he spoke had trailed off into little more than an intermittent drawl.

'Far out,' he breathed.

'What about the red snow?' Adam said, fearing that Dennis himself was on the verge of losing consciousness. 'Where does that relate to what you're saying?'

'Yeah,' Dennis said. 'Jung dreamed of rivers of blood. First he saw Europe covered by a monstrous flood, and the mountains of his homeland, Switzerland, rising higher to protect the country. He saw civilization reduced to rubble, the bodies of countless thousands. He said he realized a great catastrophe was in progress. Then the whole sea turned to blood.

'The vision recurred, with the blood emphasized more vividly, and a voice told him, "This is wholly real and it will be so. You can't doubt it."

'He had a whole series of related visions. He saw an Arctic wave descending, snow and ice to freeze the land and kill all living things. Some of his patients reported similar dreams, the ones in asylums mostly. He was having a severe breakdown too at the time. Interesting guy. He assumed he was the victim of some kind of psychosis. The visions went on for months during 1913 and '14. Then, in August 1914, World War One broke out. And he realized then that his subconscious had foreseen it and that symbolically it had been conveying the information to his conscious mind.'

'So are you saying my vision of red snow heralds a similar catastrophe, then?'

Dennis shrugged. 'Who am I, man? How would I know? But think about it. Think about this age. When the next world war comes it'll be the end of mankind and all that. So, red snow falling from the sky onto a barren, frozen landscape . . . The blood of the slain falling back to earth? Radioactive fallout descending from the skies? And your memory blackout – the annihilation of the past. I'd certainly say you're having a severe breakdown, man. Wouldn't you?'

Helmut said, 'Do you see a connection between the red snow and the earlier part of the dream? The chase?'

Dennis stubbed his joint thoughtfully into his tea mug with a brief sizzle. 'Darkness. That's the state you're in, isn't it? That's the state we're all in, but your awareness seems more acute. Death, maybe, too. Jung was always having visions of darkness and death. The night before his mother died he dreamed he was in some dark primeval jungle and he heard great crashings in the underbrush. Suddenly this gigantic wolfhound burst forth. It bounded past him and disappeared, and he said he knew it had come to carry away a human soul. The next day he heard his mother had passed away.'

Adam stared at him in stunned silence. He had often spoken to Helmut of his nightmare but had never, ever, mentioned the hound.

'That's what it suggests to me, man, anyway,' Dennis said. 'But Christ, I dunno. I'm full of crap, anyway.'

Suddenly there was a noise. A rustle, a scuffling. It came from somewhere high up in one wall. Then there was a thud behind the gas-fire. Adam started. He looked from the fire to Dennis to Helmut to the fire again. From the flue behind it a black cloud was forming, pushing out from the sides and top of the unit into the room.

'Christ,' Dennis said with a frown. He slid off the bed and over to the fire.

He shifted a small, cluttered table and a record case stuffed with toys from in front of it and crouched down. Tipping the unit forward a few inches from the top he peered into the chimney vault behind.

'Bloody hell,' he said. He reached in with one hand.

He withdrew it slowly and stood and turned around to face them both. In the cup of his large leathery palm was a pigeon. Its head hung limply over the edge of his hand, and its plumage was part covered in the same powdery black soot that was now settling on the area around the fire.

'Christ,' Dennis said. He said it again. 'Christ.'

Adam was dumbstruck, as apparently was Helmut.

'You know, I've been hearing spooky noises up in the wall for some days,' Dennis said. 'Poor bugger. It must've got trapped in the chimney and starved to death. It's still warm. Must've died just this minute. What a way to go. Christ. Gave me a fright, did it you?'

He carried the body of the bird over to the edge of the bed and sat down, placing it on his lap and staring at it in perplexity.

'There's something going on, man,' he said to Adam. 'Birds are an omen of death in several cultures. Jung talks about them, too.'

'Whose death?' Helmut enquired lightly.

'Dunno,' Dennis said. His grey face was lined. He was clearly upset by the incident. 'Something's going on, though. Something big. Bigger than us.' He looked at Adam. 'And you're the centre of it, man. It's all hanging around you. I thought there was something.'

There was a fierce light burning in those dark sunken eyes, and the solemn voice was rising with a note of genuine alarm.

'There's death in the air, man. I can feel it. I don't think it's a good idea to be too close to you.'

The Life And Soul

'Be calm,' Helmut said quietly from his seat beneath the slatted window. To Adam he added, aside, 'Don't worry, my friend. It's the smoke.'

'I am calm,' Dennis said. He looked wildly at Adam, then at the pigeon. 'But this is weird. I'm not sure that this character's safe company.'

'At this moment he might quite justifiably be thinking the same about you,' Helmut pointed out. 'Don't you think you might be overreacting somewhat? After all, look, nothing has happened. We were all sitting here having an interesting, intelligent conversation and a dead pigeon fell down the chimney. Everything else is in your imagination.'

'Come on, man. You're not going to tell me it's coincidence,' Dennis protested.

'I am jumping to no conclusions one way or the other, simply looking at the facts. And the same cannot be said of you. Perhaps it is coincidence, or indeed, perhaps there is "something big going on". Perhaps it is true that Adam is seeing visions of the end of the world as we know it, and maybe powerful psychic energies are active within and about him. Personally I remain to be convinced, but that is beside the point. What is to the point is a) Adam needs our help if we have any to offer; b) one cannot suddenly decide to shun a person simply on the grounds of unsubstantiated superstitions, that is tantamount to bigotry; and c) we are all three still here and quite capable of continuing with our very interesting discussion in a calm and civilized manner.'

'It's not superstition,' Dennis muttered.

'Quite right. I apologize. A bad choice of words. But it is supposition and it is unsubstantiated, you will grant me that. And as philosophers we cannot afford to work with such inadequate tools. We must be fearless investigators, open-minded seekers of knowledge and truth. Nothing else will do.'

Dennis, drawing several strands of his beard into one corner of his mouth, began to gather his tobacco, papers, cannabis and matches about him.

'And more, my friend,' Helmut went on. 'Let us say that there are invisible forces at work within this room. Does it matter? If they should tear the room and its contents asunder, even destroying the three of us in the process, does it matter? If Adam does see the end of civilization as we know it, does it make any difference, effectively, to us? We, like many others, have already acknowledged that man is nearing the end of his existence on Earth. We should be acting accordingly, surely, not reacting with unreasoning alarm every time something occurs to further reinforce that fact. "Anything Goes", after all, in today's world. We acknowledge that and must live by it.'

'Yeah, Anything Goes,' Dennis conceded a shade reluctantly. He studied with a wistful gaze the pigeon on his thighs, then said, 'Yeah, but I've been thinking about this. If "Anything Goes", Helmut – and I'm not arguing that it doesn't or anything – but if "Anything Goes" then why isn't it fine for me to think whatever I want and act whatever I want, superstition or not? You're right, it doesn't matter, does it. But now you're saying it does. I mean, if "Anything Goes" why do we have to seek truth or knowledge?

We can seek lies. We can seek half-truths. Or we can seek Kellogg's Cornflakes if we want. With sugar and milk or not. Or we don't have to seek anything at all. You know, why bother? Conscience is Dead, isn't it, so I can boil both of you in acid and not feel a thing. Lawlessness is the only Law. So why give a damn about truth when we're all on the way out anyway?'

'Ah. Well, that's true,' Helmut said, 'to a point. But you are missing a vital factor. Elemental to the construct of "Anything Goes" is the concept of survival against the odds for the longest possible time. Now, to take advantage of your last example, I would argue that boiling your friends in acid is not pro-survival. It surely lessens your own hopes of surviving when the bad men come to visit, if nothing else.'

'Yeah, man, but that's not what I'm trying to say. And anyway, he's not a friend. I've only just met him for the first time and he could be anyone. I mean, even he doesn't know who he is. So I could still put him forward as a candidate for the acid bath, right?'

Helmut shook his head. 'You have greeted him as a friend, or at least a potential ally, through my agency. And he you.'

'Yeah, but who's to say I'm not lying? Or he's not? Or you're not? We could all be, it doesn't matter. But that's not my point. I could go out and boil a couple of strangers in acid. I'm not saying it has to be you. And that's not my point either. I just mentioned acid off the top of my head.'

'Yes, I understand that. But I must still contend that to remain in accord with "Anything Goes" your actions must be able to be judged as pro-survival within the parameters of highly exceptional circumstances. And whereas murdering, raping, looting, or just lying in bed all day waiting for the end to come might, under these conditions, be the choice of the many, they will not be the choice of the thinker. The thinker will see that for what it is, the manifestation of a herd instinct, or the equivalent of cutting your own throat when your doctor tells you that you have only ten to fifteen years to live. He will not see it as pro-survival.'

'So what are you saying, then? That the world might not end? That we should all hold hands and sing songs together?'

'No. "Anything Goes" is based on the belief that things have gone too far to prevent the world's demise, and that this has induced a specific form of insanity within society. Nevertheless it does not mean we should immediately begin boiling one another in acid.'

'But you said we should assume an attitude of *carte blanche*...'

Adam switched off. He felt stifled and oppressed in this crowded room, and as the other two continued their debate he began to look around him for diversion. A disturbing notion had seized him, that more unwanted items were actually coming into the room, as with the pigeon in the fireplace, even as he was sitting there. He was suddenly worried that if he did not move soon he might never find a way of getting out.

His eyes fell on a book that lay on top of a pile of housebricks nearby. He picked it up.

It was a slim, pocket-sized volume bound in green leatherette. Its title, in gold lettering, proclaimed: *The Book Of Imaginary Hauntings* by Iddio E. Scompiglio. He flicked through it idly; it appeared at first glance to be a collection of epigrams and short pieces of verse. He allowed it to fall open on a page at random, and read:

Seeing without eyes is the mark of the madman or the seer. Make your choice!

Adam closed the book again quickly. He did not want to think about that. It seemed too directly relevant to him. Or was it gobbledygook? He did not want to think about it.

'Ah, I see you have discovered Dennis's *vade mecum*,' Helmut said. He seemed grateful of the opportunity to extricate himself from his discussion with Dennis.

'You mean this?'

'Have you read it?' Dennis asked with sudden animation. 'It's amazing, man. He's a great writer.'

'Who is he?'

'He is Dennis's spiritual master. And from all reports the spiritual master of many others, too. He apparently has followers in various parts of the globe.'

'In that little book,' said Dennis, 'you can find the answer to any question that might be bothering you. You don't need the I Ching any more, man. Scompiglio is what it's all about today. And he's alive, too. He's in the world working to change it.'

'Yes, a mysterious fellow by all accounts,' Helmut put in. 'It appears that nobody has ever set eyes on him.'

'Yeah, but he's going to show himself one day soon. He's going to have a Day of Declaration. And when he does I want to be around to see it.'

'Not quite my cup of tea, exactly,' Helmut said, 'though I must admit to finding a certain power in some of his writings.'*

Adam shook his head. Dennis said, 'I've got his other works here somewhere. You should read them. I dunno what it is sometimes. Sometimes he seems so simple on the surface, but the way he writes, it just floors you. It's like you know you've just tapped into something, but you can't say how he did it. Like the last essay of his I read. It's called 'The Poisoned Land'. It's about this land that's dying because people have polluted it so badly, and how the people have all got to be made aware that they are responsible. Because they don't know. That's the crux. They don't realize that they're doing the damage. They just keep blaming everyone else and, well, I can't explain it, man. It's dead simple but it speaks right to you.' He put his hand next to his heart to corroborate his feelings.

Once again Adam was shocked numb by what he was hearing. He did not dare try subjecting it to analysis, was not capable of doing so at present anyway. He just sat there and held on tight to his chair.

Dennis said, 'I've got his other books here somewhere. Hang on.'

Lifting the body of the pigeon and placing it gently on top of a stack of gravy tureens at the foot of his bed, he stood and stepped carefully through his debris to the wardrobe which lay on its side beneath the slanting roof.

'I think they're in here.'

He sank to his knees and lifted the wardrobe door and his head and shoulders disappeared inside. Helmut smiled at Adam. 'Bear with him,' he whispered, nodding.

'I thought they were in here,' Dennis said, his voice sounding hollow and even more muffled from within the wardrobe. 'I put

* Readers wishing to know more about the enigmatic Iddio E. Scompiglio are directed to *The Great Pervader* by Philip First, in which the mystery of the man and his works are discussed in greater detail.

them here the other day when I was having a tidy up. Hang on, what's this?' He began his backward retreat out of the gaping maw. 'Aw, no.'

Still kneeling he straightened his back slowly and a little unsteadily. In his hand he held a tiny furry body, stiff as a board.

'It's a kitten. It's a bloody kitten. I'm bloody sick. That's the fourth now.'

Helmut knitted his brows. 'But how did it get there?'

'Oh Christ.' Dennis seemed close to tears. He stood up and picked his way back to the bed, carrying the kitten with both hands as though it were a bomb primed to explode at the slightest jarring. He sat down. 'It's a long story . . .

'I had mice, man. I was getting overrun with them and I just couldn't get them to leave. I didn't know what to do. I tried talking to them but they took no notice. So I tried smoking them out and that didn't do any good either. And they were driving me crazy, man. I couldn't get any sleep or anything.

'So in the end I got a cat. I didn't want to kill them or anything, just frighten them off. I thought if I kept the cat on a leash just its presence in the room would be enough to keep them out. You know, once they knew there was a cat about they'd steer clear.

'But the bloody cat didn't have anything against mice anyway. In fact they got on like a house on fire, and she just lay around all day and got fat and so did the mice. So I asked the landlord and he gave me this stuff for the mice. I said would it hurt them? because I was worried, and he told me it was quite painless but that the mice hated it and wouldn't stick around. But I was a bit concerned about the cat, I said, and he told me it didn't affect cats or dogs or things. He pointed it out to me on the box, where it said it.

'So I put this stuff down and it was marvellous. The mice all vanished in days. And then I discovered that the cat wasn't really getting fat at all, she was pregnant. And about six weeks ago she had five little kittens. You should have seen them, man. They were so cute. Little fluffy mewling things . . .

'And then about two or three days later I found one of them dead. And then another one. And I found they'd been eating this stuff the landlord gave me for the mice. This makes four now. That means there's only one little kitten left, and I haven't seen it for more than a week. Thinking on it, I haven't seen the cat, either.

'Bloody landlord!' He thumped his leg impotently. 'I'll bet he knew all the time. I'll bet that stuff killed the mice, too. I'll bet it didn't just make them move away. I'm sick of it, you know. I'm sick of all of it. This bloody house. The people here are really weird. Half of them don't talk to you. There's an old bag downstairs keeps calling the police and telling them I've murdered someone! She nearly got me busted one night! I opened the door and there were two bloody great coppers standing there! Christ, that's not right, is it?

'And the guy across the landing ... He moved in a couple of months ago and on his first night I thought I'd do something to welcome him in. You know, friendly gesture, help him settle into his new home, meet the neighbours. So I cooked him a vegetarian curry and took it across and knocked on his door. "Hello, I'm Dennis," I said. "I live next door to you. I've made you a curry." Do you know what he did? He stood there and looked at me, then at the curry, then he shut the door and left me standing there. I mean, what do you do, man, with people like that? I'm sick of it all. Really. Sick.'

He pushed his hair back from his forehead and glared hard at Adam.

'My friend, you are getting yourself excited,' Helmut said soothingly. 'It does no good. It does not help the situation. I understand your feelings and I am very sorry.' He glanced at his watch. 'But the evening draws on. Perhaps we ought to be thinking about going out soon.'

'Yeah,' Dennis said. 'Perhaps we should.'

He placed the stiff kitten carefully in the gravy tureen with the pigeon and stood up to put on a jacket and a pair of old track shoes.

'Now, about our friend on the stairs,' Helmut said when the three of them were ready to leave. 'Ought we to take an offering just in case?'

Dennis scowled. 'He's usually crashed out by this time, but three of us going by might disturb him. I'll take something.'

He reached under the bed and pulled out a beer bottle and then found a discarded top which he thumped into place with the heel of his thumb and secured with a nutcracker. Adam remarked on the bottle's being empty.

'Yeah,' Dennis said. 'By the time he's got it open, though, and worked out why there's nothing coming out we'll be gone. He never remembers who gave it him, so I'm safe.'

He propped up the tv with a box of magazines. His voice rose again. 'Anyway, that big moron! One of these days I'm going to smash a bottle over his big bloody head! I mean, why should I have to pay him every time I want to get in or out of my own home? I live here, for Christ's sake. Who does he think he is?'

The party at which Helmut was due to give his reading was reached with no further major incident, much to Adam's relief. On the stairs the giant was asleep and they were able, all three, to slip quietly by. Dennis hid his empty bottle behind a dustbin outside, planning to recover it later in order to regain access to his home.

They crammed themselves into Helmut's tiny Fiat. Being the slightest in build Dennis took the back seat, arranging himself lengthwise across it then, as the others were strapping themselves into the front, suggesting that as the party was only in the next street, they might prefer to walk. So they walked.

Upon arrival Helmut was announced as *the* Mr Wasser of 'Anything Goes' fame and *Life With The Dogs* renown – *Life With The Dogs* being a collection of poems he had published a year or so earlier. Probably not one of the assembled partygoers had heard of him but in the absence of a more illustrious presence he was welcomed like a saint. Beaming and pink with pleasure he was led away to be fed and watered and catechized on his Weltanshauung.

Dennis quickly attached himself to a pint mug and a Party Seven. Acquainted with many of the people there he joined a group of intellectuals on a sofa to talk politics and smoke hash.

Adam, happy to be left alone, took a bottle of mineral water and drifted like a spirit through the busy rooms and, eventually, out to the back.

He stood on a step overlooking the back garden and breathed in the cool night air. The garden, from what he could see of it, looked extensive. It was illuminated here and there in unreal patches of light thrown down from upstairs windows. He could not make out its boundaries.

He was experiencing a great desire for solitude just now and was wondering whether to simply disappear for a while. Helmut would not take offence should he leave without saying anything, but he would be concerned. Under the circumstances probably very concerned.

So in fairness Adam knew that he should search Helmut out and tell him. But he also knew that Helmut would either do his best to dissuade him or insist upon driving him home. Adam didn't want to be chaperoned, he just wanted to think for a while, alone. The last few hours ... or days? – he had no comprehension of time – had developed into a continuing nightmare. He could not in any way work out what was happening, but was deeply frightened. Equally, he was determined he would not allow himself to be defeated.

He sat down on the step and sipped thoughtfully from the neck of his bottle. The noise of rock music and party laughter and chat came from inside, and from a window above him a number of desperate persons were loudly voicing complaint as a queue for the lavatory formed on the stairs. He thought about Dennis.

He would have been quite happy never to have to set eyes on the fellow again, but he knew that could not be so. Envisaging Dennis's home and thinking of words spoken to him by Doctor Geld at some indeterminate point in his past ... well, he could formulate no clear thoughts on that, but he was in no doubt that he needed to speak some more with Dennis.

He would have liked to have grilled him some more about his views on his dreams and the other events of his inner life. Of course, it was obvious that Dennis was far from being an expert on the matter, but nevertheless his comments had gained Adam's interest. Adam was even considering mentioning something to him of the brutish Slav and his hound, describing it perhaps as another dream.

A more productive approach, he thought, might be to make a study of Jung, even seek out a Jungian analyst. Until tonight his knowledge of Jung had been negligible, but now he was intrigued. But these thoughts were for the future. How was he to deal with the present?

More than anything, possibly, he was anxious to quiz Dennis further about Iddio E. Scompiglio. Adam was not a man who devoted much time to religious matters, be they cultist or more established. But that glimpse into Scompiglio's little book, and then Dennis's startling reference to his work, 'The Poisoned Land', had raised questions in Adam's mind that could not be expected to lie down.

People suffering varying degrees of intoxication were beginning to emerge in ones and twos from the doorway behind him, to make their way, some not too successfully, into the darkened shrubbery beyond the lawn. For some reason the bathroom had become inaccessible and tacit judgement had been passed that this was the most reasonable alternative.

He had taken little notice at first, but now a fairly regular stream of both genders was passing noisily by him, hindering his thought.

A woman, returning to the house, decided to seat herself on the step alongside him and congratulate him on his musicianship. He was not aware but he'd been blowing a regular, deep bass note into the neck of his bottle.

'Are you a musician?' she said, and laughed.

Adam shook his head. He thought at first he knew her, then dismissed the idea.

'Let me guess. An architect?'

He frowned. 'No.'

'Are you, then, a dreamer?'

He looked round sharply, searching her face for a sign of something hidden behind the words.

'A dreamer! I knew!' She laughed again, throwing back her head. But he had detected nothing, and when, with her next question, she enquired as to his birth sign he decided it was time to move back indoors.

Passing along the hallway he noticed people entering a room from which no music or party noise issued. He followed them, closing the door behind him. He was in a fairly long room, one end of which had been cleared to allow plenty of space around a bar-stool upon which Helmut was perched, sorting through his manila folder. Before Helmut, seated and standing, was an audience of twenty-five or so persons.

The main light had been dimmed and a single floor-mounted spotlight, previously set to highlight a mass of houseplants, had been re-directed to illuminate the poet. From its low position it threw Helmut's shadow up across the wall and ceiling behind and above him. It also accentuated some of his facial features, bringing out odd lumps, folds and furrows in less than complimentary relief.

Helmut had apparently forgotten the gash that Dennis had earlier applied to his throat. The 'blood' had dried on his skin and the collar of his shirt. Seated squatly on his stool, with his long sparse hair, his bloodied neck and the unusual illumination, he presented a figure resembling a comically malevolent gargoyle.

Adam smiled to himself and took a place at the rear.

Helmut waited, his eyes travelling good-humouredly over his audience until gradually conversation ceased. Then he began.

'As some of you may know,' he said, 'I call myself The World's First Radioactive Poet. It is indicative of the era we find ourselves born into that I can no longer claim to be the only one.' He watched the faces in the audience. 'Nonetheless, my title still holds true. I am the first, if not the last, and shall always remain so.'

He grinned and took the first sheet of paper from his folder.

'I've chosen to open with a short, unfinished poem because I feel that in its brevity and incompleteness it transmits a message, certainly to myself, that is most pertinent to our times. I have spent many hours in search of the climactic ending I feel it demands, so far to no avail.' He opened his hands. 'Perhaps someone here can suggest one. For now I have called it "World – Without End".'

There were smiles in his audience. He cleared his throat and took a breath, then drew himself up. Pausing a moment longer for effect, he began. His voice, commanding and assured, dominated the room:

> 'Almost darkness.
> I, alone in this doomed room
> Stare out
> Through transparent wall fixture,
> At endless empty grey no matter world,
> Wondering.

And wait
Like forgotten pet in glass jam-jar,
Dreaming that destiny, yours and mine,
May meet,
One day.

I question,
Eyes raised to sky.
Being seeking,
And jagged soul beseeching
While the question, spoken or unuttered,
Is unanswered: . . .'

The few seconds of silence that followed was broken by polite applause and murmured compliments from those gathered. Helmut, visibly pleased, nodded his thanks and sifted another poem from his folder. Adam, though not always a great fan of his friend's artistic endeavours, was moved. But he was not tempted to remain for more. He had noticed that Dennis was not present, and had decided to seek him out. He slipped unnoticed from the room.

Following the beat of soft-rock up a flight of opulently carpeted stairs he found himself in a large room. Two rooms, in fact, which had been knocked into one, running from the front to the rear of the building. At one end couples danced closely, and around them, on chairs, sofas or the floor, others sat drinking, smoking, talking softly, or smiling into their own stupors. The air was rich with the smell of burning marijuana.

At the bottom of the room, behind an oak dining table supporting a largely demolished buffet, Adam spotted Dennis. He was seated alone on the floor, his back against the wall. His head was low, his wrists hanging over his knees which were drawn up in front of him. From one limp hand a bottle of Gordon's gin dangled. Adam, his senses swimming slightly, moved down to join him.

Dennis raised his head as Adam approached and his deep, pond-dweller eyes made an attempt to focus. But they gave up, rolled towards the ceiling, and his head tipped back and hit the wall with a dull thud.

'I'll bet you've got a hell of an aura, man,' he drawled as Adam slid down the wall beside him. Adam frowned. 'Some people can see auras. I've never been able to, but some people can. I'll bet they'd find something to say about yours. There's something about you. I dunno what it is, but you're not normal, I know that much. Drink?'

Adam shook his head. Dennis raised the bottle and took a swig.

'Actually, I wanted to ask you something,' Adam said.

'Have you sampled the crystal?'

'What?'

'The crystal. White stuff. You know, *cocaine*. There's some ace samples going round tonight. D'you want a taste? Morpurgo's the man. I'll find him for you if you like.'

'No. No, thanks,' Adam told him. He doubted whether Dennis was capable of finding anyone at that point anyway.

'You sure? It's no problem.'

'I'm sure. Thanks all the same.'

'What did you say?'

'I said I wanted to ask you something.'

Dennis nodded expansively. 'Go on then, man. Anything you like.'

'I was hoping to continue the discussion we began earlier.'

'You mean your dreams and things?'

Adam nodded.

'I know what you mean, man. It's hard to drop that once you get into it. Don't you go to a psychiatrist, man?'

'I did. Not now.'

'I mean an analyst, not one of those shrinks. Someone who knows a bit about the inner world. I could put you on to a few, if you want. I've been to them all. Trouble is they're no good. Nobody is when it comes to this kind of stuff. You're on your own.' He stared dejectedly at the bottle between his knees. 'Except for the drugs, man. Thank God for drugs. I'd never make it through a day without them. This life just beats hell out of me. Do you know what I mean? It's scary. Drugs, man, that's all I've got. Drugs and a roomful of junk. What do you think of that?'

Adam said nothing. He had the uncomfortable feeling that Dennis was about to break up and sob on his shoulder.

'I've never told anyone that, man, because they don't understand. Or they don't want to. Just keep pretending, that's what
life's all about, isn't it? Don't ever let on about anything. But I
don't mind telling you, man, because you're different. I can tell
you're different. You know what I'm saying.' He turned his head
and looked at Adam with a sudden fierce curiosity. 'I didn't mean
to get at you earlier, man. I really didn't. But there's something
weird about you. A lot of things going on. Who'd you go to,
anyway?'

'Pardon?'

'Shrink, man. Shrink. Which one did you see?'

'I doubt if you'd know him.'

'Try me. I know them all.'

'His name was Geld.'

'Theo Geld? Weymouth Street?'

'You do know him?'

'Know of him. I'll tell you, man, you're lucky you dropped that
one. Or got dropped. Whatever.'

'Why?'

'Government man, man.'

'What?'

'He works for the government.'

'In what capacity?'

'Research. Don't know what exactly. Hush-hush. But I can tell
you you're better off without him. Whatever you do, man, if you're
having thoughts about going back, don't. A man like that is a
curse on anyone's good fortune.'

'Government research? Are you sure? How do you know that?'

'Did a raid on a laboratory a couple of years back.'

'A raid?'

'Yeah. Animal Lib.' He raised a finger to his bearded lips. 'Not
a word, man.'

'But what did you find?'

Dennis belched and his head tipped forward and sideways and
rested on one arm. One eye surveyed Adam sidelong. 'Horror
show. Rabbits, monkeys, dogs with their brains cut in half. Bits of
wire coming out of their heads, pieces of brain taken away, micro
experiments, things implanted in their heads, all sorts of sick
stuff. I'll tell you, man, no wonder you're such a mess if you've

had that guy working on your head. He was head of research there.

'We got him in the papers, and mounted demos outside his home. And some of his cronies, too. But there was a clampdown on publicity. Then the cops started getting underhand, visiting people's houses and stuff. Planting stuff. A couple of unexplained burglaries and muggings. I had to back off. I couldn't have them getting dirty on me. With that old bat downstairs calling them every few days and all. I didn't want to get busted. There's nothing you can do, anyway. People like Geld, they're untouchable.'

Adam could not decide how seriously to take him. Could all of this be true? Or was it the concoction, or part-concoction, of a paranoid leftist drughead? And if it was true, how did it affect him, Adam, if at all? He tried to put into perspective what Dennis was telling him but his attention was suddenly caught by something new.

Two people, a man and a woman, had just entered the room and were standing talking at the far end. The woman was the one Adam had encountered on the step in the back garden, and the man, who wore a pale suit, also seemed familiar.

They stood near the door, and as they talked seemed to be glancing in his direction. It could have been his imagination, but something in their manner made him uneasy.

'You don't believe me, I can tell,' Dennis said, his head lolling on his shoulders. 'Well, I've got the proof at home. Kept the clippings.'

It was impossible to decide whether the two were discussing himself or Dennis or both. More likely, he tried telling himself, they weren't discussing either. It might have been the buffet that had their attention, or a picture over his head or something. Or maybe they weren't really looking his way at all; in this light it was admittedly difficult to be sure. But he remained unsettled, and moreover, he thought now that he had recognized the man.

'There's more,' slurred Dennis. 'You really picked a downer there, man. Really.'

'I didn't pick him.'

The man had taken a notepad from one pocket and was writing something down. At the same time, there was no mistaking it now, he was giving Adam a long appraising look.

'God, I'm so sick about those kittens,' Dennis said.

'Dennis, listen. Do you know those two characters by the door?'

Dennis screwed his face up as though the act of altering the focus of his gaze was something that demanded a great concentration of muscular effort. He peered towards the door.

'Nope.'

'Please, look again. Are you sure?'

'Hang on. Know the babe. Ruth. Jewish woman. Spends half the year in Berlin.'

'And the man?'

'Can't see him very well.'

'You don't recognize him? I think he was hanging around outside your place earlier this evening. He seems to be very interested in us.'

'Yeah?' Dennis straightened. 'I dunno.'

The pale-suited man was putting his notepad back into his pocket. He gave the impression that he was preparing to leave. The woman seemed reluctant for him to go. She had her arms around his neck and was kissing his face. Then he said something and they both turned to look directly at Adam.

'I'm going to go and speak to them,' Adam said.

'What for?'

'I want to know why they're talking about me.' He stood up, determined to catch the man before he could leave the building.

But as he stepped forward something extraordinary started to happen. All the people at the other end of the room began to rise slowly towards the ceiling. The floor beneath them was rising, too. Sluggishly at first, then more rapidly. He had a vertiginous sensation of movement, then he was looking at the demolished spread on the buffet table. It was coming up at him with an alarming velocity. There was not even time to cry out before he felt and heard a shattering, resounding crash. All the lights went out.

Dennis, who had seen nothing, put his clay-coloured face into his hands.

'I didn't know it was poison,' he sobbed to nobody but himself, 'I would never have done it if I'd known. I'm sorry. I'm so sorry.'

Back From The Deep

When they brought Adam home the next day he was giving voice with maximum intensity, and Judith was having lunch with Simon Partridge, a colleague from her Section. Partridge, an infrequent visitor to the Shatt household, had contrived to call on the pretext of delivering some items of paperwork. They required Judith's approval, as his immediate senior, and in some cases her signature. With the South East caught up in a postal dispute he had considered it unwise to commit the documents into the hands of the Post Office, and though he might reasonably have committed them into the hands of an approved courier service he had preferred to deliver them by hand. It was really no trouble for him to pop over, he had insisted, and there were one or two details he rather needed her opinion on.

That Simon Partridge was afflicted with an interest in Judith that went beyond the professional was a secret he could not successfully keep.

Judith had tried to put him off, for she was not greatly enchanted by Partridge. A smallish, roundish person in his thirties, too neat and fussy, he was a man who wanted to be liked. To this end he affected a boyish air which got on most people's nerves and which emphasized, if anything, the underlying insecurity it was adopted to conceal. His speech and body movements were quick and too eager and tended to make her impatient to be elsewhere.

She knew relatively little about him, other than that he was a 'temporary', ex-public school, and had gravitated to government service following the collapse of a family pharmaceutical business. He had been transferred some months earlier to her branch of the Foreign Office from south of the river. And as part and parcel of the profession she occupied, there was always the nagging suspicion that he might be not quite all he declared himself to be.

Of necessity much of Judith's work was graded with an official classification of some degree or other. Much of the paperwork that passed routinely across her desk was to be kept from the eyes not only of unauthorized personnel, but of other civil servants with whom she worked. The problem, in the labyrinthine system in which she pursued her chosen course, was one of specification. It was made all but impossible, even for those with years of dealing with such matters, to know which documents, if any, contained genuinely sensitive material, and/or to whom they might or might not be shown.

Essentially the situation had degenerated into a condition beyond reason or redemption long ago. The burden of administrative secrecy, so central to all government proceedings, had grown to become a gigantic parasite crouched on the back of the system, bringing it virtually to its knees and threatening to bury it deep beneath the jungle of its own bureaucracy. Were the rules to be followed as form decreed no work would ever be done. Every file, every single document, would need to be booked in and out, severely limited in its distribution, never taken home, hidden from porters, cleaners, windowcleaners, as well as colleagues, security cameras, and even superiors, and kept clear of desktops. The rigmarole of locking, unlocking, signing, passing, checking, and keeping an eye at all times over one's own shoulder would take up the entire working day.

So generally classification and form were not given too much heed. They lurked in the background like a strict but unwanted aunt, tacitly acknowledged but rarely taken seriously.

Of late, though, the aunt had succeeded in bringing her influence much more to the fore. Over a period of a year or so there had occurred certain leaks of confidential documents to the press and commercial or industrial concerns. Nothing about to cause an international crisis, but a distinct irritation within the system nevertheless. Enough to indicate that some person or persons were not playing the game, that the bonds of Official Secrecy were being casually slipped in the belief that some other cause might be more effectively served.

Now it was just conceivable in Judith's eyes that Simon Partridge was that person, the tiny spanner in that massive works, the 'mole' as popular parlance now prefers it. Equally plausible was the notion of his being the 'Smiley', an investigator infiltrated through Security to unearth said mole. Such persons would not necessarily come with their true designation emblazoned across blazer lapels.

The initial leak had originated from Policy, then Legal, later

Analysis and Assessment. But the documents involved had a wide circulation, restricted in heading only, so it was not easy to narrow the source down to a particular location. And the source had to be located before its activities gained consequence; an entire organization could be undermined, distracted from its day-to-day operations and turned completely upside down by the mere suspicion that there was an enemy working from within.

Partridge had access over a wide area, he fitted both bills quite comfortably – as, it had to be admitted, did several others Judith knew personally, herself included, plus countless persons she did not. Most likely he was simply what he pretended hard not to be: a lonely and inadequate little man, a lost soul who could never admit it, a boy with a pash.

His persistence had won through in the end with the assurance that the day's business would be concluded within an hour. A professedly addicted tennis player, he claimed a desire to have done as quickly as possible so that the rest of the weekend might be his. Judith, unconvinced but not relishing the prospect of having to deal with him first thing on Monday morning, had conceded.

She was unnaturally guarded when receiving him in her home, and today was no exception. She was beginning to regret her decision, for just after his arrival she had received a call that her husband was being brought home 'in a state'.

They had finished lunch, a quickly heated pizza followed by fresh fruit, and Judith was making coffee. Having alluded to Adam she was hoping to see some indication that Partridge was ready to leave. But he was lighting a cigarette and indicating nothing of the kind. He'd begun to pass comment on the difficulties involved in Service recruitment, something she suspected he could have little firsthand knowledge of.

'Had a little tête à tête with Shirley, you know, on Selection,' he said. 'A couple of days ago. She supports what I was saying. Made some pertinent observations herself, too. Says she sees a new breed emerging. Young people. Don't view the job in the same way. Since Fulton, she says, she's seen the change.'

Judith brought the coffee in on a tray. She set it down on the table at which they'd just eaten rather than on a coffee table alongside the more comfortable chairs.

'Too young to fear dismissal, I suggested to her, but she said that with today's unemployment she wasn't so sure about that. Which is true, of course. We're opening the portals to more of the rank and file, you see. They don't care. Attitudes don't carry through to the poorer classes. Respect, you know. Patriotism, if you like.'

'The qualities that made Britain great?' She pushed his coffee towards him, a little slopping over the rim of the mug as she did so.

'Of course, now we've had Tisdall and Ponting,' Partridge went on, thanking her, 'the assumption that the law is there only to be broken has gained ground. Flaunt the rules with impunity, that's the attitude now. Trample on custom and be damned with the consequences. And with unemployment bringing ever longer queues of less-desirables for whatever positions become available, well, hardly likely we develop kinks in the system. Do you know, I know personally of two clerks who are avowed Marxists! And have you seen how many ethnic types are filling the typing pools these days? And the Caribbean cleaners?'

'Sugar?' Judith nudged a Wedgwood bowl his way.

'Yes. Two, please. Oh, I'll help myself. Thank you. Not that I harbour racist tendencies, you understand. It's just that I see standards slackening. Old Shirley, she's a good stick if you get on her right side, she puts it down to vetting. Says the admission procedures nowadays are laughable.'

'They always have been. The Service has been a catalogue of blunders in one area or another since its inception. Vetting is only a minor part of it. If a person wants in badly enough they'll get in no matter what. And if they manage it despite stricter vetting they're going to be potentially more able to cause real damage and to avoid detection longer.'

Partridge gave this a moment's thought then nodded in a rather self-congratulatory way, as if he had made the observation himself. 'Mm, a cogent point.' With a manicured pink fingertip he tapped ash from his cigarette into a lead crystal ashtray at his side.

'Aren't you putting the knife to your own throat with remarks like that?' Judith said archly. 'After all, you're common stock yourself?'

Partridge was visibly stung. 'Redbrick, it's true,' he spluttered, 'unlike yourself. But I do have an authentic military background, as far back as Victoria.'

She felt suddenly sorry for him and regretted her abrasiveness. He was really barely out of short trousers, and, like so many who were quick to pick up faults in others, too sensitive to withstand or successfully return sarcasm. She sipped her coffee as he waffled on in an attempt to reinstate himself in her favour. 'My point is, you see, that many of them can't even claim a full education. Comprehensive schooling, some. I mean, that might be all right for porters and typists and the like, but we're talking about executive – even, I am reliably informed, administrative in one case! Astounding! You would think that at a higher level we might rely on a little more discrimination, wouldn't you?'

'I don't see that as the crux of the problem,' Judith said. Why was she bothering to humour him at all? 'It's more wrapped up with secrecy. The unavoidable fact is that aspects of all government work must be kept from the public gaze, or from the gaze of an opposition party, or some other group or foreign agency. But if you let it be known that you have secrets you must expect others to want to know what they are. Secrets are for attention seekers.'

Partridge pressed himself more firmly into the seat of his dining chair. He puffed meticulously on his cigarette, listening as if her words were showers of gold.

'Most of what we deal with is of no possible value to anyone, least of all ourselves,' she said. 'But habits are ingrained. It goes back to the last war. For our present ruling class that was such a powerful psychological experience, coming at an impressionable age. When it ended they didn't know it. They continued to believe they were still at war, and still do, though they can never be so sure who the enemy is now. The habitual secrecy has taken on a life of its own.' She tipped her head back slightly and stretched her shoulders and neck to ease a tenseness there. She realized she had been led onto a subject she'd had no intention of discussing. Her mind was on other things.

'Yes, the historical perspective. I can see that.' Partridge watched her with bright, always mobile little eyes over the tip of his cigarette, hesitated, then came out coyly with, 'Do you give much thought to our mole, Judith?'

'Not a lot,' she said. Was this what he'd been leading up to? Why not just come out with it in the first place? 'Do you?'

'Well, I can't help wondering about it. I mean, with such perfidious goings on we're all secretly looking one another over with rather suspicious eyes, aren't we? Can it be him? Can it be her? There's a different ambience to the place these days. In its own way it's quite stimulating.'

'For some, I wouldn't doubt. Anyway, I'm sure that whoever is responsible he or she will be sifted out in time, suspended on full pay pending investigation, and either given a hearty slap on the wrist or shunted somewhere where they can do little harm.'

'You don't foresee a prosecution, then?'

'How should I know, Simon?' she replied in a voice that ought to have left him in little doubt now how wearisome she was finding his company. She put down her mug. 'Do we have everything covered now?'

He turned to a bundle of papers on the table top at his elbow. 'Very nearly. Just a couple of tiny items here that I thought you ought to cast your eye over.'

Judith took the file he passed her. She had already registered the fact that two of the documents they'd dealt with came under a 'Restricted' cover. Strictly speaking they should never have been removed from work other than via official channels. But it was an accepted fact that overworked and, ironically, duty-bound officers frequently took work home at weekends and evenings. And 'Restricted' was something of a bodyless piece of Whitehall officialese: objectively it carried no meaning, being liberally interpreted along the lines of 'having little significance whatso-ever'. All the same, it was worth making a mental note of.

She began scanning through the contents of the file, then looked up suddenly.

'What is it?'

'Ssh!' She motioned him to silence. From outside had come the sound of a man shouting. It was followed by a hefty thud against the front door. She heard the key turn in the lock, then a moment later the door of the room flew open and Adam burst in.

Seeing Judith and Simon Partridge but giving no sign of recognizing either, he stopped in his tracks, staring about him wildly. His breathing was short and laboured as if he'd been running hard. His clothing was stained and spattered with something – it looked like the remains of a meal.

'Stop it!' he shouted suddenly. He fell to his knees on the carpet, arms outstretched at his sides and fists bunched. 'I'm living!' he screamed. 'I'm *living*! You don't understand! Stop torturing me!'

Beyond him in the doorway Helmut had appeared. He was flushed and looked uncharacteristically harassed. Behind him came a third man, a beefy fellow in jeans and a white T-shirt, named Elms.

Judith released her papers, and with Partridge looking on in astonishment left her seat to move over to her husband. But Adam recoiled. He wrapped his arms about himself and whimpered as if with pain. She extended a hand carefully towards him.

'Adam, it's Judy. It's all right, darling. It's Jude.'

He was eyeing her suspiciously. She edged forward to gather him slowly into her arms as Helmut and Elms stood by, ready to come to her assistance if the situation demanded it. At her touch Adam looked startled, then he folded in upon himself and erupted into sobs.

'You're killing me. Please, stop it. You don't know. You don't understand what you're doing.'

Judith cast a questioning glance upwards at Helmut. 'What happened?'

Helmut shifted his weight uncomfortably from one foot to the other and tucked his long fair hair back behind one ear. 'I'm not exactly certain about the minutiae of the affair. I – '

'What do you mean? You were with him, weren't you?'

'Well, I was there, yes. But at the crucial moment we were in separate rooms.'

'The crucial moment? What happened? Where *were* you?'

'It was at a party late last night. It seems – '

'A *party*? You took Adam to a *party*?'

Helmut cleared his throat, glancing quickly upwards as if for help. 'In all honesty I thought it would do him good. Under the circumstances.'

'Under the circumstances ... What circumstances?' Not waiting for an answer she demanded angrily, 'Did he have anything to drink?'

He answered no with a movement of the head.

'Are you sure?'

'He never touched alcohol.'

'Dope?'

'Of course not. But there was a lot of it about. Something may have got into his system.'

'May have? Did, you mean. You know how susceptible he is.' She rocked Adam gently, kissing his hair. 'And you say you weren't there? So how do you know what he did or didn't have?'

'I was there, Judith.' Helmut fiddled unhappily with his trilby in his hands. 'But I was giving a poetry reading in another room when it seems he collapsed. Right into a buffet table as you can see. He'd been with me only moments before.'

'You should be at his side all the time! You don't need me to tell you that!' Giving him a look that made him want to shrink beneath the carpet she turned her attention back to her husband.

After a little while she asked, 'Has he been like this all night?'

'No. I was able to take him home with a minimum of trouble. He was very dazed. It seemed the most advisable course as the hour was so late. He was exhausted. When I put him to bed he went out like a light. Then he awoke at about seven or eight, raving.'

'What's he talking about, anyway? Who's torturing him? Does he have any consistency or is it all delirium?'

'Ah. Now this is really rather fascinating.' Helmut perked up tentatively as the opportunity to swing the conversation onto his own ground presented itself. 'I must confess I was baffled to begin with. But as he persisted in hogging the limelight I decided eventually to try listening rather than attempting to silence, in the hope of ascertaining something of his gist. He's been screaming the same things at everyone he's seen – Elms, here, myself, one or two of the neighbours, innocents abroad in the street. He rather put a panic into the lady next door to me. At one point I did fear things were going to get out of hand. I was on the verge of summoning assistance but fortunately Elms turned up in the nick of time.'

Elms, as if in corroboration of this last statement, expelled a short blast of air through his nostrils and rippled the muscles of his jaw.

'Yes, but what is he saying?'

'It seems he has developed, or rather, come under the inexorable influence of a most uncommon kind of empathy with the planet.'

'Planet? What planet?'

'Ours. Planet Earth. He is of the impression that he is the personality of planet Earth. And I suppose that for all intents and purposes one might say that is what he has become. He keeps insisting that we are causing him a great deal of unnecessary pain, and that if we don't quickly cease he will die. A rare state of mind, don't you think? An "altered state" is the popular generic term these days, but I don't think I've ever heard of anything quite this altered.'

Judith sighed. 'God, Helmut, how can you be so bloody irresponsible? This is the first time he's been out of the house unsupervised in weeks, and you decide to take him to some whoopee party! You could have set us back months, or worse! You fool!'

Helmut winced. He fidgeted and tugged at the ends of his hair. 'I don't think the blame should be laid entirely at my feet, Judith. I took him out with the best intentions. I thought it was what he needed and that it would be to his benefit. We had already agreed that he was ready and that he should be encouraged to get out more. I didn't plan on taking him to a party but when it came up I couldn't easily avoid it, and I thought it might be an opportune occasion to test him.'

'To test him for what? Do you really know your intentions, Helm?'

He lifted his eyebrows. 'What do you mean?'

She shook her head. 'Come on, we'd better get him to bed while he's quiet. Give me a hand, will you. Oh, what's this?'

Slipping an arm beneath Adam's to help him to his feet she had encountered a bulky, irregularly shaped something inside his jacket. She reached into the pocket and pulled out Bruno, the smallest and most treasured member of Helmut's personal entourage.

'Oh Lord! Bruno!' Helmut exclaimed. By way of explanation he went on: 'He was in such a state when I put him to bed this morning that I thought I'd better assign the whole crew to him for company. I thought I had them all accounted for after he woke, though. I had *no* idea he was trying to sneak one home.'

Judith handed him the little bear without a word, and he patted it fussily then slipped it quickly into his own pocket. Then her eyes fell on Simon Partridge who had been temporarily dismissed from her thoughts. He was looking on, wide-eyed.

'Ah, well, if there's nothing I can do to help perhaps I ought to be getting along,' he blurted out with sudden animation, glancing at his watch. 'Obviously you have your hands full.'

He gathered his papers and put them into his briefcase, thanked her profusely for the lunch, and exited.

Between the three of them, Judith, Helmut and the burly Elms, they got Adam downstairs to the bedroom. He was little trouble now, just dead weight. The full charge of his madness seemed to have passed and had left him with an absorbing self-pity. They removed his soiled top clothes and got him into a dressing-gown. He lay still on the double bed and stared silently at the ceiling. Tears gathered slowly and rolled from the corners of his eyes to wet his hair and, eventually, the pale green cotton pillow beneath his head.

Outside in the hall, as Judith pulled the door to behind them, Elms made a comment that caused her to look up in mild surprise. Shaking his head and massaging the back of his ape neck with a big hand, he said, 'If he ever gets his old skills back and has a turn like that one, I for one won't be hurrying around to subdue him.'

'I thought you were strongarm,' Judith said.

He pulled a face. 'Both of us together would've been no match for that boy.'

Helmut nodded his agreement. 'There were some perturbing moments. I can only be thankful that he was not actually moved to perform violence. The old Adam, with his faculties and skills intact, is not someone I would wish to confront in any arena of conflict. To talk of ignominious defeat would be drastically understating things, I fear.'

'The old Adam would not consider you an adversary,' she reminded him.

'Let us hope that remains the case.'

'It was like there was an animal trying to get out,' Elms said. 'The look in his eyes. Like he was at the end of his rope. If it ever gets loose God help anyone standing in its path.'

'Yes. Well, he's quiet now,' Judith said. 'I think the worst of the crisis is over.'

'D'you want us to stick around?'

'No. I think he'll be okay. I can get help if necessary, but I'll sedate him now. I expect he'll be out of it for some time.'

At the front door as they were preparing to depart, Helmut, donning his grey trilby, turned to face Judith. 'Again, let me say how sorry I am for what has happened, Judith. But I really do not feel that I can be held solely responsible. It might have come at any time, and now is as good as later. And I don't necessarily view it as a setback. It is too early to tell yet, but it may even prove to have some therapeutic value.'

'We'll see,' Judith said, her voice softening. 'But you're right, I overreacted. You are not entirely at fault. I should have told you to bring him home when you telephoned. We were neither of us being very clear-sighted. I apologize for shouting at you, Helm. I had no right. It was the heat of the moment.'

'No apologies necessary.'

'It's so difficult.' She leaned forward to kiss him goodbye, then frowned, seeing him clearly for the first time since his arrival. 'What's that? What have you done to your throat?'

'Oh.' Helmut raised a hand to his neck where a thin red line still extended from his larynx up towards one ear. 'Ah. Party capers. I'm afraid that since last night I've not had an opportunity for a decent wash.'

He seemed about to add something, then changed his mind. He turned and went down the steps to the car, a red Cortina driven by Elms. Opening the door he looked back and doffed his hat, then climbed in and they drove away.

For a week Adam remained more or less fully interiorized, incapable of recognizing or communicating with anyone. He rarely left his bed, other than to gaze in perplexity for hours on end out over the back garden, or stand before the blank wall of his room, whispering inaudibly to himself. A further three weeks were to pass before he again felt confident enough to leave the house.

Gradually pulling free of his autism, the teeming, fragmented and focusless images and relentlessly distressing emotions that composed his world began to fade. Objectivity returned slowly and he became aware again of an external reality. He found himself in a state of detachment, an emotional vacuum, observant but almost untouched by sensations from within or without.

The night of the party was uppermost in his mind, but little of it was available to recall. It came to him in flashes of vivid surreality. Random and potent, they had more the character of dreams than memories. Though troubled by what he felt had occurred he could not at present rouse himself to investigate it more completely.

Another impression that returned to him repeatedly was that somewhere during his delirium Doctor Geld had been to visit. Once, twice . . . he could not say. He just felt he'd been there. But it was just as likely that Geld had not called at all; for it seemed to Adam that in those past days and nights he had been to all manner of places, done all manner of things, whereas in truth he could only accept that the opposite was the case.

For a while he had no particular reactions to Geld, present or not. As with everything else he could not bring himself to feel concern, but later it would begin to prey on his mind.

With his continuing recovery he felt a desire to talk things over with someone, someone who had been with him on the night he collapsed. He could not turn to Judith because for her none of it would make any sense.

The ideal person seemed to be Dennis. The paranoid attic dweller apparently had a way of keying in to questions which were permanently on Adam's mind. That his answers only served to raise more questions was not, just now, a discouragement. They moved him a small step beyond the isolated position he had occupied for so long, and that was the important thing. But Adam was afraid to pay Dennis a call. A meeting just now might be more than he was up to. There was something about their last encounter that terrified him more profoundly than he could comprehend.

He telephoned Helmut one day and invited him over for dinner. A conversation with Helmut did not hold the same risk of precipitation back into the chaos he was just emerging from, and in discussing the party night he could broach the subject of meeting with Dennis again. With luck Helmut would volunteer once more to act as chaperon.

When Helmut arrived Judith was taking Adam through a series of mental exercises. She was reading him questions from lists set out in a book. The list she was using comprised about one hundred questions, all but the last fifteen or so of which related to past situations. The idea was that the patient, Adam, would project himself back into his past to describe the situation called for.

For instance, a question would read: It is your ninth birthday. Describe the day. Describe your birthday cake, your presents. How many friends are at your party? What are their names? What food are you eating? What games are you playing?

or: Recall a pleasant conversation with your mother. Where are you? How old are you? What is your mother wearing? Describe the tone of her voice.

And Adam would attempt to travel back in time and relate as many impressions with as much detail as possible. That in his case the answers were composed from imagination rather than pure memory was at this stage not particularly important. The main thing was to induce a receptive state of mind where genuine memories might more readily be stimulated.

Within the book were also certain lists containing questions designed to arouse less pleasant memories. Anger, fear, jealousy, hatred ... emotions which in the past might have been suppressed but which were considered to be still dangerously active, locked within the recesses of the subconscious and quite capable of wreaking havoc in present time. These lists, though, were kept from Adam. For now it was the gentler, more pleasant experiences that he was encouraged to relive.

They had been doing this for an hour or so and Judith was preparing to end the session. The final fifteen questions in the set had the function of bringing the patient back up into present time, and establishing a more solid relationship with himself and his surroundings. She had run through several of these and Adam was more relaxed than he'd been for a long time, stretched the length of the sofa with his head resting on her thigh. Sensing him to be in a relatively constructive frame of mind she decided to throw in a final, optional question. She asked him to project himself into the future and imagine something he would like to do or achieve, visualizing bringing this about.

For Adam this was not such a simple task. His goal for the future was to rediscover his past and unravel the complex mysteries of his present. Nothing else had any place in his thoughts, for until this was accomplished there *was* nothing else. But to visualize bringing this about . . . where did he begin?

He was thinking about it when Helmut pressed the front door bell, and he looked up questioningly. Neither he nor Judith were expecting visitors. He had failed to tell her of his invitation to Helmut and had since forgotten about it himself.

Judith answered the door, and returned, slightly embarrassed, for she and Adam had already eaten. Helmut quipped understandingly at her shoulder, not greatly put out; such things fell almost as a matter of course in the overall randomness of his lifestyle, and he insisted he wasn't too hungry, though in truth he had come with an eager stomach, anticipating a more than adequate repast.

He strode straight to the dining table and sat down with a show of dignity, continuing to make light of the situation as Adam quickly uncorked a bottle of claret. Judith, meanwhile, went off to the kitchen to heat a frozen lasagne.

'I'm pleased to see you are looking much healthier, my friend,' Helmut said as Adam poured a glass of wine. Despite his levity he intended feeling his way carefully this evening. Judith's tongue-lashing of a few days ago had not left him unscathed. Words which from a man would never have touched him had found the power to penetrate his really-not-so-leathery hide, and he was anxious that no misplaced remark should rekindle her wrath. 'How does it feel to be back amongst the living?'

Adam smiled. 'I'm not so sure that I am,' he said.

'You put on a mighty performance. Did you know? It's a pity you weren't there to catch it.'

'Was I wild? Jude says I got quite violent.'

'You remember nothing?'

'I remember being out of control. I even knew I was doing it in a mixed up sort of way. I felt like the pilot of some crazed battle machine that had somehow taken over its own controls. Much of it's blank, though.'

'Yes, you were very dramatic. Had you witnessed your finale I think you would have been impressed.'

'I didn't hurt anybody, did I?'

Helmut chuckled. 'No, but you put the fear of God into several. Myself included.' He glanced across at Judith who was watching from the door. 'When we brought you home I did have reservations about leaving dear Judith here alone with you. I needn't have worried, though. Where we musclemen had failed over hours she had you subdued in seconds. The woman's touch! Ah, the man who bottles that will die a blissfully happy billionaire!'

He raised his wine glass to his nostrils, assessed the bouquet, then put it to his lips. He swilled it around his mouth, swallowed and smacked his lips approvingly. 'Médoc?'

'St Emilion.'

He nodded. It had been a wild, if near accurate, guess. He knew nothing about wine. He pushed the glass aside.

A minute later Judith returned with the freshly microwaved lasagne. As Helmut tucked in she made to refill his glass but he stayed her with a raised hand.

'I have Boadicea to think about. Besides which, you seem to have forgotten that I rarely, if ever, drink alcohol.'

'Oh Helm,' she flushed slightly. 'Of course. I'm sorry.'

'No, no. Adam's mistake. Perhaps a little sparkling water, though, if I may.'

Adam passed the bottle of mineral water from which he'd been drinking. Judith filled a clean glass.

'You know,' Helmut said, 'I've been giving some thought to the condition of your mind that morning. It was quite fascinating. I don't quite know what to make of it.'

'Maybe it's best not to make anything,' Adam said.

'You came out with some provocative comments in the car. At the time I was too busy trying to keep you from climbing through the window to take much notice. But you kept insisting quite vociferously how you loved humanity, how you felt protective and maternally inclined, wanting to help us all. But on the other hand you were equally insistent that if we did not stop hurting you, you would be forced to the tactics of destruction. Self-preservation, you said. Why did we keep ignoring the signs? you kept asking me. Why could we not see?'

Adam sipped apprehensively from his glass. 'It certainly brought out the Messiah in me, didn't it. I was in pain, you know. Actual, physical pain. I remember that well. A persistent, twisted, scorching pain. It made me feel mad.'

'He came out in welts,' Judith added. 'Red and white blotches over much of his body. At one point he couldn't bear the touch of the bedsheets against his skin.'

'Really?' Helmut exclaimed in genuine wonder. 'Good Lord! Have you written any of it down?'

Adam shook his head. The World's First Radioactive Poet thought deeply for a minute then busied himself with the remainder of his meal in silence. When he had finished he put down his knife and fork and rose and leaned across to kiss Judith on the cheek, complimenting her. He poured himself more mineral water as she left with his empty plate to bring dessert.

'Dennis sends his best for a speedy recovery, by the way. He was very distressed when he realized what had happened. At the time I don't think he knew quite what was going on. He didn't see your collapse. He's very involved in his own crisis just now. Has been since I've known him, to be truthful. Poor fellow, he's most dispirited. Can't fully reconcile his concern for animal welfare with the fact that he inadvertently destroyed those five kittens and their mother. Not to mention the mice. He feels strongly about such things. He's rather torturing himself.

'In his own idiosyncratic way he took quite a shine to you, my friend, though it might not have been obvious at the time.' His eyes widened in delight as Judith set down before him a dish of lemon meringue and a small Wedgwood jug of cream. 'My favourite!' He sank the edge of a dessert fork into the fluffy mixture. His eyes closed in a simulation of ecstasy as he took his first mouthful, then opened again and he beamed happily at the two of them.

'I think he'd rather welcome the opportunity to discuss his

Jungian symbology further with you,' he went on. 'I thought what he had to say was quite interesting, didn't you?'

Adam nodded. 'I was hoping we could meet again.'

'Then we must arrange it.'

'He worried me at first,' Adam said. 'I wasn't sure how to take him.'

'Yes, he is rather unique. A lambkin though, really. Wouldn't harm a fly. Not deliberately. Does have a tendency to extrapolate, though. I think you should be on guard for that. It's a not uncommon failing amongst Jungians, I suspect. Marvellous though the philosophy is it does leave itself wide open to the easily led. The semi-occultists, you know, the sensation seekers. Not that Dennis falls into any of those categories. He just gets a bit excited.

'By the way, you've not suffered any further visionary encounters with Dicemen, have you?'

'No. At least, nothing quite as lucid.'

'I mention it because I discussed it recently with Dennis – I hope you don't mind. I was curious to hear his view.'

'And what did he have to say?'

'Not a great deal, as it happens. He seemed of the opinion that your Diceman might be some kind of psychoid archetypal figure thrown into consciousness in a modernistic guise – I believe that was the phrase he used – but as far as he is aware Jung has not described anything quite like it. He is anxious to hear it from the horse's mouth, however. Mmm, exquisite!' He helped himself to more cream in preparation for a final assault on the remaining dessert.

'But we had a discussion,' Helmut went on, 'an unexpectedly enlightening one in a manner of speaking, about catalysts and cataclysms. Those events which occur in life, often quite out of the blue, and radically alter the course of one's existence. You provided the springboard from which it took flight. Or more precisely, your Birth did. It's such a fine example.

'We debated the religious experience, the way it can descend upon an individual and totally affect his or her views and approach to life. And love – meeting someone, often quite by chance, who influences you in such a way that nothing can ever again be quite the same. For better or for worse,' he added as an afterthought. 'The list goes on, but the changes such events can precipitate are extraordinary.'

He chased the last crumbs around his dish, caught them with the aid of a finger and disposed of them. 'Where was I? Yes. Dennis got around to disclosing to me – in confidence, I should add – the one event that he claims has had the most dramatic effect upon the rest of his life. He told me it happened three days prior to his twenty-second birthday. He even dug out an old diary and insisted I read the entry he'd made. On that day, all those years ago, he discovered during a lunchtime drink with an acquaintance that for the whole of his life up to that point he had been sitting in the bath the wrong way round.'

'And that altered the course of his life?'

'From childhood, as far as he could remember, he had always bathed with his head between the taps,' Helmut explained. 'It had never occurred to him that there might be a better way. It had its own logic, since that way he could reach the taps to adjust the flow of water more easily. But his friend explained that if you are lying the other way around it is just as easy to adjust the taps with your toes. And Dennis experienced the light! He agreed that he had always suffered a minor degree of discomfort sitting on the plug, and with his head sandwiched between the taps he had limited freedom of movement. On top of that, he often scalded one shoulder or froze the other when altering the water temperature. But until somebody actually pointed it out it had never, ever occurred to him that there might be another way.'

Adam glanced across at Judith with a smile, and was shocked to see the expression on her face. She was watching Helmut. She looked so weary, so wan; but more than that. A look almost of horror had appeared on her features, as though she had glimpsed a spectre. He stared at her for a moment in dismay, feeling suddenly terribly guilty without knowing quite why.

'And this taught him to question everything, you see,' Helmut said, oblivious. 'Every single aspect of his existence. Never again, he said, would he be content to accept things at their surface value. Never again would his world be quite the same. Ah, Dennis! Dennis the Menace! I love him so!'

'It doesn't appear to have done him an awful lot of good,' Adam said distractedly.

'That is a judgement founded on your own predetermined value system, my friend.'

'Who is he, anyway?' Judith asked, collecting herself. Her expression had faded but the fatigue was deeply etched.

'A very good friend of mine,' Helmut said. 'A capital fellow, if somewhat prone to his darker emotions. You must meet him sometime.'

Not thinking clearly, Adam asked, 'Was there anything that changed the course of your life, Helm?'

The atmosphere seemed to close in suddenly around them. Judith, to cover the brief silence, stood and took Helmut's dish and the jug of cream. After a momentary and barely noticeable hesitation Helmut answered, deliberately evasive, with just the tiniest catch in his throat.

'I don't know that I could put my finger on any specific thing. Not in the way you can, or Dennis for that matter. Many things have affected me quite profoundly in one way or another.'

Adam gathered the hint and searched for another topic. He drummed his fingers against the side of his glass. He said, 'He told me some interesting things about Geld.'

Helmut raised one eyebrow. 'Who? Dennis?'

Adam nodded. Judith, on her way to the kitchen, looked around. 'Doctor Geld? Does he know him?'

'I get the impression he knows every psychiatrist in London,' Adam said, and Helmut chuckled. 'He claims Doctor Geld has been party to some pretty unpalatable activities.'

'What kinds of activities?'

'Scientific. Government research, animal experiments, things like that. The kinds of activities that are not broadly publicized.' There was an anger rising in him.

Judith shrugged and went on to the kitchen.

'Does it bother you, my friend?' Helmut asked.

'It makes me wonder. Dennis claims he was a member of a group that tried to expose him. Some time ago. He said there was a clampdown on publicity.'

Helmut, who had leaned back with a show of comfort into his chair and half-closed his eyes as if to indicate he no longer wished to contribute to the conversation, said, nevertheless, 'It may be worth considering statements of that ilk with a modicum of scepticism. Dennis, as I've explained and as you yourself have witnessed, my friend, is prone to a certain disproportion of view. His imagination rarely slumbers.'

'He said he had proof.'

'Even so . . .'

Judith came back. 'I don't think it's anything to concern yourself over, darling,' she said. 'We know it goes on. Experiments on animals happen, however unpalatable. It isn't a secret. It's an emotive issue, and whether they should be permitted is a highly debatable question, but for now they are. That's the world we live in.'

'So you knew about it?'

'It's no secret, Adam. Doctor Geld is a brilliant scientist. He leads his field. Of course he's involved in research, and he's hardly likely to turn down lucrative government sponsored work, is he? The nation's best resources at his fingertips . . .'

'What kind of work?'

She gave a sigh. 'That's anybody's guess. I expect details are published in the relevant scientific and psychiatric journals. I really don't think you should give it too much thought.'

'Why didn't you tell me?'

'I didn't give it a thought, Adam. It never entered my head.'

He flared suddenly. 'What about *my* head? That's the one he's been fooling around with. Surely that's worth giving a thought to? Don't I have the right to be informed?'

'Adam, I've told you, it is no secret. Psychiatrists are continually involved in research of one kind or another. That's the nature of their profession. It never occurred to me to bring it up.'

'My friend,' Helmut interceded, 'I would not allow yourself to dwell too deeply on this. Doctor Geld is well known and well respected. You could hardly be in more capable hands.'

Adam slumped. 'That's what worries me.'

'Adam – ' Judith began, but he cut her short.

'Was he here? Last week or whenever it was? Did you call him in?'

'I had to. I wasn't sure of how best to handle you. I needed his advice.'

'But you know I don't want him around. You know that. Why didn't you get someone else?'

'He's the only one familiar with your case history.'

'And what did he say? Did I tell him anything?'

He was perplexed to see a nervous smile on her lips. 'Not a great deal that he understood. You were having a Russian Day.'

'A what?'

'The few brief words you spoke to anyone that day were in Russian. Snatches from Slavonic nursery rhymes and fairy tales, a few lines of dissident poetry. It was all Greek to Geld.'

Helmut burst out laughing. 'You are an international fellow, my friend. When I telephoned to enquire after your health one morning Judith informed me you were in the middle of an Italian Day.'

'Well, I don't want him coming back,' Adam said, feeling the potency of his argument failing. 'Government research or not, I want you to keep him away from me. Especially when I'm not capable of affecting what's going on. There's something about that man, with his pedant's phrases and his vile smile. I don't trust him and I don't want him near me.'

He wrestled in silence with himself, then said, only now remembering, 'Dennis told me he knew something else.'

'About Doctor Geld? What?'

'I don't know. It was all getting crazy by then. I didn't pursue it. But he said there was more.'

'Perhaps you can ask him when we next meet,' Helmut said.

'I'd like to.'

The conversation moved on to other matters in which Adam could find no particular interest, and a short while later he excused himself. He went downstairs, leaving his wife and Helmut still chatting in the lounge, and lay down on his bed.

His mind would not free itself of its misgivings over Doctor Geld. Just why the knowledge that the man was engaged in government work should disturb him so was unclear. He knew he was being irrational; after all, Judith worked in a government department; as Judith and Helmut had pointed out, there was no real attempt to cover up the facts. Experiments on animals were objectionable, but they were established practice, widely acknowledged as such. In themselves they did not represent anything sinister. And yet he could not rest easy. His intuitive feelings about Geld remained too strong.

He lay on the bed, half-consciously fingering a small scar just above the bridge of his nose – one of many visible reminders of the extensive surgery he had undergone. Later, when Helmut had gone home and Judith was asleep beside him, he found himself going over and over the last words he had spoken with Dennis. And as he recalled what Dennis had told him concerning Geld something new came back to him. He remembered the couple who had entered the room where they were sitting. The man in the pale suit and his female companion, Ruth. It was they who had distracted him, preventing him from listening to what else Dennis had to say. But why had they been talking about him, even taking notes?

He slipped uneasily into fitful sleep, still uncertain whether what he was recalling was real or some monstrous fantasy spawned by his advancing madness.

Blood

He awoke the next morning feeling that he had not slept at all. His thoughts were clogged with remnants of dreamstuff shifting dangerously just below consciousness like silt beneath the tide. The clock's studied tick reverberated in his ear and in his head. He was not sure at first of his whereabouts.

As he came to himself he identified sounds from upstairs. Judith was moving around in the kitchen, making breakfast before departing for work. He listened for a time to her muted footsteps, remembering how, not so very long ago, she would sing or hum to herself, even at this early hour. She did not do that any more.

From outside there was no sound, no indication of anything living. The unwelcoming black of early morning was revealed through a slender gap between the bedroom curtains, and the cold had crept into the room, despite the central heating. Winter had moved up with sudden intent during the past week, using the night time to tighten its remorseless grip.

It struck him as he rose groggily from his bed, that for some time now he had not been woken by his usual nightmare. The immediacy of his recent crisis had brought him other, if equally unfathomable, dreams. Unknowingly over the months he had become so habituated to it that he experienced now an almost tangible sense of loss, which lingered for some hours, a feeling of having stepped into a void. The passing of the red snow, in particular, he acknowledged as he would the sudden and unannounced departure of a trusted but somewhat mysterious ally.

The remainder of that day he spent wandering a little vacantly around the maisonette. He sat in the window and dreamed, and as the mood took him wrote down his thoughts.

Over the following days he began to notice signs of an improvement in his physical condition. Vague aches and pains which had been part of him for as long as he could recall seemed to have blown off. There was an easing of the stiffness in many joints, and an easier responsiveness in his limbs, as if the mental storm he had been through had somehow released internal energies that had previously been held in stasis. Other changes, too, that he did not yet have any intimation of, were taking place.

As a result he began to exercise regularly each morning. Simple stretching and bending routines to begin with, improving circulation and flexing under-used muscles and joints, then graduating onto a slightly more strenuous programme as the days went by. And one afternoon he made the decision to call on Dennis.

Unable to recall the address he telephoned Helmut, hoping at the same time to hear his friend offer to accompany him. But Helmut was not at home. So he set out virtually blind, prepared to cover every street in Notting Hill if necessary until he located the house. He knew he would have no difficulty in recognizing it once he set eyes on it again.

It was dark and had begun to rain heavily when he left home. He caught a tube to Notting Hill Gate station then hailed a taxi so as to avoid the worst of the weather, hoping they would pass the house before the ride became too expensive. He'd been in the cab for less than ten minutes when he instructed the driver to pull over.

And it was as he stood in the cold by the low front wall and gazed up the rainlashed concrete steps to that big double door that his fear truly came back in upon him. That same apprehensiveness he had felt when he came the first time with Helmut had returned, intensified twentyfold. It spread through his veins like a rush of some neutralizing chemical, paralysing his will so that he was unable to move.

He glanced about him at the street. It was totally deserted this time, no pale-suited figure lounging between brick pillars. The darkness was deeper, the asphalt road surface and paving stones appearing insubstantial and treacherous beneath the freezing, hissing rain. In a bay window across the street coloured fairy lights on an imitation Christmas tree blinked off and on behind old ruched lace, debasing rather than celebrating. He turned back. There was not a single light glowing this time in the windows of the house where Dennis had his lodging.

The rain as he stood there soaked through the shoulders of his overcoat and through his shoes and socks. He shivered, and at last forced himself to move. He had the mien of a condemned man as he climbed the steps to the big forest green door.

It was off the catch as before. He pushed it open and stepped out of the rain into the underlit hall. Now he realized he had come unprepared. He had brought nothing for the big man on the stairway. There was little he could do; he knew that if he went outside again, to buy a bottle or for any other reason, he would never find the courage to re-enter the building unaccompanied.

He turned his ears to the noises of the house; the creak of a stair, the settling of a floorboard, the rattle of a latch as the gathering wind gusted up the stairs, the rain beating on window panes ... there was no indication that the big Scot was present. In fact he had the impression that the entire house was empty, though common sense told him this was unlikely.

He climbed to the first floor. The odour of neglect and decay seemed more pronounced this time. Encouraged by the damp it almost clung to his skin, effortlessly penetrating his clothing. And there was another, faint, scent, both associated with the house and alien to it, which did not immediately register on his consciousness.

The lightbulb had not been replaced and he kept a hand to the wall as he moved to the foot of the second flight. As before a dim light shed its weary glow from the landing above, painting the edges of the upper stairs a lifeless red. The staircase was empty. The Scotsman's wife was evidently not expected home this night, though indications of an earlier vigil were present in the form of used cans and bottles.

He ascended to the next level, then along a series of passages. He froze at one point, seized with a sudden conviction that nearby, in the impenetrable darkness, a presence waited. But he moved on, became lost, then eventually found himself at the stairs to the attic. The house was still uncannily quiet. He had neither seen nor heard a soul.

The steep attic stairs bore their former litter of discarded junk, and the landing, when he stepped up onto the top stair, was as cluttered. The rain thrummed alarmingly on the black skylight overhead. A crack at one corner of the frame allowed a steady stream to enter, spilling down the wall and forming a sodden patch on the carpet at its base.

The pallid yellow door to Dennis's haunt was slightly ajar, a fact which drew Adam's attention as he recalled the sliding bolts and chains of last time. He knocked twice softly. There was no response. He knocked again, more loudly this time, and called Dennis's name.

When there was still no answer Adam, after a moment's hesitation, eased the door open a few more inches and put his head inside. The crammed room was unchanged. The old black and white television had keeled onto its side and was flickering wildly, its picture given up to a horizontal hold that had lost its grip. The orang-utan on the wardrobe stared impassively down at him. There was no human occupant.

Disappointed, he withdrew. He would have put a message on the door but had not thought to bring pen or paper. But it struck him that if the door had been left open Dennis was unlikely to be far away. Perhaps he was even on the floor beneath, answering the call of nature.

Adam retraced his steps to the foot of the attic stairs. Sure enough the room at the end of the passage, which Helmut had disappeared into on their last visit, was occupied. A rectangular thread of yellow light outlined the door, which was otherwise lost in the darkness. Adam seated himself on a low stair to wait.

When, after some minutes, no one emerged, he grew restless. Eventually he stood to approach the door. A feeling of dread overcame him. He saw again the blood he had envisioned last

115

time, creeping out beneath the toilet door. He began to tremble, and could not prevent himself from glancing down. There was no blood. He exhaled shakily.

At the door he listened self-consciously. He caught no sound from within so raised a hand to knock.

'Dennis,' he said. No one answered.

Strangely, this door too was unlocked. Under the pressure of his knuckle it swung inwards an inch or so.

'Is there anybody there?'

He was greeted by the same silence.

So it was empty. And there seemed little point in waiting any longer. Dennis might be anywhere; it could be hours before he returned. Adam decided reluctantly to make his way home – but before leaving he needed to relieve his full bladder. The door resisted slightly to his push, and there was a muted crackling sound on its other side. He gave it a little more weight and stepped forward to enter – and stopped suddenly, immobilized on the threshold, rooted to the floor.

Dennis was in there, sitting on the lavatory. He was dead. Somebody had cut his throat.

Part Two

'Homo sapiens gives every indication of pushing hugger-mugger and pell-mell for its extinction. Should its end be achieved I can only ask, What then?

'Earth's evolution will have retrograded by perhaps a billion years, but what does this mean? Time has no substance, after all. It is a mere conception of consciousness. It has no actuality. God does not wear a watch.

'The body Earth and its life-forms, then, will evolve as before, minus humanity which, having declared itself the foe, will have had itself removed ... And I don't think the monkey will be allowed near the top of the tree again.

'... The thought has come to me during this lifetime in the company of mortals, that perhaps the real tragedy is not that homo sapiens may make itself extinct, but rather that it may yet fail to do so.'

Iddio E. Scompiglio
(extracted from *THE UNSEEN WORKS*).

Mystery deepens and the night grows darker before the dawn. All that is lost cannot yet be found. The sleeper strives to wake, but the nightmare will not end.

Adam slept.

He dreamed.

He dreamed of deceit and betrayal, of formless conspiracies and sinister masquerades, of faceless characters moving like shadows with murderous intent. He saw the glint of moonlight on blood-guttered blades, saw death in the smiles of persons he half-recognized but could not place.

He saw Doctor Geld, a grinning, spectral figure in a room that was little more than a cubicle, hung with drapes, bathed in a soft reddish luminescence. The doctor was in conference with another man, once more someone whom Adam knew – had known? – but could fit no specific identity to. Moving closer to where they talked, as if moving through walls and furniture, he stood behind Geld and listened to their words. But though he heard quite clearly he could extract no sense from their sound.

He had the feeling that the subject under discussion was himself. *No doubt!* And then the man with whom Doctor Geld conferred looked up. He looked beyond the psychiatrist, curiously, directing his gaze at Adam. Doctor Geld's thin body twisted and his head swivelled around on his narrow shoulders and their eyes met.

And Adam felt a spasm of fear. Into his mind came the certain conviction that the man with whom Geld conferred was not all that he claimed to be.

An impostor.

But then, who was he? Why were they together? And what were they saying?

He backed away. Something was not right. The ground dropped without warning from beneath his feet and he was falling.

He pushed at a door in a passage in a large house. On the other side something prevented the door from opening more than a couple of inches. He knew what it was but could not bring himself to remember. He could barely breathe, half-sobbing with an unreasoning terror as he pushed harder. He did not want to enter the room, but he was compelled to. He had to see what it contained, had to *remember*.

A sound from behind. A muffled thud, and he swung around. At the other end of the passage, bearing down upon him, a giant figure.

'Y' did it, y' bastard! Y' did it!'

He cowered, shrinking back into the door, which still refused to give. He shook his head, signifying no in the absence of words caught somewhere in his throat. He had the feeling, though, that the man meant something quite different. He tried to cry out that this was a mistake, that he did not know what was going on. But the Scotsman's massive hands had encircled his throat.

He struggled, choking, tearing, imploring, as the vital force was wrung from his body. The blood pounded in his temples. He was thrown to the floor, an unbearable weight crushing his ribcage, and he knew himself to be dying.

And his last thought was of the man he had seen a moment earlier, in conference with Doctor Geld. He recognized him, and with recognition came the inevitable acceptance that his madness was surely now complete. For it was impossible, it could not be, it made no sense at all. The thought, thrown up from the furthest, darkest, most tempestuous reach of his departing consciousness, was that the man, whom he had perceived as hiding behind an illusory persona, was God.

Adam woke.

He lay gasping for breath, drenched in sweat. Something was invading his mind, clamouring for his attention, something he wished to avoid acknowledging at all costs. He closed his eyes, burying his face in his hands, and rocked from side to side in an effort to keep it at bay.

He grew still. It was already there. There could be no ignorance of knowledge already possessed.

He viewed again the scene that had sent him reeling in horror back down those narrow passages, down the blood-tinged, beer-littered stairs and outside into the cold night's storm. Dennis sat sprawled in front of him, bereft of any last vestige of dignity. His shabby brown cords were heaped about his ankles, sinewy, white lower limbs exposed. His life's blood had gushed and spread a tacky wetness over his sweatshirt and abdomen.

His head, half-severed, was thrown back and rested on the cistern behind. His deep-sunk, pebbly eyes were open. They gawked stupidly at the naked lightbulb overhead.

His fleshy lips were bluish and all but concealed beneath the bush, parted and stretched in an unnatural broad grin. The facial muscles had fallen back under the pull of gravity. The skin was the colour of lard.

But there had been no frozen scream there, no terminal expression of terror, or even pain. If anything his features had conveyed only sorrowful surprise ... probably not even that.

His throat had gaped sticky black-red and wide. It too grinned, as if mocking the brutality of his end, dribbling perversely like the misshapen maw of some toothless Hadean hag.

And on his thighs had been spread a glossy magazine, its pages spattered and floresced with blood. And it came back to Adam now with the clarity of a photograph. For the first time he saw the title of the article Dennis had been reading: 'Annihilation Of The Self – The Way To True Happiness?'

There had been a bundle of something behind the door, something heaped and shapeless that he had only caught a glimpse of and not identified.

'Oh God!' He exhaled a long shaking breath. 'Anything Goes', Helmut had declared, meant survival at any cost against the odds for the longest possible period. It was the common-sense response to a time of No-Law, a precautionary emotional protection to alert you to the possibilities, keep you awake for when the bad men came to visit. But the bad men had come and had found Dennis without a friend.

There was something else that had to be taken into account. The fact was that he, Adam, had known it was going to happen. He had seen it, had witnessed in a vision the blood creeping under the lavatory door. He had had no way of knowing then what its interpretation might be.

Dennis too, in that unnerving episode with the pigeon, had foreseen something. He had clearly been very frightened, claiming there was death in the air, accusing Adam of being at the centre of something. None of them had understood then. Now, it was too late.

So was it possible? Was he somehow unknowingly the cause of another man's death?

He was too shocked to fully comprehend it or to look logically at the implications, both of his apparent prescience and of the murder itself. But he was involved, there was a direct connection with him, he could not reasonably assume otherwise. What was he to do?

Something was welling up inside him. He pressed his head back hard against the pillow as he fought to contain it. Something was demanding to be let loose.

He cried out, 'Help me! What is happening? What has all this to do with me? My God, *WHO AM I?*'

Waiting For Gard

Doctor Geld, having glanced frequently at his gold fob watch with the apprehension that time really was of the essence, resolved to set the meeting in motion. Apart from anything else, the tense silence being generated by the other four assembled members was making him uncomfortable.

'It appears that our Apostle may be exhibiting signs of increased absorption in things subjective,' he began. 'Out of which recognizable behavioural patterns are slowly emerging as he attempts to piece together the elusive elements of his past.'

He lifted the flap on a folder which lay on the desktop beside him. 'You have each been given a transcript of the papers contained herein and, I might be so bold as to assert, will have studied some if not all of what is written there. They do not make an easy or particularly entertaining read – ha-ha! – but they are the most up-to-date examples of his attempts to describe his inner conflicts that we have.

'I have been called upon to provide an answer to the question, Do these papers, or the condition of his mind at present, constitute a security risk? Well, before putting forward my opinion I should perhaps refresh your memories and give you a brief analytical breakdown in order that you might better understand how and why my verdict was arrived at.'

He glanced about him quickly as he slipped some sheets of typewritten foolscap from the folder, then rose from the chair he occupied. He cleared his throat and adjusted the black-framed spectacles on his nose, then began to read out loud:

'In this, my own created world, a madness is rife. It finds its way like a cancer. Inherent within itself it carries the death-wish, the darkening craving for oblivion, the unrealized mass-motivator; paradoxic, gaining strength from its own urgings not to come into existence.

'This world knows fear and uncertainty. There is a suspicion here, almost a knowledge, that all truth is tainted, that ignorance is to be fostered. There is an underlying conscious acceptance of life without value, of existence without purpose. Out of the perpetual night which conceals it from itself this world has spawned the means by which to achieve its own end.

'This world is an unborn child in the womb of its Mother. Eternal Mother. Like the child in the first violent throes of its birth it experiences trauma. It knows terror – the pain and the awful twisted rejection of the Mother – no longer, nor yet again, the love. In these moments, out of the teeming chaos of the nightmare that precedes consciousness, a decision may be made. The child does not have to be born.

'And I, being the Mother who weeps for her stillborn babe, am the sorrow and the torment of mothers of all lands and ages whose child has come from the womb inert, never to draw the first breath of life, never to open its eyes.

'Is this world truly so blind? Can it not conceive the immensity of the process, the nurturing, the unfolding, the terrible yearning, loving, groping effort it has taken to arrive at this point?

'Be aware. The tragedy is this: This world *can* end, before it has begun. The decision *can* be made. The child does not have to be born.

'None will ever know save the Mother, left alone to grieve and begin again.'

The doctor let the hand which held the papers drop to his side.

Small beads of perspiration had gathered on his crown, as they tended to do whenever he felt himself to be under pressure. Some ran and were trapped in the thick dark hedge of his encircling hair. One or two managed an escape through the open 'gates' at his temples: errant sheep chasing one another in panic down the steep, slippery slopes of his face. With his free hand he produced from his breast pocket a vivid tangerine foulard printed with an emerald fleur-de-lys design. With this he successfully curtailed their bid for freedom, then mopped his shining brow.

It was admittedly warm in this windowless room. But although Geld sweated, the air, filtered down through an antiquated conditioning system, was dry and charged with static.

In the aftermath of his reading still no one spoke. The almost featureless, dull yellow walls, floor and ceiling glared oppressively under fluorescent striplights. The silence intensified, or so it seemed. And then the room came alive, filled with the whirring, buzzing, humming, clicking, skreeking and flickering of computers, printers, monitors, a cipher machine and other less easily identifiable modules of electronic hardware, all of which seemed to have found vent for expression in the same moment. Doctor Geld was obliged to raise his voice.

'Now, this may not seem a particularly obvious example to choose, containing as it does no overt references to us, or indeed to Gospel. However, it is one of the shorter pieces – some of the others are far over-extended, and rather impenetrable and tiresome. And it does provide some quite fascinating insights into the patient's thought processes and the manner in which he is, not necessarily comprehendingly, attempting to come to terms with his predicament. Permit me to elucidate.

'Contained in a somewhat cryptic manner within this essay I see a quite concise and, I think, pertinent commentary on the way in which our Apostle is experiencing himself and his world. And that, of course, is most relevant to us.'

He lifted the papers close to his face, scanned them briefly, then let them fall again. 'He tells us, "In my own created world a madness is rife." This is most surely a reference to his own condition, the inner world of fantasy and delusion which has risen out of himself and wrested control from him. He talks then of "the death-wish", "the craving for oblivion". I do not take this to be an indication of a desire to end his own life, but rather of his desire to have an end to what is happening to him, an end to the fears and uncertainties, the deep suspicions of deceit, the feelings of persecution that he cannot rid himself of. And "the perpetual night which conceals it from itself", a further reference to the all-obscuring vacuum he feels within himself, the dark void where memory of the past should be.

'And now things become more specific. "The unborn child" can surely only be the past which, whilst constantly rising to torment him, yet refuses to be "born" into consciousness. He feels it to have a life of its own, beyond his control: "The child may make a decision, it does not have to be born".' Doctor Geld paused a moment. His eyes were shining. He was almost beginning to enjoy himself.

'"I am the Mother", he goes on to state – that is, he contains, nurtures, cares for that which is within him and which refuses to be born into the world. Or – an ambivalent element here – perhaps it does indeed enter the chamber of consciousness, but it is "stillborn", i.e. the past which he discovers contains no meaning for him, no "life". It is arid, empty, unrecognizable. It is alien to him. So he finds himself cut off again, alone in grief and despair, his only choice to try once more to bring to the surface that which prefers to remain buried.

'Now, such delineations apart, we can also discern here – and even more so in several of the other pieces he has produced – an emergent compensatory paradigm, an incipient messianic complex, if you wish, born out of the very core of his suffering. This one might describe as an autonomic psychological response to the terrible feelings of inferiority and persecution that torment him.

'In practical terms, what does it mean? Well, let me say that when he turns his vision outwards he is faced with a world engulfed in turmoil and strife. He witnesses what he has termed "the fostering of ignorance", something he envisages as being responsible for the world's problems, generating catastrophic effects all across the globe. And when he looks within he experiences what to his acutely sensitized subjective eye appears quite suddenly to be a reflection of that outer condition. In a flash of so-called intuition he comes to identify his inner world as a mirror-image of the outer. And vice versa. And, perhaps more importantly, he sees – or is convinced he sees – a definite causal relationship between the two. They are interdependent. The one engenders the other, and again, vice versa.

'Well now, something is set in motion. From that initial flash commences the process whereby he comes to see himself as set apart from, and slightly above, other mortals. He sees and understands things that they – we – do not.

'Put simply, he wishes to save the world. An admirable sentiment. He sees it as beset by evils of one description or another, and becomes subject to the most intense and ostensibly profound personal insights into the character of these evils. Potent visions and intuitions concerning the true nature and purpose of existence become commonplace now, and he envisions the way to personal and universal salvation. Fortunately for us he has been driven to commit many of his most personal feelings to paper. Unfortunately for him he has committed himself to a truly impossible mission, ha-ha! For where on Earth is he now to begin? His inner world, despite his new understanding, remains chaotic and defiantly intractable. And the real world . . .' Doctor Geld allowed the words to trail off with a slight lifting of the shoulders and a rueful expression intended to inform the others that they might draw only one reasonable conclusion.

'He has set foot along a ruinous road, and I am afraid this is far from uncommon – though not irreversible, I hasten to add. Over the years I have studied many, many examples of written works which bear no great dissimilarity to these. Our institutions overflow with individuals gifted with a perfect understanding of Life's hidden meaning, and who, moreover, enjoy the dubious privilege of a direct communication with God.'

He gave a humourless chuckle, adding wryly: 'Which is a

privilege, it would appear, that even we can no longer lay claim to.'

Nobody else laughed.

'The fact is,' he went on, 'that the individuals I refer to are generally kept apart from society ... for their own good as well as in the interests of public welfare. Their inner urgencies explode so easily, directing them into many forms of anti-social activities, violence against self and others included. Others, of course, maintain a greater self-control and consequently roam the streets as they please. And then there are those who, despite or because of their inner convictions, do successfully gain a degree of fame, or indeed infamy, in the world. But I surely don't have to point out that many of history's most heinous crimes have been committed in the name of a Lord and Creator.

'But I digress. My point is simply that these particular writings should not be considered unique, nor even far beyond the median line. And in spite of their apparent relevance to us they remain indicative purely of the patient's state of mind, of which we are already aware and which is in any case being monitored constantly.'

Still nobody troubled themselves to pass any comment. He was not really expecting them to. None of them had come here with the intention of giving him an easy time.

With the possible exception of one, these persons were to Doctor Geld less amenable than wayward schoolchildren. They had little genuine interest in what he had to say, their considerations were dictated solely by a desire for personal advantage. And, like children, they were alert for the smallest chink in his armour. They would knock or drag him down if his weaknesses showed through, or simply play gleeful witness to his fall. They did not dislike him as such, they were simply without feelings one way or the other.

And of course he was effectively on trial here. It would be unreasonable to expect clemency.

He swooped back to the open folder on the desk. 'Let me quickly give you one more example. This one is very brief and does contain certain references which might be construed as having direct relevance to us:

'"In the beginning there was God, and God created all"' he

128

read. '"He created the universe and filled it with stars and planets. He created the worlds and among them the Earth. He covered the Earth with lakes and seas, mountains and trees. He gave it flowers, fruits, insects, birds, beasts and fishes. God breathed Life into the world and made it a beauteous place.

'"And then God created Adam.

'"And Adam lost his mind."'

Doctor Geld elevated his gaze. 'So he mentions God. Ought that to worry us? Millions of others do every day, after all, and we don't – ha-ha! – we don't fly into a tizzy over every one of them! In another much less coherent jumble of scribbled outpourings he makes reference to The Gospel. Not "Gospel", mind, but The Gospel. So what does that imply? Alarm bells may ring, but have they reason? Let me again break this piece down into its discrete elements. That way you will see how one of the things I detect here – '

'Just get on with it, Theodore, would you,' came a bored voice from across the room. 'Leave out the technicalities and the analytical mumbo-jumbo. We already know what a jolly intelligent fellow you are. Just let's have the gist, there's a good chap.'

Doctor Geld's cheeks darkened slightly and he took out his foulard once more and applied it to his shining brow.

The speaker was Asprey, Co-ordinator and Technical Liaison Director, Whitehall's Head Prefect to Intelligence and head of a Select Advisory Board. Or something of the kind. Geld had no memory for nomenclature. And in any case, official designations or other means by which knowledge of one another might be gained were not encouraged in the crepuscular world in which they all co-existed.

Personal names were coded. Asprey, for example, in keeping with the cynical tone in which the whole operation had been contrived and mounted, was known officially as Angel One. Doctor Geld was Angel Two, and so on as far as Six. But other than on paper code names had long been dispensed with. Grown men and women could not in all seriousness address one another happily in such a manner.

Geld, for his own part, had no interest in the specific identities of those persons with whom he found himself obliged to co-operate. Unless called upon professionally to compile an analysis report he troubled himself little to find out anything about anyone.

But these particular individuals were important. In a couple of cases higher echelon important. Asprey himself, grey Gieves and Hawkes suited and partially shrouded in a portable cloud of mellow blue Havana smoke, habitually strode the corridors of power. His role here was effectively to monitor Gospel's progress, reporting back regularly on the turns of events to Those Who Should Be Kept Informed. Asprey, as exigencies warranted, had access direct to the Prime Minister.

Indicative of the degree to which he was assured of his own importance was the manner in which Asprey flaunted the rules. 'STRICTLY NO SMOKING' notices occupied prominent positions around the walls. They were to bring attention to the fact that ultra-sensitive electronic equipment was housed in this room, equipment requiring optimum conditions to function correctly. But to Asprey both equipment and notices were invisible. And nobody there would ever have considered making them otherwise.

Geld, obsequiously, said, 'Yes, of course. I simply wished to illustrate the manner by which I came to arrive at my decision.'

'But it's the decision we're after, man. Hang the illustrations,' Asprey said. He considered a moment, then turned to his nearest neighbour with a chortle of pleasure at the witticism he had quite inadvertently originated. 'Hang the illustrations!' he repeated, grinning, in case they had failed to get the joke.

'Very well, my decision, then. My professional opinion. These papers, and the developments we are currently investigating, do not in themselves constitute a security risk – at least, that is, ha-ha, not one more severe than the one we already face. I am happy to be able to disabuse you of any fears you may be harbouring. They are groundless – within limits, of course.

'So ... no cause for alarm. The patient, suffering increasingly dramatic fluctuations of mood, soaring to euphoria, plummeting to degradation and despair, tossed between megalomania and self-pitying introversion, does not have the faintest idea of what is happening to him. A watchful eye remains necessary, it goes without saying, for he is determined to find out. But essentially nothing has changed. My recommendation is that no further measures be taken. And most emphatically I must advise against the termination of Gospel just now. There can be no justification. It would serve no practical purpose whatsoever.'

'I was under the impression it had been terminated in effect from the day it began to go wrong,' Asprey remarked blandly.

'Not terminated,' the doctor replied, effecting a wide grin, a vile smile as the late Adam Shatt had christened it, but not looking directly at either Asprey or any of the other three, 'merely held over pending developments.'

Mackelvoye, Angel Three, the overburdened Deputy Director General, now spoke, 'Do you foresee him becoming a danger to himself?' He scribbled agitatedly on a piece of notepaper atop the table he sat at.

The psychiatrist's mouth twisted thoughtfully. 'As I have said, I do not believe he has any intention of taking his own life. But as a necessary part of his recovery he must successfully bury the details of his horrific experience in a part of his mind from which they cannot be dug out. This, to an extent it would seem, has occurred. The only thing now which grazes those memories is an earthquake or tremor.'

'But these earthquakes seem to be becoming more powerful, and more frequent.'

'The memories refuse to be completely buried, which is to be expected. They refuse also to come all the way to the surface. Result: tremendous conflict. However, after the burial must come the resurrection. Who knows at what point? But the memories will burst through. What their effect will be, and whether he will be capable of distinguishing between the true memories and the false, I cannot predict. Whatever, there is likely to be a great deal of anger. It may be directed at himself, or us. A complete personality change is not out of the question. Should that occur, and he fully realizes what has been done, or what he believes has been done ...' Again the doctor allowed his words to hang unspoken in the air.

Before he could resume his speech another voice chipped in. This time Doctor Geld grew noticeably more tense. Whereas Asprey's comments and Mackelvoye's questioning had demanded responses, they had not been intended to necessarily disconcert him. They were not aimed as slurs upon his person. Now, though, he knew himself to be under attack.

It was Nevus who spoke: Geld recognized the voice. He was Angel Four, a fat little dark-haired ministry man, short-sighted to the point of near blindness. He sat off to one side of the room, his chair tipped back against the blastproof yellow concrete wall. His stumpy little legs swung rapidly back and forth beneath him, the feet some inches free of the floor.

'You tell us you do not believe this constitutes a security risk,' Nevus said, adopting a tone of mock humility. 'And given the evidence at hand, plus the quite daunting degree of your professional expertise, I can understand how you might formulate such an opinion. But would it not at the same time be true to say, and pertinent, what's more, that you have a vested interest in arriving at that conclusion?'

Doctor Geld's single eyebrow shot high and divided. He emitted a sharp, involuntary burst of staccato laughter, and his small eyes darted like fireflies behind his bifocals. It became vital now that he locate Nevus physically as well as aurally.

Speaking in company Doctor Geld, to all intents and purposes, spoke to himself. He had never found public speaking a joy, no matter the decades of accumulated experience. It was only through the resourceful exploitation of a dominant physical handicap, his inadequate sight, that he was able to make of it the success that he did. The simple expedient of blotting his audience from visual consciousness enabled him to dislocate himself in space, so to speak, creating the illusion of near solitude in a room that could be bristling with company.

This, crowned with his formidable intellectual capacity, effectively gave him leave to rattle away for hours if need be. He could speak with a confidence that belied his real feelings, and with little fear of contradiction or rebuttal, for when questions came they were as from disembodied voices about him, or voices within his own head, and were treated as such. He had no small experience in dealing with voices of that nature.

But just occasionally, under specific pressures, it could be another story. Provide voice with body and personality, give it a measure of dogged hostility that declined propitiation or dismissal, and the doctor might be seen to falter. Deficient eyesight, as with the diminution of any sense faculty, may be a subconscious endeavour to remove one's self from life's firing-line, but at the day's end the real world has ways of making even the most inventive fugitive sit up and take notice. And on this day it had Geld taking notice of something he had never dared imagine he might have to confront: the possible end of his career. His reputation, his position, his credibility . . . a life's devotion. They were all at stake here.

So he pinpointed his accuser in space and glared at him.

Nevus, despite the heat, was wrapped up tightly in his customary thick black velvet-collared coat. Wide, powerful hands on short arms were finger-linked on his chest. He grinned in the doctor's direction, though it was evident that, even with the aid of the pebble glasses his inquisitive turned up nose supported, he was not finding it easy to descry his target.

'A vested interest?' Doctor Geld echoed, producing a glazed and insincere smile. 'I think it would be true to say that each one of us has a vested interest in the outcome of this affair, Mr Nevus. I am merely putting forward my professional judgement, which is what I was initially called upon to do.'

Nevus snickered. His fleshy face, permanently creased by little squinting eyes and a wrinkling nose, furrowed itself more pronouncedly. He lifted a hand and smoothed it over the close-cropped, luxuriant soft black hair that covered his head, growing low on his forehead and neck and even appearing in sparse tufts on his cheeks and jowls. 'Quite so. We most certainly do. But some of us more than others, I'd say. Wouldn't you?'

He emitted a thin squeal intended as laughter.

They glowered at one another, the short-sighted angular shrink and the fat purblind ministry man. And, as if by some prearranged signal, the machines in that hot, almost airless room, fell silent.

For a few seconds all that could be heard was the phantom throb of a baffler secreted somewhere within the walls. Its numerous tentacles stretched unseen around them, terminals picking up sounds originating within the room, swallowing and digesting them, and regurgitating them in altered form. Thus, even with the aid of the most sophisticated audio-surveillance equipment, anybody listening from outside would have been rewarded with nothing but an earful of white noise. This was distinct from standard tradecraft, which requires the installation of hidden microphones in all rooms so that conversations can be recorded for later case officer inspection and transcripts passed to relevant personnel. Here there was no case officer, and officially no relevant personnel. Officially there was nothing, and for a moment each of them was reminded of the gravity of the matter they were attempting to resolve.

Mackelvoye rat-tatted the end of his pencil on the table. 'You know, I'm just wondering whether this meeting ought really to continue with Gard not present.'

From within his dilating cloud Asprey gave a gasp of simulated horror. 'You *dare* to speak that name out loud?' he said, irresistibly bound to perpetuate a joke the others had long since tired of.

'It's just that we seem to be entering into areas of decision making which rather require the sanction of a higher authority.'

A soft-spoken, thoughtful, diplomatic man, Mackelvoye was growing increasingly ill-at-ease with his role. As Gard's number two he seemed to have assumed, involuntarily, administrative control over an operation he would have preferred having nothing to do with from the outset.

'Couldn't agree more,' Asprey said. 'But is he likely to show up?'

Geld said, 'With all due respect, I do not think it wise to place too much faith in Gard just at the moment. He has not graced our company *in persona* for quite some time, and I'm sure that if his intention were to join us today he would have made his appearance by this time. That is why I felt it proper to commence, and by the same token I see nothing to be gained by curtailing the meeting just now. His presence is not actually essential, after all. Any decisions may still be referred to him for final approval later on if need be.'

Asprey gave a judgemental nod. 'Agreed. If we sit and wait for him to show we could be here till Doomsday. I don't know what his game is. I'm rather of the impression he doesn't love us any more, aren't you?'

Nevus giggled and Doctor Geld threw him an icy glance.

'Carry on without him, then,' Asprey pronounced. 'Muddle on through as best we can, the way we always do, eh? That's the name of the game. I can see Roger's not especially keen on the prospect though.'

Mackelvoye sighed softly and regarded his scribblings. 'To be honest I see no other course. Events are hardly going to stand still while we sort things out. I was just hoping for some indication that he might be considering taking on his responsibilities again.'

Asprey clapped his hands. 'How *are* things on high anyway?' he said with a boom, having registered the pettish tone that had crept into the Deputy D-G's voice. 'Has *anybody* had any word at all? I mean, he does rather appear to have lost interest in us, doesn't he. Forsaken the whole shebang and moved on to pastures new. Given us up to our fate. How long since anybody here last gazed upon his sublime features?'

'I don't consider us to be forsaken, Geoffrey,' Mackelvoye hastily rejoined, as if regretting his last words. 'He is being kept aware of developments, and it goes without saying he maintains a strong interest still. Caution does dictate that he keep a low profile at present. You can see that.'

'Not a million miles removed from the proverbial policeman, it strikes me! Don't you think a personal appearance about now might be just the tonic we need. Morale-wise if nothing else. After all, he was and is the Prime Mover. Seems unfair to bunk off and leave the lackeys to deal with the mess at such a critical juncture.'

'I think Gard is wise to dissociate himself from Gospel for a time,' Doctor Geld said. 'If he is under surveillance from any quarter and the extent of his involvement were discovered, or if the nature of the experiment itself became known, the consequences could be catastrophic and far-reaching. And apart from that, he is rather preoccupied. He has many pressing matters to attend to, I'm sure.'

'Royal accolade among them, no doubt!' piped Nevus. He smirked. 'It's imminent, I hear. And I would be mortified to see the sword slip and bite into his neck!'

He was ignored.

Mackelvoye looked at his pencil tip, then at Asprey. 'There are still communications, as deemed necessary.'

'As deemed necessary!' Asprey scoffed. 'How charming.' He sucked vigorously at his cigar and his cloud swelled and thickened ominously. 'I don't understand why you're all so eager to stick up for him. The man is quite obviously guilty of dereliction of his duties. As I see it he's no longer fit to occupy his office.' The humour had left his voice. He leaned forward on his chair, knocking ash from his trouser leg with a flick of one hand. 'You know, the picture I get, Roger, old boy, is that Gard has made himself bloody unreachable. And quite deliberately, too. And you are all content to sit here and be fobbed off with his "too busy", "other matters" bunkum, without taking into account what his absence really means. *Nobody* seems able to get to him any more! I can't even approach his office, let alone get a glimpse of the Inner Sanctum. And I don't think he's ever there anyway. He doesn't answer calls, rarely gives out directives. Conducting himself like a bloody ineffectual ghost!

'And the brutal truth is that you need him right now. We all do. In the flesh. He's responsible for this mess and I think he owes it to us to at least be around while we try to muck out of it.'

'Point taken, Geoffrey. But as I say, I simply don't consider us to be abandoned. I confess I'm not altogether happy wearing Gard's hat, but, let's be objective about this, until there is a more positive development, something more decisive to act upon, he would be needlessly subjecting himself to risk by joining us.'

'Your loyalty does you great credit,' Asprey replied with barely disguised sarcasm, 'but I think you're cutting your own throat. Still, why should I worry? I'm only the All-Seeing Eye around here. When the proverbial truly hits I won't have to trouble myself to blink. It won't be flying in my direction. Wouldn't be in any of your boots though.'

Creatures

'Perhaps what really has him worried is our mole,' Nevus suggested.

'Mole!' Asprey spluttered. His manner had become quite scathing. 'What's a little mole to Gard? It's nowhere near him, is it? What bearing can that have on his attitude?'

'Don't underestimate the mole, Geoffrey,' Mackelvoye cautioned. 'It could be anywhere, and we wouldn't necessarily know until it chose to break the surface. Whoever he or she may be they have certainly dug close enough to warrant our investigation.

Their activities have been irritating rather than seriously damaging, it's true, but they've nevertheless succeeded in causing chaos in a number of areas. Nobody knows quite who is who any more. I've had to send in Smileys here, there and everywhere, and even I don't know who they are. None of us can afford to look upon this lightly. We're all walking on eggshells, not just Gard.'

'Well, hiding away like this is not going to do much to bolster his credibility, that's all I'm saying. He should be giving a little more thought to his image. At this rate he will find himself removed in no time. Nobody's going to respect him or have faith in him any more, let alone fear him!'

'On the subject of animals, by the way,' Nevus said in a syrupy voice, re-directing his attention and the conversation to Doctor Geld, 'how are yours these days? Any left?'

The doctor froze. It was still not known how news of his test subjects had leaked, and short of a thorough house-cleaning (which was out of the question) it was unlikely it ever would. But that which should have been a closely guarded secret, even from those persons here in this room, was instead becoming virtually common knowledge.

He groped for words. 'Mr Nevus, I am not sure what you are insinuating – '

'Nothing, doctor. Nothing at all,' Nevus said, extending his little legs out horizontally in front of him with pleasure. 'Merely enquiring. Out of concern.'

The fifth member, Angel Five, who had so far made no vocal contribution, now spoke. 'What do you mean, Nevus, "any left"?'

'You don't know?' Nevus piped merrily. 'I thought everyone was informed. Well, they are dying. One by one. Kaput!'

'Is this true?'

'There have been fatalities in recent weeks,' the psychiatrist said. 'But not necessarily as a result of experimentation. There are many factors to be taken into consideration.'

'How many fatalities?'

'Two. Rabbits,' Nevus snickered. 'And a capuchin.'

'Is the patient at risk?'

Doctor Geld twitched uncomfortably. 'I do not believe that to be the case. As I say, there are many factors. The animals in question died as a result of a delayed traumatic response which manifested as a sudden hypothalamic seizure – not necessarily connected with my experiments. In addition, our Apostle was not subject to the same treatments these animals received.'

He took out his fob watch. 'Now, I have given my opinion, and that is all I came here to do. I do not think my presence is required further. So if there are no more questions . . .'

He slipped his papers back into the folder, which he closed and pushed into a briefcase alongside the desk.

'None, it would appear,' said Mackelvoye after a pause. 'You'll be informed of any steps resulting from this meeting.'

Geld nodded, snapping the briefcase shut. 'Mr Mackelvoye, I leave it with you to ensure that none of these transcripts are allowed to leave this room. They are for the shredder, as I am sure you are already aware.'

Taking the briefcase he strode with what dignity he could muster to the single electronically sealed entrance in the corner of the room. He tapped out a code on a small key console embedded in the concrete.

Above his head a red light blinked. Inserting a plastic card he tapped a second combination of digits. The flashing red changed to green and the door opened with a whirr and a metallic click. Doctor Geld exited the room, with relief, though at the same time conscious that no one else there had yet indicated their intention of leaving.

Of Trust And Understanding

The late Adam Shatt had realized that it was no longer advisable to rely upon his wife, Judith. In the days since his horrifying discovery in the house in Notting Hill Gate he had not taken her into his confidence. Nor had he told anybody else.

She declared herself an unworthy confidante by reason of her good upbringing. Moral circumspection and an inbred, unquestioning regard for society's mores would have afforded her, had he told her, a single course of action. She, like any normal person, would have gone without hesitation to the police.

Naturally Adam had considered going to the police. Through omission he made himself an accessory to the crime, but he could not do so without even further complicating his dilemma. For he would surely be their principle suspect. And his case history, his blank-outs and breakdowns, stacked as evidence against him, would provide them with a substantial case for his prosecution.

He was under no misapprehensions concerning his ability to withstand sustained interrogation. Despite the facts he felt he lacked any defence, and feared the way things would be twisted – a deft inquisitor might without any real difficulty have him actually believing himself the killer. He had to accept that in itself that was not such a ludicrously far-fetched proposition. It was not something he cared to think too deeply upon.

A sparse comfort had come initially with the reassurance that the murder would have been promptly reported; but to his perplexity Adam discovered that this was not so. Curiously and quite inexplicably none of the local newspapers covered the finding of a tenant's body in the lavatory of a Notting Hill Gate private residence with its throat slashed and head all-but severed.

True, the newspapers did upon closer inspection read like Black Museum guides. Mayhem prevailed in the city and its environs to an alarming extent, which might have accounted for the failure of one more violent death to make it to the page. But that was not an entirely convincing explanation. It came to Adam just a little too conveniently.

So he found himself enmeshed in a delicate trap. On the one hand he wanted nothing more than to prove himself a law-abiding citizen and unburden himself of the knowledge he held. And on the other he was obliged to keep silence, fearful of what might otherwise ensue. The one person he might conceivably have spoken to was not available. Helmut's telephone rang and rang, but the Nuclear-Age Thinker was not at home. He had probably taken off on one of his not infrequent jaunts to God-knew-where.

Adam stood alone, absorbed in his thoughts, in the back garden of his home. It was a raw December afternoon. During the earlier part of the day a biting wind had been rising, and under the distant pallid gaze of the sun gathering patches of grey-white cumulus were herded eastwards across a winter blue sky.

The garden had a lifelessness about it now. The trees at the end, their branches swaying and groaning lightly, had given up the last of their leaves. There was no new growth, the grass of the lawn was still and no flowers bloomed. Adam was lost. He had no idea of where to turn or what step to take next. Filled with an urgency to move, to be doing something, he nevertheless held back.

Any decisive move on his part, it seemed, led him deeper into confusion. And with this latest development he had become fearful to the point of an inability to act again on his own volition.

For days he had been going over and over events in his mind, trying to discover some pattern, something other than madness that ran through all he was experiencing. But all that presented themselves were endless entangled plots and fantastically interwoven paranoias, twisting and plunging through domains where reason could not follow.

Still he could not bring himself to abandon the conviction that somewhere in there a correlation, no matter how tenuous, had to exist. Something – a link, a connection, a clue which he was somehow failing to descry. His world was complex and irrational, and he was hopelessly caught up in a plexus of events, but surely it could not be utterly without design? He felt he might have become blind to what would under different circumstances be obvious. He needed an indication, a sign. But where now was he to search?

His eyes roamed over the walls which surrounded him on all four sides, and beyond them the walls of neighbouring gardens extending to left and right as far as the ends of the terrace. There the backs of the houses rose four and five storeys high. They enclosed the individually sectioned properties within a tall, unbroken rectangle of yellow-brown brick, like the perimeter wall of a fortress. He gazed towards the trees which, throughout spring and summer, had formed a natural screen between his house and that of his neighbour opposite. The rear of that house was plainly visible now through the network of bare branches.

It had been some time since he had given any thought to the brutish Slav, or the crazed animal he kept chained in his garden. Since his accustomed nightmare had ceased disturbing him he had found too many other things occupying his mind. He had neither seen nor heard them, not even a whimper from the hound during the bitterest days and nights.

Adam had little more than a notional recollection of his last journey out to the wall, when he had climbed up in the early mist onto the overhanging chestnut bough. Weeks had passed, maybe longer, he could not accurately judge. He felt that he looked back on it now from the viewpoint of some other person, someone who, if not actually capable of understanding, could at least regard it with a distanced and perhaps dispassionate eye.

Instinctively curious he took a step towards the wall. The sense of ritual that had always, if not quite consciously, coloured the act on former occasions was not present this time. He was under no compulsion, and neither was his brain fogged or dream-laden. And though he approached cautiously it was without the anticipation or exhilaration, or the former irresistible, fearful craving for the encounter with the beast.

This was the first time he had conducted the exercise in daylight. And when he ducked beneath the branches and stood before the wall he was unsurprised that no enraged and slavering creature came flying at him out of the jungle of long grass. He rested his palms on the upper course of brick, having no intention this time of hauling his body up onto the bough, and let his eyes take in the garden.

He was seeing it free of mist for the first time. It was spattered with patches of sunlight, switching restlessly off and on with the movement of the trees and the passage of the clouds overhead. The long grass bent and shivered, susurrating at the cold wind which buffeted it and ran through its stalks and blades. He sensed the emptiness of the brutish Slav's basement. The curtains were drawn, as they always were, and the door and windows closed. Other than the dog being absent there was no visible change. But he knew without question that no one was living there any more.

All that remained as evidence of the brutish Slav's occupancy was the post to which his pet had been chained. A length of tubular iron sunk deep into the soil midway down the garden, it was as thick as a man's arm. It rose eight feet or more out of the earth and pointed skywards like a metal finger at the clouds driving east. The chain was nowhere to be seen.

Adam leaned on the cold brick wall. In the manner that he had first acknowledged the passing of his nightmare and the red snow that always followed, he was uncertain of his emotions now. He sensed relief but was haunted by a melancholic languor associated with loss. The 'prescient sorrow' he had known before returned. He felt that something had been taken from him, or had passed on. Many things. The nightmare, the red snow, the brutish Slav and his dog, perhaps even Dennis, shed like layers of dead skin, hardly related any longer in any way to him.

But these things, he could not help feel, were part of it all. Changes, the nature of which he could not comprehend, taking place in order that the future might form. Within and without, physical and psychic energies gathering and subtly discharging; the release of things impalpable and evasive of rationale.

Some minutes passed. He breathed in the dark, earthen, vegetal smell beneath the trees. He watched a cat, a sleek, smoke-coloured female which appeared suddenly on his absent neighbour's wall. She slipped silently into the garden and disappeared in the long grass where previously she would never have dared step.

Adam pulled himself up onto the wall, then let himself down on the other side. He approached, with a slightly heady feeling, the metal post. He placed his hands against it, breathing deeply, feeling its cold hardness on his palms. He leaned his weight against it.

Eventually he turned, walked back and climbed over the wall into his own garden. He made his way back across the grass to the house, his head bowed and his hands deep in his trousers pockets, troubled but inwardly attuning to an almost subliminal whispering within himself which he could not yet quite translate.

Indoors he removed his Wellingtons and flak jacket and went to the lounge, intending to write. But he sat down and closed his eyes for a moment, and was immediately drawn into a long sleep and a series of unfathomable dreams.

The Big World

When Adam informed Judith that they no longer had as neighbours the brutish Slav and his hound, her curt and incurious response was a barely perceptible shrug of the shoulders, preceding the words, 'I'm not surprised. It wasn't much of a life.'

She had arrived home late from work, exhausted and preoccupied, and did not seem eager to talk. So he'd mixed her a mug of hot chocolate and left her to herself in front of the television. He didn't pursue the matter, nor did he trouble her with his new thoughts and plan of action.

In point of fact it was more a resolve than a plan. He was going to venture out into the world again. He felt strong enough, he felt able enough. He felt that for too long he had been taking shelter in the womb of his walled garden and home.

Admittedly that had never been his intention, but only now was he beginning to see clearly how the combination of unforeseen circumstances and his own patterns of behaviour and response had been consistently guiding him on a closed track. With each new and unexpected event he had been sent reeling back to the same spot he had so recently debarked from.

So he was resolved now that this must end. It was time for him to get out and do something. He was ready to be born.

Adam sealed his decision with a ritual act. He went to the bathroom cabinet and located the medication earlier prescribed for him by Doctor Geld, which he had always kept there just in case. Now he took the phial and flushed its contents down the lavatory, sending a few valedictory phrases in their wake.

Almost immediately the big world began to reveal itself. Adam's returning strength and inner resources were tested to flashpoint as he ran head-on into a sequence of mystifying and apparently unrelated incidents. Far from seeing things with a greater clarity, he was instead drawn yet deeper into intractable mysteries.

The first in these complexes of circumstance arose one afternoon, quite late, towards the end of a long hike.

On the whole Adam had been much inspirited by the continuing improvement in his physical condition. He was exercising more vigorously day by day without discomfort over gradually extended periods of time. He was increasing the distance he could walk, and on this day had covered a little under five miles. Jogging intermittently he was not, as he made his way back towards home, feeling unduly tired.

As he walked, his thoughts on no one thing in particular, he found himself suddenly transported back in time. He was with

Judith, in Oxford. For some moments he was seeing and thinking it before he really became aware of what was happening. They had taken a bicycle ride out into the country and had ended up by the riverside a little way from Marston. The day was warm, it was early June, and they were enjoying a picnic together just prior to going down for the summer. They sat on a chequered woollen blanket spread over cropped green grass in a meadow where Friesians grazed.

Adam smiled to himself as the memory came back. Judith, her hair long and tumbling about her shoulders, was looking at him sidelong and smiling as he poured Dom Pérignon into two glasses. She looked happy, with none of the cares that were etched seemingly so indelibly into her features now. She was younger. She wore a simple blue cotton frock and had removed her sandals.

It was one of those long forgotten memories that flood back suddenly into consciousness in a wave of emotion. He felt it all so intensely, almost hearing her laughter, catching the scent of her perfume in his nostrils, feeling the sun as it fell gently on his head and bare arms. It was an occasion he would always remember. It was the day he had asked her to marry him.

Unknowingly he came to a halt in the busy street. The most crucial element had all but passed him by. It was not the content or the details that were important; they, in this case, were mere embellishments distracting him from the reality in which they were contained. What *was* important was the experience in itself: the occasion *remembered*. Until now he had not possessed the faculty to look back and recall that day.

He stood excitedly and rigidly still. He could not quite grasp what this meant, and already it seemed to be fading. Not from recall but, strangely, from significance. He should have been moved, instead he now felt little reaction. His excitement had come in a rush and was gone. And in its place now there was moving in something else.

A heaviness came over him, an oppressive gloom mingling with an indistinct sense of foreboding. Chilling tentacles crept from somewhere low in his spine and spread through his bones and veins. Something was trying to make itself known to him. Like a spirit from the other world striving to pass a last message to the living, something apart from the happiness of that day in Oxford with Judith all those summers ago was attempting to break through into conscious memory.

He shook his head, the gloom did not disperse. Instead it intensified into a feeling of dread, tainting and destroying any trace of joy or elation his returning memory should have brought him. He found he was trembling. He knew, he just *knew*, that this was connected with that memory. His experience was genuine: a vivid recollection from his past which had previously been inaccessible to him, and this ... this shadow, belonged to it.

But it was not going to come. Its residue clung about him but the body was not to be seen. Somewhere its passage was barred.

It was like passing from one altered state of awareness to another. He stood on a busy shopping thoroughfare, outside a brightly-lit newsagent's premises somewhere in that uncertain region that is neither Islington nor Camden. The night had come down rapidly as he'd walked, and through the incessant roar of the first manic rush-hour traffic people swept by him in all directions, driven like particles in a storm.

His attention was drawn to the glaringly illuminated interior of the shop where a staggering variety of Christmas goods had been placed on open display. Vying for pride of position on the limited shelf-space available were jolly plastic Santas, tinsel trees and inflatable snowmen, reindeers with sleighs, colourful fairy lights, baubles and gew-gaws glittering in myriad forms and dimensions. They had gained temporary domination over the more mundane displays of stationery, coloured crayons, combs, cheap transistors and everyday household items. The counters were decked with seasonal confectionery in tasteless packaging, and to one side of the shop Christmas cards were racked in their hundreds.

Other than an Asian assistant behind the counter at the rear there were four persons in the shop. The nearest to Adam was a middle-aged lady with a small child and a shopping buggy, selecting sheets of gift-wrappings from a revolving display stand. He watched her for a moment, then noticed the young woman in a quilted blue anorak and grey pleated skirt who had been talking with the counter-assistant. She was approaching the street-facing window. In one hand she had a sheaf of small bills or posters, rolled into a tube. In the other she carried a roll of sticky tape and a pair of scissors.

The other person present, a tall, grey-haired man in a light overcoat and dark blue suit, stood apparently unheeded by the others. Though better garbed and obviously of a different social standing he had managed to make himself blend in with his surroundings. Initially he had been flicking through some glossy magazines. Then, standing obliquely to the girl in the anorak as she chatted with the assistant, he had feigned interest convincingly in some boxes of over-priced crackers. Now, as the girl leaned into the window to affix one of her posters to the inside of the glass, he changed his position. He took up a new stance about a yard away to her rear.

Adam had been paying scant attention. Now he frowned in puzzlement as the nature of what he was witnessing slowly dawned on him. For the man had casually let part the flaps of his overcoat, and like the Christmas gifts that surrounded him, had placed himself on open display.

The girl in the anorak had no conception of the metabolic changes her presence had wrought upon this particular specimen of human malehood. She was plainly not the type to deliberately draw attention to herself. And the man, for his part, was patently not aware that he was being observed from without. With his perceptions limited, presumably by a combination of the heights of his transport and the obscured view of the street outside caused by the shop's reflected interior, he had passed caution to the breeze. The precise content of his thoughts at that moment was less a secret than the colour of his socks.

Adam remained a little undecided and not overly dismayed by this exhibition that greeted his eyes. To his unsettled mind it could be only an additional feature within an already overwhelming sense of displacement. He gazed, therefore, but did not fully absorb.

Had he assimilated the scene in all its aspects he would have fallen prey to a further shock. The man's silver-grey hair was dishevelled and his suit had the uncustomary appearance of having been slept in; he was not in characteristic command of himself; his broad shoulders were raised and his features flushed and somewhat contorted. All the same he was recognizable as someone Adam had seen before, in a vision. On that occasion he had been playing intently with a set of six dice in a room with arched and mullioned windows. Adam had subsequently trailed him, or his likeness, as far as the door of a gentlemen's club down Pimlico way.

Inside the shop the girl, having Sellotaped her poster to the pane, straightened and briefly appraised her handiwork. She turned and smiled her thanks to the assistant. Her admirer, anticipating her, stepped to one side and removed himself from her immediate line of sight.

The girl left the shop and he, unabashed, the fingertips of one hand lightly supporting the undershaft of his erection, followed her.

She stepped outside into the unwelcoming evening and spotted Adam staring in. Her lips parted in a smile.

'Are you going?' she enquired warmly.

Adam gazed beyond her. The tall man was stepping into the frame of the doorway. As he did so their eyes met. Adam was subject to a sudden disorienting sensation of déjà-vu, as if this were someone he had seen in a dream.

Spotting Adam for the first time the man stopped dead. His jaw dropped slack as simultaneously his head darted backwards and his eyes widened in amazement. It was as if he too were confronted suddenly with a ghost, or with the one person he had least expected to see.

He recovered himself quickly. With a hurried motion he drew his coat about him, stepped out of the door and strode rapidly away.

The girl repeated her question. Adam, perplexedly gazing after the tall diminishing figure, failed to catch her words, though he grew aware this time that she had spoken.

He blinked. 'What?'

'To the lecture,' she said. 'Are you going?'

He looked at her. Her face close to was not unappealing. Her skin was white and freckled. She had large, expressive grey eyes and brown hair tied unfashionably in a ponytail. She wore no makeup and her unflattering choice of clothing gave few clues as to the form of her body underneath. She was about twenty-four or -five, he estimated.

'You ought to, you know,' she insisted, and it came to him that she was referring to something on the poster she had just put in the window. She had assumed him to be studying it.

For the first time he ran his eyes over the poster. It was a standard enough piece of advertising, black print on a yellow field. It proclaimed:

THE SAVIOUR IS HERE. HE IS SOON TO BE RECOGNIZED.
Prepare yourselves for the Day of Declaration.
A rare discourse – A Time For Change, by Iddio E. Scompiglio.
Admission Free.

Below this, in a smaller fount, were printed the date on which the meeting was to be held, two evenings hence, and the time and venue: a local infants' school assembly hall at 7.00 P.M. There was also the address of the organizing body, 'The Sons And Daughters Of Scompiglio', and a telephone number for enquirers.

Adam scanned the notice a second time.

Iddio E. Scompiglio!

He was back in that absurdly cramped and pokey attic room, reaching out to pick up a slim, pocket-sized, green leatherette bound volume entitled *The Book Of Imaginary Hauntings*. He was allowing it to fall open again randomly and reading the words printed there: 'Seeing without eyes is the mark of the madman or the seer. Make your choice!'

Those words, which had disturbed him then, had little impact now, but he recalled how both Dennis and Helmut had proceeded to fill him in on details of the little volume's author, Iddio E. Scompiglio. The details had disturbed him further, and they did so again now.

Iddio E. Scompiglio had written a work called 'The Poisoned Land'. According to Dennis's brief description this piece bore an uncanny similarity to Adam's own unfinished and unpublished 'The Poisoned Garden', the treatise on earthly decay which still lay hidden, along with so many others, in his bedroom cupboard.

And Helmut had made reference to the mystery that surrounded Scompiglio's identity. It seemed that nobody had ever set eyes on the man. Nobody knew who he was.

At that time an idea of exorbitant magnitude had struck Adam. Mercifully, perhaps, events had not given him any opportunity to pursue it. And on latter occasions, finding it slipping into his thoughts, he had treated it to a forceful dismissal. It was not the sort of notion to be seriously entertained, especially by a person in his condition.

But he was encouraged to consider it again now. Under the circumstances it would have been madness to do anything else.

The idea that had struck him at that time was that he, the late Adam Shatt, was Iddio E. Scompiglio.

He had personally produced those books, written the multifarious works and done all the other things attributed to the man. This would include, it would seem, having founded a sizeable modern-day religious movement. And he had done them all, been that person, founded that religion, in his former existence, of which he now possessed no knowledge.

Following that line of reasoning, though, led him into confrontation with some daunting propositions: The inference as of this moment could only be that he, Adam, was imminently to declare himself the new Saviour of mankind. In just two days, in fact.

This he could confidently dismiss. But there were other points to be considered. For instance, should all of the aforementioned turn out to be fact he would be forced to embrace the revelation that, with his past life inaccessible to him, he was purposefully being fed utterly false data about himself. He was being made to live an unnatural alternative existence, deliberately and perversely deprived of his real background.

Wild-eyed before the poster he let out a long breath. It was too big, much too big. He could not allow himself to contemplate it. For what possible motive could there be for withholding such knowledge from him?

Plenty, he had to admit, if it were true.

And ... God, it was too horrible. For it would mean that *everyone* he had any kind of contact with was involved in a cover-up, was lying, always had been ... determined for reasons unimaginable that he should never learn the truth about who and what he really was.

He focussed slowly back on the girl in the blue anorak. 'I'm sorry. What did you say?'

A wariness had crept into her eyes. The warm smile was contracting ever so slightly. She had the look of someone just remembering a prior engagement.

Adam would have laughed had he been capable. Ignorant of what he had just saved her from she was seeing him as a potential threat. He wondered how events would have evolved had he not been brought to a halt just there.

'I said you ought to go,' the girl repeated. She took a step away, preparing to move off up the street in the same direction her proud worshipper had taken. 'You'll have a wonderful time!'

She slipped away. Adam watched her until she was swallowed by the night.

He turned back to the poster. This, surely, constituted proof positive that his outlandish notion was just that – outlandish. A notion. A fantasy. In two evenings from now Iddio E. Scompiglio, the real Iddio E. Scompiglio, was scheduled to stand up in public and give his message.

Dennis's doleful voice came from far away. 'He's going to have a Day of Declaration. And when he does I want to be around to see it.'

Dennis wouldn't be there, but Adam would. He made a mental note of the time, date and venue. Nothing short of his own death was going to prevent him from attending that lecture.

He was moving off when he happened to glance across the street.

Opposite, dominating a corner of a side-road which stretched down and away towards King's Cross, was a pub, The Man In The Moon. A man was standing outside its rejuvenated Victorian frontage.

He leaned in casual stance against the wall of its pilastered entrance, alongside a double door which let into a cosily lit saloon. He wore a pale suit, and he was watching Adam intently.

Adam gave a start. Even in the bad light he could not doubt what he saw. The man stood almost ghostly, just beyond the rim of a pool of pale luminescence thrown from an overhead lantern. He held a pen to his lips and a notepad on which he seemed about to write something.

'Hey!' Adam started forward, intent on crossing the street to accost him. His heart beat fast. He was suddenly breathless.

But as he made to step out from the pavement the traffic lights at an intersection a little way off changed from red through to green. Immediately two taut columns of vehicles surged forward, headlamps ablaze.

He stepped quickly back. For a second he was dazzled by the lamps of the nearest advancing car. For a second he was no longer standing on a busy London thoroughfare, he was in a dark and narrow country lane. He was blinded, terrified. A violent piercing pain stabbed through his head, and with the stomach-churning jar of impact his whole body cried out as bones splintered and flesh was torn and mutilated.

Then he was back, adaze, searching for a gap in the flow of vehicles. He ran with the traffic and managed to reach the centre of the road. Now he was blocked by the flow from the opposite direction.

A glance towards the pub told him what he had already guessed. Of course, there was no longer anyone standing there. The pale-suited figure had vanished.

Adam weaved with an exasperated cry between two oncoming cars. He sprang onto the opposite pavement. His right leg gave way as he landed, a lancing pain shot from his hip down to his knee. The cars raced on into the night, a single horn blaring mournfully. Adam made for the corner.

There was nothing to suggest that the man in the pale suit had ever leaned casually there. With ample time for escape he might by now be in another street, or in any one of the premises lining this one.

Adam threw himself through the doors of The Man In The Moon, into the saloon. It was too early for customers. The sole occupant was a barman with a walrus-moustache. He was slouched across the bar reading a newspaper. He did not trouble himself to raise his head.

Adam marched into the public bar. No one. He checked the toilets, then returned to the saloon. The barman raised his head.

'D'you wanna try the cellar, fella?' he asked. He was Australian. He winked, then leered with implied camaraderie. 'Or maybe she's hiding down here behind the bar with me?'

Adam swore as the barman grinned. He walked back out onto the street, with little option now but to continue on his way home.

More Of The Big World

And the very next morning the big world knocked his feet from under him yet again. It had the local postman slip a letter through his door. The letter was from Dennis.

Before he had even glanced at its contents he noted the signature at the end and had to reach out for support, the nearest kitchen chair. He sat down heavily.

'Man,' the letter began. It was written in a haphazard, almost childlike script that plied a tortured trail across two sides of pale pink recycled notepaper. 'I really feel I ought to apologize for not helping out the other night. Truth is, I didn't catch on to what was happening. I was just right out of it.

'Don't remember much about it now but H. tells me you got pretty sick. If it's any consolation, man, so did I. But I hope you're getting over it. I know things affect you, but don't go letting it get you down. It isn't worth it.

'Listen, it has stuck in my mind that we started a conversation about that cheap creep shrink, Geld. I told you he was no good for you, and in case you think I was bullshitting, I've enclosed something that ought to make you think again. If it doesn't then there's nothing I can do for you. You're lucky, though. Lucky you pulled out when you did.

'There's more on him if you want it. A.L.F. kept a file. None of it has a chance of getting public, of course. Not now. He's got cover. Characters like that always have. The press just don't want to know. Heavy pressure. So keep away, man. That's the best you can do.

'One other thing – the nice Jewish girl, Ruth, you wanted to chat up before you fell in the food – I got her address for you. In case I don't see you for a while, here it is.

'Interesting chick. Does Jung, *very* seriously. And the Kabbalah, too, I think. I've heard she's a spiritualist, and she's in with some German-based mystical sect. But she's a bit reticent with me on some of these things. I've tried talking to her about it but she's not to be drawn. Tells me I'm a terminal neophyte, which I take to be her pleasant way of saying 'Piss off'.

'Mysterious lady.

'Anyway, I reckon you and she would have things to talk about, somehow. I've told you there are things going on around you, man. I dunno what, but there's something. I reckon Ruth and you would get on.

'Come round again when you're feeling up to it. Bring H. and we can talk some more. I'll make a curry.

'Take care,
    Dennis'

The letter gave Adam's experiences of recent days a very dubious aspect. He ran through it twice more, then made a cursory appraisal of the other contents. There were several Xeroxed newspaper clippings and another piece of recycled paper, this time in green, upon which was scrawled in large, irregular capitals, the name Ruth, followed by a Kensington address.

Again he went over the letter.

Dennis was alive!

And yet he had seen the body, seen the blood. He had truly seen it. That could not have been pure hallucination. Could it?

Could it have been a prank? He recalled his first encounter with Dennis – the trick knife that had appeared from nowhere to slash Helmut's throat . . .

With a shaking hand he picked up the Xeroxed clippings from the table in front of him. There were five, each quite brief. Two had photographs accompanying.

Each of the reports covered the same subject: the attempts by a group of animal rights activists to bring to public light the nature of certain experiments being conducted in the name of scientific research. The activists had broken into Oxfordshire government research laboratories and freed many of the test subjects. They claimed the animals had suffered appallingly and unnecessarily at the scientists' hands.

Protesters had mounted a permanent demonstration outside the home of Doctor Theodore Geld, a member of the Institute of Psychiatry and head of experimental research at the offending laboratories. The walls of his house and garden had been daubed with red swastikas and anti-Nazi slogans. He was receiving insulting and often threatening letters and telephone calls. When entering or leaving his home he regularly, under police guard, had to run the gauntlet of eggs and rotten fruit and vegetables.

The first of the photographs was a head and shoulders shot of Doctor Geld. The other showed the protesters, some wearing masks and holding placards, on the pavement outside the doctor's smart suburban home. It was not possible to tell from which newspapers the cuttings had been taken, or the dates. The reportage, though, bore the earnestness of provincial journalism rather than the glib self-assurance of the nationals.

In one of the pieces a sentence had been underlined in red, presumably by Dennis's hand. It was an allegation, for which the liberationists claimed to be able to produce documentary substantiation, that in his private life the doctor was involved in some pretty seedy activities. He was accused of being an enthusiastic collector of pornographic literature and films, and worse, far worse, an erstwhile subscriber, under an assumed name of course, to PIE, the recently disbanded Paedophile Information Exchange.

Adam put the papers down, too stunned to make anything of their claims. Was Dennis alive? Certainly, there had been no newspaper reports of his death. Nor anything else to support what Adam alone had witnessed. But why a hoax? And ... no! Nobody could have faked what he had seen.

And additionally, Dennis had not known, nor could he have known, that Adam had planned to visit him that evening.

Adam sensed his surroundings beginning to withdraw. He gripped the edge of the table with both hands. Where was all of this leading him? How could he know what was true and what was not? Was it necessary for him to go back to the house to find out? Was he capable now of doing that?

He questioned the wisdom of his ritual disposal the other day of his medication. He asked himself seriously whether the most advisable course just now would be to go out immediately and have himself admitted to the nearest, most secure, psychiatric hospital. For nothing, absolutely nothing in his world, was making any sense.

Until finally . . .

Finally he discovered himself staring at the postmark on the face of Dennis's envelope. The letter had been mailed by second-class post. Dennis had dated it a week or so after the evening Adam and Helmut had spent in his company. The postmark on the envelope confirmed that he had posted the letter some two days after writing it.

Hazily there was coming to Adam's mind some recollection of a recent postal dispute. It had been resolved now, but at one point local post boxes had been sealed over several days, and deliveries appeared to have ceased altogether. The disruption had created a backlog of mail that was still being cleared.

So something did make sense, or at least formed an impression of solidity, though he could still not grasp it very firmly. The letter had undergone temporary suspension, held in a kind of Post Office bardo. It had been there for two weeks, or even longer.

No illusions, then. Dennis *was* dead. Committing it to the post would have been one of his final acts.

Adam picked up the letter again and stared at the scribbled words with eyes that had filled with tears. What was he to believe? Dennis, with this letter, had made a declaration of friendship. Was it conceivable that this friendship had been the very reason he had died?

He faced losing all motivation again. Sitting there at the kitchen table and forcing himself, as the day passed by, to examine the options open to him. He could not see that they amounted to very much.

The fact that he had Ruth's address was the one significant advance. It gave him hope that he might discover something of the identity and rationale of her mysterious companion at the party. Other than that he had a collection of articles damning Doctor Geld further in his eyes, but which really told him nothing new. The letter had thoroughly shaken him, but it left him now feeling more fatalistically inclined towards every aspect of his dilemma. He could not see a way through.

A Third Encounter Of The Close Kind

The infants' school in which the putative new Redeemer of humanity was to make his public debut was not difficult to find. It was situated in a side street no more than half a mile from the spot where Adam had first viewed the poster. A London three-decker enclosed within high brick walls, it was one of some two hundred schools built in the eighteen-seventies by the London Schoolboard to provide education for under-privileged children. The original building had expanded with the years, sprouting annexes and single-storey prefabs in almost every undeveloped space.

Judith parked her Metro in the road outside. She had not initially shown any great enthusiasm at the idea of accompanying Adam. Surprise had been her first reaction, for neither of them was religiously inclined. But Adam was insistent and she had been reluctant to let him go alone. Of late his behaviour had given her cause for renewed concern, and she recognized the need for being with him and providing him with a kind of moral support.

They located the assembly hall without difficulty but upon entering discovered themselves in a large room occupied by persons practising T'ai Chi Chuan, the slow-motion form of Chinese exercise. A bright-eyed young instructor informed them of an administrative error which had caused the venue for their meeting to be changed to a classroom on the floor above.

When they entered the right room Adam was mildly surprised to find it almost full. He had conjured up in his mind a rather sorry congregation of troubled teenagers, ageing hippies, a few down-and-outs and sheltering homeless and other lost and lonely souls. In fact close on a hundred people were here, from varying strata of society.

To accommodate them rows of chairs had been arranged in wide arcs radiating from a low dais at the front end of the classroom. A central aisle some two yards wide allowed access to the chairs, most of which were taken. People were still arriving and it seemed the attendance was exceeding the organizers' expectations. A lively conversation was in progress just inside the door between three Sons And Daughters Of Scompiglio and the school caretaker over the provision of additional seating.

The caretaker, a proud and crusty veteran of North Africa and the Normandy campaign, was endeavouring to explain the nature of the problem. He was not happy at being called upon to render service. He liked to pass his evenings locked away in his office re-enacting World War II battles with miniaturized hand-painted models on table-top landscapes he had painstakingly and lovingly assembled over several years. This week he had set aside for Arnhem. His US Eighty-Second Airborne was currently bogged down on the outskirts of Nijmegen, German reinforcements were pouring into the town and the British Second Army was still held up at Grave. The situation was critical and the old caretaker was resentful of the interruption.

The problem was twofold, he pointed out, stressing the latter two syllables by pressing two gnarled fingers against his left palm. Firstly, the school was taken up reguller five evenings a week with Adult Education classes. Being reguller these got priority. And as Mr Scuppidlio had only phoned a month ago to book, and as his class was a one-off, he had only been allicated those chairs which weren't allicated to other classes. And as far as he had been informed anyway, Mr Scuppidlio had not requested many chairs in the first place. What he'd asked for he'd got.

And secondly, the school itself, being only an infants' school, didn't have that many full-sized chairs in the first place. Most had to be brought over for the evening classes from the junior school up the way, and what with rate-capping and the like, the local authority couldn't lay out for any more.

Adam, overhearing the conversation, took a glance around the room. Sure enough, interspersed amongst those persons who had managed to find adult-sized seating were crouched others of varying shapes and sizes upon items of furniture plainly designed to accommodate bodies of more modest proportions.

So what are we to do? The Sons And Daughters enquired of the caretaker, who responded with a shrug, then a shrewd narrowing of the eyes. 'Well, there're chairs ... in some of the classrooms. Littl'uns, mind. You'll have to make do with what you can find. But don't go disturbing the other classes.'

He heaved a sigh, then, as if suddenly entering into the spirit of the occasion, straightened his shoulders and adopted an authoritative air. He crooked a finger. 'Come with me,' he said, and departed the room. Immediately two young followers in grey trousers and navy blue cardigans were dispatched in his wake.

One of the original three now disengaged himself from his companions. Wearing a welcoming smile he approached Judith and Adam.

'Hello, I'm Sebastian,' he announced in tones of disarming candour, as if this were information guaranteed to elicit approval and respect. He too was dressed in unassuming grey and blue which Adam surmised to be a kind of uniform, along with the anorak for out-of-doors. Adam glanced quickly about for the girl he had met outside the newsagent's, but she was not in evidence.

'Everything's all set,' Sebastian told them. He waggled his head with a chumpishly apologetic expression. 'A little prob parking bottoms,' he grinned.

'I'm so pleased you could come,' he said, as if they were a couple he had personally invited. 'It's going to be a most enlightening evening. I can sense it, can't you? There's something here tonight. Do you mind if I ask, are you members?'

They looked at him blankly.

'Ah, obviously not. This is your first time, then? Oh, that's fantastic. Let me give you one of these, and then perhaps you ought to find yourselves a seat whilst there are still some left. Oh look, over there seems to be the only space still available for two.'

He had handed them each an information sheet containing some notes on The Sons And Daughters Of Scompiglio and their enigmatic founder, and was gesturing towards a row of chairs. Midway along two adult-sized chairs were unoccupied.

'Scompiglio be upon you,' he said, and wafted away to greet a woman just entering.

Judith and Adam squeezed along the row. By the time they reached the chairs, however, one had been taken. Adam gave Judith the other one and eased himself onto one of three vacant infants' chairs alongside.

A minute or so later an old lady in a woolly overcoat and scarf made her way along the row towards them. Judith made to stand and offered her the large chair, but she declined in that endearingly adamant way old people often have.

'I wouldn't dream of it!' She eased past them, clutching tightly to a walking-stick and shopping-bag. 'I'm used to these baby ones. They're no bother to me.'

Indeed she was child-sized, though not as tiny as the occupant the chair was designed to seat. Bearing her weight on the stick she lowered herself, a little unsteadily, onto the seat beside Adam. She arranged herself, stick and bag clasped firmly in front of her knees, then took stock of her surroundings and leaned towards Adam.

'You don't trouble yourself so much about things like that when you get to my age,' she told him with a confidential shout. 'You have different priorities. You wait, you'll see soon enough. Have you been here before?'

'No,' Adam admitted. 'Have you?'

'Not to this one, no. But I come here most evenings. Just to get out of the cold. I can't afford to run the heating at home. I'm a pensioner, you know. But I'm not one to sit there and moan about my problems, I'd rather be up and doing something about it. Resourceful, that's what my George used to call me. "You're very resourceful, Joyce." He was always saying it. Course, he's not with us now. Died almost ten years ago, with his heart. But he was a lovely fella. You'd've liked him. Everyone did.

'But I like it here. It's nice and cosy, isn't it, and you get a bit of company. Both my boys went to school here. Long time ago now, though. Mrs Bentley was headmistress then, but she was crippled in a car accident. Then they had Mrs Kavanagh. I didn't get on with her as well. She was good at her job but I didn't like her as much as Mrs Bentley. Their classroom used to be just next door to this one . . .'

Maintaining a flow of nods and smiles Adam gave his attention to the details of the room. There was only one entrance, at the side of which was a camp table containing books, cassettes and other items pertaining to Scompiglio and his Church, all of which were for sale.

Mounted upon the dais at the front were two microphones on stands. Behind these stood a seat where presumably Iddio E.

Scompiglio was to take his place. A small table had been positioned alongside, and on this was a glass tumbler and a carafe containing juice. Slightly further back stood two Wharfedale public address speakers, one each side of the dais, facing the auditorium. Another small table held a tape recorder.

Behind Scompiglio's chair three green baize-covered screens had been set up. Displayed on these were posters and notices, and arranged on tables in front of the dais were more of the same articles and books penned by the man. The little green *Book Of Imaginary Hauntings* was there but Adam could not make out its price.

Near the dais several Sons And Daughters, dressed predominantly in blue and grey, conversed amongst themselves. As Adam peered over the heads of the people in front of him, they each took seats and a middle-aged man stepped from their midst up onto the dais.

He wore pastel yellow and beige, a quietly commanding figure with a shock of dark hair not yet turning to grey. He strode to stage-centre and took up position at the microphones, standing. As yet he said nothing. He gazed out over the assembly seated before him, a serene half-smile on his lips, and in his eyes an expression a softness and depth which implied an uncommon knowledge and inner conviction which somehow placed him apart from, if not above, others.

He looked down upon the faces of businessmen and -women, punks, pensioners, secretarial and office staff, a smattering of hippies and salesmen ... all drawn for reasons of their own to hear the message of Iddio E. Scompiglio.

The figure on the dais made no movement. He waited in introspective but alert and receptive repose, giving the impression of absorbing and assimilating an atmosphere or vibration in the room that others were oblivious to. Two minutes passed, and then he raised his arms.

The hands floated upwards, drawn by invisible strings, the arms loosely outstretched. At their fullest height, they rested. The palms faced outward over the congregation, slightly forward of his head and a little over shoulder-width apart.

Silently his calm, smiling eyes began to move from person to person. And one by one everybody in that room was becoming aware of his presence. The sound of their many voices was dwindling, until it finally died away altogether. The room grew silent and expectant, all eyes fixed upon the figure before them.

For two minutes more he stood there, his waist rotating very slowly so that his gaze and open palms passed over every person, perhaps imparting a silent benediction to each one, whilst simultaneously, Adam could not help but think, somehow assessing aspects of their individual characters.

There could be no doubt that something was happening in that room. The atmosphere had changed, had grown calming, receptive. The air at the same time seemed charged with energy and expectancy, as though something wonderful was about to take place. Even the old caretaker, who had just re-entered bearing two more small chairs, was reduced to respectful silence at the back of the room. He stood and gazed with a partly open mouth at the man on the dais, his conflicts for the time being vanquished from his thoughts.

The man let his arms sink slowly back to his side. He sat down facing his audience. He poured fruit juice into the tumbler and took a sip, then replaced the tumbler on the table at his side. Then he turned to a woman who had seated herself at the tape recorder to his right, and nodded. The woman depressed the play button and set the tape spools in motion.

Some moments passed and Adam thought he detected the first distant strains of human voices chanting in unison. He attuned his ears more closely. Yes, barely audible at first, the sound was growing by degrees, swelling, fading, swelling again rhythmically – several persons, male and female, intoning mantric syllables over and over.

The words they used were not English, and if they were of any language at all their sense was lost on Adam. But the effect of the chanting was to further enhance the classroom's agreeable ambience. As Adam listened he was drawn in by their mesmerizing rising and falling. His mind began to clear, empty, and involuntary tensions he had been sustaining in both body and thought seemed to slip away. He found himself waiting, open and accepting, for something marvellous.

The audience, mostly absorbed as he was in the sounds issuing from the speakers, sat quietly and unmoving. Some were smiling to themselves, others had their eyes closed; one or two looked bemused and even a trifle embarrassed. One woman's eyes, Adam saw, had filled with tears which spilled freely down her cheeks. And the chanting continued, building and surrendering, ascending and discharging, single syllables, mantric phrases, evoking memories and pleasant thoughts in the minds of its listeners and inducing an emotional state that for the vast majority was all too rare.

Presently, after twenty minutes or so, the sounds began to fade. Their passing was barely detectable at first, but slowly the volume ebbed and did not return. As the voices grew more distant all ears strained to catch their last sweet tones, until they were gone, swallowed in a vast silence that held the room in total and perfect suspension.

There was a click as the tape recorder was switched off. Once again all eyes became fixed on the man seated on the dais. His gaze flickered from face to face as he allowed a few more seconds of silence. Then he spoke.

'Good evening. For those of you who've not met me before my name is John Stevens. On behalf of myself and The Sons And Daughters Of Scompiglio I extend a cordial welcome to you all. I must say I'm pleased to see such a good turnout on this decidedly chilly eve.'

For some reason Adam was surprised and even disappointed to note that John Stevens spoke with a gently lilting but quite sonorous Canadian accent. But it was with relief that he heard him announce his name.

From the moment he had set eyes on him he had been wondering whether this could be Iddio E. Scompiglio. And he'd been praying, without quite knowing why, that it was not. John Stevens somehow did not fit the mould that Adam had semi-consciously fashioned for Iddio E. Scompiglio, though what kind of person would have he was unable to say. It was as if the mystery of Scompiglio, having been presented to him, would have been shattered unbearably by his appearance in human form. Contrastingly, at the same time he had powerful personal reasons for wishing to come face to face with the man.

'Before the commencement of this evening's lecture I would like, for the benefit of those who may never have attended any of our meetings, to just briefly fill you in on who and what we, The Sons And Daughters Of Scompiglio, are, what our aims and aspirations embody, and the kinds of activities we are involved in,' John Stevens went on.

Adam settled back in the tiny chair, becoming aware for the first time of the discomfort it was causing him, its hard, moulded plastic edges biting into his buttocks. And he became aware also, as John Stevens began his account of the worldwide organization that was The Sons And Daughters Of Scompiglio, of deep and even breathing sounding distinctly in his left ear.

He turned. The little old lady beside him, her aged limbs responding to the school's central heating system, had fallen asleep during the recorded chanting. Her head with its wispy grey hair still tucked beneath her scarf, had fallen forward. The chin rested on her shrunken chest.

As she slumbered she muttered from time to time beneath her breath, and gave little spasmodic jerks of her shoulders or arms. In sleep her small hands gripped more tenaciously than ever the handles of her bag and walking-stick.

John Stevens explained how The Sons And Daughters Of Scompiglio, with administrative headquarters in both Italy and California, had grown to become a body of dedicated people intent upon carrying out the wishes and instructions of their leader and founder, Iddio E. Scompiglio. Their aims, he said, were to bring about a more stable, peaceful and harmonious world by utilizing the practical philosophy propounded by Scompiglio.

He spoke of the manner in which he himself had first come to hear of them, and of subsequent developments which eventually persuaded him that his life's mission was to become active and productive in their cause. He described how The Sons And Daughters Of Scompiglio were organized, how they conducted their day-to-day affairs, and how each of them waited patiently for the promised Day of Declaration. On that day Iddio was to return to the world and announce the Time in which the creation of the new world would occur.

'That Time is upon us now,' John Stevens informed them, permitting a forceful note to slip into his voice. 'Scompiglio is preparing this minute to declare himself to the world. Even as I speak Scompiglio works, preparing the route that will bring us change!'

A voice at Adam's side said, 'Stewing steak.' Adam turned abruptly. The old lady still slept. 'No, half a pound, silly!' she scolded, then rolled her dentures around her mouth and lapsed back into silent dreams.

John Stevens began to speak about Scompiglio himself. He was a man, he explained, a mortal like the rest of us, who had cast off the shackles that chain us to our passions and miseries. He was a man who had discovered the True Knowledge. He had schooled himself and grown to become a leader and spiritual educator of immeasurable magnitude. And then some years ago, having called his followers together before him, he had suddenly and quite unexpectedly left them, never to be seen again.

At the time it was a great shock to all involved, John Stevens said. In our limited understanding we could not at first understand how he could abandon us when all seemed to be progressing so well. But we were not abandoned. Scompiglio had left clear instructions as to how we might establish his Church across the planet. He had allotted each of us tasks to this end, and had given us assurance that once his aims were achieved he would return. He had conceived it in such a way that upon his return he would find himself head of a large and potentially influential organization, capable of effecting the changes he would instigate in order to bring the world into the New Enlightened Age.

Adam's neighbour spoke again.

'Ooh no,' she said. 'Not on your nellie.'

There were smiles on faces nearby but John Stevens carried on unperturbed. There was a changing timbre to his voice as he allowed his enthusiasm to mount. His face and limbs were taking on a degree of animation as, with consummate oratorical skill, he titillated the conscientious ardour of his audience, raised their hopes and expectations, and began to bring them with him into his own dream, towards a point where it might be said they were no longer under their own conscious control. Without ever revealing quite what it was, John Stevens was promising them something. Something they had always wanted but could not identify and had never possessed, that should have been theirs by divine right, something all of them sought unendingly and desperately.

And when he seemed satisfied that they were fine-tuned to the best of his considerable abilities, John Stevens brought his speech to a close.

'The lecture,' he announced in tones heavy with import. 'That is what you have all come here for and I shall not keep you a moment longer. Ladies and gentlemen, listen now with me, if you will, to the words of Iddio E. Scompiglio. "A Time For Change."'

The woman at the tape recorder, who had loaded a new tape, pressed play.

'It's a bloody recording!' Adam breathed loudly. He slumped against the back of his chair. 'Jesus, after all that!'

But he could not be wholly certain that the indignation he felt was not tempered with a degree of solace. For there was no doubt that his guts had been stirring as this moment approached. Why exactly should he experience such feelings? He looked up at Judith seated on the big chair next to him. She was staring intently ahead and paid him no heed.

As the tape leader wound onto its receiving spool John Stevens addressed his audience once more. 'The voice you are about to hear,' he purred into the microphone, 'is that of Father Ken, our Chief Proclaimer across the American Jurisdiction. He it is who holds the reins in Iddio's absence. He is based in Southern California, and the words you will hear him recite are taken verbatim from a manuscript penned by Iddio E. Scompiglio.'

Now Adam felt strongly that he should complain, or in some way give expression to his discontent. 'Just as well we didn't have to pay,' he hissed aside to Judith. But he folded his arms across his chest and kept silence. Deprived of the opportunity to see or even hear the man whose reputation and personality had drawn him here, he was curious enough, for now, to at least listen to the words of Scompiglio.

Earlier misgivings were once more rising to trouble him, but with an effort he suppressed them. He could accede to them later if they persisted but just now he was eager to stay with the proceedings.

From the tape, through the twin Whartedales, the voice of

Father Ken was projected in clear, rich American tones. He read slowly, enunciating his words precisely, with conviction and with a rhythmic concentration which, like both the chanting and the voice of John Stevens which had preceded him, bordered on the hypnotic.

He spoke of the trouble the world was in, the terrible plunderings man was wreaking upon his planet, the chaos that was the consciousness of mankind. In such a vein he carried on for some minutes, all of it cogent and thought-provoking stuff, but essentially nothing that was particularly original. After a while Father Ken's disembodied voice began to shift the subject towards possible ways in which these unwelcome conditions might be alleviated, but by now Adam was losing interest.

And he was not alone.

It was about twenty-five minutes into the discourse that he felt a weight descend onto his left shoulder. When he turned his head to investigate he found a little grey female head resting there. The old woman had tipped sideways in her sleep, and Adam had become her pillow and support.

He tried gently to rouse her. He tapped her arm then shook her shoulder, carefully so as not to alarm her. But she merely muttered something about a naughty puppy called Pog, and smiled and slid her teeth noisily around her mouth. Her eyes remained shut and Adam did not have the heart to try any harder. Her weight was by no means unbearable so he allowed her to rest there, turning with a shrug of his free shoulder to Judith who was observing his plight with quiet amusement.

Father Ken's voice pursued its course, and again like John Stevens's before him it was growing more forceful. He was weighing the words he read, loading them with urgency, with meaning never fully delineated but calculated to arouse the passions of his listeners. His monologue continued for a full hour and with its close there was an electricity in the room that all but hummed.

The audience was inspirited. Eyes shone, postures were alert and responsive. They wanted to be up and doing something to remedy the injustices of the world. All, that is, bar a handful, for whom the warmth and comfort of the schoolroom had provided all the inspiration they required. These, plus Adam and the old lady who snoozed on his shoulder.

Now John Stevens asked from his chair on the dais, 'Does anybody have any questions?'

Somebody near the front, an intelligent-looking fellow in a suit and spectacles, rose from his chair and asked an obscure question concerning a 'spiritual hierarchy' which purportedly watched over and guided this planet. He wanted to know Iddio E. Scompiglio's station in it.

John Stevens gave his reply in similarly obscure terms. He referred to the new Spiritual Age and the masters who throughout recorded time, and certainly long before, too, had been nurturing mankind in its progress along the evolutionary path. He told of remote areas where these masters reside – the Himalayas and the Gobi Desert were two locations he mentioned – and hinted at levels of being which far transcend the ability of mortals to (as yet) attain or even to comprehend. The masters dwell in these states of being as a matter of course, he said, and explained that Iddio E. Scompiglio was one of their number and that he had re-adopted human form in order to lead us.

But then John Stevens seemed to grow evasive. This really was a vast and complex topic, entering into levels of esotericism that few were acquainted with, he said. He suspected from the wording of the question that the enquirer already possessed some knowledge of the subject, to which the man in the suit and spectacles nodded a touch complacently.

It would be inappropriate, John Stevens said, to embark upon the detailed discussion the question demanded when so many here were receiving perhaps their first introduction to Iddio E. Scompiglio and the subject of spiritual evolution. He invited the questioner to attend further more advanced study groups if he wished.

A girl then stood up with a question about the reputation The Sons And Daughters Of Scompiglio had acquired. She claimed to have read of certain allegations that the Church sometimes resorted to 'nefarious methods' of recruitment or conversion into its ranks. There were reports that members had been coerced into handing over large amounts of money and possessions. She made particular reference to one dark incident in which certain

167

members of Scompiglio's Church were reported to have committed ritual suicide by throwing themselves from the balcony of a high-rise apartment block in central London.

John Stevens, his eyes narrowing, fielded her question quickly and skilfully.

'There have been allegations,' he agreed, 'but none have ever been proven, or even brought so far as a court of law. The Church Of The Sons And Daughters Of Scompiglio is an open organization. Anyone who so wishes may freely question its members,' he spread his hands. 'Witness this meeting . . .'

He pointed out that journalists had been invited to meet them on several occasions, and those who had accepted had not subsequently had any harsh words to say. In many cases quite the opposite, he said. 'It is always easy to criticize from without – and let us not be misled into believing that the newspapers exist to print news. In the main it is the reporter's job to create sensation and controversy, to dig dirt and, where there is little or none to be found, to create it. The press exists to manipulate the minds of its readers. It appeals to their basest appetites in order to sell its product. By its very nature it also becomes open to manipulation by those who would seek to benefit in some manner by the content of its reportage, and who also have the power and knowhow to influence it. There are exceptions, it goes without saying, but largely the press, the media as a whole, should never be consulted by any person searching for truth.

'As for the last item you referred to,' he said with a stern look, 'it is an undeniable and unfortunate fact that religious bodies, and particularly those which either deliberately or not have acquired a cultist or quasi-occultist reputation, tend to have an appeal for a certain type of character. Someone who might be inadequate or even mentally unstable to some degree, the misfit who finds no comfortable slot in society. Fortunately these persons are in the minority. It is equally true that very often the church or group is able to provide something that is lacking in their lives, to alleviate the pain and isolation they suffer. Sometimes this is not the case, not necessarily because of the insufficiencies of the organization but rather because of the emotional state of the person involved. In the case you are alluding to that may have been the case, but let me make it plain that no direct connection with the Church Of The Sons And Daughters Of Scompiglio was ever established in that instance. And might I also politely suggest, young lady, that in future you pay more attention to discovering the truth of a matter for yourself rather than heeding the scurrilous reports and rumours of others. You will find the benefits are enormous.'

John Stevens was finished with the girl, who sat down, blushing furiously. He had acquitted himself satisfactorily but there was no doubt that the question had displeased him.

Now Adam spoke.

'Where is Iddio E. Scompiglio?' he demanded, more loudly than he had intended. 'I was under the impression the lecture was to be given by him in person.'

John Stevens's unruffled visage scanned the audience as he sought his questioner. 'I'm sorry,' he said, 'I can't seem to locate you. Would you mind standing? I like to see who I am addressing.'

For Adam standing was not so easy, burdened as he was with a sleeping pensioner. But it was true that perched on such a small chair he did not make an easy target. He could himself see John Stevens clearly only by sitting up and craning his neck.

So he very tenderly slipped one hand under the old lady's head and the other under her shoulder and lifted her from him. He rose, supporting her torso as he did so as her weight began to incline towards the space he had occupied.

Once on his feet he was obliged to bend awkwardly at the knees and waist, twisting himself in order to maintain support and also speak to John Stevens.

'I want to know,' he repeated, 'why Iddio E. Scompiglio is not here today. You talk about misleading the public – well, I feel I've been misled by your publicity handout.'

He was reacting emotionally, but the difficult position he occupied was not helping him express the scope of his feelings on the matter. He felt slightly ridiculous, but at the same time he could hardly leave the little woman to tumble to the floor.

John Stevens smiled enigmatically. 'Friend, Scompiglio is here. Believe me, Scompiglio is with us, each of us, right here and now.'

169

'That is not what I mean and you know it!' Adam rejoined tartly. 'Why doesn't he show himself? Why doesn't he speak to us in person?'

'My friend, your question has a facetious ring. I have already explained to you, Iddio E. Scompiglio is preparing to show himself as soon as all conditions are met. He – '

'It is not facetious! I want to meet him. I want to know who he is. That's what I came here for.'

'The Day of Declaration is at hand, friend. Scompiglio will come in person to all of us, providing *we* are ready for him.'

'I'm ready!' Adam's shoulders and arms were beginning to ache. Slight though she was, the old lady was becoming difficult to support at such an angle. 'I came here wanting and expecting to see him. And now, like many others, I'm beginning to wonder whether he exists at all.'

John Stevens laughed a coldly dismissive laugh. 'You do not appear to have understood much of what I've been saying. Time, I'm afraid, does not permit me to go back over every point. Perhaps you should attend another meeting. Or join one of our study groups to clarify your mind.' He shifted his gaze. 'Next question?'

With a calculated lack of expression that somehow conveyed more than words ever could John Stevens reduced the late Adam Shatt to nothingness. Not only for himself but for the greater part of his audience too. They seemed to be hanging on his every word, and as his concentration was re-directed to the person he was now inviting to speak, their minds followed.

A man somewhere to the rear of the room began to speak, but Adam was not prepared to be silenced.

'Just a minute!' he cried. 'I haven't finished!'

The old lady's weight was making his arms tremble. He wanted her to wake and relieve him so that he might concentrate more fully on what he had to say. John Stevens seemed content to ignore his protest. Adam twisted uncomfortably around to address the man speaking.

'I'm sorry but I'm not happy with my answer,' he said. 'If you wouldn't mind hanging on a minute I'd like to clear this up with Mr Stevens. You'll have your turn, don't – '

He stopped short as his eyes fell on the figure seated at the end of a row, four ranks back, across the aisle.

'*You!*' he cried in a choked voice. 'What are you doing here?'

The man in the pale suit – only this time it was almost white – regarded him nonchalantly. He sat casually, one knee crooked over the other and a notepad resting on his thigh. In his right hand a pen rested, its tip poised above the paper.

'I want to talk to you!' Adam yelled, and was alarmed by the near hysteria in his voice. He began a scramble along the row to reach the man before he could escape again.

In his consternation he had let go of the old lady. He remembered just in time, his conscience came uppermost and he dived back.

She had toppled sideways but Judith had caught her head before it collided with the seat. Now though, the weight of her lower limbs was causing her to roll forwards. She was about to tumble from the chair onto the wooden floorboards. Adam bent quickly and grabbed her hips; and she woke up.

Her first sight was of a stranger looming over her, his hands grasping her middle. She screamed. Her tiny body jerked violently, and in the same reflexive action her hands, which had never relinquished their grip on her walking-stick, flew up in a defensive gesture. The curved handle of the stick caught Adam a smart blow beneath the nose, which immediately began to gout blood. He straightened with a groan, his hand going to the offended area.

Now she started to thrash and struggle wildly, crying out with all the gusto she could muster from her shrunken lungs, 'Pervert! Animal! Help! Help! Somebody! Police! Help me! Murder! Murder!'

Her stick struck Adam several times about the legs and body as with tremendous spirit she tried to fight him off. Struggling to right herself, for she had slipped now into a semi-sitting position on the floor, she became aware of Judith's hands on her head and neck. Assuming a second assailant she re-directed her blows blindly over her head, and Judith was forced to cower back out of range.

And Adam, his eyes streaming from the blow to his nose, glimpsed the man in the white suit. He was rising from his seat,

171

unhurriedly slipping his notepad and pen into his jacket pocket as he did so.

'No! I want to talk to you!'

Abandoning the old lady, whose thin voice was growing thinner and whose blows were losing their initial vigour, he leapt again along the row of startled onlookers. Most moved to give him passage, but when he reached the end it was to discover that the aisle which had earlier been clear was now congested with people seated on miniature chairs brought in by the caretaker and his aides to cope with the unexpected influx.

The man in the white suit was already halfway to the door. He threaded his way carefully and without haste through the river of bodies.

'Stop! Stop!' Adam hurled himself bodily forward, aware that somewhere off to one side the little old lady was calling between exclamations of shock and distress for somebody to apprehend *him*.

He strove to make headway, the people in front trying to draw back and let him through. But one foot became entangled in the straps of somebody's shoulder-bag, and as he attempted to free it he tripped on a stray leg, overbalanced, and went sprawling amongst the scattering bodies.

He fell into a writhing undergrowth of human limbs and chair legs, clothing and other accessories, blood pouring over his mouth and chin. And as he landed he caught a last glimpse of a white-clad figure stepping through the door at the back of the room, closing it behind him as he departed.

The Big World Continued . . .

Adam wasted no time. After a sleepless night passed struggling to thrash something cohesive out of the random bombardment of events that befell him, he went the following morning to the Kensington address Dennis had given him, that of the woman at the party, Ruth.

But she was no longer in residence. She had taken herself away. The big world was showing no mercy.

On a tortuous route homewards he found himself passing through St James's and Whitehall, and had the notion of calling in on Judith at work. They had seen so little of each other lately, day or night. She was exceptionally busy, putting in unsocial hours at work, and at home she seemed tired and preoccupied. Adam had been pleased and grateful when she had agreed to accompany him to the Scompiglio lecture, but it had not afforded the opportunity he had hoped for communication between them. He sensed, or believed he sensed, a distancing, a failure to meet on common ground. His own condition could be held largely to blame, of course, but merely apportioning blame did not touch the root of the matter. He needed Judith, was reliant upon her for so much. What he was beginning to conceive of as their growing estrangement was cause for much additional concern.

Could he be alienating her with the sheer weight of his demands? Was she finding it finally too much to cope with? Or alternatively, was he victim to his imagination? Maybe she was around more than he realized. Maybe he was the only one sensing discord? His own preoccupations had a habit of distorting his experience of their world.

He didn't know. Everything was jumbled.

He halted yards from the portals of the monolithic grey-brown fortress in which his wife spent her working hours. He had been here before and weighed it a soulless place. With its plumbless, neglected interiors, mazed with corridors and countless office-cubicles, staffed with remote and disdainful minions, he found it discouraging and oppressive. He had been glad on those earlier occasions to escape, and this time was reserved about entering.

Perhaps, anyway, Judith might not welcome his unannounced arrival. She could be busy, or might be elsewhere, in some other department or even in another building entirely.

The wind keened around the dead stone walls and sliced sharply along the meter-lined street where he stood, making him shiver. At a first-storey window a solitary, sober-suited man, hurrying along a corridor with an armful of files, had happened to glance down. He paused in his step, as faceless behind the reflecting glass as the building in which he stood, and briefly regarded Adam, then hastened on. Adam turned and walked away, under an impulsive desire to be gone from this place.

It was about five minutes later that someone stepped from a

sloping side-passage and approached him. A plump, trim, incon-spicuous young fellow with a rounded face and a fitful smile. 'Mr Shatt!'

He slipped from the mouth of the passageway just ahead, making Adam halt. Adam did not recognize him, he didn't know him from Adam, but the man was obviously acquainted with *him*, and that stirred his curiosity.

'I wonder if I might have a word?'

The man was wheezing and flushed, as though from recent unaccustomed exertion. There was a moment's uneasy silence between them, then he said, 'Ah, forgive me. You've obviously not recognized me.' With a quick jabbing motion he was proffer-ing a hand. Adam remarked mentally that beneath the grey raincoat he wore the man's physical form was not dissimilar to that of the person he had seen minutes ago at the window. 'Partridge. Simon Partridge. I work with your wife.'

Now his other hand was at Adam's elbow, maladroitly essaying to draw him towards the entrance of the passageway.

Adam resisted.

'I do apologize,' Simon Partridge hissed. He relinquished his hold with an open-handed gesture of appeasal. His eyes darted wildly about the street. He could not relax. He was as uncertain of himself as a laboratory pup. 'But this is a matter of some urgency. Please, let me buy you a drink.'

'Look, what's this about?' Adam demanded.

'*Please!*' Partridge was all but shimmying on the spot. 'I have to talk. I'll explain inside.'

With misgivings Adam permitted himself to be shepherded into the mouth of the passageway. They walked down a few paces and entered a door over which hung a sign carrying the name of a bar, and he followed Simon Partridge down a flight of carpeted stone steps into a cellar. It was smartly furnished, reasonably spacious, and popular, offering hot and cold food as well as liquid sustenance.

Partridge went immediately to a juke-box in one corner and slotted in several coins, punching selections at random. Rejoining Adam he indicated a vacant alcove, a shallow, low-arched affair, once storage for wine or coal, now fitted with leather-upholstered benches and a varnished table. As Adam seated himself Partridge crossed to the bar.

He returned with Adam's requested tonic and a large whisky for himself. 'Apologies again for my less than civilized conduct,' he breathed, wincing with displeasure as heavy metal chords, one of his own selections, crashed from wall-mounted speakers wreathed with silk-polyester foliage. 'Not usual behaviour, but I was most anxious to speak to you. When I saw you there I simply couldn't pass up the opportunity.'

He looked more closely at Adam. 'Have you hurt your nose?'

Adam said, 'It's nothing.'

Somebody, presumably one of the bar-staff, reduced the volume on the juke-box amplifier. Partridge winced again, this time out of apprehension.

He appeared mildly more composed indoors, though anxious. But throughout the ensuing conversation he kept an almost ceaseless vigil over the other customers in the bar and, particularly, the stairway, the only public entrance, by which he and Adam had entered.

'You have obviously recovered something of your former vigour,' he remarked in a limp attempt at light-heartedness. 'I barely managed to catch you.'

Adam was impatient. 'What is this about? I'd appreciate an explanation.'

Partridge repentantly fluttered a hand. 'Forthcoming.' He gulped a mouthful of whisky. 'Gah! Yes, I'll be direct. I have some information. Information I don't think you would wish to be without, though doubtless you won't thank me for it. I intend to divulge it in a moment, but firstly there are certain things I would like to know myself. So bear with me for a short time if you will. It will help us both if I can ascertain just exactly what you have discovered.'

'Discovered about what?' Adam demanded.

'About yourself, Mr Shatt. Yourself. Now, I have little time. I am, as I said, a colleague of your wife, Judith. I was under the mistaken belief when I approached you that you would remember me — we have, well, "shared the same space", if briefly, on more than one occasion. But no matter. Judith and I work in the same section, though I know I'm not far off target in saying that she would prefer it if that were not the case.' He gave a short reflective pause. 'Mr Shatt, do you know what Judith does?'

Adam shrugged. 'She's in Research and Co-ordination. Some kind of Government Communications liaison body between Home and Foreign Office. I'm not genned up on precise details.'

'No. Of course,' Partridge nodded, pursing his lips. 'Do those terms mean anything to you?'

'No more than they should,' Adam said, guarding his response. 'Why?'

Partridge's small mobile eyes came to rest for some seconds on his face. 'The Research Division of the Government Communications Bureau is indeed a sub-division of the FO. And the section myself and your wife both operate in does liaise and co-ordinate resources between FO and HO. At least on paper. Interministerial and -departmental distrust and traditional rivalries are in fact so high as to render any attempt at genuine, helpful communication between the two bodies dead on its feet. Always has been and I suspect always will.

'But there's more to it. Those titles, and others equally pedestrian, are in fact designations of specific elements of the disparate intelligence communities, which are more numerous than you might suspect. Ours is a small co-ordinating section set up to utilize the resources and facilities of those "departments" which, in certain instances, cannot officially exist – this despite the humble taxpayer's obligatory perennial contribution towards their upkeep. Has your wife mentioned anything of this?'

'She doesn't discuss her work,' Adam replied with gathering suspicion. The muted thump of a disco-beat now penetrated the alcove where they sat. Partridge took a pack of Dunhill from his coat pocket, offered them then took one himself and touched the flame of a gold pocket lighter to its tip.

'That doesn't in any way arouse your suspicions?'

'Why should it?'

Partridge elevated his rounded chin and blew a cloud of uninhaled smoke into the air over Ádam's head. 'The fact of your wife's being a government employee has never concerned you?'

The tone and possible implications of the question took Adam by surprise, but he had determined to let nothing slip until he had better gauged Partridge's motives. He affected indifference –

'Again, why should it?' – and wondered whether the little man had the skill or the presence of mind to catch his hesitation.

Partridge was scanning the bar, bright gaze flickering over faces and forms. His fleshy cheeks no longer bloomed with their earlier flush, but had begun to acquire an unnatural sheen. What the hell was he in such a stew over?

He shot out another question. 'Does the name "Gospel" hold any significance for you, Mr Shatt?'

He was scrutinizing him closely. Adam signified in the negative.

'But you are acquainted with the psychiatrist, Doctor Theodore Geld?'

His senses already prepared, Adam was this time quick to field the unexpected. But Geld's name coming from such a source gave him no comfort. He nodded. 'I know him.'

'Yes,' Partridge said. 'Apologies, Mr Shatt, mysteriousness does not become me, I am well aware. But you must understand, I have certain knowledge of you, your background and recent life experiences. And I know that there is something going on around you, though precisely what it is or who is involved I have not yet discovered. I come to you with a paltry amount of evidence, a mountain of suspicion and many unanswered questions – in many ways not unlike yourself. By questioning you now I hope to learn more. Quite extraordinary measures are being taken to try to ensure that this business, whatever it entails, remains a closely guarded secret.'

Adam was rapt attention. The words 'something going on around you' had a darkly familiar ring, hurling him momentarily back to that cluttered attic, the unfortunate Dennis making exclamations of fear and alarm.

He thrust forward over the table. 'What do you know? Do you have something on Geld? *Tell me!*'

Three individuals in business attire entered via the stairway. Partridge shrank. 'Mr Shatt, *please!*' he exhorted in a hoarse whisper. His eyes followed the three as they moved to the bar, calling loudly for drinks.

'I assure you,' Partridge said, 'I actually know very little. And if I tell you everything now it may adversely influence your responses. So please, bear with me. Answer truthfully and I shall do likewise in a moment. And Mr Shatt, please. You are hurting my wrist!'

177

Realizing for the first time that he had been applying pressure to a very vulnerable nerve Adam released him and sat back. Simon Partridge kneaded his forearm with a pained expression.

'One other thing. I must ask for your absolute assurance that not a word of this conversation will pass beyond the two of us. Not even to your wife. Not yet anyway. This is vital. Will you promise me this?'

Adam assessed him thoughtfully, then shrugged. 'Very well.'

The businessmen, their orders delivered, retired with refreshments to another part of the cellar, out of sight and hearing. Partridge seemed relieved. 'Mr Shatt,' he said, 'do you recall *anything* of your life prior to the incident in Northern Ireland?'

'No. Nothing.'

'And the incident itself?'

Again he shook his head.

Simon Partridge ruminated, grooming a non-existent moustache with two pink fingertips. Adam noticed that the fingertips were raw, the nails chewed down to the quick. 'What of your earlier career? Any recollections there?'

'Nothing reliable. No, nothing.'

'Do you fraternize with former colleagues or associates?'

'Judith and I called in at the office a couple of times. To pick up files and other bits and pieces. Those were the only times. I don't socialize much these days.'

'But you met your erstwhile colleagues?'

'Two or three. We didn't stay. I wasn't in good shape.'

'But you knew them?' Partridge could not disguise his mounting excitement. Cool inquisitor he was not; his emotions had totally the better of him.

Adam hesitated, then replied: 'No. They knew me.'

'Hah!' Partridge was both thwarted and triumphant at once. His eyes darted to and fro, unfocussed, glistening. Febrile cerebral currents fluxed behind that schoolboyish brow. Adam, a deep and yawning fear beginning to open in the pit of his stomach, watched him uncomfortably, feeling himself considerably disadvantaged.

Evidently coming to an agreement with himself on some point Partridge put his next question: 'Does it ever strike you as odd,

Mr Shatt, that you have no memory of those events in Northern Ireland, nor of your life preceding them?'

'Yes. No. Things strike me as odd, period.'

'Of course. But I can't help thinking, putting myself in your shoes to some degree, that you must at times entertain doubts. It would be perfectly understandable.'

Adam refused to be drawn.

'You rely totally upon others for information about your past, is that not so? Surely you are bound to question from time to time the authenticity of that information? Having no concrete support of your own you must wonder whether that past life was the one you really experienced? Any sane person would.'

A creeping chill had set the flesh at the nape of Adam's neck crawling. The muscles there were slowly and involuntarily contracting, and he was aware of a tightness in his chest, a constriction in his breathing. 'Amnesia of the extent I've suffered isn't particularly uncommon,' he said. 'And my past is fully corroborated. I have reams of evidence to substantiate it. What – '

'Quite so. Mr Shatt, I must stress that I have placed myself at some considerable risk in seeking you out today. It isn't safe for me to stay. Now, I want us to meet again so I'm going to tell you something which will ensure your wanting the same. It's quite evident to me that you harbour suspicions about your former life, despite all that would seem to render them groundless. Is that not so?'

Reluctantly Adam nodded.

'And in your endeavours to follow up these suspicions you have come up with virtually nothing? Nothing concrete anyway?'

He hesitated. How far should he take this man into his confidence? Was it safe to tell him anything at all? What did he already know? Who the hell *was* he? Adam would have preferred caution and a play for time but Partridge was making it abundantly clear that time was not on offer. He nodded again. Partridge smiled whimsically.

'Well, that's as intended.'

'Intended? By whom? What do you mean?'

Partridge's fingers were tickling the sides of his glass, plump pink spider legs skating on ice. He seemed to resolve something in his mind, and they ceased.

'Mr Shatt, you never were in Northern Ireland. I can tell you that with one hundred per cent certainty.'

'That's absurd,' Adam murmured. He actually felt little. Partridge's words were what he had wanted most and least to hear, and his mind was rejecting the paradox. He had dropped suddenly into a protective stupefaction.

'Yes. Quite absurd.'

'Everything . . .'

'. . . is fabrication. You are a living lie, Mr Shatt. Your life is a fiction. It has been created for you by individuals with the knowledge and power to mould and direct the experiences of others, and who consider themselves sufficiently above the law to justify doing so. Quite covertly, I might add, though sealed with the approval of the very highest authorities.'

Barely taking it in, Adam muttered, 'But why?'

'Oh, that's obvious, surely? With a little imagination. Control! That lure of countless ages and civilizations. A step towards Utopia, if you happen to be holding the strings. What else could it be? Manipulation, be it of masses or individuals, has always been a primary concern of ambitious men, and women. The distinction in your case lies merely in the means, the technology. And . . .'

'And what?'

'Well, I can't quite believe that you as you now stand represent an optimum end product. And I would like to know what it was they were trying to achieve. This creation lark, building a new identity, a "legend" as we like to term it, is a cover-up. But a cover-up for what? What precisely was their aim?'

A Little Third-Eye Technology

Partridge's eyes danced feverishly.

'Do you know of a man called Gard?' he asked.

Adam didn't.

'He's the moving force behind all this. Or he was. It seems he may have tried to separate himself from it. He's a distant and

180

mysterious fellow. Very powerful when he puts himself to it. He's also my boss, far-removed. Judith's too.'

'Partridge, you're talking in bloody riddles!' Adam suddenly flared. 'What are you saying? What the hell has been done to me?'

Partridge held up two hands, palms outwards. 'I've very little to work with. I had hoped to gain more answers by questioning you, at least fill in one or two gaps. But ... There is a wall of secrecy surrounding you, one which I cannot risk being found trying to penetrate. So I simply don't know all the answers.'

'Well, what do you think you know?'

'I'm trying to tell you.' He cast a furtive glance at his wristwatch. 'Do you know anything of micro-bioelectronics, Mr Shatt?'

Adam frowned.

'It's very hush-hush. A recent field of research, hardly out of the womb. In fact, should you come across any mention of it you will find it played down. A theory, nothing more, resident solely in the minds of science-fiction writers. This is the view that official-dom will do all in its power to encourage, as it always does when attempting to disguise the true facts of an emergent technology.

'Believe me, whenever you encounter statements to that effect you can be just about certain that the truth is somewhat different. If official sources so much as bother to comment on a subject the chances are that some of the finest minds available are currently engaged upon its development. In the case of micro-bioelectronics I know that millions of pounds of taxpayers' money has already – '

'Just tell me what it is, Partridge,' Adam cut in sharply. 'What is it and what's its connection with me?'

'We are talking about the development of a "chip", Mr Shatt. An electronic circuit or memory-device constructed with carbon-based molecules akin to those in our own bodies. Whilst micro-scopic in size it is calculated to be capable of boosting circuit densities one hundred-thousandfold or more. It is much faster than anything currently conceived and requires only the minutest amount of power. A little marvel! Destined to render obsolete even the most sophisticated of today's micro-technology. A phrase I picked up recently was, "Kiss your silicon goodbye and say hello to the real thing."' He chuckled.

'So where do you come into all this?' He drained his whisky tumbler of its contents. He was evidently beginning to enjoy himself. 'For some years now micro-bioelectronics and its applications in the fields of psychiatry and human behaviour has been a favourite area of research for our friend, Doctor Geld. Under conditions of great secrecy he has been conducting a variety of experiments on animal test subjects – to what precise end I can't claim to know. However, it would appear that under his sedulous ministration the science has advanced in leaps and bounds.

'Quite logically, a crucial juncture has been arrived at where nothing more of value is to be gained under such restricted test conditions.'

He paused here to allow his words to sink in, then went on, 'It is my belief that he, and perhaps others like him, who knows? has taken that most significant and unconscionable step into forbidden territory and begun to experiment on at least one human subject.'

Adam's mouth had turned dry, but though he clasped the glass of tonic water, now warm between sweating palms, he could not bring it to his lips. He sat motionless and suspended as Partridge's voice, like some alien voice inside his own head, told him what he had always known.

'The experiment went disastrously wrong, though possibly not irredeemably so. Doctor Geld and his associates now live in the hope that it will not have to be terminated, that something may yet be salvaged – such effort and expense has been necessary to bring it this far, after all. And in the meantime the sorry individual to whom the deed was done has been let loose to roam as he will, half-mad, aware that something is hideously amiss but ignorant of just what it is, or what has happened to him. I need hardly add, I'm sure, Mr Shatt, that that unfortunate soul, the original human test subject, is you.'

The most absurd incongruity came to pass just then. The Beatles' 'Yesterday' began to play on the juke-box, and as the melody filtered through to the alcove where they sat Adam found his attention focussing on the lyric, all else receding for a moment from consciousness.

Several more people had entered the bar. Office staff from somewhere nearby, ordering drinks and lunch. Partridge paid them little heed. He was beginning to fidget and Adam eventually grew aware that his silence was making the plump fellow uncomfortable. Slowly, shaking the song from his thoughts, he said, 'Do you have any idea what was done to me?'

Now Partridge pushed himself forward and scrutinized Adam's features enquiringly, quite insolently. 'That small blemish over the bridge of your nose. Is it a scar, Mr Shatt?'

Adam lifted a hand, then let it drop self-consciously. 'I'm covered. I took a lot of damage when I got hit – '

' – in Northern Ireland. Yes.'

'Go on.'

'Doctor Geld's experiment, I am certain, involved the implanting of a carbon-based molecular "biochip" within the body, probably in or uncomfortably close to the brain.'

'Do you know this?'

'Guesswork. Inspired.'

'I don't believe it.'

'I think you do.'

'You're telling me that I'm walking the streets with some lump of electronic hardware installed inside my skull? That it's influencing, or is supposed to be influencing, everything I do, say, think? The way I experience the world?'

'Not quite. "Hardware" would be something of a misnomer in this instance. The "chip" after all is organic. Effectively it is a tiny – one thousand of these things can be fitted onto the cross-section of a human hair, Mr Shatt – a tiny new "cell" functioning harmoniously with your overall metabolism. Rather, that is, it should be. Harmonious is I suppose hardly the term one would most readily choose to describe your current condition.

'And as for what it is actually doing, I have already indicated that I am reduced largely to conjecture. The experiment went wrong, remember. So not only are you not the man you have been made out to be, you are not the one you were intended to be either.'

'So it isn't actually functioning?'

'I wouldn't say that.'

'It can't be!' Adam thumped the heel of the palm of one hand against the table edge. 'There's no power source!'

Partridge shook his head. 'You are not thinking clearly. It

derives the negligible flow of power it requires for its function from the ceaseless electrical activity going on all around it. That of the brain itself. The diversity of the doctor's talents is quite impressive. It seems they have found their point of focus here. Potentially at least it is functional. But the question remains, what does it or should it do?'

Adam dwelt on this for some time before saying, 'If any of this is true, tell me one thing. What put them on to me? Why did they choose me and not some other poor sod?'

Partridge smiled. 'Ah, that's an easy one,' he pronounced in enlivened tones. 'They didn't. You volunteered.'

'*What?*'

'Yes. Revelation upon revelation, I'm afraid. Shock upon shock. And there's more to come.' The smile took on the character of a thin smirk. There was little doubt in Adam's mind that he was taking pleasure in his role, regardless of the risk he professed to be running. He had assumed a position of power, that of a cat pawing a mouse, a gaoler before a prisoner he had the authority but perhaps not the inclination to set free, a scientist with a test subject and an experimental frame of mind.

'Understand, Mr Shatt, that prior to your unfortunate "accident" and subsequent amnesia you were a radically different personality. Startlingly so, by all accounts. You, like I, inhabited that murky world of secrecy and mistrust, that densely-populated, self-perpetuating and unimaginably complex world in which Doctor Geld and his ilk ply their immoral trades. You, like them, and like me, deceived yourself into believing that what you did was essential, in some way productive, constructive, of value to society. You struggled with us in this tacky, far-reaching web.

'The secret world is a world of manipulation and dissimulation, everybody seeking the right leverage, the right method of execution to gain control over others. Individuals, industrial concerns, media, populations, governments, neighbours, friends, colleagues, they can all be controlled and need not be aware of it. The mechanisms are intricate, insidious and really horribly attractive in their shades and delicacies. There are times when I must confess to admiration little short of awe.

'We who are drawn into it fail unanimously to understand until it is too late the real inner workings of the secret world. We fail to realize that by its very nature it can never allow any escape. We volunteer to be swallowed whole, crawl blindly like grubs in its teeming, lightless belly, and only later grow sick on the diet of tainted meat we feed constantly on. We are slaves to misconceived laws, prejudices, corrupt ideals and rotten judgement, and we can't do a thing about it. We stand in the dark, unable to move and unable to admit it, so thoroughly infected that we dare not even investigate the seeds of our original motivation.

'Which is one reason why you are of such great interest, Mr Shatt.' Partridge dangled his glass between finger and thumb, waggling it to and fro. Adam realized he was a little bit drunk. Either he had a very low tolerance, or he had been drinking before they met. 'You've escaped, you see. You sit here in front of me with no idea of who you are or how you came to be, and yet without knowing it you have found a way out. That makes you a symbol. A paradox standing both for what we have become and what we would aspire to be. And with your next step you can either be completely free of our vile world, or you can be led back into it. I drink to your future.'

Whatever effect Partridge was intending to create was diminished when, bringing the glass to his lips, he discovered it empty bar some slivers of melting ice. He returned it to the table top with a rueful glance.

But Adam had missed the tail-end of his speech anyway. Something in Partridge's words had triggered an unconscious reaction and Adam found himself cast back suddenly into total darkness and paralysing fear.

He was in another world, an earlier world. He could see nothing and felt only the ground beneath his feet, but close by a large dog growled and bayed furiously. He could hear it thrashing in the undergrowth, racing back and forth just feet from where he stood.

Some distance off twin beams of light suddenly pierced the night sky. He made out trees against the skyline, and a winding black snake that was a hedgerow bordering a country lane. It was this that kept the dog from him.

The two beams spread, united, tilted and fell to horizontal. He watched them speeding towards him, partially blocked by a hedge some distance away. The roar of a powerful engine grew in his ears, then the vehicle rounded the corner just yards away.

He heard men's voices calling, off to one side. With one arm he shielded his eyes from the dazzle of the headlamps as the vehicle bore down on him. He leapt aside but was too slow.

He jerked back in his seat with a thud. Partridge, with concern in his voice, enquired, 'Mr Shatt?'

The vision faded. Adam stared at him, ashen-faced and breathless.

'Are you unwell?'

He shook his head. 'I'm all right.'

'You see,' Partridge went on after a further moment's solicitous pause, 'your question as to "why you?" only deepens the mystery. For if, as is the case, they already "had" you, and if as you now stand you are not the perfect result of the experiment that you were intended to be, then what, once again, were they hoping to achieve with you? It stands to reason that as you were a willing subject it cannot have been judged so utterly terrible – though it's true that in those days you were something of a fanatic to the cause. But then, for that very reason, why "alter you"? The whole thing is quite baffling, to say the least.'

'Something else,' Adam observed. 'Why the subterfuge? If I was one of them, why go to such lengths now to keep that fact from me?'

'Ah, now that's another easy one. Operation "Gospel", as some wit saw fit to christen it, is an unlawful and highly risky enterprise. We would seem to be talking about the engineering of human consciousness, after all. The state-backed secretive manipulation of emotions, thoughts, actions ... our very being. It rather has a ring of Big Brother to it, doesn't it. So if some human rights group should get wind, or by some means it becomes public knowledge ... well, I'm sure you can follow my gist. This is the United Kingdom, let's remember, not the Soviet Union or some barbarian state. Our humanitarianism stands as an example to the world. We openly deplore the very idea of any such malpractice.

'So you are allowed to roam more or less freely, yes, for the hope is always that your former personality will win through once more and you will voluntarily return to the fold. But what you know *in potentia* makes you a tremendous liability. Your actions are unpredictable and your loyalties moot until proven. Therefore, a counterfeit past, a bogus identity. Though it might confuse the issue, and even delay your speedy recovery, it at least affords a measure of protection.

'All that publicity, you see. Who now would listen to you should you claim to be someone else? The public already knows you. They've read about you, seen your story on television, and they sympathize. But should you come forward now declaring that all of that was lies and that, moreover, you have uncovered a monstrous government-backed conspiracy involving the implanting of bits of electronic gadgetry inside people's heads! You're mad, Mr Shatt. Mad as the proverbial hatter. You won't even get the time of day.

'And of course, should your behaviour tend to lean that way I have no doubt that before you can truly begin to make a fuss you will be nipped expediently in the bud. You are being monitored, and though termination is undesirable it is a long way from inconceivable.'

'They're monitoring me?'

'It goes without saying! You are their precious but wayward pet, their plaything, their Frankenstein's monster. They can let you roam, but only as long as they know where.' Partridge gave a little jerk as the implications of this last statement suddenly registered home with force. 'I must be going,' he said, rising quickly from his seat.

'But Gospel ... what is it, then?' Adam said, half to himself. 'Experimentation of the kind you describe isn't feasible on a broad scale. It must be down to selected individuals. Why? What's it about?'

'I lack firm foundations, as I've already made plain,' Partridge said. 'But whatever Gospel is it should be borne in mind that it is only a beginning. I can say that with absolute certainty. When we next meet I hope to have more answers.'

'Wait!' Adam reached out and took his arm. Partridge stiffened. 'Partridge, please. Just a couple more questions.'

Partridge hesitated, the beleaguered expression on his features of a man in two minds over a matter of great magnitude. 'Be brief, then.' He sank back into his seat. There was a gleam in his eye now, an ominous eagerness in his poise. He seemed to be anticipating something.

'Who?' Adam said. 'If they're watching me, monitoring me. Other than Geld, how can I know?'

The little eyes widened infinitesimally and a twitching smile danced across his thin lips. 'On a per capita assessment I can't say, though they are necessarily very few. It's highly unlikely that you would in your present condition come into direct contact with many of them. But of course they have enormous resources. Watchers can be employed as required. They would have no knowledge of Gospel. But they would rarely be necessary, if you think about it. On a more, ah, intimate front I think a little deductive reasoning might bear yield, Mr Shatt.'

His expression had become quite malevolent now, gloating. Adam, whose thoughts had already pursued the line he was indicating, found himself fighting down a sudden inner rage.

'You mean,' he said, struggling with the urge to commit violence upon the man, 'that if I was once party to all this . . .'

Partridge lifted a pale eyebrow a fraction. His tongue, snakelike, wetted his lips then vanished. 'Yes . . .' he breathed.

'Judith.'

He nodded.

That Many-Splendoured Thing

Adam took this in silence. He pushed himself slowly back in his seat and rested his head against the cool brick behind him, filled with loathing for the neat, rotund figure opposite, yet aware that his rage, though far from unreasonable, was not wholly rationally directed.

Eventually he said, flatly, 'How do you know all this?'

Partridge hesitated. 'I know of Gospel through having once glimpsed the name on a document. The document bore no imprint to betray its origin, though it was patently "in-house". Your name was also on it, as was that of Doctor Geld. All I picked up in that brief glimpse was that you were being referred to as "the Apostle", that Doctor Geld was known as "Angel Two", and that Gospel, whatever it was, involved both of you.'

'And that's it?'

'Not entirely. You see, the paper was on your wife's desk, flagged to her. So obviously she was involved too. And she, when she realized I was looking over her shoulder, gave every indication of being, well, frightened, as well as extremely anxious that the paper not remain in my sight.' Partridge was beginning to button his coat. His satisfaction was apparent, if not explained, but so too was his returning nervousness, hardly vanquished by the alcohol. 'Intrigue is a magnet to me, Mr Shatt. Witness my chosen profession. I felt impelled to dig further, and everything else has just followed in ones and twos, adding up to what I've just told you.'

Adam, galvanized once more by a reluctance to let him leave, threw another question: 'Do you know anything about a murder?'

He was rewarded with the sight of Partridge's fingers flying wild of the button.

'Who?' Partridge demanded with an abrupt pallor.

'A man I met just once. He lived in Notting Hill.'

'So they've gone that far,' Partridge whispered, and shuddered, his feathers well and truly ruffled. 'I don't know about this, but it comes as no real surprise. I must go. Listen, you will receive a telephone call for a Mrs Merrick. You will inform the caller that he has dialled a wrong number, and replace the receiver. Exactly five minutes later I shall call the public call box near the bottom of your street. If it's engaged, or for some reason you cannot get to it I shall call again five minutes later. If I still fail to make contact, don't worry. I will find a way.'

He pulled a pair of suede gloves from his coat pocket.

'Partridge, a final question,' Adam said. 'What's your role? Why are you helping me?'

Once more Simon Partridge was undisguisedly torn between his fear-filled concern for his own preservation and – what was it? Adam watched him, fascinated. The musculature of Partridge's face worked feverishly as he wrestled with his consternation. Finally it seemed his passion to get whatever it was off his chest gained the upper hand.

'I'm glad you've asked me that.' He took a new cigarette from his pack. With his resolve to stay a new excitement fanned the light in his eyes; he seemed barely able to contain himself. 'In all honesty I can't claim to act out of compassion or altruism or any of the more ennobling instincts. Such feelings are virtual strangers to me. And I really care little about or for you. If the information I have brought is to some degree illuminating I think you must acknowledge that it also exacerbates your suffering. This causes me no pangs of conscience. So, there, you are at least relieved of any need to feel indebted. I am not motivated by any particular desire to save your soul.'

In fingers that were now trembling the blue and orange flame of his gas lighter made a brief marriage with the long cigarette. He consummated it with a deep, shuddering inhalation, and his eyes met Adam's. 'No, the truth is, I'm in love with your wife.'

He had endeavoured to impart the words in a steady voice but after a courageous opening they disintegrated into a sequence of croaks and yodels. Their impact was nevertheless unreduced, and left Adam speechless. Again the totally unexpected. He could find no appropriate response.

Partridge then made an attempt at a wry smile which became a series of rapid muscular convulsions affecting much of his face. Reddening slightly he dropped his gaze.

Presently he found words to continue: 'You can't know what a wretch I have become. I am in love with a woman who clearly finds my company unbearable. I don't think you can know what that means.'

A curled forefinger rose suddenly to his mouth and he bit hard on the flesh. Adam found himself opposite a small broken boy.

'I'm condemned, Mr Shatt! Condemned to a life of misery. You can't understand ... I worship the ground she walks upon. Eighteen months, more, and I have thought of nothing, *nothing* but Judith. Each minute, each *second*, possessed, driven, *tortured* by the knowledge that however much I may love her she cares nothing for me, nor ever will. And I can't help myself.' He was able to look at Adam once more. 'I've never experienced anything as awful as this before. I've never known what it means to love somebody with such passion that you can live only for them. I had not realized myself capable. I'm a cautious man, a shy man. I am conservative in habit and not given to extremes of emotion or action. For someone like myself to find himself consumed by this terrible power ... It is cruel and devastating. I have no defence.

'Love!' He fairly spewed the word. 'It is driving me to madness.

I was turned on my head, utterly transported. I saw the possibility of real happiness, for the first time. I saw the possibility of life! Love promised me everything a man could possibly want; it placed all those things so temptingly within my grasp, and then it wrenched them away. It raised me to unimagined heights and then threw me down again. Now I am reduced to nothing. I have only a ceaseless griping in my gut and a squalid bitterness pervading my entire being. I am eaten up and poisoned by love, Mr Shatt. I know it and I hate it, but I'm its victim and can do nothing about it.'

He took hold of his empty glass again, remembered, and replaced it forlornly on the table top. He continued in sullen tones, 'You are wondering how my loving your wife applies to this situation. Well, it's simple. I want to ruin her. That's what she has done to me. And you are the means I have to achieve it. When you leave here today her world will have become a less comfortable place. She will be just a little more alone. You can never confide in her again. You can never trust her. And if she truly loves you – and despite what she does I believe that in some warped and incomprehensible way she does – then she will suffer, for she has lost you.'

'Partridge, that's insane.'

'Insane, yes.' Partridge was eager to agree. 'And let me tell you what insane is. Insane is the day I first set eyes on your wife and found unleashed within me this ungovernable, irrational force. Insane is the days and nights I spend thinking of her, nothing but her. Insane, the gifts I have left on her desk, the pathetic plotting and scheming I evolved for some excuse to bring her and me into contact, no matter for how brief a time. Insane is the hours I have spent outside your home, in all weathers, praying for just so much as a glimpse of her (and incidentally, that is how I initially came to know of you). Insane, oh yes, insane the way I somehow *ludicrously* succeeded in persuading myself that she was responding, that she, even when I knew it was not possible, felt some reciprocal attraction for me. Insane, insane, that is love. I am telling you, Mr Shatt, you cannot possibly know. It is the very opposite of itself. Yes, I have become something of a philosopher in my most miserable hours. I see the world more clearly now and I understand love's place. It is the most potent energy, Mr

Shatt. Look around you and you will witness its symptoms everywhere. You will see the carnage it inspires. Out of it all other destructive forces are born!'

Partridge's cheeks had suffused an unreasonable crimson. His chubby fists were tightly balled on the table's surface. His teeth had begun to chatter and he drew in a deep breath and held it.

'I told you, revelation upon revelation,' he wheezed presently, his mouth writhing in an unsightly manner. 'But I'm sure it can't come as such a total surprise to know that another man is capable of loving your wife? She is a very attractive woman; I can tell you I'm not the first – well, you are yourself testament to that. But she has to be stopped. What she is doing is wrong, the power she has is far too damaging. She must be brought down.'

'You need help,' Adam informed him softly.

Partridge succeeded in producing a smile of sorts. 'We *all* need help, Mr Shatt. Every single one of us. That is a universal truth. We all need help and there is none. We exist, life is cruel and God is without mercy. That's all there is.'

He rose, stiffly, and eased himself out from between the bench and table. Looking down at Adam he said, 'I do pity you, Mr Shatt. Truly. What can you do now? I come bringing you news which, whilst providing answers you seek in your quest for the truth about yourself, can only really worsen your situation. Your deepest fears are realized. What you now have to confront . . . is it bearable? The world has turned upon you, there is nowhere to turn for sanctuary. Even those purporting to help only bring more suffering.

'What will you do, Mr Shatt? Can you continue? I suppose you must. Giving up might hold certain enticements, but to do so now, well, that's surely impossible. It is the truth, the whole truth and nothing but the truth that beckons you. You can have nothing less, but oh! what a price to pay!'

He swivelled, a little clumsily, and was gone. The atmosphere in his wake felt dangerously unsettled, as though some passing demon had kicked a vipers' nest.

Adam sat as he was for some time, his hands in his pockets, motionless. Revelation after revelation. Shock after shock. And they left him numbed, unable to think.

He seemed to have stepped out of himself, to have somehow become the detached observer, impartial witness to the storm in which he was simultaneously embroiled. Questions were whipped up like frenzied shards of debris, hurled at him with searing ferocity, but he let them pass through him and away, declining in any way to contemplate them.

He became aware once more of his surroundings and moved from his seat. He, like Partridge, had grown stiff. His limbs felt cold and heavy, drained of blood or life. He pulled his coat about him.

He was leaving the bar when he grew conscious of the piece of paper he was holding in his hand in one pocket. He drew it out and unfolded it. It was less than three hours since he had called at Ruth's. There had been no answer to his repeated ringing at the front door of the decaying Regency mansion where she lived. But as he'd turned to leave, barely registering the uneven clack of high heels on the pavement outside, he had come face to face with a youngish woman with a lipstick-clad smile.

'Looking for me, luv?'

She was a pale, dark-haired creature with the slack gaze and ungainly stance of a smackhead or a lush. She wore a short leather skirt, dark tights or stockings, a beaver-skin jacket and red leather shoes. Adam had asked her if she knew Ruth.

'Top floor?' She stepped past him up to the front door, taking keys from her handbag. 'Ruthie? She's not here now.'

Adam moved up beside her. 'Do you know where she is? It's important.'

'I'll bet it is.' She surveyed him sidelong. 'If it's business, luv, Ruth's not your girl. Far from it. And I'm not well disposed at the moment. You know how it is.'

She had unlocked the door and was entering. Adam slipped in with her. 'You are sure she's not here?'

'I said so, didn't I? Look, if you want I can phone Tricia. She's a mate of mine. You'll like her.' She let herself into a ground floor flat, off to the left of the main hallway.

Adam took two ten-pound notes from his pocket. 'I have to get in touch with Ruth.'

'My, you are in a paddy, aren't you?' She stood in the doorway to her flat, a hand on a hip, cynical but not unkind. Then she took the money and disappeared inside.

Through the crack of the door Adam glimpsed her sifting through assorted papers at a table in her sitting-room. She returned, 'There was no need for that,' and handed him a slip of notepaper, 'but seeing as you're offering.'

He thanked her and left. Now he stared at the new address she had given him. It seemed to add up. He folded the paper carefully and put it in his breast pocket. By many reckonings this flimsy scrap with its hurriedly scribbled message and faint hint of Poison might be all he had left.

Miracle

He stepped outside into the ghostly afternoon.

From further along the passage a wave of coarse laughter drew his attention. A small crowd had gathered outside a bar and brasserie, mainly businessmen from inside. It was attracting other passers-by, and a ragged circle of onlookers had formed around some spectacle Adam could not see. Despite the biting wind some of the brasserie's customers stood in their shirtsleeves. Adam moved closer to look.

From outside the circle he saw a woman. She was aged somewhere in her thirties and pushed a skeletal, rust-pocked pram wanderingly to and fro. Barring a shabby oversized man's grey jacket which hung like loose sacking from her thin shoulders, she was unclothed.

Her limbs and face were undernourished, streaked with grime; she also seemed oblivious to the winter. She manoeuvred the old pram, which must have come from a skip or council tip, within the circle, and cooed and clucked into its interior. She glanced from moment to moment towards her audience, smiling a secretive, superior, tragic lunatic smile.

The businessmen, lagers in fists, urged her on. They playfully joshed one another and laughed raucously at their own lewd suggestions.

The woman was responsive to the attention she had gained. She let go of the pram's push-bar and reached inside. From beneath the remains of a torn canvas hood she withdrew a loaf of sliced white bread wrapped in Sunblest cellophane. She held it to her cheek. She pressed it tenderly to her lips then cradled it to her breast.

The audience voiced its appreciation. Adam ran his eyes over the faces. Men, women, even some children, intent, all but a few, on extracting the maximum possible amusement from an unscheduled lunchtime diversion.

The object of their attention opened her mouth now to sing to the packet in her arms. From trembling lips came a warbling sound, hardly audible. The tune was recognizable as 'Away In A Manger', but beyond the first line she seemed unsure of the words and substituted some gibberish of her own concoction. Her song nevertheless inspired hoots of approval from the respectable men at the brasserie door. Adam closed his eyes.

Unbidden and unwished for, words from Simon Partridge's pre-parting speech came like a voice at his shoulder: '*We all need help, Mr Shatt. Every single one of us. We all need help and there is none. We exist, life is cruel, and God is without mercy. That's all there is.*'

He walked away, deeply ashamed, angered and distressed by his own impotence. But he did not go far. A small boy who had detached himself from the onlookers rushed past him as he was about to exit the passage, calling excitedly to two friends in the square beyond. All three ran back, clutching one another's garments, followed by an overweight woman carrying Christmas presents.

Adam, after another moment of contemplation, went back after them. He squeezed through the crowd and stepped into the circle. The woman still nursed the loaf in her arms, still singing her pathetic cradle-hymn. But a staunch nurse in a blue cloak had entered the circle and was about to lead her away.

The nurse's presence threw him momentarily, then he dismissed her. He strode to the mad woman and grasped her by the shoulders. She made no measurable response, just stared through him idiot-fashion, still singing softly. But the nurse, at first taken aback, and then with fury and utter contempt, opened her mouth to lash him. But no words emerged. Something in the look he passed her influenced both her intention and the tone of her expression. She was silent. The brasserie crowd, sensing something was about to happen, fell abruptly silent too.

With a hand beneath the woman's chin Adam gently raised her head and looked into her eyes. They were empty. She lolled at him vacantly, making no attempt to resist. An energy pulsed in his veins. His hands moved to the sides of her face, fingertips applying the slightest pressure to her temples.

He detected the first glimmer of response. Her eyes grew pained then troubled. She had ceased singing and stiffened, a small animal sound escaping her throat. And Adam, outside of space or time, did not know what he was doing or why. A hand shifted to the nape of her neck, the fingers close to the protrusion of the seventh cervical vertebra. The other rested at her temple as he focussed his mind, the energy welling like a sudden springtide born of a source somewhere deep within and beyond him.

At first she tried to pull back, and he held her. She was breathing rapidly, her head straining to turn against his hands.

The tide rose and flooded from him. It poured along invisible meridians, from the very centre of his being, along the length of his arms, out through the tips of his fingers, a conscious vitality that came through him but was not his, that he directed but did not initiate. It commanded him as he commanded it, and every nerve end, every cell and atom in his body had become alive.

The woman ceased to fight him. She relaxed quite suddenly, her hands dropping to her sides. The loaf which she had been clutching to her chest rolled onto the paving stones. There was noticeably a swift and subtle transformation of her facial features. An accumulated tension lifted, the taut muscles that had shaped her facial expression unknotting. Her agitation was blown away, and with it went the spiritual death that had been her longtime lover. Adam sensed her own strength flowing back into her limbs.

Her eyes opened wide, and without a thought he released her and stepped back. They stared at one another, both uncomprehending. Soundless and unseen, dispersing energies in the atmosphere around them reverted to previous, latent, unconceived forms.

She had a bright, if bewildered focus to her gaze, a clarity and fixity that had not been there before. She took in her surroundings uncertainly, as if seeing them for the first time. She sought words but found none, and then she realized she was naked.

She gave a cry and shrank, tried to withdraw completely into the jacket. The nurse who had stooped in a dream to gather up the fallen bread, was quick to unclasp her cloak. She wrapped it around the woman and put her ample arms about her. Adam turned quickly and walked away.

He exited the circle of onlookers, which parted like fronds to a rolling breeze, and strode from the passage to the open square. His fingers tingled; he was exhilarated and disturbed simultaneously, and walked as though he glided on air.

Entering the square he heard footsteps and something lightly touched his arm. As he turned two small warm hands took his. The woman's eyes and cheeks glistened, and for a second he had the ghastly feeling that she was going to fall down in front of him. The nurse at her side was also in tears.

He averted his gaze, embarrassed and as lost for words or explanation as they were. His eyes went to the crowd behind them, and then further to where, at the far end of the sloping passage, where he had originally entered with Simon Partridge, a familiar figure stood.

In the dying winter light of early afternoon Adam concentrated his vision to take in better what he saw. He was not mistaken. The figure was silhouetted against the off-white stone facade of the building beyond. Even at a distance the compact, powerfully muscled body and squat head seated on wide shoulders were instantly recognizable. The feet were set firmly apart, the forearm and midriff tense, encircled with chain, the whole body taut, leaning backwards slightly, restraining. And had any doubt remained it would have been immediately dispelled by the sight of the great hound which heaved, forelegs off the ground, towards Adam, straining to gain release.

He looked again towards the crowd, which fully blocked the passage. More than simple curiosity was expressed in their faces now. Some were beginning to edge towards him in a darkly menacing fashion. He sensed hostility in the air.

Adam slipped his hand from the woman's, smiling at her with brief reassurance. He gave a last glance beyond her then turned to walk quickly across the square, away from the woman and the nurse, the advancing crowd, and the brutish Slav and his monstrous slavering pet.

Of Angels, Ghosts, Pensioners and Small Feathered Friends . . .

Doctor Geld, in the windowless, airless, sunken room, sweated again before his fellow Angels.

'This time it is serious,' he said, and he meant it. The machines around him whined and hummed emphatically.

'You're damned right it's serious,' Mackelvoye, Angel Three, Gard's deputy, rejoined. 'This is what I've feared all along.'

Mackelvoye looked strained and more than a little discomfited; the weight of unwarranted responsibility was leaving an unmistakable imprint.

'Would somebody mind telling me what is going on?' Asprey demanded. He had just arrived, the last, in an absurd green suit. An A-One-Double-Priority summons had found him midway to luncheon at the Reform, necessitating cancellations at unforgivably short notice of what had promised to be an informative chin wag with the Cabinet Secretary. And with his discovery now, as he seated himself on the vacant tubular-steel framed office chair, that he was without cigars, he was primed to be intolerable company.

'We have a crisis,' Doctor Geld informed him carefully. 'The Apostle. There are new developments.'

'Yes, I gathered that. What are the details?'

Doctor Geld stretched his lips and swallowed and turned to Angel Five, seated to his left. 'Perhaps, my dear, now that we are all assembled, you might like to recount events as you experienced them. Mr Mackelvoye and myself can fill in as necessary.'

Judith, crisply attired in a blue suit and cream blouse, stood. After a moment to collect her thoughts she proceeded upon an account of the evening she and Adam had attended the lecture at the infants' school. In the glare from the overhead fluorescent strips, their light reflected unkindly from the barren yellow walls, she looked pale and tired. Dark circlets hung beneath her eyes as though she had not slept well for some time.

She had hardly completed two sentences before she was interrupted by Asprey.

'Who did you say? Iddle-aye, addle-aye who?'

Judith enunciated the name precisely. 'Iddio E. Scompiglio.'

Asprey cast mocking glances about the room. 'Who the bloody hell,' he demanded imperiously, 'is Iddio E. Scompiglio when he's at home?'

'You've seen the report,' Judith said.

'I haven't.'

'Why not?'

'Haven't had one.'

'Yes, you have,' Mackelvoye put in. 'I dispatched a copy to each of you.'

Asprey offered him a blank stare. 'First I've heard of it. What was it about?'

'Scompiglio. We ran him through the computer.'

'It's news to me.'

'You haven't read it?'

'Can't have.'

'It was flagged: *Your Eyes Only.*'

'Don't recall it. Probably didn't get the time. Such a clutter in my trays.'

'But where is it, then?' Mackelvoye demanded.

Asprey shrugged. 'How would I know? If you dispatched it as you say, Roger, then I must assume it lies unopened on my desk. I'll make a point of checking when I get back.'

Mackelvoye made a sound somewhere between a groan and a sigh. Nevus, black-coated and smug against the wall, sniggered. 'I read it.'

Mackelvoye grew angry. 'Are you honestly saying that you've just left it lying around where anybody might open it?'

'Honestly can't say, old boy. But not to worry,' he winked. 'I keep exclusive company.'

Mackelvoye swore and would have delivered the full content of his opinion had not Doctor Geld intervened. 'Gentlemen, please. The matter of the missing report can be investigated later, but there is little time. Perhaps we might stick to the topic in hand?'

'Absolutely. Delighted,' Asprey said. 'If somebody would be good enough to enlighten me with an answer to my original question.'

'Iddio E. Scompiglio,' Judith told him, 'is the founding head of a relatively modern religious sect. His followers look upon him as the new world Saviour, though we have as yet been unable to determine whether he is in fact a living man, as they claim, or merely some kind of figurehead. His church is active in several countries and boasts a worldwide membership of some several thousands.'

'Thank you.'

She resumed her account. 'Adam and I attended one of their meetings. It was at Adam's insistence but I don't quite know what was behind it.'

'Sounds marvellous,' Asprey said. 'Were your prayers answered?'

'I can say,' she continued coolly, 'that the evening had some interesting moments.'

'Ah. So you're converted now?'

'Geoffrey, be quiet!' Mackelvoye let fly, colouring up. 'You are out of line on this. It is not an inconsequential parlour game.'

'Now, now. Let's not lose a grip on ourselves,' Asprey returned, though without the comfort of his customary cigar and tobacco cloud he was feeling just a touch vulnerable himself. Doctor Geld was obliged to step between them once again.

'Gentlemen, *please*.' He turned imploringly to Judith who, raising her voice a little, went on, 'Towards the end of the evening events began to get a little out of hand.'

She paused to ensure she had regained their attention. 'Adam grew upset. Mr Scompiglio had failed to turn up to speak in person, and for some reason he took this almost as a personal insult. He grew quite emotional and was virtually shouting the speaker down. Then he suddenly turned on a member of the audience. He ... he became hysterical, tried to grab this person.'

'Identified?' Asprey shot out the question.

She shook her head. 'The situation was far from easy. The room was overcrowded, things got very confused. The man was able to slip away before Adam reached him. But Adam knew him. He insisted later that the man had been following him for some time.'

Asprey's flippancy was fast dissolving, at least temporarily. He glanced towards Mackelvoye. 'One of yours?'

'No. I sanctioned no one. Angel Five was sole nursemaid that evening.'

'And presumably unknown to you?' Asprey said to Judith.

'I didn't actually see him.'

'Oh? Where were you?'

'I was there, with Adam. I did see the place in which he indicated this person to be, but I didn't see anyone fitting his description.'

'Which was?'

'He described him afterwards as a tall man, approximately his own age. Dark hair, long but smart, well cut. He wore a white suit, shirt and shoes and was taking notes. The way Adam told it, he got up and walked unhurriedly from the room the moment he was spotted.' She paused, then said, 'Even in the confusion a man of that description would have stood out. I'm sure of that. But I didn't see him.'

Asprey guffawed. 'A ghost, then? Oh Lord, that's all we need. A holy ghost, what's more, with a touch of radical chic!'

Nevus emitted a little squeal of mirth.

'He had an accomplice,' Judith said. 'At least, we think so.'

'Seems to me you're rather high on thought and lacking in the concrete stuff,' Asprey said. 'I suppose this accomplice simply drifted out on a cloud of spiritual well-being and hasn't been seen since?'

'She's a little bit too good to be true,' Judith said, evenly. 'We've had her questioned, informally, and if she's lying she's damned good. The best. At the same time though, she did employ some very effective delaying techniques. Both Adam and I were prevented from reacting with any kind of efficiency.'

'Can't you wring it out of her?'

'We can't put undue pressure on her while there's still the possibility of her being an innocent member of the public, Geoffrey,' Mackelvoye growled, rattling his pencil on the table top.

'Why not?'

'She's an old age pensioner, for God's sake! If she's genuine and we push too hard she could croak on us without warning.'

'An old age pensioner who's bloody well working for the opposition!' Asprey fulminated. 'So what if she "croaks" as you so eloquently put it?'

Judith lifted her hands to calm them. 'It could have been what it seemed at the time: sheer coincidence. We've put a team of watchers down. Twenty-four-hour surveillance. If she's up to anything we'll know soon enough.'

Asprey shifted in his chair. His hands wandered like questing ferrets through his pockets until he recollected his cigarlessness. He scowled. 'So where does all this leave us? Our Apostle has acquired a yearning for salvation; he may be hallucinating, he may be paranoid; he may be completely bonkers, but on the other hand there's just a chance that someone else might have an interest in him. Well, it's hardly news. And for the most part firmly in your province anyway, Theodore. Did it really call for an A-One-Double?'

Doctor Geld replied thoughtfully. 'Hallucination or paranoia, possibly, but we would be foolish to dismiss the possible intervention of a third party. Which brings me to the next development.' Nervously clearing his throat he turned to Mackelvoye. 'Perhaps you would like to take over . . .'

Mackelvoye opened a pale pink folder on his lap and scanned a sheet of paper inside. He said, 'On the day following this incident the Apostle was in contact with one of our small boys. More accurately, a little bird from Research with no direct connection with us. One Simon Partridge, a name I think familiar to us all?'

'Ah, Partridge!' Asprey declared, and beamed at Judith with the implication of welcoming Partridge to an exclusive club. 'Your little feathered friend! What did he want?'

'As far as we can ascertain, Geoffrey,' Mackelvoye informed him with deliberation, 'he wanted to blow the whole bloody gaff. He wanted to open Gospel wide.'

'He knows about Gospel?' Asprey's surprise showed on his face.

'We don't know what he knows,' Mackelvoye said, 'or what exactly passed between the two of them. But we're assuming the worst. The Apostle was extremely agitated when they parted and has been uncommunicative and very withdrawn since.'

'Any action?'

'We have him under tight surveillance, allowing him to think he has a free rein until we discover just what his game is. He'll be taken care of.'

Asprey raised an eyebrow. 'I'm sure he will, but I ought to tell you – as a friend, you know – that your handling of the terrorist chappie did not go down well on high.'

'Terrorist?'

'That oddball in Notting Hill. The animal activist. It was frightfully messy.'

'He was taken out at my recommendation,' Doctor Geld said quickly. 'He was a serious risk.'

'Accepted. But what about the method? Mightn't he have just disappeared or something? Been tucked away in one of your institutions for the duration? I mean, he was an unknown. You could have experimented to your heart's content.'

'They are already overcrowded,' the doctor said between his teeth.

'Then you might have shown a little more decorum. Leaving him in such a state for any Tom, Dick or Harry to find, it's, well, it's rather loud. I mean, we have such a marvellous selection of clean and effective, not to say discreet, chemicals at our disposal. Why on Earth must our man resort to ritual slaughter? Is he a pervert or something? Does he like the sight of blood?'

'He carried out his orders,' Mackelvoye said blandly. 'The end result was the same.'

'Quite so, but discretion is the watchword, you know. The boys in blue made a terrific fuss and it was a job keeping the newshounds at bay. It doesn't look good, that sort of thing. And the word upstairs is that whoever is donning Gard's hat is failing to display the requisite judgement. I thought I'd mention it here, considering Partridge. I hope, if you find it necessary to put him away, that you will show a modicum of taste. It will go down so much better.'

'As circumstances dictate,' Mackelvoye muttered.

Nevus now spoke quietly from his place on the sideline. 'Our mole has finally surfaced, then.'

'It would appear that way,' Mackelvoye said, a grimness in his manner suggesting that he was not entirely satisfied.

'So what can we predict now for the Apostle?' Asprey asked.

Doctor Geld, shaking his head, heaved a little sigh. 'In a case like this prediction is impossible. His behaviour is in fact becoming more unpredictable and extreme. We must assume that he is highly suspicious, but until we can determine the extent of Partridge's knowledge, and what he has told the Apostle, we can't know that he is actually on to us.'

'Why not haul Partridge in and find out?'

'In time,' Mackelvoye answered him. 'But I've judged it expedient for the nonce to wait. It seems implausible that he is operating alone. He could lead us to bigger fish.'

'Then Theodore, what in your psychiatric omniscience do you suggest?'

Doctor Geld inserted the end of his Parker between his yellowing teeth. 'As I see it this situation need not be to our disadvantage. Partridge has obviously revealed something to the Apostle which has catapulted him into a state of severe agitation. Whatever it is that he has put to him it could turn out to be the vital trigger which will permit a flow of genuine memories to come back into his conscious mind.'

'And then what? Is he going to be capable of recognizing them as such? And if he does is it likely that he'll come running back to us?'

'Ah! Ha-ha! That I certainly cannot predict. The balance could tip either way. We must watch and wait and be ready to act upon any sign he may give us.'

Mackelvoye rustled his paper and made an unusual respiratory sound and said, 'Before we go any further I ought to perhaps just fill you in on the other developments.'

'There are more?' Asprey asked.

He nodded. 'One: on the same morning that he made contact with Partridge the Apostle first visited a woman, a . . . lady of the streets, in Kensington.'

'Good Lord!' Asprey turned back to Judith. 'My dear, I had no idea!'

'He spent less than two minutes in her company, Geoffrey,' Mackelvoye told him with renewed impatience.

'Even worse! Good grief! You have my every sympathy,' he went on, still talking to Judith, 'I do have an understanding of these things, though I say it myself.'

'We don't know the purpose of the visit,' Mackelvoye went on steadily, his eyes on the paper on his lap. 'Angel Six is following up.'

Judith, with a note of concern, said, 'Is that wise?'

'In view of the sensitivity, who else is there?'

Asprey stole a glance at his watch. His thoughts had never strayed far from the possibility of a late luncheon. 'You said "developments" in the plural?'

'Yes. Theodore was hardly overstating the case when he referred to "unpredictable and extreme" behaviour. It seems – and I have absolutely no explanation for this – that our Apostle has cured an unknown female of a chronic schizophrenic illness.'

Asprey was puzzled. 'Cured her? What do you mean? How?'

'By the, ahem, "laying on of hands".'

There was a short silence before Asprey emitted a burst of harsh laughter. 'Miracles now, is it!' He gave himself over to a further moment of perplexity. 'Theodore, does this have anything to do with your jiggery-pokery? What exactly did you do to him?'

Doctor Geld threw up his hands. 'Ha-ha! Were that it did! No, I am as lost for an explanation as anyone.'

'But it's verified?'

Mackelvoye nodded. 'There were witnesses. In abundance.'

Shaking his head and massaging the back of his neck Asprey exclaimed, after a pause, 'Well, what with miracles, ghosts, pensioners and little-feathered friends . . . I'm damned if I can find anything suitable to say.'

'Join the club,' Mackelvoye said.

'The world revolveth backwards and neither Gard nor all his Angels can explain,' Nevus remarked, and squeaked with laughter.

'Try singing "The Twelve Days of Christmas",' Judith suggested sardonically.

'All things considered, Theodore,' Asprey said in annoyance, 'do you still feel it wouldn't be wiser to bring him in?'

'The Apostle? Not yet.'

'I don't like it. And they're not going to like it upstairs.'

'I have decided to take it to Gard,' Doctor Geld said. 'The situation is critical and warrants his personal attention. Mr Mackelvoye can hardly be expected to continue to run the show.'

'Not before time,' Mackelvoye breathed with evident approval. 'But I don't think you'll find him in.'

'I have a suspicion ...' the doctor said shrewdly, and let the words trail off. 'I think he will have some comment to make now.'

Sleuth

The tall, well-dressed gentleman who stepped from a black London cab on one of Westminster's less salubrious backstreets was, to anyone who knew him, a poor imitation of his former self. The straight back had yielded to gravity's inexorable will, the confident military bearing giving way to a slight stoop, as though at the removal of some essential internal support.

His expensive blue suit lacked razor creases and did not appear such a perfect fit. He carried a raincoat over one arm and his silver-grey hair was a touch long and windswept. Only the black leather shoes retained a shine, a visible lustre, an assertion, perhaps, that no matter other indications, his feet remained firmly on the soil.

He paid his fare and took a step backwards, merging into the shadow of a doorway, protected from the dispersed illumination of the streetlamps overhead. He took stock of the street while the cab moved away, and when it had passed from sight around the corner stepped out and walked back in the direction from which it had brought him.

He slipped across the road and turned right, then right again into the neighbouring street, a slanting brick-paved alley with faulty street-lighting. Here his pace slackened. A close observer would have seen his eyes taking in the entire street before crossing once more and approaching a building about midway along. He paused for a moment at the door, then pushed it and entered, having failed despite his precautions to espy the figure that stalked him.

Doctor Geld was far from happy. The activity he was engaged upon fell well outside the pale of his routine. It filled him with mordant pangs of anxiety and guilt, the fact that he was snooping on a man he had come to respect and possibly even revere. His mouth had dried up and his sphincter puckered tight but volatile.

He could not rid himself of the absurd notion that discovery now would lead to his receiving a sound whacking on the bottom, and as he skulked along the deserted street he wrung his hands accordingly.

Riding this complex admixture of emotion was the heady frisson of adventure, and an intoxicating adolescent pride at having successfully followed up what had been, after all, little more than a hunch.

He was cold, too. Two near breathless evenings huddled at the darkened window of a gutted travel agent's at the end of the street had done little for his health. He walked with an awkward stiffness, his bones feeling brittle and unreliable.

He too hesitated at the varnished oak door. On the wall at his shoulder was a small brass plaque, which read 'SOCIETY. Club Amour For Gentlemen'. His apprehension mounted at the thought of the treatment he might expect once inside. His heart, which had commenced thumping with alarming vigour the moment his eyes had spotted the man he was suffering such extremes of discomfort for, now threatened to burst into his mouth and choke him. But he had made his resolve and it was binding. At such a critical juncture any failure on his part to address the situation directly could end in catastrophe. He pressed the buzzer, conscious of the little fish-eye camera peering at him from above the door.

There was a pause then a buzzing sound. He laid his hand trembling on the brass doorknob and pushed.

He stepped into a welcome blast of warm air from a convector over his head. He was in a closet-sized vestibule, bare but for a damask curtain in front of him. The outer door closed automatically and as he parted the curtain another electronically-sealed door behind it opened to receive him.

He entered a reception lobby which let onto a much larger room, regally furbished with reproduction, or even genuine antique, eighteenth- and nineteenth-century pieces. A Regency sofa, a Sheraton couch, a large Classical-style cabinet, a mahogany table with corresponding chairs at one wall.

Elegant mirrors, Regency-striped wallpaper and plush drapes and velvets provided a rich ambience, tending towards red and muting in a tasteful if sensuous manner what might otherwise have been a rather formal effect. Palms and trailing or climbing plants in ceramic pots and vases decorated both the large room and the reception area where he stood, and a Mozart divertimento played softly and somewhat reassuringly in the background.

At the furthest end of the large room a wide red-carpeted staircase swept upwards to a first floor landing. There Doctor Geld, craning and squinting, was almost certain he glimpsed a pair of blue-suited and black-shoed legs just exiting left.

At a desk a pretty and shapely young woman looked up from an elaborate computer and telephone system and smiled, revealing twin rows of pearly whites. 'Good evening, sir. Welcome to Society.'

Doctor Geld nervously passed his tongue across his dry lips and approached the desk. 'I am looking for somebody.'

The girl pursed her lips understandingly. 'I'm sure Society can provide just the person. We take pride in being able to cater to every taste. That's what we are here for.' Slender fingers with red-varnished nails tapped out something on her computer keyboard while her smiling eyes barely left his face. 'May I ask, sir, is this your first visit?'

'Ah, no. No. You misapprehend me.' The doctor writhed and produced a gaping grin, disconcerted by the generousness of exposed cleavage his eyes could not help falling on. The girl balanced her chin on a curled forefinger and looked up at him with wide warm eyes, throwing him into deeper confusion, rendering him mute.

'Don't worry, sir. Membership is quite simple. You just pay your appropriate fee here and you'll receive your card upon leaving. Once you've registered the house is yours. Perhaps you would like to see our tariff, then, if you wish, you could start with a relaxing drink in the lounge upstairs.'

She presented him with a triple-gatefold club tariff and he moved away, thankful for the respite. Already the sweat had broken out on his dome and he had gone from cold to feverishly hot in seconds. Something in that girl's look unnerved him. Too kind, too warm, too promising, too ... It was as if she knew something. He could not think clearly, his mind whirled. What on Earth was he doing here?

He was panting. He felt faint and closed his eyes. He opened them again. What was he to do? The urgency of his mission denied him the opportunity to escape, but he was so afraid. He fumbled for his foulard and raised it to mop his brow. Then, on a sudden panic-impulse, he flung aside the tariff and made a dash for the staircase at the end of the large room.

He had some fifty to sixty feet to cover. He had gained twenty before the girl's silken-voiced but anxious appeal sang out behind him. 'Sir! Sir! You can't go up yet. You must register. Sir! Sir! Please!'

He sped on. Her tones abruptly acquired an acid timbre. 'William! *William!*'

Doctor Geld made the foot of the stairs and hared on to the top, his elbows tight to his ribcage, forearms flapping furious arcs like the wings of some grotesque flightless bird. A croaking in-breath of terror sounded deep in his throat as he became conscious of another presence appearing off to his rear, a tall figure, swift and dark.

He had made a terrible mistake. He was in dire trouble, but he could not stop himself now. He veered left along the landing and bolted into the only available corridor.

Several closed doors whizzed by him, and the blurred faces of one or two startled club-members and girls. He could hear a high-pitched, erratic keening sound and realized as he came to a halt at the corridor's end, facing a high, double swing-door, that it was the emissions of his own throat. He hesitated for less than a second then lunged forward into the room beyond.

He was totally disorientated. He had stepped into a blackness where odd, indistinct patches of brightness and colour stood out without form or meaning. Recognizably human figures moved in the artificial dusk and the thick scented air was like an intoxicant.

He careened forward several paces. He crashed into a table, brought himself up, reeled away and collided with someone. The man, off-balanced, turned with an indignant grunt. 'What the – !' Then, in astonishment, '*Theodore!* What in the name of heaven!'

Doctor Geld gasped and gulped, supporting himself on the back of a chair, and pawed at Gard's sleeve. He understood now that he was in a sumptuous, spacious lounge. The outcrops of coloured light clarified themselves. He made out a softly-illuminated bar, lamps on table tops. Young waitresses glided, platters in hand, between the tables, and – Good God! – he looked again – they were topless. *They were bottomless!* They had on nothing but bits of satin ribbon, stockings and suspenders, the skimpiest of black skirts and even skimpier frilly white aprons!

He passed his eyes around the room, quickly took in some of the clientele. Middle-aged to elderly males predominantly, many in the company of much younger, barely clad women. Gard himself was arms intertwined with a full-breasted hostess less than half his age.

It would come to Doctor Geld much later that amongst the male visages he had glimpsed before leaving the establishment that evening more than one was familiar. Men he had had dealings with in the course of his duties, or men he recognized from their publicity: men of high office and renown; an MP, a Crown Court judge, a high-ranking member of the clergy, others he could not quite fit an identity to.

But for now such things did not concern him. His concern, most pressingly, was the figure looming quite suddenly at his shoulder. A silent, towering presence in dinner jacket and tie.

Geld cringed. He quaked and tried to grin and find words of explanation. Then Gard's voice, with something of its old authority, calmly intervened. 'It's all right, William. He's my guest. I'll take care of it now. Apologies to Suzie. I'll have a word in due course.'

William loomed more completely, just enough to be fully appreciated.

'Very good, sir.' Glacially polite. He directed a hooded stare at Doctor Geld and withdrew.

Geld sank onto the padded velvet chair.

'Theodore, what is the meaning of this? Are you drunk?' Gard, seeming to recollect, gave a word to the toy on his arm and she too slipped away. He assessed the neighbouring clientele, assured himself that they had resumed, after the fracas, more leisurely pursuits, and took a seat beside the doctor.

'You can't blunder into an establishment like this! What can you be thinking of, man? Society won't tolerate behaviour of that sort. It has a reputation to consider.'

Geld blathered apologies, his eyes following a waitress. He gathered breath to impart something of his reasons for coming here. His perception was arrested by yet another unguessed at spectacle and he reverted on the instant to slack-jawed amazement.

He saw a low stage a little way off upon which a youthful quintet performed what he had at first taken to be slow modern ballet. They were attractive and well-formed and their motions were complemented by a wide spectrum of coloured lights alternating to unobtrusive electronic rhythms. But it was only now that he realized that they were all *in puris naturalibus*, or very nearly so. And it was only now, if his weak sight did not misguide him, that he perceived that they were engaged in activities he had never previously witnessed in real life.

Doctor Geld's mind became a vacuum. All thought scattered. He slipped his spectacles from his nose, hurriedly wiped them and replaced them to take in more fully the mesmerizing sight.

'Theodore! What's the matter with you? Answer me, dammit!'

Geld wrenched himself from the floor show with a start. 'It was vital I got to you.' He spoke in a daze. In a matter of five minutes or less he had passed through a lifetime. 'It's Gospel. There are serious complications.'

Gard stiffened.

'Come with me.' He rose and strode towards the double door through which the doctor had made his uncourtly entrance. A bedraggled Geld tagged reluctantly in his wake, his eyes glued to the last to the antics of the performers on stage.

Gard led him down the corridor and through a door into another passage. They passed several more doors and a variety of men and girls in various states of undress. Through one half-opened door Geld glimpsed, or thought he glimpsed, a lady in lace teddy, stockings, stilettos and Santa Claus robe standing elbows akimbo astride a writhing Yuletide sack from the drawn neck of which a pink and hairless head protruded.

He had no time to better assimilate the scene; Gard strode on, taking a key from his pocket with which he unlocked an unmarked door near the end of the passage. He showed Geld into a cubicle-like room, carpeted and draped and bathed in rubescent light. Its only furnishing was a substantial leather-upholstered couch and a small, locked cabinet on the wall near its head. Gard closed the door and turned the key behind them.

He turned on the doctor. 'Damn you, you know better than to mention that name!'

Geld attempted another garbled explanation but Gard was not yet prepared to hear. Had they been in a larger room he would have been pacing it, as it was he stood in minatorial contemplation, eyes burning holes in the wall hangings.

'How did you find me here?' he demanded presently.

'There was a strong element of guesswork,' Geld told him contritely. 'Necessity compelled me.'

Gard mulled this over. 'No matter.' He stretched the muscles of his jaw and throat. 'William isn't to be fooled with, you know. Had I not been here he could have done you considerable damage, or marked you for subsequent attention. Society has an exclusivity to maintain, and he's a thorough man. One of our running-boys until a couple of years ago. He will not sit by and see us besmirched.'

'Running-boy?' Geld queried distractedly. He had regained his composure enough to begin making mental notes of Gard's mien and was disturbed by what he saw. Gard was haggard and doughy-eyed, undoubtedly had lost weight and was far from immaculately turned out. There was alcohol on his breath, more than a whiff, and intimations in his speech and manner of an uncharacteristic estrangement. You're close to breaking, thought Doctor Geld. He had seen the signs before, many times.

'Special Branch,' Gard informed him. 'Useful man, too, until he strangled that Libyan attaché.'

Geld shuffled his feet in unhappy recollection. He had compiled William's psychological assessment, though he had never met the man. Superintendent William South had evaded court proceedings but the psychiatrist's personal recommendations had been instrumental in his dismissal from the force. He could not avoid wondering whether William had any idea who he was.

'Now what do you have to tell me?' Gard demanded.

As concisely as he could Doctor Geld gave his account of recent events, as he knew them, that had befallen the late Adam Shatt. And as the details were disclosed Gard, who had propped himself with his buttocks against the side of the couch, could be seen to go into decline. His shoulders slumped and his chin sank closer to his chest, and Geld observed a persistent gripping and loosening of his sinewed hands on the couch's edging.

Gard, in dealing with William, had shown himself still well capable of commanding a natural authority, but the doctor had not failed to notice the alacrity with which that authority dissolved as his mind shifted elsewhere. And even in panic Geld's subconscious ear had not deserted him. It had detected, and reminded him now of, the subtlest wavering in Gard's voice, a nuance betraying the fact that his authority had been summoned. It had required thought in its bidding and contained emotion in its delivery. This was not the old Gard. This was a changing Gard, a Gard who was *actually unsure of himself.*

When Geld concluded Gard had closed his eyes and could only murmur, opening them and slowly shaking his handsome head, 'He haunts me.'

'The Apostle?'

'The Apostle. Our Adam. The late Mr Shatt. He worries me to distraction. This whole shebang does. Why on Earth did I set it in motion? It's going to destroy me.'

Struck by his despondency Doctor Geld made a thoughtful sucking sound, drawing the soft flesh of the inside of his bottom lip against his yellowing lower incisors with his tongue, and releasing it. He did this several times.

'When you say he haunts you, are you saying you have encountered him again? Since Victoria Street?'

Gard looked up. 'Of course!' he exclaimed, answering an unspoken question of his own rather than the one Geld had put to him. 'He led you here! He followed me that day, is that it?'

Doctor Geld affirmed this.

'Why wasn't I told?'

'You were, ha-ha. At least, we tried.'

'Yes.' He gave a vague nod. 'Yes, I expect I was.'

The doctor repeated his question and Gard nodded again.

'I think so.'

'You think so? You *think* you have encountered him?'

'I believe.'

Geld puckered his lifting brow, ever more perplexed.

Gard said, 'It was coincidence,' but he didn't sound wholly convinced. Then he told Geld, with certain details omitted, about the evening he had run into the late Adam Shatt on the pavement outside an Islington newsagent's shop.

'It unnerved me, I don't mind telling you,' he said, and Doctor Geld made note of the confession.

Gard's hand had dipped into his jacket pocket as he was speaking. Now he withdrew it. He held a small, elongated cuboid box, the containing section of which he slid from its outer sleeve then tipped the contents into one palm. He loosely bunched his fist and shook it; the contents rattled. Lethargically he let fall a set of six white ivory dice onto the couch, regarding with little apparent interest the combination of black dots their upturned faces revealed. He collected them and tossed them again.

For the next minute or so Doctor Geld watched without comment as Gard played dice on the massage couch.

'There was another occasion,' Gard now said in passive admission. 'Quite some weeks ago. Do you want me to tell you about it?'

Doctor Geld nodded. Almost unconsciously they had individually adopted the respective personas of troubled patient and professional therapist.

'I was in my inner sanctum,' Gard said. 'Playing dice just like now, except that until recently I used to take note of combinations. That's what I thought it was, you see. The combinations. But that's irrelevant.' He lifted a hand and made a flicking motion, swatting away the irrelevancy like an insect. 'I had ... a feeling. Something made me look up from my desk. He was standing there, at the door, watching me.

'I was far from pleased, Theodore, to say nothing of surprised. I had not given anyone permission to enter, nor had I been informed that anyone was waiting to see me. I couldn't think how he'd got through the security doors, let alone the outer office. I was ready to carpet him *and* my staff in no uncertain terms.

'Then it struck me that something was really extraordinarily amiss. I mean to say, he *couldn't* have come through my door. I hadn't released it. And even if there had been some sort of malfunction I would have known. I would have heard the door. No, it simply had not been opened.

'You'll think I'm mad. I thought I was. Because when I opened my mouth to speak he had gone. No word. Didn't turn and leave, or back away. Just faded.' Gard made a soft, aspiratory popping sound, 'Puh!' and accompanied it with an appropriate gesture of the hands. He laughed humourlessly. 'And now you tell me he is performing miracles!'

'Ha-ha!' Geld said.

Gard took no notice. He gathered his dice and rolled them again. 'I knew something would happen today,' he said.

'That I was coming to see you?'

He gave a melancholic shrug. 'Something. Just something. I knew. Through the dice.'

The Truth About Gard

'It isn't the combinations, you see,' he reiterated. 'The numbers count for next to nothing, contrary to what I had always assumed. My approach was one of trying to influence the roll of the dice, having them land on a predetermined combination. Or I would try to divine some kind of meaning or relevance out of the random numbers that did come up. But neither of these is a factor. The dice can fall as they may. I do not influence them, and I make no attempt now to read anything into the combinations. No, it's the concentration.'

Inclined over the couch, watching the dice tumble, Gard's features were stained a curious albinal pink in the red light. His skin appeared semi-translucent, giving an impression of insubstantiality. It was as though he were not wholly in the world, emotionally or physically.

'Playing induces a specific concentration, a meditative focussing of the mental faculties, and it is that which is all-important. I'm sure of it now. One gets a certain feeling . . . sometimes. An impression comes, a . . . a thought or an idea. I can't describe it. It comes and then it has gone. But it leaves a subtle imprint. That's what told me. About this evening.'

He turned his head, his face at an angle, and peered at Doctor Geld with a particular intensity. 'You see, Theodore – ' and abruptly his features changed. He was staring, not at Geld but beyond him, with an expression of puzzlement which moulded in the instant into pure horror. A hand bolted out and clamped onto the psychiatrist's wrist. 'Theodore! Behind you!'

Doctor Geld, his grin frozen in sudden unfathomable dread, twisted his thin body. His eyes swivelled and he looked behind him and for a second, just for a second, he thought he saw something. He thought he met the gaze of his former charge, the Apostle, Judith's enigmatic husband, the late Adam Shatt.

His eyebrow leapt and divided, but before it could stabilize the apparition was gone and he was left with some doubts as to whether he had actually seen it. He blinked at the red-bathed velvet-draped wall, and turned back.

Gard had released him. He passed a hand over his silver-grey hair, hollow-eyed, and said, as though the question cost him some considerable effort, 'Did you see anything?'

Geld's hesitation lasted less than a second. He replied that he had not and Gard bowed his head. He looked for a moment as though he might topple over and Doctor Geld moved to offer him support but was motioned off with a gesture of irritability. And Gard said, quietly, as if in confession of some mortal sin, 'I'm having a breakdown, Theodore. You know that, don't you. You, of all people.'

'You are under some strain, I am aware of that,' replied the doctor.

'Behaving strangely of late,' Gard said. He did not enlarge. 'Miriam's gone. I expect that's already public. Went off with a bloody art teacher, and I can't really blame her, I suppose. Seems she couldn't take any more, but I hadn't even realized there was a problem. Glaringly obvious now, of course. The signs – right back through the years. But at the time . . . always far too busy.

'Would you credit it? Spending more than half your life with someone only to discover one day that that person is not the one you thought you knew? It came like a bolt from the blue, you know. I always thought I'd provided her with everything a woman could wish for. Wealth, position, two wonderful homes, children. But I obviously never understood her needs. So wrapped up in my own, I suppose. Had no inkling of how unhappy she was all that time, how damned lonely.

'She wants everything now, of course. No holds barred. She seems ... *bitter.*' He shook his grey head mournfully. 'She won't talk. She says I should have done that long ago, which is true enough. She says she tried and I wouldn't listen and now she's having none of it.

'Theodore, I can say with total honesty that in all those years of marriage I never talked to her. Not about the truly important things. Didn't take the time to try to get to know her. No understanding of a woman's real needs. Little sympathy, either. What a fool.

'The boys have taken her side, predictably. They were always closer. It's only now that it's hitting me. What it all means. Too late now, though. Merry bloody Christmas.'

He trailed off into brooding introspection whilst Doctor Geld entertained a quandary. His primary objective was under threat, for prior to coming here he had given little serious consideration to Gard's mental state. He had been prepared for resistance but the unanticipated collapse he found himself confronted with now was a different matter. With little relish he was obliged to ask himself whether, in the unlikely event of his successfully drawing Gard back into office over Gospel, the man was actually fit to be toting responsibilities of such magnitude.

Gard might have been deliberately fuelling his doubts, for he was saying, 'And here I am now hallucinating all over the place! Hah! Rough justice! You are quite positive you saw nothing? You wouldn't lie to me? No. Nothing at all? Well, there we are then. Case proven.'

He cast his eyes around the little room, into every corner, every cranny. 'Not even a flicker?'

For the third time Doctor Geld denied him.

'Seemed so real to me.' Gard straightened his shoulders and adopted an unconvincing levity. 'Well, what's the diagnosis then, Theodore? More important, what's the prognosis? Any hope, or am I a candidate for one of your isolation wards?'

Geld measured his reply with a degree of caution. 'Obviously this is a trying period for you but I always advocate trying to come to grips with one's problems as opposed to what may seem the more attractive course of seeking to escape them. Which brings me to my main reason for coming here – '

'I am not a child, Theodore! Don't patronize me!' Gard flared with sudden hostility. 'I know full well why you came here. You want me to take control.'

Geld laughed. 'Ha-ha-ha! Well, you see, we Angels are making heavy weather of things without you. The Apostle grows more difficult to deal with. Gospel has grown into something that we do not have sufficient knowledge or authority to oversee. As a body we cannot reach agreement upon crucial decisions. We are all unsure of ourselves. We need you.'

Gard snorted. 'Look at me, Theodore. My mind wanders, my hands shake, I can't concentrate on one thing for more than a minute at a time, save for when I'm casting dice. I'm not in a condition to take control of anything. You can surely see that for yourself?' Distracting himself with his own mention of dice he gathered his set of little ivories into the palm of his hand and nodded at them. He spoke again and it was again with that leaden remorse that had characterized so much of his speech since they had entered the tiny room. 'How I regret having originated this entire set-up. Look what I've done. What right did I have? There's that poor fellow out there, staggering around not knowing a jot; there's you people plotting and panicking; there's a world waiting to tear out my throat should it ever learn the truth; there's my family turned upon me because of what they experience as my blatant lack of common goodness ... And let me tell you something, Theodore, in regard to your allusion to my "seeking to escape" as you put it, let me tell you that this – ' he gestured at the four walls, ' – is nothing. There is nothing here. It's empty.

'Yes, I saw your eyes all a-goggle. I watched your massive brain calculating the delights Society might offer you. But they are specious delights, my friend. You will find they pale very quickly. By which time of course it's too late. Society is just another huge step down a well-trodden descent into hell, but by the time any of us grasps it we're too far gone to be capable of hauling ourselves back.

'Still, it's no good telling you. You've glimpsed and now you won't be satisfied until you've discovered the truth for yourself.'

He tossed the dice contemptuously. 'What on Earth can I have been thinking of?' he resumed, staring as if still hoping to descry something of significance in their configuration. 'Look at the mess, look at the suffering. And for what? What purpose? Tell me, Theodore, because I've certainly forgotten if ever there was one. I've gained nothing but trouble and more trouble.'

'We still need you,' Geld persisted patiently.

'No!' Gard was adamant. 'You don't. I am not what you think I am. I'm not what *I* thought I was. Look, Theodore, this isn't Gard. This is a crumbling and deeply fallible human being, an old man, crushed and repentant. Premature dotage is my only recourse. Is that what you want to rely on? You mustn't. You will be making a grave mistake.'

'Asprey is threatening to go over your head.'

'Then let him.'

'For selfish reasons, apart from any other considerations, I would prefer not. He will opt for immediate termination. All my work will have been in vain. But if you return, even if only provisionally, the others will know that you at least maintain an interest, and Asprey will be discouraged from rash decisions.'

Gard nodded, smiling grimly. 'It's a scapegoat you're really looking for, isn't it. All of you. Has been from the start. Let's be truthful, I was never in control. I originated it all, yes, I set the damned applecart rolling, but then you immediately grabbed the reins. And you kept a firm hold of them, just as long as the cart didn't tip. But it did tip and you were suddenly all too happy to hand over again. Only I wasn't there any more. I'd hopped off some miles back and you were all so carried away with yourselves that you had failed to notice.'

'It isn't quite that way.'

'Isn't it?' Gard, having scooped the dice again, let them fall in a trickle. 'I've been a fool but I was never blind, though I'll admit the pretence was often preferable in the face of reality. But I've done a great deal of thinking.

'So listen carefully, Theodore, and consider this: If I were to come back now it would be to do one thing and one thing only. It would be to *set him free.*'

Doctor Geld's eyes widened, his eyebrow skittering. 'You mean – '

'I mean I would haul young Adam in and tell him everything. Repair him if it's at all possible, make him well again and then let him go. Just let him walk away, free to follow whatever course he chooses, take any decisions he likes. And we would *not interfere in the least.* Bugger the consequences, let's restore his birthright. Yes, let's do it, Theodore, for God's sake. Let's give him a bloody chance!'

'Were that it were that easy,' stammered Doctor Geld, for whom the prospect was as appalling as handing over authority to Asprey.

'It is, Theodore. It's the honourable, humane, and incredibly easy way.'

'There is another detail I didn't quite get around to mentioning.'

'Which is?'

'The Apostle has disappeared.'

'Disappeared?'

'He has been lost to us for almost eighteen hours. He shut himself away in his room for the best part of two days, refusing to speak to his wife or even eat. He was apparently behaving in a most extraordinary manner. Despite being unable to gain access to him she has recorded strange noises and movements in the room. He then went out abruptly, without a word, and made a second rendezvous with Partridge. This we judged explosive and tried to prevent. Unfortunately we were unable to act quickly enough. Partridge has now been taken care of but the Apostle was alerted. He did not return home last night and we have not been able to locate him. Mr Mackelvoye is in a terrible tizzy over the entire business. He is threatening to resign. We really can't carry on without you now.'

But he saw that his words were falling on deaf ears. Gard had turned away; he had had enough. He let his dice tumble, stared at them, gathered them and tossed them again, mechanically, distantly, bereft of interest or concern. Doctor Geld made one or two further appeals but was unable to penetrate the dark cloud of sad implacability that had descended. Gard steadfastly refused to even acknowledge him.

When Gard did eventually cease playing it was to slip a hand into an inside pocket and take out a small leather wallet. He held it fondly for a moment between his two palms, as though it were something precious and friable. When he flipped it open Doctor Geld, by craning his wiry neck, was able to peek over a bowed shoulder and see what it was that was claiming Gard's one hundred per cent attention now.

The wallet contained a photograph of Miriam, Gard's wife. It had obviously been taken some years ago; she was young and smiling and the colour had faded quite noticeably. She was holding two small, fair-headed boys, the elder of whom could not have been aged more than about five or six.

Gard stared fixedly at the photograph, and after a while he said, quietly and definitely, 'I want to go back. I got it all wrong. Everything. I want to go back there and start afresh. I'd give anything, you know. Anything at all.'

And Doctor Geld was rather embarrassed to see a tear gathering in Gard's right eye. It brimmed there for a moment, sparkling like a living gem in the strange red light, then tumbled down Gard's cheek and splashed onto the couch where his six white ivory dice were randomly cast.

The Stranger In A Strange Land

The snow fell heavily on unfamiliar streets. For some hours it had fallen steadily, a gusting, dense white flux from the fraught blackness overhead. It had settled on the wide city streets to be churned and discoloured by the passage of traffic and hurrying feet; on the high roofs it formed shifting blankets, pure, white and untouched except by the wind.

The late Adam Shatt, not aware of who or where he was, walked a broad pavement, his head and upper torso bent into the freezing wind that whipped up the new snow as it fell. Regardless of the weather, or the hour – his quartz wristwatch had failed and showed only a rapidly changing date – there was activity in the streets. The bars and eateries were full, the nightclubs doing good trade. Private cars and taxi-cabs pulled in and out of sidewalks, dispersing wealthy passengers about a thousand different destinations. The city spared time for neither sleep nor rest, it was a driving, or perhaps driven, place, a shouting metropolis with a will to be heard.

There were the vaguest recollections, like dim flashes of distant memories, of a journey. A long and tortuous journey, often broken, hours of waiting in frozen railway stations, snatches of fitful, fright-filled sleep . . . He thought he recalled passing through dead and dying forests, vast barren areas like war zones, shocked and infertile. But he could not be certain of it, or of anything. It all had the aspect of dream. His limbs ached and his skin was raw and tender to the touch of his clothing. He acknowledged that he was almost certainly delirious; the demarcation line between imagination and experience was unrecognizable, its validity an enigma to him.

He had reached the end of the great avenue and stood before an open plaza ringed with the brightly lit facades of cafes, restaurants, shops, clubs and high-rise office blocks and modern municipal buildings. At its hub stood a gaunt stone structure, the blackened, bombed-out tower of a great church, its ragged top disappearing into the snowy dark.

Incorporating the ruin was a complex of two modern constructions, a squat octagon like a lady's powder box, and, the matching lipstick tube, a hexagonal tower. The external walls of both were a honeycomb of square concrete cells, and within these blue glass glinted, lit by arclights and the gaudy confusion of the surrounding nightlife.

A Christmas fair had been set up within and around the complex and across the open plaza. It was a ghost village now. The miniature period shops and colourful stalls were shuttered up, and in its centre the dodgems and roundabouts of a children's funfair were quiet and still. Apart from one or two couples wandering like spirits between the little huts and houses the area was deserted.

As Adam stood and stared the ground beneath his feet began to tremble. He both heard and felt a distant vibration, growing closer. He glanced about him, unnerved, and then as quickly relaxed. The train passed harmlessly way below him. He turned and looked back through the swirling snow at the broad avenue. He had been here, he knew this place, but for the life of him he could find no name or memory to fit.

He raged inwardly at his own inadequacies but found no answers. Instead, what was brought vividly to mind with renewed fear and bewilderment, was the memory of his second, and last, meeting with Simon Partridge.

How long ago? A night? Two? Three? More than that? The

nightmare obfuscated temporal perception. He could not tell, but the meeting had erased the lingering doubts he had harboured about Partridge. Simon Partridge had not been lying, and whilst his motives could still be called to question his sincerity was now dramatically proven. So too was the risk he had claimed to run.

The telephone call for Mrs Merrick had come late in the evening. Judith was already in bed and Adam, having hauled himself out of the spare room in which he had passed the hours since his bizarre encounter with the lunatic woman, had gone out onto the balcony overlooking the garden to breathe the frosty air and try to clear his thoughts. The phone jangled several times and fell silent without piercing his consciousness. But when it started up again he was pricked into a recollection of Partridge's earlier instruction.

And again with the unshakeable sensation of being trapped within a dream over which he had no control, he had answered it. He had passed on the agreed-upon message to the anonymous caller, recognizably Partridge, and had replaced the receiver. He had stolen outside and padded down to the public call box a minute's walk away at the bottom of the street.

There was no one about. The night was undisturbed but for a clarinet-player practising scales in a nearby house. The booth smelled of stale ash and urine. He stamped his feet and blew into his hands, for he had come out without a coat or gloves. His breath formed brief vapour clouds in the air. He felt anxious and self-conscious like a boy out on a midnight prank, and very afraid, without knowing quite what it was he should be fearing. But there was another feeling about this exercise, something deeply and subtly unsettling. It had come upon him as he picked up the telephone receiver at home, and had remained with him. Déjà vu. He had done all this before. It was standard procedure.

The phone rang. He grabbed it.

'Mr Shatt?' Partridge was breathless again. Adam acknowledged him. 'I have more information. We should meet. Tomorrow. St Paul's. West Front. Eleven-thirty.'

The earpiece clicked and a dialling-tone hummed. Adam put back the receiver and returned home where, by all indications, he had not been missed.

* * *

The cathedral presided with solemn sober dignity in the uncertain mid-morning light. Above the great central dome a low umber-toned sky hung motionless and cast a gloomed shade over the city as if in forewarning of the world's end. The tourists still came, many to worship, for this was the fourth Sunday of Advent, others to look and wonder. Some, the majority of whom would undoubtably have forsworn any impulse of an even remotely religious association, came nonetheless in the hope of finding something. Friendship. Happiness. Love. Whatever small miracle it took to touch a flame to the waiting candles of their lives. Was it too much to hope for?

Adam arrived eleven minutes early. He took up a position on the chequered marble terrace, beneath the Conversion of St Paul. From here, at the top of the double flight of granite steps and in the lee of a massive Corinthian column, he commanded a wide view of the cathedral forecourt and main approach.

Satisfying himself that Partridge had yet to arrive, or was at least not making himself visible, he took to observing the sightseers. On the forecourt an old drunk was endeavouring to entertain anyone who would give him a minute. He was unshaven and wore shabby handouts and a bowler. His repertoire seemed to consist of vocal renditions of various old standards alternating with snatches of Irish jigs and folk tunes played on a tin flageolet with a red plastic mouthpiece. His singing was maudlin and often wincingly off-key but he played his instrument with noticeable skill. Dirty, stumpy fingers flew nimbly over the stops and his feet simultaneously parodied dance as they worked to maintain his body at an upright angle.

At over-frequent intervals he would cease playing and swiftly whip off his hat and offer it around. This effectively dispersed any small crowd he might have attracted, but it gained him a few coins too, probably a not inconsiderable sum at the day's end.

Still no sign of Partridge. It was early but Adam was in the grip of a growing apprehension. He wished he had waited; he felt vulnerable here. He should have situated himself somewhere further away and less exposed and allowed Partridge to make his entrance first. But Partridge would probably take that tack too, creating the absurd situation of the two of them, hidden one from the other, each waiting for the other to make the first move.

No, the West Front, Partridge had said, so rather than prolong the agony, that was where Adam would be. He just hoped that his arriving early was not a fatal mistake.

The drunk drew his attention again. He was climbing the first flight of steps intent on pestering a two-family group chatting in Sunday best below where Adam stood. But he had also caught the vigilant gaze of an assistant virger stationed outside the West Door, who, whilst disapprovingly tolerant of the antics on the forecourt had evidently drawn a barrier at the foot of the steps. He descended quickly in his black gown, stern but a little bit muppet-like, and shooed the offender off.

The drunk stumbled away but in doing so caught his heel on the lip of a step. He toppled and sat down heavily, limbs all asplay, but somehow not losing hold of his flageolet.

He was unhurt and muttering comic but, mindful of location, mild imprecations, succeeded in gaining the vertical once more. He looked about him, at the assistant virger who, with the two families, had moved back to the top of the steps, and then at Adam. He winked, a sly wink, uncomfortably, intelligently intimate, superior and mocking. Adam found himself looking away.

Now the drunk placed the mouthpiece of his flageolet between his lips, but he did not yet play. Instead he crept with deliberately exaggerated cartoon-character steps up behind the assistant virger. Undetected, he delivered a shrill, blast into the man's right ear and darted away down the steps before anyone had time to react.

He looked back and grinned, then stumbled off across the forecourt towards a group of young tourists, Italians by the yell of their garb, gathered near Queen Anne's statue.

Adam spotted Simon Partridge. He was a good distance off, and in full view. A diminutive figure beneath the bright blue iron railway bridge at the foot of Ludgate Hill. His gait was noticeably hurried and as he came up the hill Adam could see that he was whistling while casting harassed glances all about him. His face was flushed and between the fingers of his right hand he held a cigarette.

He was dressed in fashionable and highly unsuitable leisure-wear. A spanking new beige and green blouson was zipped to the throat; light grey tracksuit bottoms were drawn at the ankles.

The trousers, intended as loose fitting, had in fact to stretch around his plump thighs and buttocks and were longer than his short legs. On his feet he wore red and white running shoes and tucked beneath one arm was a tennis racquet in a matching Slazenger case. Crowning the outfit was an American baseball-player's peaked cap. He was a universal butt.

Opposite the cathedral, outside a firm of solicitors' premises, Simon Partridge paused at the kerb to allow a couple of tourist coaches to crawl past. Then he crossed the road with quick mincing steps, the cigarette jutting stiffly from between his fingers, heading directly towards Adam's position though he had given no indication of having seen him.

He had to alter his course slightly to get around the young Italians who were enthusiastically encouraging the drunk's version of 'The Rose of Tralee'. As he did so the Irishman launched into an instrumental on his flageolet, attempting to accompany himself with a spritely dance, hopping first on one leg and then the other.

The Italians laughed and applauded but the piper, inevitably, lost his balance. He careened backwards, still playing and swivelling at an angle as he tried to right himself, and crashed into the passing Partridge.

Partridge, who was looking elsewhere at the time, leapt nervously and dropped his racquet and cigarette. The drunk scrabbled about on hands and knees. The Italians giggled. Partridge, at first frightened, looked flustered, then angry. He bent to retrieve the racquet and dusted himself down. Then, circling wide of the Irishman, he continued on his way, limping slightly and one hand massaging the side of his neck.

He came up the steps.

'Mr Shatt!' His hand was still at his collar. 'You saw that? Damned oaf! He landed right on my instep and caught me with the tip of that tin whistle.' He withdrew the hand and inspected the tips of his fingers. 'Sharp, too. I don't know why people like that aren't made to clean the streets or something. Something useful.'

He had positioned himself behind the pillar a yard or so from Adam and was pointedly not looking at him, speaking in a low voice as if to the wall.

Adam had little interest in his opinion of the drunk. 'You have something to tell me?'

'Yes, I have.' Partridge's bright little eyes swiftly assessed the terrace. 'Something to show you, too.'

He eased his left shoulder up and gingerly backwards in a circular motion, grimacing before responding to Adam's intensely demanding gaze. 'Evidence, of a sort. I've managed to secure documents. I think they will persuade you as to the veracity of some of my earlier statements. I also have a couple of names.'

'Names?' Adam leapt on him. 'Who? Tell me!'

But Partridge shook his head. 'It isn't wise here.'

He looked down at the floor then screwed up his eyes and blinked blearily several times. He seemed tired. The bright flush that had burned his cheeks had faded rapidly. 'I suggested this location because the most conspicuous can often be the least . . .' He eyed Adam now in a curious manner '. . . the least obvious. But we mustn't stay.'

Partridge passed a hand around the back of his neck, rolling his head against it, then rested it on the fluted, acid-pitted stone of the column. 'I've instructed a cabbie to wait . . . at the back of Ludgate Court. Follow me, thirty seconds behind. It will be better.'

He made to move off, swayed, and had to reach out again for the column. 'Gosh,' he said in a breath, and hung his head. 'Do you know, I – I think I might have overdone it this morning. I've come over . . . woozy.'

'Are you all right?' Adam said.

'I . . . I think so.'

But he evidently wasn't. As Adam stepped around and put a hand to his elbow Partridge's brow contracted in pain. He was panting, short, shallow breaths. He lifted his eyes, with difficulty it seemed, and focussed them questioningly on Adam. His mouth hung open.

'Partridge? What's wrong?'

Partridge stared a moment longer. His face was ashen and poured suddenly with sweat. 'Oh. Oh God,' he said. The question that was in his eyes resolved itself. He turned and looked back out over the cathedral forecourt, shaking. He no longer seemed to have full control of his body. When his gaze returned to Adam's the eyes held a glazed panic.

Partridge's legs folded beneath him.

Adam caught him under the arms. He lowered him to the flags, supporting his head and shoulders. 'Partridge! Simon!'

Partridge's eyes rolled, he let out a rasping sigh and his head fell to one side.

'Simon, is there anything I can do?' The face was a shock to see now. The skin had turned a mottled grey and a thick white salivation had gathered around purple lips. The sudden sweat had soaked his hair and still streamed from all his pores. His eyes found Adam again.

'Mr Shatt.'

'Yes. I'm here.'

'Tell her.'

'Tell her what?'

The lips trembled as he fought to form words. His eyes strained to maintain their focus on Adam.

'She . . . she must . . . know.'

'What? Know what?'

'I . . . loved her.'

It was too much like the movies. Adam stared, devoid of an appropriate response. 'I'll tell her,' he said, and Partridge stiffened. His face contorted in a spasm of pain, the eyes rolled upwards in their sockets once more and he lay still.

Adam leaned over him. There was no breath. No heartbeat. He looked up to take stock of his situation. One or two persons were directing curious glances his way but mercifully none gave indications of wanting to get involved.

The same thought that had evidently struck Simon Partridge just seconds earlier came to Adam. He twisted his body and looked out over the cathedral forecourt. The Irish piper was nowhere in sight. He turned his attention back to Partridge's body, lifting the head and tilting it slightly to one side. It was there, low on the side of the neck, below and behind the ear, within the first sparse pale short hairs. A tiny red pinprick.

A figure materialized alongside him. 'Can I help?'

It was the muppet-like assistant virger, shyly grinning and crinkle-browed.

'Stay with him,' replied Adam curtly. He slipped his hands from beneath Partridge's head and shoulders. 'I'm his doctor. I must get my bag.'

The assistant virger took the weight and Adam rose. He quickly descended the steps and turned into St Paul's Churchyard. There he quickened his pace, cutting through the deserted shopping centre. Emerging onto Newgate Street he spotted a number twenty-two bus which he ran for, caught, and stayed with to its Putney Common terminus.

Now, as he wearily circumnavigated the great city plaza where the ruined church rested between the glittering facets of its new self, ersatz village clustered around its feet, as the snow, whipped and spuming in the wind, distracted and half-blinded him, Adam reproached himself for having neglected to search Simon Partridge's corpse. The old Adam would have done it on reflex, swiftly and unobserved. Partridge had said he had documents. The racquet case was such an obvious receptacle. He had mentioned names; he could have had them written down. But Adam had panicked and made off empty-handed, without so much as a glimpse of a prize.

Consolation took the coldest forms: what practical value could documents have now? He had long suspected deceit, he had long felt himself snagged at the centre of an invisible web of manipulation and disinformation. Partridge had supported this and the only real surprises had come when he had learned the identities of the organization and personalities involved, and the fact that he had once been a willing partner. Now, with the deaths of the two men who had tried to help him, he needed no further proof of the lengths these people were prepared to go to keep him from discovering the truth about himself. The documents might have served to bolster Adam's confidence in Simon Partridge as an ally – hardly a matter for consideration now – but they could have done little else.

And names? Similarly, he knew he could trust virtually no one. Could specifics have told him any more?

His past remained beyond his reach yet never ceased to exert its malign influence over everything he attempted. But there was real consolation to be had. Out of the deep obscuring fog he was just beginning to descry the subtlest of clues, indications that perhaps not everything was as far distant as it had been.

The strange wave of sensation he had experienced when he had taken Simon Partridge's telephone call, for instance. And, more telling, the fact that he now recognized that on the steps of St Paul's he had not acted as he would formerly have done. *This was knowledge of himself as he had been.*

He dragged his body on through the nightlife around the rim of the plaza. He lacked any notion of direction or destination but felt he had to keep moving, following an instinct. He was here for a reason, he had to be, and providing he did not allow himself to stop, providing he did not succumb to his exhaustion or his fear, the reason must at some point present itself.

He tried to keep a rhythm to his pace, slurred and uneven though it was. The rhythm helped his brain keep ticking over, helped the thoughts to keep forming out of the dream-delirium through which he struggled. If he kept moving he would find something, if he ceased something would find him. Terror or discovery, illumination or death. Why was he so certain he had been here before?

He left the plaza and entered a wide street, another world, poorly lit and deserted, silent in comparison. There were no shops, no cafes, no warm and welcoming interiors, nothing to distract him from the ever present snow. It fell more heavily here, or so it seemed. It was a wall through which he somehow moved. And he moved on, leaden feet barely leaving the ground, and pushing, pushing forward.

After some yards, as his eyes adjusted to the darkness, he began to make out physical features. To his right, behind high fencing and hedge, some kind of parkland. Visibility was too restricted to see much detail but there were small, low-roofed buildings inside high-fenced enclosures, and criss-crossing snow-covered pathways. Possibly a detention-centre of some kind, or an open prison; but something about these descriptions did not fit and it puzzled him. Then he grew conscious of the smell, a rich, feral, faecal odour that even the snow could not keep down, and the answer came immediately. A zoo, locked in silent night, its detainees shut away in their communal cells.

On the other side, when the wind parted the snow sufficiently, he saw an elevated railway which ran parallel with the street. He recalled having passed a station back near the plaza. For some distance the road and railway hugged one another along the same straight course, then the road curved at a right angle and cut beneath the track. A bicycle path led off to Adam's right, staying with the railway, and he took it without pausing to think, entering a new intensity of darkness. The line loomed above him to one side, the zoo's precincts, lost to sight now, dropped away slightly to the other.

The snow had formed into drifts a foot or more deep in places along the path. Though it was generally shallower at the midpoint where he walked, it was soft and untrodden and more tiring to walk through. His feet were frozen and wet. His overcoat too, well-lined but only showerproof, had begun to soak in the snow and felt heavier as a result.

He forced his body on, muttering, singing to himself, anything to hold on to consciousness, to keep himself moving. He crossed a wooden footbridge, slippery beneath his feet, which spanned a frozen canal. Another path led him over a second bridge and then he was in forest. An absorbing darkness gathered suddenly about him, seemingly sucking him into it. He could see nothing, nothing but the grey flecked blur of snow against the dense black backdrop.

It gave him the sickening illusion of movement. Instead of the snow falling he was rising, on a tiny island in a vast wild emptiness. Then, as the wind took the snow in all directions at once, the motion became slewed and lurching. He cried out as nausea swept through him, flailing with his arms until a hand smashed against the trunk of a tree. Then another. He hugged the tree, sinking to his knees, afraid to release it lest he be dragged back into the void.

Gradually his senses returned and he grew aware of the silence here. It was unexpected and complete. Not even the wind in the trees, just the startling internal roar of his own breathing. It was pleasant just to lie there. The snow was soft and comforted him and he was sliding into a warm drowsiness, wanting nothing more than to sleep. But he could still recognize the signs of exposure and slowly forced himself back to his feet, and moved on again between the trees.

The path was no longer discernible but he remained aware of it by blundering from it into the trees or undergrowth on either side. When this happened he would have to relocate the path by touch, sometimes almost on his knees. Twice he stumbled and fell and it was only by the sheerest effort of will that he was able to resist the temptation to lie where he was and sleep. His overworked limbs protested, his mind cried for rest, but a deeper part of him took charge and made him move on. The path was endless and he could not guess where it was leading him. He was lost and did not know if he was wandering deeper and deeper into a frozen wilderness from which he could not hope to return. Where was he?

Back in London. The final spur that had persuaded him – as if Partridge's murder was not persuasion enough – that he had to flee. He had needed somewhere to stay for the night. With the knowledge he had he could no longer consider returning home, and very few places offered sanctuary.

He had found a public call box and was on the point of calling Helmut, whose silence had been unbroken since the evening he had shown up invited but completely forgotten for dinner. The lack of communication implied that Helmut was still away somewhere but Adam wanted to confirm it for himself. It was not unusual for Helmut, when he was writing or engaged upon some particularly absorbing task, to shut himself away for days on end.

He did not get as far as dialling the number. Something occurred to him which stopped the blood in his veins. *They knew Helmut!* Doctor Geld and his thugs. *They knew everyone with whom he had even the remotest connection. Judith. Oh God, why Judith?*

Which meant that anyone he might think of contacting would be in very grave danger.

The second factor in the equation – Helmut's silence – broke through from its resting place. Adam groaned. He reeled from the telephone box, wild-eyed. An elderly lady out walking a pair of white toy poodles halted in her tracks and regarded him with haughty disquiet. He barely saw her. Before his eyes was a vision of his friend lying in a pool of blood, surrounded by his crew of teddy bears, on the floor of his pokey Victoria sitting-room. They would have killed him within hours of Dennis. He had no way of checking. Victoria was out of the question, and whilst he had addresses or telephone numbers of a couple of Helmut's friends, they were at home, and he could not take the risk of contacting them anyway.

He made his way up the suburban Putney street, observed, he was vaguely aware in some distant corner of his mind, by the lady with the poodles. Apart from her there was no one about. The afternoon sky remained overcast, little light managing to penetrate the heavy cloud cover. There seemed to be nowhere left to go.

A hotel would provide shelter but he needed more than that. He craved company. Human contact. Warmth. Sanity. He had to tell somebody, to describe his helplessness, his confusion to somebody who would sit quietly and listen in sympathy. Someone dispassionate and sufficiently distanced from the nightmare he would reveal to enable them to apply a rational and realistic perspective to his experience. He needed to be told he was dreaming, that all of this was the illusory product of his own distraught psyche, that he was mad, if you like. Just as long as he could be assured that it wasn't real and would soon be over. Just as long as somebody would take him in their arms and hold him tight and rock him back and forth till he slept like a babe.

There was one person. It might be a mark of his insanity that he could even think of it, he could not judge. His desperation dispelled objections he would have raised at any other time. This was the only course still open to him.

He had arrived at the once sedate residential Kensington street shortly after dusk. As much as possible of the afternoon had been spent nursing a fruit juice in a nondescript Putney pub off the riverside. At throwing-out time he had taken refuge in a local cinema and waited, oblivious to the programme, for the psychological and actual cover of descending night.

Had he been looking for it he would have been aware of the flashing blue light before he entered the street. It played faintly off walls, trees and windows, but his thoughts were elsewhere and it wasn't until he came around the corner that he noticed the patrol car, a ragtag knot of people gathered near it. It was parked at the side of the road, outside the house he had come to visit.

Better judgement advised immediate withdrawal, but he couldn't. Not until he knew. He approached cautiously on the opposite pavement. There was a uniformed officer at the front door of the house; the door was partly open and the light from the hall gave him a glimpse of other figures in plain clothes moving about inside. A second uniformed policeman sat at the wheel of the stationary patrol car and the pavement in front of the house was cordoned off.

Adam watched from the shadow of a cypress for some seconds, judged it safe and moved up to join the ghoulish assembly. All eyes were expectantly on the exterior of the house, and in particular, he realized with a tightening of his stomach, at the twin rectangle of curtained-off light that was the front window of the ground-floor flat.

He listened to the whispered conversation around him but could make out little, even less from the garbled chatter of the car-radio. So he asked an old man standing next to him, a neighbour if the red carpet slippers on his feet were anything to go by.

'Murder!'

It was said in a hushed voice but with hardly contained relish. Adam's world dropped away. There was only himself and the old man he addressed, whose hairless face and intense watery stare were illuminated on and off by the revolving blue lamp like a mask at some bizarre fancy-dress ball.

'Who? Who's been murdered?'

'Young girl.' The rubber tip of the old man's walking-stick lifted some inches from the road's surface, prodded towards the ground-floor window and dropped again. 'In there.'

His desire to say more was written large across his features but he held a respectful silence. A thin, maculate hand wobbled in agitation on the handle of his stick. The police lamp continued to blink disconcertingly. *Why the hell didn't they turn it off!*

'Do you know her?' Adam gently prompted, trying to steady the emotion in his voice and inadvertently holding the victim in the present, living tense.

'Tart,' the old man said as if it explained and perhaps even went some way towards justifying everything. He quickly covered himself. 'Not a bad girl, mind you. Don't get me wrong, I'm not saying that. She always used to stop for a chat when she saw me. I gave her some tomatoes once, out of the garden. But she got down on her luck, you know. I've seen her in some states, and it wasn't just the bottle, I don't think. I felt sorry for her, but what can you do? She had to pay the rent, didn't she.'

'Do they know who did it?'

'Hmph!' The old man's jaw clamped hard. He glared at the kerbstone near his feet. 'One of her, you know, watchemecallits. One of her "*clients*". Had to have been.'

'They haven't arrested anyone then?'

The old fellow shuffled a degree closer to Adam, leaned into his ear. 'Must've been a right nutcase. I overheard two of those policemen. Inside. They were shook up. It wasn't just a murder.'

He drew back, leaving a gaping silence which Adam, turning cold, had to fill. 'What do you mean?'

'Well, he had his way, see, but not in the normal way. Not like you or m – ' He checked himself. 'Not like a normal chap would.'

His stage pauses were infuriating. He waited now, his eyes on Adam. Nobody could accuse him of being a blabbermouth. Adam sang for his supper. 'What did he do?'

The old man nodded. 'Used a knife.'

'A knife?'

'Did it with a knife. Terrible things. Then left her propped on the bed with her throat cut.' A new thought played briefly across the old neighbour's face. 'Are you from one of the papers?'

He had emerged from the forest onto a whitened road which cut a broad swathe across his path. At his left shoulder a tall statue loomed suddenly out of the snow-blurred dark, a composite of beasts and heroes locked in mortal combat. He paid no heed to its detail. He dragged himself across the road, though following it would have been preferable, and re-entered the forest on the other side.

If it was possible the darkness was deeper here. Nothing moved, the wind had died. The trees were packed more closely, the path even narrower than the one he had left. The snow crunched softly under his step and he heard his own voice saying over and over again, 'Now is the time, now is the time, now is the time . . .'

The path took him over another footbridge, along the wooded strand of a frozen black lake, out onto another wide and empty road. This too he crossed and once more entered the forest.

He did not know how much further he had walked before it came to him that he could see again. The trunks and branches of trees were plainly visible for some distance around him, standing out against the snow. Lime, beech, birch, conifers, oak. The path through them stretched ahead, latticed with the delicate and strangely beautiful plexus their shadows cast. Everything was bathed in a soft silvery luminescence.

The snow had stopped, along with the wind. The great pall that smothered the heavens had passed on, and with the passing of the last stormcloud a full moon had burst resplendent into the clear night sky.

Adam stared, wonderstruck with the sudden beauty of it all. The chiaroscuro of tangled shadow-work, deep black over the silvered white-blue counterpane of snow, opened out on all sides, occasionally stirring like a living thing as a last ripple of breeze played through the branches. In the moonlight the snow was fired with innumerable tiny coloured lights, and far overhead the velvet sky was lit with an infinity of impossible stars.

Such a complete transformation was not lost on him. It had a profound and deeply moving effect. The sudden shifting of opposites, the emergence from a state of terrifying chaotic darkness into one of indescribable beauty touched something deep within him. It was some time before he moved on and when he did he walked with a lighter step, still weary but aware again, without the biting wind, of the warm blood flowing in his veins. His spirits had risen and if his destination was still a mystery he was at least rid of the feeling of wandering in a void.

A hundred yards or so further on he stepped from the trees. A new obstacle confronted him, this one man-made and possibly the last thing he had expected to find. It was a wall, ten or eleven feet high, rising abruptly out of the snow-covered earth. It was constructed from smooth up-ended slabs of concrete crowned with bullnose coping and coloured with a variety of graffiti.

In the moonlight it stood out starkly and disquietingly, stretching away to left and right in a straight unbroken line as far as he could see. Between Adam and the wall was a steel mesh fence of lesser height. It had been ruptured close to where he stood, and in other places he could see it had been pushed out of shape and bent close to the ground, presumably by the graffiti artists. Above the wall on the other side the tops of tall lamps were visible like strange spindly flowers, throwing down their light on a landscape that was hidden from him. Beyond the lamps he could see nothing but the cloudless night sky.

He knew where he was. Quite suddenly. Indeed, the signs were everywhere. He had been passing them ever since his arrival, on hoardings, in window displays of shops and stores, restaurants and bars. They were on streetsigns and hotels, at the railway station he had passed, at the entrance to the zoo. And for anyone who still failed to see it the city's name was written in the sky, neon-emblazoned on the tallest buildings as well as the lowest, in every conceivable brilliant colour and at just about every aspect. There was probably no other place on the planet so obsessed with promoting its own image. It was as though the city itself lacked a sense of identity, as though it too had suffered a great crisis and was fearful that without constant reminding it might lose sight of itself.

And he *had* been here before, more than once. He was not mistaken. He knew the place well. He stared at the wall, knowing that were he to turn now and follow it, in whichever direction, he would find no way around it. It had no end. He would walk and walk and after a march of some days and some hundreds of kilometres would find himself back here again, at the same point from which he had started out.

And he knew, or at least he thought he did, what it was that had brought him here.

Part Three

'Nothing is ever quite what it seems.
   And that's the truth.'

Iddio E. Scompiglio.

When the night is long and all rests upon the sleeper and the Earth; when the Mystery should be known but darkness lingers, the red snow will fall.

'He is living under eighty per cent delusion,' Doctor Geld said in answer to a question no one had yet asked. He took careful measure of his colleagues' reactions, Asprey's in particular, as they inspected the copies of the document he had passed them. 'Little of what he experiences is true. It's possible he may not even know where he is.'

Surprise was, unsurprisingly, written large on three faces – Mackelvoye's marginally less so: the psychiatrist had already briefed him by phone on selected aspects of the morning's agenda – but Geld knew he was treading a very trippy line. So he kept talking, in part to fend off his own impending breakdown of nerve, but mainly as a diversion, an irritation that might help keep at bay doubts or questions arising from a too close inspection of the document's contents.

'He has assumed the characteristics, to all intents and pur-poses, of a prototypical "Humean" being. Subjectively he is a bundle or collection of different sensations and perceptions succeeding each other with inconceivable rapidity and in a perpetual flux and movement. He – '

'That rather applies to each and every one of us, doesn't it,' Mackelvoye observed, his eyes on the paper. Doctor Geld gave a blank grin.

'That was Hume's intention. He was attempting to define Self. Or rather, repudiate it,' Judith told him.

'Yes.' Mackelvoye raised his eyes reprovingly. 'I know.'

'Well, it certainly describes you at the moment, Theodore,'

Asprey let fly. 'For God's sake, man, you're as jittery as a tomcat in a dog's home. What's the matter with you? Pull yourself together, and do stop waffling.'

The macerated stump of an extinguished cigar pitched and tumbled between his lips as his eyes for the nth time ran over the printed sheet he held. Clearly, as Geld had had no problem in anticipating, he was displeased by what he read.

'How did you find him?' he demanded.

'Who, the Apostle?' responded the psychiatrist deliberately.

'No, Gard, you fool!'

'I can assure you it was not easy. Ha-ha! A case of sheer persistence in the face of determined indisposition.' Geld had begun to perspire freely. He did not wish to be drawn on the details of his encounter with Gard. Certainly he could not risk revealing anything of the means by which he had come to possess this paper, nor those others he had prepared and set aside for back-up as and when it should be required.

If the truth be told he was still somewhat in awe of himself as he recalled how, in the subdued light of that redly illumined private cubicle, he had sedated the demoralized and unprotesting Gard; how, on the firm leather couch so conveniently positioned for the application of therapies far removed from any he was accustomed to administering, he had quickly and with a deftness born of long practice, placed his broken master under hypnotic reverie.

He could scarcely now believe the manner in which he, with parched throat and hammering heart, had escorted Gard from Society. They had drawn hardly a glance – and certainly not a censorious one – from the fetching young creature on reception.

Once outside in the cold night's embrace they had walked slowly, arm in arm, until Geld had spotted and hailed a taxi. They had driven the short distance to the anonymous grey St James's government block, paid the driver and entered, using Gard's access code, via the night-access door.

Higgins, the night security guard, had posed no problem. Sleepily compliant in the face of such authority he had willingly concurred to their directive that no record of their entrance or exit be entered in the register. Higgins was an old soldier and a good one; he could be counted upon to commit crimes of any magnitude providing he could claim, honestly, that he acted on orders from above.

Of course he would have to be taken care of. An operation such as this could not be allowed to balance on the shoulders of a nobody, and Doctor Geld had not wasted a minute in activating a pipeline which would this afternoon summon Higgins for a routine medical check. Geld himself, arranging an incidental inspection of the report, would detect the first indications of an illness which would call for Higgins's immediate hospitalization, and which would sadly prove fatal with unsuspected and brutal swiftness.

On the fifth floor, locked in Gard's inner sanctum, it had been a relatively simple matter for Doctor Geld to administer further sedatives and deepen his new patient's trance. He had then prepared the document the Angels were now reading, and the others he had anticipated he might need. Once done it was merely a case of obtaining Gard's impress and his signature in its customary green ink, and the job was done.

As a final precaution Gard himself had been removed to a secure cell in a wing of a safe hospital. With forged admission and sectioning papers he languished now, unbeknown to all, under the name of Ernest Turner, an impoverished thriller writer in the grip of premature senile dementia. He had after all been *in absentia* for so long that it would be days if not weeks before anyone thought to question his whereabouts. By that time Mr Turner would have been released back onto the street, his memory and quite possibly his brain destroyed by the strict diet of reserpine and aminazin that was his current regimen. In fact – Geld glanced anxiously at his fob watch – it would soon be time to fly off and top him up.

These things were very regrettable, but what could one do?

The doctor wiped his brow with a carmine foulard.

'Good,' Mackelvoye declared, and laid his copy of the document on the desk in front of him, smoothing it with the heel of one hand. Geld relaxed a little. He had known that failing a personal appearance by Gard this document was what the Deputy D-G most wanted to see. He counted on Mackelvoye's enthusiasm and ready acceptance to help dispel possible objections from other quarters.

Asprey shifted belligerently in his chair. 'Hmph! So Gospel rolls on as before. Nothing changes. Gard is in his heaven, or says he is, and all's well with the world, eh? Pity the poor bloody taxpayer, that's all I can say.'

Again Geld was hard put to hide his satisfaction. Asprey certainly did not like it but he did not seem to suspect anything.

'It's unlike you to empathize with the "poor taxpayer", Geoffrey,' Mackelvoye retorted. 'And as it happens he would have far greater cause for complaint were you to be given your way. Termination of Gospel at this stage would be an unjustifiable waste on all counts, not least expense. At least with Gard overseeing the operation again we have a chance of seeing it through.'

'To what end? The whole thing's a damp squib that can still blow up in our faces. We've lost control of our man and he could do anything. Anything at all. And what's our response to such a disaster? We watch, and we watch some more, and then dammit all if we don't blow further expenses by carrying on watching!'

'Precisely. We watch in readiness to move in on him the moment things show signs of getting out of hand. But whilst there's the slenderest chance – '

'And *Berlin*!' Asprey spluttered. 'What on Earth is he doing in Berlin? I mean, Belfast I could have understood, but why Berlin?'

'That is what we are trying to find out. He has been there many times before, as you know, in an operational capacity. But he seems to be making no attempt to reach any former contacts. We must assume an ulterior motive.'

'Or no motive,' Judith said. They turned, surprised.

'He's terrified,' she went on. 'Just look at it from his viewpoint. He's got no memory, he's hallucinating and delirious. Those he trusted have betrayed him, and those he has turned to for help have died. My God, what else can he do but run? Anywhere!'

Doctor Geld made a mental note of Judith's distress. It was evident in her face, voice, posture ... He said, 'There may be some truth in what Judith is saying. He may have had no specific reason for choosing Berlin, may have simply ended up there. As I've said, it is possible that he is not even capable of recognizing it and so does not know where he is.'

Nevus, who, since reading the purported missive from Gard,

had been unobtrusively polishing the lenses of his pebble glasses, now spoke. Without directing the question at anyone in particular, he said, 'Might I ask, when entering the city, was he by any chance riding on an ass?'

'Shut up, Nevus!' Mackelvoye fumed, and Nevus, shaking with suppressed mirth, slipped his glasses back on.

Asprey waved his dead cigar. 'Hold your horses, now! He has a point. Let's not be dismissive. What's the update on the miracle front? Anything new? And how about his holy ghost? Have we managed to trace the invisible man?'

'There are no developments in either case as yet,' Doctor Geld replied softly.

'I half-expected to hear that he'd revived the dead Partridge,' Asprey guffawed. 'That would have been a turn-up for the Good Book, wouldn't it! Oh, and in regard to that squealing wretch, by the way, that was a greatly improved job, Roger. Effective, simple, clean. The folk on high are suitably mollified. Just a pity you didn't get to him a tiny mite sooner.'

Wearily Mackelvoye passed a hand across his face and glanced across at Doctor Geld, whose features had darkened considerably.

'I wish we could all be in agreement on that,' he sighed.

'I think we are, aren't we?'

'We are not!' the doctor spluttered. He was suddenly beside himself. 'It was an unforgivable act! It should never have happened!'

Asprey swivelled in surprise. 'Theodore, what on Earth has gotten into you? You were as anxious as anyone to have done with him.'

'Have done with him, yes. But ...' the doctor now appeared speechless. Behind yellowing teeth his purple tongue could be seen to hurl itself repeatedly from side to side, giving his hoarse breathing an unusual sound.

'It's the location rather than the act,' Mackelvoye interceded on his behalf.

'I'm sorry, I don't think I understand.'

'Consecrated ground, Geoffrey. Theodore is profoundly upset at my failure to take that into account when I had Partridge taken out.'

'Oh Lord, is that all! We'll have it blessed on Sunday for you, Theodore, if that's what's bothering you.'

Geld gripped his papers and turned away. With chattering teeth he struggled to contain his emotions.

Mackelvoye, in a voice that had become tired beyond expression, said, 'You know, there was a rather terrible irony to this Partridge affair. His father was a top-flight chemist, you probably know that. He had a thriving business once, did regular research and development for us. Covertly, of course. Brilliant man, quite brilliant. Quite unlike his offspring.'

'Yes, I was aware of that,' Asprey said.

'Well, he ran into trouble. No head for business, as is often the case. The company foundered, and at about the same time Partridge senior found himself exposed in a rather unseemly episode involving some budding rose from a local prep school. It finished him off. Topped himself when it became public. That's how we came to take young Simon under our wing. Act of compassion, really.'

'I see,' said Asprey, puzzled. 'I see.'

'No, you don't see, Geoffrey,' he bristled. 'In true Whitehall Liaison Director style you do not see at all, you just make out that you do. I hadn't finished. How can you bloody well see when no one's yet given you a peep at the bloody gorgeous view?'

'Pardon my breathing. Please carry on.'

'I was about to go on to explain that Partridge senior was involved in – headed the team, in fact – the development of certain chemical products utilized by us from time to time in a variety of circumstances. One in particular, one of his last, was a particularly efficacious method of sub-cutaneous assassination. So suited to our needs that we stockpiled it in some quantity. For a rainy day. Just as well we did, as it turned out.

'It was virtually undetectable, and devastatingly effective in minute amounts. A tiny droplet introduced into the bloodstream induces a fatal seizure within moments. And all traces pass from the body within a few more minutes. Partridge senior was justifiably proud of it. He christened it "Product O". I'm sure he would never in his wildest dreams have imagined that it would one day be used to kill his only son.'

'Ah,' commented Asprey with a respectful nod. He allowed a

second or two of silence to pass, then said, 'Well, a commendable job nevertheless. Not quite so happy about the whore, though. Angel Six again, I gather. Was that really necessary?'

Mackelvoye slowly massaged his eyes. 'She was just a whore, Geoffrey. Who's going to make a fuss?'

'Quite so. No, I was just querying whether there might be something seriously adrift with Six. I caught a glimpse of the police report. Not a pleasant read.'

'It's just his method,' Mackelvoye said.

'Can we discuss these matters at a more convenient time?' Judith intervened. 'We are supposed to be making decisions about Adam. I'd like to know what we are doing about him.'

'Well, if Gard is in the driving seat,' Asprey said archly, 'I suppose we just go wherever he takes us.'

'And where might that be?' enquired Nevus.

With an effort Doctor Geld gathered his inner resources. He was furious with himself for having lost control at such a critical juncture. He had drawn unwanted attention to himself at the worst possible time, when he needed to be maintaining an unflinching aura of knowledge and control. But his feelings on the matter were so aroused that even now he had to fight to remain calm.

'We have instructions,' he said through his teeth. 'With a fair insight into the Apostle's state of mind we can accept that he has seen, or been shown through, our subterfuge. He knows his world is not as we have tried to make it appear, so he is seeking to escape us and find some imagined truth. He – '

'If he knows who we are,' Asprey interrupted, 'and, as would seem likely, now knows something of who he is, or was, why has he not simply come back to us like a good chap?'

'He's a different person,' Judith explained as though addressing an obtuse child. 'Can't you understand that? We cannot judge Adam by what he was. However little or much he really knows about us and his past relation to us, he is not going to come back. Ever. We represent everything he would now repugn.'

Asprey puckered his brow. 'He'll become his old self again, won't he? With time? I mean, it's hardly credible, is it. Such a complete personality change. Theodore?'

'"Two souls, alas, are housed within this breast,"' the doctor replied.

'What?'

Mackelvoye, nodding, completed the quote. '"And each shall strive for mastery there." Faust, Geoffrey. Have you forgotten?'

Asprey scowled.

'Matters of the mind can be remorseless in their defiance of intellectual analysis,' Geld informed him. 'In view of the intelligence we have I would not be unduly surprised if, even with the return of genuine memories, the Apostle came to regard us as his enemies rather than his friends.'

Asprey threw open his arms. 'And yet we still let him run around freely? In another country, dammit! He could be passing Gospel to anyone! Gard's instructions, Theodore. Enlighten us.'

From a folder inside his briefcase Doctor Geld withdrew another document. He did not pass it out. He was in possession of the only copy and eager to retain it. He held it up to his face. In the event of anyone's demanding an inspection of its contents after he had read them out he had calculated that the single copy would prove a valuable hindrance to their appraisal. With all four, or at least three, vying to view simultaneously, their attention would be distracted in his favour.

'Gard has sanctioned certain precautions,' he announced. 'To wit: "Surveillance to be tightened; select teams to be on alert and ready to pick up target at any time. A Specialist to be sent out to make contact. As a further safeguard a device to be emplaced providing access to instant termination should the nature of the situation demand such."'

'A device?' Judith queried.

'A remotely-controlled explosive device,' Mackelvoye explained gently, 'satellite tracked and activated, to be planted on or about his person. It's a fall-back, a last resort. Nobody wants to employ it, but if we should lose him, or he should lose control, run amok or try to take Gospel to the other side . . .'

Doctor Geld added, 'Be assured, my dear, we are not treating this lightly. Ha-ha! But events as they stand create a need for a reflexive response capacity to any situation that may arise.'

Geld himself was far from overjoyed at this latter inclusion, but his pragmatism had opened his eyes to its advisability. Apart from anything else it would do much to keep Asprey at bay.

Judith's eyes had reddened. 'How can you plant something like that without his knowledge?'

'That does present a problem,' Mackelvoye acknowledged. 'Ideally it would be placed by someone he knows and trusts, but such persons are in lamentably short supply.' His voice contained no hint of reproach but Judith lowered her eyes; she fished in her sleeve for a tissue. 'It's impossible to determine precisely how short but we have to assume the worst. So the alternative is to get him as he sleeps, or arrange an accident or diversion of some kind. Something that will permit emplacement without arousing his suspicion. But we will make every effort to bring him home first.'

'And who has responsibility for the device?'

'Its activation? It will be a joint decision, taken and subsequently executed here, in this room.'

'And the Specialist?' Judith asked, her voice trembling.

Mackelvoye said it with obvious reluctance. 'Angel Six.'

Nevus chuckled.

Judith raised her eyes. 'Why Six?'

'There is no one else. You know that. Six fits the bill on several crucial counts.'

'With what orders, then?'

'That upon word from us the Apostle should be contacted and every endeavour made to persuade him back. That failing verbal persuasion the device should be emplaced, thus enhancing our future response capability. And that, in the event that it is not successfully planted, or for other reasons cannot be activated and termination becomes necessary, whatever measures it requires should be employed to bring about Gospel's swift and expedient conclusion.'

'You see, Mr Asprey, we are not as you seem to think, eager to place ourselves at risk,' Doctor Geld sang out loftily. 'Termination is never out of the question, but neither do we run to it with the alacrity you prescribe.' In deference to Judith he then went on, 'By its very nature the device can have the effect of preventing Gospel's demise. Safe in the knowledge that we have the means to instant termination at our fingertips we need not overreact to every minor crisis that turns up.'

Asprey rubbed his jaw thoughtfully. 'All things considered, though,' he said, also with a sidelong glance in Judith's direction, 'do you really think Six is the best person for the job?'

'That question has already been answered, Geoffrey,' Mackelvoye answered tersely, and Asprey, with a shrug, took a fresh cigar from his inside breast pocket and did not pursue the subject any further.

Doctor Geld, all tremble and sweat, shuddered with relief and made ready to escape.

'If there's nothing else . . .' he pressed shut his briefcase. '. . . I have a clinic to attend.'

A mood had descended. The machines were silent, the baffler hummed, the air was close and still. The others, too, were keen to be away.

Whilst . . .

It was in Berlin that Adam's second miracle was performed.

Again it was unanticipated, and certainly unpremeditated; again it was in a crowded place and he removed himself quickly from the scene, sensing a dazed but predacious fascination if not actual antagonism in the air. Again he walked away with a feeling of walking on air. He was exhilarated and perplexed, cognizant of a potent, unseen energy that could not be measured.

This time there was no sighting, either real or hallucinatory, of the brutish Slav and his pet. Neither did he give them any thought.

And it was within hours of this that Judith, back in London, arriving home exhausted and depressed, was subject to an experience she would never satisfactorily explain.

Berlin, divided, enveloped in cold, became a place of dilemma and renewed uncertainty. Recalling his purpose in coming here and knowing something of what he was about, hardly eased Adam's fears. Ruth, whose almost illegibly scrawled address he had transferred from its damp and tattered paper scrap into a newly-purchased and less easily misplaced pocket-address book, was a wholly unknown quantity.

He balked now that he was here, so close. He was afraid of what she represented to him, what she might, or might not, turn out to be.

At times he reproached and even ridiculed himself for having made the journey at all: his reasoning was untenable, this was further evidence of his advanced dementia. He was about to make an utter fool of himself and witness the shattering of all his hopes in the process. For Ruth, whom he had after all spoken no more than ten words to at a party, would not know him, would find herself confronted by a maniac at her door and would be alarmed and perhaps terrified by his anguished entreaties for information she could not possibly possess.

But at better moments he reassured himself that this could not be so. She had to know him, he could not doubt it. But in what capacity? *Why* would she know him, and what would she know?

And more importantly, perhaps, her companion, that silent unworldly character who had observed Adam and dogged his footsteps, *making no secret of it.*

Who the hell were they?

He could not entirely dismiss the possibility that they were in league with Geld and the others. Judith's response in the aftermath of the Scompiglio business had been no source of comfort. And with what he knew of his wife's duplicity he could give her words only token credence. But if Ruth and her companion were part of the same vast incomprehensible conspiracy then any last vestige of sanity, logic or hope fell away. There would be no more point in running, fighting, hiding, seeking . . . no point in anything. He could, given the opportunity, deny them their final triumph over him as a last desperate act, but that was all. And that would leave the mystery unsolved; and whilst he could contemplate it he was not sure that he could willingly commit himself with such a condition still prevailing.

The final possibility that struck him concerning Ruth was this: that he would find, when he got to her door, that someone had been there before him. He shuddered at this. It seemed that the cost of his continued freedom was the deaths of others; the vilest and most paradoxical blackmail – for he could not give himself up to save them. That was not what was demanded of him.

His hope in this respect was that his whereabouts were as yet unknown in London. He had to take the risk of contacting Ruth, she *was* his last hope. And whatever the outcome of his visit he really no longer had anything to lose.

But still he balked.

He had found a hotel. A cheap, for Berlin, decaying remnant of a more glorious era. A great granite staircase leading upwards between ornately carved oak balusters to long, hollow hallways behind monumental antique doors. The rooms were big, grimy and baroque, furnished with creaking, ill-matched beds, wardrobes, chairs, couches. The place had a permanent smell of Gallic cigarettes, and changing, unidentifiable cooking seeping from the private residences below. Odd snatches of conversation and television and radio broadcasts filtered through from the other rooms. The decor, warring purples, reds and oranges, crooked wallpaper, haphazard rugs and smeared, patchy paintwork, assaulted his senses in a dismal light.

He lay on his bed for a day and a night, being eaten by bugs, not sleeping. The room was overheated and stuffy. Outside the wind rattled and buffeted the window panes. His head was teeming with too many questions, but when he gave himself to one or another his concentration fled. In the ceiling a tarnished chandelier hung from a leaf-and-garland central boss, swaying from time to time in the erratic air currents, and somehow cast a bulbous shadow on one wall and part of the ceiling resembling the profile of a hanging baby.

And when at last the feeble grey light of another morning began to edge between the heavy red curtains into this mad, violent room, Adam sat up and remembered his hunger.

He had eaten nothing since his arrival. Gathering clothes which had mercifully dried over a radiator and hot-water pipes, he left the hotel. Outside the snow was falling heavily again. It was bitterly cold and the streets had not been cleared, which surprised him, making passage heavy for both pedestrians and drivers.

He found a cafe, a smoky, steamed-up place where predominantly immigrant workers gathered for coffee or schnapps before moving on to their respective trades. He ordered eggs, sausage, black coffee and bread rolls at the bar, speaking German effortlessly and not yet registering the fact.

And it was as he was moving away with the coffee, easing between the groups of sleep-subdued men to find an empty seat at a table, that he felt a sudden irresistible weight at his shoulder.

There was no time to react, he was knocked aside, the coffee cup flying from his hand and leaving him gripping the empty saucer. The body that had collided with him had fallen face down on the dirty floor. It was a man, dark and curly-haired, tanned skin. He writhed and jerked in a continuous spasm and Adam stared, too stupefied at first to understand.

Someone at his side bent quickly and rolled the man onto his back. The nose and upper lip were smashed and bloody from his impact with the floor. Little vermicules of blood and mucus mingled with the mucky wetness that had been traipsed in from the street. His eyes were open but rolled into his skull so that only the whites were visible. He seethed and shuddered helplessly as the man who had stooped to help him tried to insert the handle of a dessert spoon between his clenched teeth, cursing in Turkish then, looking up at Adam and not realizing he had understood, saying in German, 'I am sorry. He is my brother. He is epileptic.'

A space had cleared around them as others moved to avoid the convulsive kicking of the unconscious man's booted feet. And Adam for a split second tried to resist, fighting himself, unwilling to be involved. Then there was no thought, inhibition was gone, and he lowered himself onto one knee beside the epileptic and his brother.

'I can help.' He held out the saucer and somebody took it.

'You are a doctor?'

He nodded. He took the man's head in his hands whilst the brother supported the upper torso and shoulders.

It was swifter this time. The reluctance that in the woman had, perhaps by reason of gender, succeeded her initial apathy, was less of a contending force. And Adam knew more what he was looking for. His hands went to the man's upper spine, the fingers of one remaining alongside his head, pressing lightly to the temple and cranium. He quickly sensed what he sought, the subtle depleted vitality that was the man's own life force, blocked and dischannelled; a reservoir fallen into stagnation. And the energy burst from him like a bolt of electricity. It was so sudden that he too jerked violently, once, and let out an involuntary shout. The shout, too, was like a healing power expelled in conjunction with that which poured from his centre and leapt from his fingertips.

The seething breath ceased. The enspasmed limbs relaxed and the man sank into his brother's arms. The brother stared at him, stroking his brow, then turned to Adam, smiling but unsure. 'I have never seen anything like that.'

Adam straightened, breathing deeply. 'He'll be all right now.' He was trembling slightly. He felt warm and pleasantly tired and light-headed, his fingers tingling, his knees weak. He motioned to two men who, with the cafe's other customers, looked on undecidedly. 'Help him. Get him onto a chair.'

They moved to comply.

'Doctor,' the brother asked. 'What should I do?'

'Nothing,' Adam said. 'Give him water if you wish, if he wants it, but nothing else is necessary. He is in charge now. Clean up his face. He is not ill any more.'

He knew he could no longer stay in this place. He quickly slipped through the watching men and outside into the cold morning, confused, troubled, elated, his belly still empty.

Judith did not go straight to bed as she had intended. She was beyond tiredness and the thought of a mug of hot cocoa before settling between the sheets, which had seemed such a good idea during the late drive home, had lost its appeal. She could not hope to relax, let alone sleep.

Closing the front door behind her and barely shrugging off her coat to leave it lying where it fell, she went downstairs to the spare room where Adam had locked himself before slipping away to meet Simon Partridge.

She sat down on the bed, her head aching, her eyes red and puffy and sore with tiredness and tears, her thoughts clouded with a fog of uncertainty. It had all become too much.

Gospel – what did it mean? What had it turned into? What had *she* turned into? The depths of complicity and conspiracy to which she had somehow allowed herself to descend shocked her. It was as if she had been blind and deaf. She could visualize now the subtle escalation of events, the remorseless unfolding of a process that would, eventually, piling complexity upon complexity, swallow them all. It was of their own making. No one had possessed the foresight to envisage its development, and now it had taken on a life of its own, possessing them and manipulating them, keeping them so engrossed that escape was never even thought about, let alone sought.

What was it all for? She could not see any way through, had lost sight of any reason, any morally justifiable purpose in what they were doing. Pulled one way and then the other she no longer knew what was right, a condition she found insufferable. Uncertainty was a stranger to Judith, as it had been to her husband, before this. Now doubt ran through everything, everything she had ever believed in.

She sank slowly onto the pale blue coverlet and as her head touched the pillow her eyes closed. Her darkness teemed in agitation, flashing angrily, red-orange, black. Possibly her need actually blotted out consciousness for a second, a minute, two minutes, even five. But she came to a sensation of something alien, out of place, not as it should be, and was instantly awake.

It was another second or two before she located the source. Beneath the pillow where one hand had slipped, her fingers had come into contact with something cold, smooth and comparatively unyielding.

She withdrew it. It was a small notebook, Adam's. She must have failed to notice it when tidying the room after he left. She flipped it open. Printed on the first page, boldly, in writing that was unmistakably Adam's, was a single statement: 'I AM NOT NOR WILL I BE A MERE PARTICLE IN THE MASS, RULED ONLY BY THE MINDLESS SPIRIT OF GRAVITY'.

She stared at it for some time, acknowledging its Nietzschean derivation but recognizing too its relevance to Adam's plight. She turned the page.

On the next sheet he had written: 'THE EARTH IS MY MOTHER, I SHALL NOT HARM HER. I SHALL LOVE HER AND PROTECT HER. SHE BEARS OUR CHILD'.

There was nothing more. Judith let the notebook rest for a while beneath her hands on her lap before putting it aside. She left the bed and moved to the drawer in the base of the wardrobe where she knew Adam stored much of his writing. Kneeling to slide open the drawer she hesitated. Something made her stiffen. Something . . . an intimation of movement, perhaps, or a sensing of minute atmospherical change, or simply an intuition . . . made her turn her head. Adam was standing behind her, a few feet away at the foot of the bed, watching her expressionlessly.

Judith gasped.

'Adam! I thought – ' She shook her head. 'I thought you were in Berlin.'

For a moment her husband said nothing, and it came to her like a realization in a dream that there was something very strange about what was occurring, though she was not yet quite ready to grasp what it was.

Presently Adam spoke. 'Why, Jude?' he said quietly. 'Why have you done this?'

She rose unsteadily to face him.

'It's not a betrayal, darling. Understand that.' Fabrication now, anything short of plain-spoken truth, would be unforgivable. She could see that even in her confusion. He needed to know, and she had no more spirit for deception. 'You were part of it.'

'Gospel?' His voice was tired and distant. He was pale and haggard, but he regarded her with a fierce intensity. His long, dark, untidy hair was wet, as were his clothing and skin. She did not recall it having been raining when she came in. 'I know.'

'Adam, how much do you know? Do you know that we are not against you? That you don't have to run?'

He gave a forlorn smile and did not answer directly. 'I escaped, didn't I. After the experiment. I woke up and when I remembered what had been done I ran. That big house, in the country. That's where it happened.'

Judith nodded. '"Monkswood." It's in Oxfordshire. It was a private hospital, converted for Gospel's purposes.'

'"Monkswood", yes. A hospital with only one patient. A patient who went in believing himself healthy and came out sickened.

'It's been there, on the threshold of memory, for a long time, you know. But I couldn't grasp it. That nightmare had it all – when I ran, out across the grounds in the middle of the night into the fields, and the dogs were sent after me . . . It was in the lane. I was terrified. The dog was so close, and I didn't know there was a hedge preventing it reaching me. When the car screamed around the corner I must have walked right into it. It was the car that did all the damage, wasn't it. Northern Ireland was a total myth. That's what happened, isn't it. It was all neatly packaged in a nightmare.'

Again she nodded. 'You were lucky to live.'

'Jude, why didn't you ever tell me? You knew how much I'd suffered. You saw me, night after night. All this madness. You should have told me.'

Tears streamed down Judith's face. 'Geld said no. It was too risky. You had run away once, we couldn't risk your regaining your memory but not your loyalty. I had no choice, Adam. You must know that. I was like the others, like you used to be. I believed in what I was doing.'

'And now?'

'I don't know any more. I don't know. It's only now that I see the layers of self-delusion coming to the surface. You've made me look at things differently, question things I've never thought to question. And I see what you've been going through, and the person you are – and are becoming, still . . .' She held open her hands helplessly. 'You've changed. Everything has been turned on its head and I've begun to doubt, but oh God, even now I'm not sure.'

'Jude, tell me about our marriage,' Adam said. She started visibly.

'What – what do you mean?'

'Our marriage. There's something. A shadow. I don't know, it's just flashes. Tell me what it is.'

'I don't know, Adam. I love you. I loved you before all this. I love you more now. I'm afraid for you.'

Adam shook his head ruefully. 'Even now,' he said, 'you can't let yourself see. Your loyalty condemns you.'

He watched her in her distress, wanting to step forward and hold her.

'Adam, you must come back,' she wept. 'You have to. You won't be harmed. That's not what they want.'

She wiped her eyes. She could hardly see him any more.

'Goodbye, Jude.'

'Adam, wait!' There was such finality in his voice. 'Please!

Listen! The animals that preceded you, the test subjects, they're dying. There isn't any escape. Not your way.'

She reached out to touch him, but of course there was nothing there.

'Darling, take care,' she called feebly after him. 'I think we are going to kill you.'

She stood alone by the side of the bed. She pushed back her pale brown hair, her hand clutching the crown of her head, not knowing what to make of what had just transpired. Was she insane? The thought terrified her. She closed her eyes tight, then opened them and stared wildly about the room. A dream? It was so vivid. But she was overstressed and exhausted. She must have slept without knowing it. Fallen asleep even on her feet.

She could never have simply imagined it. She couldn't have. She could *not* have simply imagined it.

Could she?

Wedding

The Jewish woman, Ruth, had a smart two-bedroomed flat on the fourth floor of a modern apartment block just off Müller-strasse, in the Berlin city ward – still technically under French control – known as Wedding.

Contrary to expectations she had shown no surprise, let alone alarm, at finding the late Adam Shatt at her door. The opposite was more the case. She gave every indication of having expected him.

'The dreamer!' she had pronounced, smiling and holding wide her blue front door to give him entry. 'We wondered when you would arrive.'

Adam, supporting himself with one arm against the jamb, was deathly tired. He still had not eaten, having made his way here directly upon leaving the cafe. Warm air flooding out of the apartment gently cocooned him, carrying with it a mouth-watering smell of a recently prepared breakfast. He felt a dull prod, of indignation. Of all the responses he had calculated Ruth might evince this was one that had not presented itself for consideration. He felt instantly disadvantaged.

Thoughts passed in wild disorder. Uppermost was the idea that he was walking into a trap, but he questioned the need for her to set a trap when he had come here voluntarily. His head was muddled and he could not think anything through. He dismissed everything, he was past caring. He entered.

As Ruth closed the door behind him the warning bells were triggered in his skull. Something was wrong. His vision blurred. A rush of panic took him. The room rocked perilously, his knees buckled and he was hit by a sweep of sudden, violent nausea.

He turned to struggle back for the door, his hands groping ahead of him. Then strong arms encircled his chest, and he found he lacked the strength or the will for even a minimal show of resistance. His own voice was drowned beneath a pounding, roaring sound which grew in volume until he feared it would burst his eardrums, and then ceased abruptly, taking with it all sense of perception.

The picture which floated in a haze of indistinct forms was familiar. It had been before his eyes for a long time prior to his awareness either of its existence or his absorption in it. It was a Monet. A large detail from one of the mural-sized 'Waterlilies'. He felt drowsy and weak. He dreamed and saw things that weren't there as he was drawn into its deceptively placid depths.

Ruth sat close by, perched on the edge of an armchair in front and a little to the right of the one he was slumped in. She had a blue-and-white Japanese bowl on her lap and was feeding him hot soup with a china spoon she held to his lips.

She smiled softly when he looked at her. 'The dreamer awakes.' Then, with gently sardonic reproach, 'A man should not take on the day without a hearty breakfast. Especially days like these. You are asking for trouble.'

He sipped from the spoon and let his head rest against the back of the chair. His eyes returned to the Monet and he took refuge there rather than confront the inevitable. Ruth said, after a minute or so had passed, 'Do you want to take over now?'

She placed the soup bowl in his hands and he caught the faint scent of her perfume. It was subdued, a natural rather than commercial scent. White Musk? Evening Primrose? How would he know? He concentrated on the soup as she moved her chair back and settled more comfortably. She said, 'I'll get you something more substantial in a minute, if you think you can keep it down.'

She was not what he had imagined. At their first meeting she had come across – cast herself, he now thought – as a hippyish party girl. Shallow talk, inviting smile, lip gloss and too-too intoxication; someone he would have quickly forgotten had not events subsequently taken a more sinister turn.

But this was not the same person. Composed and self-assured, she sat easily before him in loose-fitting woollen check trousers, a broad-shouldered fern green wool cardigan, cream blouse and house sneakers. She wore a slender gold chain at her neck and a matching bracelet on her left wrist. She wore no rings on her fingers. Her long, dark-auburn hair was thick and lustrous, falling freely past her shoulders.

Her face was slightly asymmetrical in form. One eye was a little larger than the other, and her smile, which seemed never to be far from her lips, tended to rise more towards the left. The eyes were bright and olive green, almond-shaped, and reflected the smile on her lips. Her skin was fresh and clear with little makeup. She was an attractive, feminine woman with an aura of self-motivation. There was nothing nervous or irresolute in her attitude; her brightness and vitality coupled with a healthy, secretive amusement gave the impression that for her life was a game, one which she played earnestly and with vigour, but a game nevertheless. And she had control.

Her surroundings supported his overall impression. The decor was an example of creative elegance and understatement, tasteful, restful and stimulating, nowhere ostentatious. Everywhere, it seemed as he looked around, there was something to attract and please the eye. Paintings and framed photographs; bookshelves filled with books on art, philosophy, works of literature and poetry; intriguing ornaments and objets d'art. But there was no clutter, nothing out of place or overplaced. The room had an air of comfort married with space.

All this in contradistinction to the impressions he had conjured up from their initial encounter, which had later gained flesh with Dennis's written account of the woman. Sloppiness and disarray had suggested themselves as a natural milieu: the paraphernalia of seances or popularized mysticism; incense-holders, candles, Tibetan or Nepalese hangings, mandalas, pentagrams; misty-eyed gurus peering down from wall-posters and bookshelves; unfinished paintwork, unwashed dishes, indications of soft drug use. But there was none of it. Nothing more mysterious than a couple of ornamental Buddhas, in sandalwood and soapstone, and a tatami exercise mat placed in one corner.

In a sense this deepened his dilemma, for it made her an even greater enigma to him. Sphinxlike, she represented an incalculable danger, and he, knowing nothing, was obliged to place himself in her hands. While one part of him looked around and took heart from the signs of balance and order that surrounded him, another reminded him that he must at all times be guarded, that he could trust no one, not even himself, and that he should feel his way forward with extreme caution.

All of this passed through his mind as he cleared the soup bowl of its contents. Then he put the bowl aside and asked her, 'How did you know I was coming here?'

Ruth shrugged loosely and her smile played engagingly across her lips. 'Did you have a choice? I think it was really only a matter of time.'

Adam scowled. It was hardly a satisfying answer. It told him nothing and he sensed a cat-and-mouse game of the type he knew too well – direct questions, indirect answers. Ruth was in a position to toy with him if she chose, there was little he could do about it and he felt beaten before he'd even begun.

'Do you know what has been going on?'

'Yes.'

'Everything?'

She shrugged again. 'Everything it is necessary to know, yes. But the peripheral details are not what concern me.'

'"Peripheral" details? What do you consider "peripheral"?'

'I can't tell you that at the present time. It would be unfair. I could not expect you to understand.'

Adam frowned, an anger rising inside him. 'Would it help if I gave you a few examples to choose from, and then you can tell me which ones you consider "peripheral" and which you deem worthy of your concern. Murder, for instance. Is that peripheral?

The brutal murders of persons whose sole crime seems to be that they were associated with me?'

Ruth waited as if considering a reply, but he gave her no opportunity. 'Or let's try something else more subtle. Let's try the engineering of consciousness. The systematic destruction of personality, the depriving a person of his mind. All government sanctioned. The deliberate inducement of insanity, the denial of a man's soul, his *being*! The theft of his past and the substitution of a false one. The grotesque denial of all basic human rights in favour of so-called advancement in the name of science, or is it power? Are any of these things deserving of your consideration? Or are they too merely "peripheral"?'

He had come forward onto the edge of his seat, gripping the arms. He was uncomfortably hot and sensed that he was on the verge of raving. Ruth was not disconcerted.

'I am sorry, deeply sorry about the deaths of those three. I had nothing to do with it, I promise you, but neither could I have intervened. In none of it could I have intervened, though I wish it were otherwise.'

'But you know something!' Adam accused her. His voice grew louder. 'Who the hell are you? And your friend!' He looked about him wildly. 'Where is he?'

'My friend?'

'At the party! Where is he?'

'Ah, so you did see him,' Ruth said, almost in a whisper.

'You said you were expecting me! You said he was here!' Adam rose suddenly and launched himself across the room, flung open the nearest door. 'I want to see him! Why is he hiding?'

The door let into a bedroom. A quick glance revealed no one. He wheeled and furiously made for another door but was overcome with dizziness and had to reach out for the wall. He hung his head between his shoulders as the room spun.

Ruth left her seat and crossed to his side. 'Come on, sit down.' Supporting him by one arm she guided him, as his senses began to stabilize, back towards his chair. 'There's nobody else here.'

'You said . . .'

'I said we had wondered when you would come. I did not say there was anyone here with me.'

'Then where is he?'

Ruth, standing in front of him, smiled down with an inward expression that he would never have successfully interpreted, and shook her head. 'You must be patient.'

Before he could say anything more she left him and went out of the room. When she returned a minute or so later she carried a plate of steaming vegetables and pasta in a white sauce on a tray which she passed to him.

'Aren't you eating?' he asked when she sat down.

She replied, 'I'm on a diet,' again as if the idea contained something that privately amused her. Then, when she saw his hesitation, she rose again with a tolerant sigh and went back to the kitchen. She reappeared with a fork which she dipped into the food and took a mouthful. 'Delicious, if I do say it. Perhaps a shake more paprika in the sauce would not have been amiss.'

She resumed her seat as Adam began to eat, hanging one knee loosely over the other and blithely kicking a foot in the air. 'You're not thinking at all clearly,' she told him. 'I've had ample opportunity to poison or subdue you had that been my intention.'

'Why has he been following me?'

She gave him a quizzical look. 'Has he been?'

'You know he has. You were there, at the party. He was watching me. And I saw him earlier, in the street. And again, he was in a doorway, watching, just watching, and taking notes. And – I went to a meeting – but you know all this, don't you. Why am I wasting my time?'

'And you are convinced that it is he who has been following you? Don't you think it might have been the other way around?'

'What do you mean?'

That enigmatic smile again. 'You're here, aren't you?'

There was a crash as Adam's fork came down forcefully against the edge of his plate. '*Don't play games with me!*'

She was quick to apologize. 'I'm sorry. Believe me, I understand that you have been through a terrible ordeal, and are very upset. I am going to tell you everything I can, but that is not yet a great amount. And everything I try to reveal to you will only open more questions in your mind. You can't yet be expected to understand, and it must be done slowly. My task is not an easy one; I have to inform you in a manner which will not leave you overwhelmed. I have to find a way of encouraging a frame of mind where you will be more capable of understanding.'

She lifted herself from her seat and came and crouched at his side, one hand on his arm. 'Before you do anything else, finish your meal, and then sleep. You have to build your strength, and in sleep you may find something useful. Trust me, Adam. I am not here to do you harm.'

Her face held no laughter now. Her eyes were wide and, he dared to think, compassionate. The light, firm pressure of her hand lent emphasis to her words, and he wanted to believe her. God, he wanted to believe her!

With a long exhalation of breath he allowed his head to tip back against the rear of the chair, his eyes towards the ceiling. 'I don't know. I'm confused and I don't know what to put my faith in. Everything sooner or later turns out to be false or to lack any substance or foundation. Everything cracks when I prod beneath the surface. And I can't trust my own judgement. I can't even tell whether you, all of this, are not just further elements in an unending nightmare.'

Ruth lightly pushed his arm away, and tossing her head back, stood. 'Well, you certainly know how to charm a girl!' she retorted, and then she laughed.

Her laughter cut through the tension between them, lightening the atmosphere so that even Adam was unable to resist. For the first time in many, many weeks, it seemed, he laughed. It was weary, half-expressed and shortlived, but it was laughter all the same, and afterwards he felt that a restricting bond had been removed.

Eventually Ruth said, 'Eat up, now. You can stay here for as long as you wish, and when you've slept we'll talk some more.'

He looked at his watch. It still flashed dates incessantly. He looked and found a clock on a nearby shelf. It was five minutes past ten; he could not have been here much more than an hour or an hour and a half.

With the hot food in his belly came the first glimmerings of returning strength, but at the same time his wits were growing dull. A warm langour had crept up on him and was willing him to lie back and close his eyes. It was comfortable here, and conducive to rest. His brain still persisted with a torrent of confused questions, but its voice was less clamorous, a deeper part of him pushing it to the rear. There was no urgency. Later would do.

Randomly one question detached itself from the babble and attempted to break through to the forefront of his consciousness, but before he could even call up the words to phrase it his eyelids had drooped and closed, and the world once more was spirited away.

He awoke fighting, groping frantically to recover the details of a disturbing dream which already, like chaff in the wake of a hostile juggernaut, were flying from him in all directions.

There had been a conversation, with Judith, which had abruptly been curtailed, leaving him troubled and anxious in its inconclusiveness. And there had been a chase, a car, darkness in a country lane, all electrified with his terror, all so familiar. A great hound snuffling and baying in long grass, the blinding dazzle of headlights, and behind it all a pervasive presence, a half-seen, half-sensed image seated, and like a great insect enfolded within the leather wings of his revolving chair, the psychiatrist, Doctor Geld.

But it was gone, all dissolving but the afterglow, the haunting melancholic longing, before his eyes were fully open.

He located Ruth. She sat beside a table, gazing out of an east-facing French window that let onto a small balcony. Out into a blank grey wall of snow. She must have sensed his waking for she looked round, her chin resting in the cup of one hand, and smiled.

'Bad dreams?'

He massaged his face with his hands. 'I wonder sometimes what they mean. I can rarely recapture them, but there's a feeling, as though I've actually lived them. Or perhaps will do.'

Her green eyes narrowed slightly, appraisingly. 'Why not? We go through so many experiences we don't understand. Some can be very, very painful and the instinct is to avoid them. But avoidance is delaying the inevitable. They have to be lived, or relived, to be understood. And dreams can be a key. They have to be passed through. They are leading somewhere.'

He was surprised by this reply, not sure he understood it, but encouraged, with a strange mixture of comfort and fear, to probe further. Her words hinted at a familiarity with something he had long been seeking to make sense of. 'There's something else. There's a feeling that seems to run deeper than the experiential content of the dream, a focusless sense of loss, of grief or separation; and then there's something even further back – a feeling of something impending, of moving towards something but not knowing what. It's not easy to put into words ...'

Ruth nodded slowly. 'We are strange and complex creatures, and strangers to ourselves. We think we are awake when for the most part we may be asleep. And when we think we're sleeping ... well, perhaps that's all we do.' She turned back to regard the snow, and he had a feeling that a door had opened and then been quickly pulled shut again. After a silence of half a minute or so, she said, without shifting her gaze, 'There are guides but we are not shown how to recognize them.'

Still in the border zone between sleep and waking, still bemused by circumstance and tiredness, he could not tell whether he was missing something vital in her words, or whether there was in fact nothing there to miss. He watched her curiously for a while, her seated figure semi-silhouetted against the unchanging weather outside. They had been speaking since his arrival here in German. Ruth's pronunciation was flawless and he had not been able to gauge whether this was her first language, but it seemed to him that language was not of paramount importance in her way of communicating.

Presently Ruth stirred and said, 'Come and look.'

Adam roused himself from his chair and moved to stand at her shoulder.

Outside the big white flakes continued to fall, though unhindered now by any wind, and he let his gaze roam over the landscape they had claimed. Below him was a clear area. A few cars, white roofed, booted and bonneted, stood on a white parking space traced with tyre-tracks already filling with new snow. Heavily laden shrubbery bordered the park and an adjoining pure white lawn. Beyond was an access road, which looked hardly used, and beyond that, fifty yards from the base of the building where he stood, was the wall. Grey and stark and crested with a ridge of snow, it curved and zig-zagged away on either side until it was lost behind neighbouring buildings.

On the other side of the wall was a wide area, a no-man's land patrolled just now by two armed soldiers. A rectangular guard-tower stood near its centre, and inside Adam could make out a sentry peering out through binoculars. Further away, at the far reach of this area, was the wall again, or its counterpart. And beyond that, another country.

Ruth's apartment overlooked the French border control point, manned on this side by a few bored soldiers. An elderly pedestrian had just passed through unchallenged and was making his way with careful steps along the slippery corridor towards the East German customs control, a twin-storey prefabricated building which crouched beside the pillars and barricades of a row of vehicle entry points. The pedestrian carried several bags, probably Christmas presents. Apart from this there was little activity. The place was cold and lifeless, with the aspect of an over-manned country bus station.

Ruth indicated with a slight inclination of her head. 'Beyond the wall.'

Beyond the wall, obscured by the snow's blur, Adam could only make out the streets and shattered buildings of another city. Or rather, of the same city.

'The shadow,' Ruth murmured. 'The alter-ego. The second self. Do you see?'

He responded blankly.

'It's the same place,' she said. 'Unwhole and hidden, kept from itself. You're looking at its other face, which is barely recognized and scarcely acknowledged. And it is looking back and seeing the same thing. The two are alien but inseparable. They are one personality.' She raised her face and stared into Adam's eyes. 'That is what we are dealing with here. That is the first thing you have to understand. Until you have grasped that I can't tell you anything else.'

She rose and moved away from the window into the centre of the room. Adam, following her with his eyes, entertained the unwanted notion, not for the first time, that he might have come all this way, suffered all this, merely to confront a woman whose grip on reality was as fragile and undependable as his own.

She might have guessed his thoughts. She turned on her heel and gave him a reassuring smile. 'I'm not being fair. It is difficult for you. But you actually know much more than you think you know, and I have difficulties too. I have to somehow put you back on the pathways to that knowledge. That's the only way you can ever hope to understand what has been happening to you.'

Berlin

'Professor Jung, before he died, remarked in his writings upon the existence and significance of the Iron Curtain,' Ruth said. 'He saw it as a symbol in the physical world of the split which runs through the psyche of modern man. He was acutely aware of the paradox inherent in such a structure. A man-made geo-political boundary which cuts man off from himself. By refusing to acknowledge the other side man keeps himself blind to the quiddity not only of his so-called opposite number, but to himself. His Undiscovered Self.

'Political groups are always quick to see evil in the opposite group, Jung stated. And similarly the individual will try to rid himself of everything he does not know and does not want to know about himself by foisting it off on somebody or something else.' She pushed her hands into the pockets of her cardigan and gazed past Adam to the window. 'Ah, if he could just have lived to see modern Berlin. With its walls and sectors, its energy and dissension, what would he have made of it? This seed of the West enclaved within the East, neither yet able to recognize the other for what it really is.

'There is such energy here, but it is easy to miss it and see only the objective things. The changes are happening, but slowly and not obviously. It is a place of tremendous psychic activity on the planet.'

She raised her shoulders and hugged herself, smiling past Adam at the city beyond. 'Ah, Berlin, Berlin! Divided and lost, symbol of the world of which you are a part, I love you! There is nowhere else I could live and be happy.'

She approached the window and looked down. 'One day this wall will cease to exist. The Iron Curtain, too. Except perhaps as monuments to remind us of our ignorance. Under the right circumstances that could be a day for humankind.'

'You have an enlivening capacity for optimism,' Adam drily commented.

Ruth nodded. 'There is a potential for catastrophe, it's true. There are so many indeterminate factors at play. The future is always an effect, and you are bound to be aware of that.'

She studied his face for some moments with grave contemplation. Then, as he began to grow uncomfortable, a light came into her eyes. She turned and moved away with a thespian flounce and stepped up onto the seat of her armchair. She spread her hands and announced, 'And now, into this torn and divided place comes a lost and bedraggled figure: an amnesiac, a dreamer. A man in search of himself.'

She lissomely folded her limbs, lowering herself into a half-lotus, her head slightly tilted, eyes sparkling. 'And what's more, a man who can perform miracles!' She laughed. 'What can it all mean?'

Adam gave a start. That his healing was known to her should have come as no surprise, he had accepted that she knew a great deal about him. But her reference to it was unexpected, and it unsettled him to think she had knowledge of something that had happened only hours earlier, in early morning.

'I'm not mocking you,' Ruth said.

'How can it be happening?' he asked her. 'How can I be doing these things?'

'In a response to a need,' was her quiet reply.

He frowned. 'But how?'

'We are all of us heirs to fortunes we may know nothing of.' With a touch of sadness, he thought, Ruth added, 'And for the most part will not glimpse either in this existence or others.'

Adam was puzzled but his earlier misgivings were being overridden by a sudden urgency to confide in this woman. He said excitedly, 'There have been other phenomena. Dreams, of sorts. But not dreams. I've been convinced I've been somewhere, spoken with someone, seen or done something. I've had premonitions I could not at the time interpret, but subsequently events have proven their validity. Earlier when I woke I was sure I had spoken with my wife, that something vitally important had passed between us.'

'Let me say it again in different words,' Ruth said. 'We are creatures of innumerable potential talents and faculties, if we but knew it. The projection of consciousness, like healing, like precognition, is just one.'

'So they were genuine experiences?'

'That is not for me to judge. But you are developing that faculty, yes. And others. There have been times when you and I have been together without your knowing.

'But be careful. It is not always easy to distinguish what is actual from what is not. Not every image that flashes into consciousness, in a dream or otherwise, is necessarily a mean-ingful one. We are capable of tremendous self-deceit, and you are as liable to delusion as anyone – in your present state perhaps more so.'

For the first time Adam felt that he was making progress. Her words stirred him and made his spirits soar.

'Tell me,' Ruth said, 'what was your experience when you healed those two? What did you feel happened?'

He shook his head. He did not know. 'It just happened. I didn't make a conscious choice.'

'How did you know what to do?'

'I didn't. There was an energy, and I felt compelled to use it. It was an intuitive action.'

'What was the source of the energy?'

Again he couldn't say. 'It was everywhere. It was even in the two people I healed, but in them it was blocked, pent up and growing weak. In fact, that's it, I felt I was a catalyst, or a channel. The energy just went through me. Once I had contacted and released their own energy my part was over.'

'Good.'

Ruth unfolded her legs and leaned across towards him. Unexpectedly she extended one arm to quickly caress his jaw, then she settled back into her former position.

Adam watched her questioningly. There had been no hint of anything provocative or sensual in the gesture. He could not even interpret it as one of friendship. It was more as though she had been curious about something. Now she seemed content.

'I'll make coffee,' she said, and went to the kitchen.

He made to follow her, reluctant to let the conversation lapse at this point, but as he passed the French window he paused, his gaze transferring to the scene below.

Nothing had changed but in the light of Ruth's words he had entered a new mood. He looked down at the great double wall which split the city in two and made an island of the land on which he now stood, at the guard-towers and barbed wire and the shell-shocked buildings on the other side, as if seeing it all for the first time.

The two patrolling guards were on their way back. They kept more or less to the tracks they had already made, their machine guns slung beneath one arm, their feet dragging in the snow. They talked as they walked. One of them threw back his head and Adam thought he heard his laughter. They looked very young, no more than boys.

The elderly pedestrian had long since disappeared. On the Eastern side a barrier was lifting to allow a car, an old black Lada, to approach the West.

He thought, Why all of this? What is it that we fear? Each other? But what do we see in others if not a reflection of ourselves and the possibilities that are part of us, all of us? It is the unknown that is truly frightening. The unknown within us. We shrink from it rather than acknowledge it, but if we don't confront it surely we will be condemned to be enslaved by it?

He shook his head. He felt for a moment that he stood far above the city, viewing what he saw with an awareness he had not experienced before. The thought came to him that the food Ruth had given him might have been laced with something mildly psychoactive, but he hardly cared. Something far greater seemed to be under the microscope here.

Ruth's voice sang from the kitchen and his train of thought was broken. 'What else happened? With the healing?'

He went to the door. 'What do you mean?'

'You haven't noticed?' She seemed amused. 'Something was happening before. A natural process. It gained a significant boost when you discovered and directed that power.'

She came from the kitchen with two mugs of coffee, and handed one to Adam. 'Decaffeinated.'

'Please,' Adam said, 'no more riddles.'

'Look at yourself. Haven't you noticed changes? Feel yourself.'

He remained nonplussed.

'A short time ago,' Ruth said patiently, 'you were a virtual cripple. Now look at you. I'd say, given a good sleep, more to eat and a little time to recover, that you're a very fit man. Wouldn't you?'

'I . . . I'd hardly thought about it.'

Ruth gave a laugh. 'Physician, heal thyself!'

'Except that . . .'

'Except what?'

Adam put aside his coffee to roll up one sleeve. The skin of his forearm was a mass of red blotches. 'It's all over, and very tender. I feel like I've had chemicals poured on me.'

To his surprise Ruth smiled. 'That's good.'

'What?'

'Some afflictions we need, to fulfil ourselves. Think about it. I think you already have the key.

'By the way,' she added brightly, 'when did you last shave?'

This time it was Adam's hand that went, on reflex, to his jaw. 'I don't know. Days ago.'

His fingertips explored the skin of his face as he sought to make sense of the messages they were transmitting to his brain. He flashed a distraught look at Ruth, who was sipping her coffee and watching him over the rim of her mug with amused but sympathetic eyes. He looked for a mirror and she passed him one from the table top near the window.

He stared at himself in disbelief. His face was beardless, the skin perfectly smooth.

With that the soaring optimism of moments ago was blown away. The ground opened beneath his feet and he dropped into a familiar chasm of panic and uncertainty. 'I *am* dreaming!'

Fiercely he seized Ruth's shoulders. 'I *am* insane! None of this is real, is it! *Tell me!*'

'It is not a dream.' Her face remained calm and she made no attempt to resist his grip, but in her voice and expression there was the subtlest, and sharpest, tone of admonition. He released her instantly. 'I am telling you and you are not allowing yourself to see. Be patient. It will all become clear. You are changing, Adam, and everything is as it should be.'

'As it should be? What the hell is going on here? It's all

madness! I thought it was this bug in my head, and now you're saying everything's as it should be?'

'Ah, Gospel,' Ruth said in a semi-whisper. 'Whatever murky mind thought that up had a perverse sense of humour.'

'You're not part of it?'

She shook her head. 'No. Gospel is a threat, a very real one, though not precisely in the manner you think. These people are powerful. They make the world a dangerous place. You must take care. You are free of their leash but not yet beyond their influence, and they will never willingly let you go. But even they don't know how big this thing really is.'

'Power games,' Adam said in a dull voice. 'I'm a pawn, a plaything. I'm like dust in a storm. I may as well stop fighting.'

'But you won't. You can't. Believe me, you'll soon understand why. But until then, just trust in the certainty that has brought you this far. It won't fail you.'

She stepped forward and put her arms around him then and hugged him, just briefly, just long enough to give him heart and allow him to haul himself from the chasm. Then, releasing him, she amazed him by saying, 'Listen, I have to attend a local children's Christmas party, to help supervise, and then I have a meeting. I think we should stop now.'

Catching his expression she grinned. 'Life goes on, you know!' More seriously, 'I want you to go back to your hotel and rest. Come back tomorrow, about this time.'

She left him and crossed the room to a wood cabinet against one wall. This she opened and withdrew a small chest which she unlocked. Taking something from it she came back and pressed a bundle of Deutschmarks into his hand. 'This will help.'

She led him towards the door. 'Remember, take care, *use* tonight, and expect the unexpected. Tomorrow you'll be ready for more.'

A sudden thought came, almost inanely into Adam's head. 'Iddio E. Scompiglio,' he said. 'Who is he?'

Ruth stopped. 'Ah, now there's a name to conjure with. Why do you ask?'

'It was at a meeting of his church that I last saw your friend. And there seems to be much confusion about his identity. I . . . I thought at one time I might be him.'

274

He half-expected her to laugh but she did not. But neither, predictably, did she give him a direct answer. 'There is a lot that isn't known about Scompiglio, it's true. That's in his nature, and it will remain that way for some time.'

She opened the door. The cooler air from the outer lobby pushed inside. Ruth raised herself onto the balls of her feet and kissed his cheek. 'Tomorrow.'

He stepped outside and the blue door closed behind him.

Pick Up And Shake

'No Mr Nevus today?' enquired Asprey breezily as he took his seat.

Mackelvoye responded with a withering look and snapped, 'You're not going to tell me you don't know?'

'Know what?'

'*Know what?*' Mackelvoye was incredulous. 'Know why this meeting has been called.'

'I just know there's a meeting.'

'You didn't read the dispatch?'

'Which one?'

'The one I sent you this morning.'

'I saw it, yes.'

'But didn't read it?'

'No time, old boy.'

'But it was "Your Eyes Only" again. With an A-One-Double.'

'Most of yours are. By the time I'd unearthed it and spotted the Priority it was time to be on my way. Had a deal of difficulty getting here, too.'

Mackelvoye brought the side of his fist down hard on the desk. 'Damn!'

'Now, now, Roger. There's no need for that. Just tell me what all the fuss is about.'

'It's about bloody Nevus. He was picked up late last night by a Smiley. Caught red-handed with an armful of papers relating to Gospel.'

Asprey's eyes widened infinitesimally. 'Relating to Gospel? What was he doing with them?'

'God damn you, Geoffrey. All of this is contained in detail in the dispatch. Why must you waste everybody's time? Nevus was preparing to leak them. He is our mole, has been all along.'

'Good Lord!' Asprey appeared uncharacteristically shocked. 'Nevus? Nevus? No, I don't believe it.'

'Well, you better had believe it. We're in deep trouble. When they raided his home the Smileys found all sorts of confidential material, much of it corresponding to information leaked from numerous departments over a lengthy period.'

'But what has he leaked concerning Gospel?'

Mackelvoye took a deep breath. He rested his elbows on his desk, the tensed palms held edgewise in front of him. 'We don't know yet. The Smileys want him handed over to the inquisitors at Sarratt, but obviously we can't risk that. We are seeking Gard's sanction to keep him here, give him to Theodore to work on.'

Asprey was still disbelieving. 'Are you sure about all this?' he began, then seeing the wrath in Mackelvoye's eyes hurriedly changed tack. 'But why?'

'Sheer caprice, by all indications,' Doctor Geld, who whilst stunned at the news of Nevus's treachery was nonetheless fairly pulsating with glee at the prospect of interrogating the fat ministry man, said. 'We would seem to be dealing with a pathological personality. One who derives pleasure from disruption for its own sake. We have no evidence of loyalty to a particular body or cause. Of course, much remains to be extracted.'

'Well, what about little Partridge then? Were they in cahoots?'

'It seems not,' Mackelvoye said. 'Partridge's motives are still unclear. And likely to remain so.'

Asprey pushed himself back heavily into his chair, a look of wonder on his face. 'Well, I'll be blowed. Nevus. Who would have thought? The sneaky little bugger.'

He gave himself over to a moment of contemplation, gazing across to the chair Nevus had habitually occupied. He envisaged the plump little man there now, wrapped in his thick black coat, his inquisitive upturned nose wrinkling as he seemed to test the air, peering about him myopically, fat little legs swinging free of the ground, big hands linked across his chest.

'I don't know how you didn't spot it earlier,' he said.

Mackelvoye bristled. 'What do you mean by that?'

'Well, Roger, it's been under your nose all this time. Surely you at least suspected?'

'Did you?'

'I'm not a detective.'

'Mr Asprey, with due respect, I think you are failing to address the point, ha-ha!' Geld interposed.

'Which is?'

'The consequences for Gospel.'

'And what might they be?'

'In the light of Nevus's actions we can no longer consider it advisable for the Apostle to roam free.'

Asprey fairly swelled. 'Termination time, eh? After such a spirited defence you finally concede defeat. Well, don't say I didn't warn you.'

'I don't see that we have a choice,' Geld replied with a quaver of agitation. 'Mr Nevus has wreaked absolute havoc with us, something that nobody could have foreseen. That he may not yet have leaked anything of Gospel becomes irrelevant under these circumstances. We simply dare not risk the possibility that he may have, that someone else may now be as anxious as we are to have the Apostle in their keeping. Determining the extent of Mr Nevus's treachery will be a lengthy process and we will not have an answer until it is done. Therefore it is with regret that I have made my recommendation that the Apostle be brought in immediately. Yes, you have your way after all, Mr Asprey.'

'In addition there's been another miracle. A fact thoroughly documented in the dispatch,' Mackelvoye remarked sharply.

Asprey pursed his lips. 'Another healing? Hmm, that's not good, is it. Not if he's making it a regular practice.'

'It draws attention to himself,' Geld said. 'And I feel that he's under such pressure now as to be at the point of responding irrationally.'

'He's done that all along.'

'I mean violently, perhaps.'

Surveying them coolly Asprey seemed to come to some agreement with himself. The self-pluming attitude of seconds ago was dropped. 'So what is your proposal?'

'That we pick him up.'

'Yes. And do we have Gard's okay?'

277

'I act on Gard's authority,' Geld nodded, and Mackelvoye lifted from his desktop a paper the psychiatrist had hurriedly, and reluctantly, prepared and passed via the appropriate channels early that morning.

'I have Gard's instructions here,' Mackelvoye said. 'He wants the Apostle brought in immediately, for safe-keeping. He stresses a preference for avoiding full termination if at all possible.'

'You mean he doesn't want a stiff one.'

Mackelvoye frowned and Asprey, remembering himself, quickly muttered an apology to Judith. Mackelvoye then went on, 'He leaves however no doubt as to the urgency with which he views the situation. If there is no alternative the Apostle is to be rendered permanently inactive.'

'Well then, I suggest we waste no more time. Theodore, put your infernal genius to work tout de suite on Nevus.' He rose. 'For my part I shall have to prepare a report for those on high. To give you a little time to operate I shall delay its delivery for as long as possible. It will only be a matter of a couple of hours, so move swiftly, because I can assure you that there will be panic when this breaks. They'll be on you like a ton of bricks and you'll have no leeway unless you can come up with positive results. Yesterday.'

Mackelvoye looked up with some surprise at this unaccustomed largesse, but made no comment. 'I'll order a team in to pick him up immediately,' he said.

Mackelvoye and Asprey had left. Judith, silent throughout the proceedings, gathered her things to go and was waylaid by Doctor Geld, who had delayed his usual hasty departure.

He sidled up to her with a sickly grin. 'My dear, I wonder if I might have a word.'

'What is it, Theodore? I'm very tired.'

'Yes. Er, it won't take a moment. But a, ahem, a slight irregularity has arisen, something — ha-ha! — rather puzzling. I didn't want to bring it up in front of our colleagues, but it is of direct concern to you.'

She gave a sigh but agreed to listen. Doctor Geld took from his pocket a micro-cassette recorder which he set down on a desktop alongside a blank computer monitor and keyboard. He fixed her with a glazed stare and depressed the 'play' control.

For a while as the tiny magnetic tape began to wind between spools there was no sound. Then came a series of vague and erratic bumps and an occasional sigh or breath, identifiable as human. Judith drummed her fingernails on the melamine work-surface. Then she froze.

There was a voice, and she recognized it instantly.

'*Adam! I thought . . .*' There was a short pause, then: '*I thought you were in Berlin.*'

A longer silence followed before the miniature amplifier and speaker conveyed the next short piece of speech. '*It's not a betrayal, darling. Understand that.*' Another brief pause. '*You were part of it.*'

At first Judith could not believe what she was hearing. Transfixed she stared at the recorder, then by degrees her eyes narrowed and shifted to the psychiatrist, and she enunciated in barely controlled tones her fury. 'You *bastard*!'

Doctor Geld had cautiously retreated to the other side of the desk, behind the computer terminal and interfaces. He seemed to quiver in uncertainty. 'My dear, I – '

'You bugged my home!' She was rooted to the spot. 'How dare you! How *dare* you!'

'*Adam, how much do you know?*' chimed her tinny voice from the recorder. '*Do you know that we are not against you? That you don't have to run?*'

Judith glared at the doctor, livid but desperately confused. *Adam's voice was absent from the tape!*

Geld smiled nervously and ran his tongue around his lips. 'I want you to understand – '

'*Understand!?*'

'*Monkswood. It's in Oxf –* ' He darted out a bony hand and silenced the machine. He tried again.

'Please try to understand the necessity for this. Surely it's obvious? There was no intention to pry into your private affairs, but it was essential to monitor the Apostle's progress.'

'Why wasn't I informed?'

'That, too, must be obvious.'

She digested this. 'You didn't trust me.'

'In a matter as delicate as this . . .' The doctor spread his hands placatingly.

'How long's it been going on?'

He swallowed. 'Since Gospel's inception.'

With a muted scream Judith reeled away, her fists clenched at her sides. She marched across the room to face the blank wall opposite, then turned. The doctor tried unsuccessfully to meet her gaze. He winced and shrank behind his monitor as she unleashed a torrent of invective at him.

When she had finished she left a silence that was filled with the humming and ticking of the machines. Geld said, 'You were not alone. In the interests of security electronic sound thieves were installed in the homes and working environments of all Gospel personnel. Indeed, they were instrumental in leading us to Mr Nevus.'

'And does that include your home?'

'Ah! Ha-ha!' He shrugged uncomfortably and grinned at the monitor top, saying, 'It does, yes. But having foreknowledge I was able to take countermeasures when it became intrusive.'

For a long time Judith simply stared at him, but gradually the intensity of her look diminished and her eyes dipped slowly towards the floor. The rigidity of her stance slackened and her anger seemed to ebb away. She sank slowly onto a nearby chair, the one normally occupied by Nevus.

'What are we doing?' she said. 'So much falsehood. So much deception. What on Earth are we becoming?'

Doctor Geld tentatively broke cover, stepping from behind his desk to approach her. 'Judith, if I might just re-direct your attention. The recording itself; there are one or two anomalies which cause me concern.'

She raised her head, which he interpreted as an indication that she wished to hear more.

'Well, you must realize that the content of the recorded, er, conversation, in itself constitutes a grave security risk. My impression is that you are in direct contact with your husband. Now if that is the case I feel you must let me know. For his own good as well as your own. The information you passed would be a vital factor in his development. And I have no wish to see you in trouble, but the evidence is clear. You have attempted to warn him of our intentions.

'But a lot remains unclear. Might I ask, were you using a tape recorder yourself? Or do you have a direct radio link? I confess I am somewhat perplexed.'

Judith laughed briefly, without mirth. Her head was like a dead weight on her shoulders. 'Theodore,' she said quietly, 'he was there.'

'There?'

'Adam was there in the room with me. We ... I thought, we spoke. Are you telling me you have not edited his voice from the tape?'

Receiving, as she now feared she would, his negative reply, Judith put her hands to her face. Covering her eyes she tipped her head back a little way and took several long breaths. Then, in as few words as possible, she attempted to reconstruct for the mystified psychiatrist the strange events that had transpired that night. Doctor Geld listened intently, pulling up a chair as she spoke. When she had finished he sat without comment.

'You don't believe me, do you?'

'Ha-ha! I do not know what to believe. But in the light of everything else that has occurred it would be foolish of me to make snap judgements, would it not? Nothing, it seems, is ever quite what it seems!'

'So what's next?' Judith asked. 'Are you going to put me away? Lock me up for interrogation with Nevus?'

'No, no. Nothing like that, my dear. At least, not at present. I merely want to get to the bottom of this matter.'

'Theodore, I love him,' Judith said. 'Can you understand that?' She was not sure that he could. 'I love him. He's my husband and I am desperately afraid for him. I don't know what is going on but I would betray Gospel now to save him. I believe that what we are doing is wrong. Horribly wrong. If Adam came back tonight I would tell him everything, and keep you and the others from reaching him.'

The doctor fingered his jaw. Her words had a familiar ring. 'I do not doubt it. But the fact remains that he is not here – unless you are party to information we are not – and he is in danger. I implore you, if you do have some clandestine means of communicating with him, let me have it. If we act now, together, we can still bring about his salvation.'

'I'm not in contact with him, I've already told you!' she cried. 'What happened is as much a mystery to me as it is to you.'

'Very well then, we are forced to proceed by the book.' He fiddled for a while with his thumbs in his lap, regarding her closely. Eventually he left his seat and went over to his briefcase, returning with it and delving inside. 'My dear, I think these might help.'

Judith looked up slowly, first at him and then at the small plastic phial he held in one hand, in which could be seen a score or so of small coloured capsules.

'*Damn you!*' With an angry sweep of her hand she knocked the phial from his grip. It shot across the room, bounced from a table top, hit the floor and skittered out of sight behind a bank of computer consoles.

'Is that your answer for everything?' she screamed. 'Don't handle the problem, just dole out the soma? My God, how can you be so insensitive? I am worried sick! Adam's going to die!'

The doctor seemed bewildered. 'Not if we can avoid it. We don't want him killed, we want to bring him home – '

'It isn't only that! I mean the animals!'

'Aah!' He seemed suddenly to understand. 'Aah,' he said again. 'But I told you some time ago that you need have no worries on that score. The animals underwent different – '

Judith, unable to remain seated, yelled, frantic in the helplessness she felt, '*And I don't believe you!*'

Geld gave some consideration to this, then he went over stoopingly to the console behind which his phial had fled. It was within easy reach and he bent and retrieved it. He remained squatting alongside the throbbing technology, his spine against the reinforced concrete wall. He seemed to be wrestling with something deep within himself. Finally, he looked up and said to Judith's back, which despite her efforts was beginning to shudder with the sobs she strove to suppress, 'My dear, perhaps I can put your mind at rest on that issue.'

'How?' She did not turn.

He heaved himself stiffly to a standing position. 'I have not been entirely honest with you in the past. With any of you.'

If he was expecting some exclamation of surprise from her at this he was disappointed. He went on, 'I – I must impress upon you the confidential nature of what I am about to tell you.'

'The walls have ears,' Judith caustically reminded him.

'Er, not just now, they don't.'

She nodded. 'Go on. You have my assurance.'

'Well, ha-ha! The fact is that whilst several of my animals have died as a direct – I do not deny it – as a direct result of the testing stages that were designed to lead ultimately to Gospel, and beyond, I can state with absolute authority that your husband is not at risk.'

She turned now, angry again. 'How can you say that! You've put that thing in his head and you weren't sufficiently progressed to do so. You've destroyed his mind.'

Peevishly he shook his head.

'What are you saying? That you intended him to lose his memory, to drive him crazy? Theodore, you may have proven yourself inept but we all know that Gospel had loftier designs than that.'

'Ah yes, loftier designs. It is true. But that "thing" as you term it was and is a miracle of modern technology.'

She snorted. 'Then how come it has malfunctioned?'

'It hasn't.'

'It hasn't? Theodore, you're not making sense. Gospel has been a failure, you can't possibly deny that.'

The doctor gave a bland shrug. He took himself off to the desk on which his pocket recorder still stood. 'Judith, you are not allowing me to explain. I am trying to tell you that the "biochip", to use the proper term, did not malfunction, and neither in fact did it ever function in its intended capacity. You see, it was never used.'

The words made her start and she shook her head as if to clear a fog. 'What do you mean?'

'The experiment . . . it never took place.'

'*What?*'

With a shake of his narrow head the doctor pulled out a chair and sat down. He placed the phial of capsules on the worksurface beside the micro-recorder as though it were a precious thing, and stared at it. Judith strode over and grasped his arm with both hands. 'Theodore, what did you just say?'

He let out a long sigh. 'I said it did not take place. My dear, take a seat, will you. All this perturbation is making me rather weary.'

The Truth About Gospel

When she was seated opposite him the doctor, toying with the phial of sedatives on the smooth surface, said, 'You are aware of what I had hoped to achieve?'

Mistaking her silence for an invitation to elucidate he went on, 'I had planned to install not just one but a network of micro-bioelectronic molecular chips. They were to be situated about the vital activity centres of the brain, functioning as a part of his own biological makeup whilst – I am using the crudest terminology here – sensing and picking up the minute electrical impulses of the main neural pathways. They would simultaneously be monitoring the biochemical changes produced within the neurotransmitters involved as a response to the specific impulses. Put simply, they would be recording the minutiae of specific brain events. The essential data gained would be fed to a single "mother-chip" in the posterior of the cranium. There it would be "read", analysed, codified and eventually transmitted to the infinitely more sophisticated data-and-analysis banks we have here.' He waved expansively at the machinery about them.

'In effect we would have had access to the patient's thought processes, his memory, experience and learning patterns, through an essential record of almost every neurobiological interchange and the cellular and inter-synaptic mechanisms involved, incredible though that may sound. And beyond that, with future research, the facility to replicate any or all of it by artificial means. Such, as you know, is the reason for the existence of this room and all its contents, and for the need for secrecy. It was to have been a revolution, a quantum leap uniting diverse fields of scientific research and development. It was my dream, my life's purpose,' the doctor, transported, was rubbing his palms together, his bifocals flashing beneath the harsh striplights. 'Nothing approaching it has ever been attempted.'

'So where did it go wrong?' Judith, dazed, demanded. 'Why didn't you go through with it?'

The memory obviously pained him. His face fell. 'I had barely begun,' he said. 'I had made the initial incisions and begun drilling into the skull preparatory to a full craniotomy. A routine enough operation at this stage, to expose or provide access to the cortical sites I needed to probe. But it became apparent that something had gone amiss. My monitors were indicating severe disturbances, EEG readings began flying off the graph. The magnetoencephalograph sensors were mapping multiple localized events of an unusually high intensity, but giving me no clue as to their source. In addition I had to contend with violent muscular activity; at one point the patient began to struggle on the operating table. Had he not been securely strapped down I would have had difficulty restraining him.

'I was at a loss to explain it, I have never encountered anything quite like it, but plainly the operation could not proceed. So I had him sutured and returned to his bed.'

'And you didn't make a report?'

'Ah.' He waggled a long finger. 'Not called for at this point. When he regained consciousness I planned to conduct further tests, question him in the hope that he might through conscious recollection, or even dreams, provide insight into his unconscious demurral. By these methods I thought to obviate any future obstacles and proceed once more with the minimum delay.'

'But you didn't?'

'Well, ha-ha! My dear. The next thing I knew, I was at work attempting to analyse the readings and micrographs I had, and the alarm went off. The Apostle had awoken and escaped through the window. My Lord! You can imagine my consternation!

'And then of course the car struck him down in the lane. It was all of a sudden so topsy-turvy, and a bitter blow. Bitter. All my plans, the years of failures and frustrations . . . to be robbed of success when perfection was so close at hand.'

Judith pressed her palms flat against the desktop, mulling over what she had just learned, her mind racing to gather the implications of his confession. She leaned forward intently. 'And even then you didn't tell anyone?'

'Ha-ha! Judith, how could I? It would have meant the certain abandonment of Gospel! And I did not consider just then that all was lost. I would supervise his recovery and perform the operation the moment he was fit enough to bear it. No one would be the wiser. I could never stand by and see it all come to nothing, and I perceived no reason to. It was a short-term postponement, that was all. Of course, I could not have predicted his awakening an amnesiac, nor that his personality and loyalties would have suffered such adverse effects. And by the time I had realized the extent of his psychological injuries it was too late to tell anyone. I would have been disgraced, my status gravely impaired, my dignity besmirched. I would have lost my funding.'

Judith sat back with an exhalation of breath and ran a hand through her hair. 'My God.'

The psychiatrist peered at her with a cagey grin.

'Theodore, let me get this straight. You're saying that Gospel is a fallacy, a myth?'

'I am saying that what took place is not consistent with what is believed to have taken place.'

'But we've all been operating as if it were.' She closed her eyes in concentration. 'Let me ask you something. It's been troubling me, because I'm no longer very clear about it. I want to know, what was the ultimate goal of Gospel? To what practical use would this "quantum leap" have been put?'

'My dear, surely that's self-evident?'

'It may be. But I want to hear it from you.'

Geld looked starstruck again. 'To have the ability to reproduce the characteristics, the mental processes of a model human being, down to the last biochemical detail, you cannot visualize the benefits in that? In health and mental development it would have untold results. That is why we used your husband; he was such a perfect specimen. We had to have the best in all respects. To have at hand those processes and formulae which maintained him in such optimum condition – do you not see the giant strides it would have advanced us in the eradication of disease, in understanding the human immune system and the mechanisms involved in both mental and physical health? The future could see a society without illness or handicaps, the lame and halt made fit, the unemployable becoming valued citizens . . .'

'How far in the future?'

'Well, I must stress that we are at the beginning, the very first faltering steps. The full practical applications of Gospel are a long way off, and still undefined. We are the founding fathers – at least, we could have been,' he added disconsolately.

'And Adam was sufficiently egotistic to find the idea of a future society modelled on himself rather attractive,' Judith said. 'It's pipedreams, Theodore. Admit it. You're painting this rosy, cosy picture of an ideal society whilst fumbling with a technology you don't yet understand or know how to apply. And there's a darker aspect to it which you're not owning up to.'

He looked up. 'My dear, I'm not with you.'

'To have the facility to replicate selected characteristics of a model human being? To be able to recreate chosen thought patterns, modes of behaviour? My God, Theodore, someone somewhere is going to cry "master-race" long before your first perfect Alpha has left the Hatchery.'

The psychiatrist let fly a burst of machine-gun laughter. 'Ha-ha-ha! Ha-ha-ha-*ha*! My dear, that is extremely speculative, excessively imaginative! Master-race! Ha-ha! No, no. There is no conception of a master-race!' Wheezing, he laughed again and wiped his watery eyes with a foulard. 'Even were such a concept feasible – and I assure you it isn't – it would require generations. Generations! No, no. Your New World, Brave as it may be, remains firmly in the realm of science-fiction. All of it. We have at present the facility to record, analyse and store, that is all.'

'But in the wrong hands, nevertheless . . .'

'In the wrong hands, certainly, the technology might conceivably be misapplied. Possibly. That is a paradox inherent in all great discoveries and advancements, that they may be used for good or evil. Hence our emphasis on security. But nothing of the order you are suggesting is within the realms of possibility, I can promise you. And as for myself, it is for the benefit of mankind that my efforts are directed, not its detriment.'

She gave this some thought, then said, 'Then what about Adam, now? I'm still puzzled. If as you say you did nothing to him, then what has caused these behavioural changes? How do you explain everything else that's happened?'

Geld gave her the blank and forlorn look of an ugly simpleton. 'I have no satisfactory explanation. I have worked down every avenue, gone over and over the data at my disposal, and found no concrete foundation to support what has occurred. Of course, the amnesia may have come about as a result of the trauma of the collision with the vehicle, but beyond that I can't say.'

'Then let me put something to you. Is it not possible that what happened on the operating table constituted a rejection by his subconscious of something he had previously consciously consented to? Is it not possible that some deeper part of him rose up to overrule the decisions of his conscious will, even to the extent of blotting out his past personality as if his former life was not acceptable? Is it unreasonable or far-fetched to suggest that a wiser facet of his being, his conscience, if you like, has taken control, steering him from the path he was on and directing him along an alternative one?'

Geld could not successfully conceal his cynicism. 'My dear, your imagination knows no bounds, does it. But I can't give myself to conjecture. I am a scientist and a pragmatist. I am concerned with facts.'

'But you've already admitted you have none.'

'The facts we should concern ourselves with just now involve your husband's well-being, and the grave danger he is in. It is not just ourselves he must be wary of, nor even those others who might seek to gain possession of him. He is in danger from himself. Moreover he represents a risk to others, to innocents. I fear for what might happen should he in his present state rediscover his old skills. I fear that we may have let loose a monster.'

'Or a saint,' Judith whispered. With animation she said, 'Theodore, you have to tell the others what you've just told me. You must report it. We are going to kill Adam to protect something that doesn't exist. This is madness. You can end it. You can't think only of yourself; it will come out in time anyway.'

Geld shook his head. 'Impossible,' he said, grinning repellently. 'You are not perceiving the situation objectively. If the others are apprised of the information you now have they will be left with a single recourse. There will no longer be a reason to bring the Apostle home alive, and every reason to ensure that the knowledge he has can never be passed on. Their heads are in the noose, you see, as is yours. So it is not just my interests that I am seeking to safeguard just now, my dear. The Apostle's one hope is to be persuaded back, or brought back by some means unharmed.'

'Do you really believe that Six has his welfare in mind?' Judith said contemptuously. 'You know what will happen when contact is made.' She let her head tilt forward into her hand. 'My God, where does it all end?'

'Judith, I have entrusted you with my confidence because I wish to have you understand my actions and the position I find myself in, and to work with me to prevent, if it can be done, Gospel's termination. We must work together on this. We may have dissimilar motives but we share the same goal. So I entreat you again, do you have a means which you have not disclosed of reaching your husband or relaying a message to him?'

She gave a barely perceptible shake of her head.

'You are sure?'

Wearily she raised her eyes. 'Theodore, I have told you about that evening. That's all I know, which is nothing.'

The doctor gave a sigh. Resignedly he reached out and depressed the 'eject' control on his little recorder. The microcassette flipped out into his waiting palm. 'But I may count on your silence?'

Judith stared at him long and hard but made no comment.

Rising, he dropped the recorder into his briefcase which he snapped shut. 'My dear, I apologize, this is most distasteful. But I do have to impress upon you the confidentiality of all that has passed between us. Should you still entertain any thought of disregarding my admonitions, that is, ha-ha! should you still be under the delusion that there is something to be gained by approaching some other person in regard to your husband – perhaps even in the hope of touching a compassionate chord somewhere? – well, I must warn you that this,' he grasped the tiny cassette between finger and thumb, 'played to the wrong ears would engender regrettable consequences. Even should you have some measure of success in convincing concerned parties of your solitude and lack of electronic aids when the recording was made, well, I can only add, again without pleasure, that it would not advance your aims in any way. Indeed, with the additional evidence I might bring to bear in my professional capacity, both the reliability of your statement and your, ahem, your psychological efficiency and well-being, would be called seriously to question. The outcome could be quite unhappy. And believe me, I would not like to see it come to that.'

Judith, with a look of sheer disgust, let her brow sink once more into her hand.

Geld bent from the waist to take the phial of capsules from the desk. He slid it with a slight scraping sound across the surface until it rested alongside her free hand.

'These might after all be helpful,' he said quietly. Then he popped the micro-cassette into his jacket pocket and left the room.

Fight And Flight

Four figures fell on Adam out of the night.

It was in an unlit side-alley which cut between two main streets. He was making his way back to his hotel, having spent much of the afternoon out walking.

Something warned him of the danger, a sixth sense, and he reacted on instinct, with no time for thought.

The first attacker came from behind. Adam dropped onto one knee, tucking his chin into his chest and reaching up with both hands. He took the outstretched arm which had been descending towards the back of his skull. He hooked beneath the humerus with his right, just above the elbow, continuing the forward motion of his assailant's body whilst gently levering upwards. With his left, in the same movement, he slid across the back of the man's hand, dropping it sharply down and simultaneously bending the wrist in on itself. As the man, propelled by his own motion, sailed in a somersault over his head, Adam applied pressure with his thumb to the first two knuckle joints and slipped free the blackjack the clenched fist held.

A second man was almost on him from his right. Still kneeling Adam dropped his torso, discarding the cosh and throwing his

290

hands to the floor for support as he drew in one leg for a thrust-kick up into the face. But he sensed others coming in on him from forward and rear left.

He spun and rolled and came up standing, shoulder to shoulder, with the second man. Mirroring his movement as he took his wrist, he twisted and locked and bent the man double. Stepping back he spun him around and with the locked arm as a fulcrum, propelled him under his own force into the nearest of the two, sending both sprawling in the snow.

Number four was on him. His onrushing weight caught Adam off-balance. Adam slipped and was knocked to the ground, his attacker on top of him, an arm like a vice encircling his neck, expert fingers applying paralysing pressure to a vital nerve centre.

As his spine touched the floor Adam went into a roll, continuing the natural motion of their two bodies. They came up together, but already Adam's senses were leaving him as the lethal fingers kept up the pressure at his neck. He butted back into the man's chest with his head, more to ease the pressure than to injure him. He jerked his right leg up and snapped back with his heel to smash the kneecap, then hard down, scraping the thin flesh from the shin and crushing his opponent's instep.

The man howled. His fingers left Adam's neck. Adam rolled him over his thigh and as he hit the floor, still screaming, bent and punched the face so that the head cracked back against the snow-covered asphalt. The man lay still.

There was movement to his left. His vision was blurred and his strength gone from the compression of his nerves – that man had known his business. There was no time to assess. Intuitively he fell, rolling as hands and knees touched the snow, into the movement. It worked. His body hit the legs of the oncoming assailant and took them from under him. As he went down Adam came up and over him and rammed his face down hard into the floor, knocking him out cold.

Now there were two.

On his feet Adam shook his head, his vision still hazed. There was someone in front of him, slightly to his left, moving in. Something metallic glinted briefly in his hand. Adam backed away a couple of paces to gain a vital second of recovery, and was locked in the arms of the second man at his back.

In the split second of their collision the man, trying to arrest Adam's rearward motion, pushed forward. Adam took that moment. With two hands he locked onto the man's own inter-locking hands, hugged them into his chest. Simultaneously he lowered his centre and folded swiftly forward from the waist, catapulting his attacker over his back. As the man came down and Adam released his hands, his feet descended on the head of his last incoming companion.

The last man ducked and threw his arms up for protection, attempting to sidestep. Adam made to move in to take the knife but missed his footing on the slippery road surface. The man, recovering himself, took rapid stock of the situation, turned and ran from the alley, his feet skidding beneath him. Adam gave his attention to the one he had just thrown. Winded, he was trying to sit up. He had lost all stomach for the fight. Adam let him climb to his feet and make his way dazedly in pursuit of his comrade.

He checked the other two. The man whose foot he had crushed was already coming to. He half-sat, moaning, the injured limb extended in front of him. Blood poured from a broken nose, and seeped from a boot and one trouser leg into the snow. He exchanged a mistrustful glance with Adam then, reassured that he would live to see another morning, began to drag himself away in the wake of the other two.

The last one was spreadeagled and motionless, but his injuries were not serious. He would wake before he froze, and be capable of walking away.

Adam straightened, in two minds as to his next move. Back to the hotel? He had left nothing there but an unpaid bill, and there was the strong possibility of another reception committee. To Ruth, then? He hesitated, entertaining what could not reasonably be ignored: the possibility that it was she who had put these four onto him. He had come to within a millimetre of giving her his total trust. Was that now to be shattered?

It was as he pondered this that his eyes flickered over some-thing that drew them instantly back, making him start and his body resettle instinctively into a defensive stance. A form had appeared in the deep shadow near one end of the alley, a familiar shape made indistinct as it blended in the darkness with the tangle of alley-junk around it. A human figure, stocky, compact, quite still. And at its side, crouched on its haunches, also still, was the shadow of a huge dog.

His heart began to pound. He moved up, wanting to run, expecting at any second the murderous attack as the hound launched itself from the cave-blackness of its cover. But as he drew closer the form began to change and distort, refiguring itself with other shadowy shapes until he could no longer see what it was he was looking for. And when he at last arrived there, shivering with fear or fever – he didn't know which – it was to find only a collection of bulging rubbish sacks, bins, boxes, some planks and scaffolding props. He could not tell whether the form he had seen, or thought he had seen, had moved away, or faded into nothing, or had simply not been there in the first place.

He breathed with relief, the tension slipping from him. Even so he reached out with a toe to prod the nearest polythene sack. There was a flurry of movement and a screech that froze his blood. He leapt back. A dark shape hurled itself from the shadow.

It darted past him and away down the alley before he'd had time to glimpse it – a stray cat searching the rubbish for scraps. And Adam, numb with terror, found himself back in time, staring into the flushed, crinkled face of his friend Helmut, helplessly shaking with laughter on the bonnet of his car.

He moved away, stepping out from the alley into the undefined circle of light thrown down from an overhead lamp on the pavement of a broad but empty boulevard.

'There,' Ruth said, the tip of her forefinger descending onto a location on the large map she had spread across the table. 'That is where you must go to find what you are looking for, if that is still your aim.'

'It's further East,' Adam said.

Ruth smiled. 'South East, to be precise. But that's not a problem. I can arrange your transit visas, and a car in East Berlin. It's relatively simple these days, restrictions are not what they were. And I'll accompany you to the city boundary to put on the right road. We can go early in the morning.'

He could only take her word. Behind a buoyant front her concern had been evident when he had arrived in a state of dishevelment, in her words 'stirred but not shaken', half an hour earlier. Concern, but not surprise. Never surprise. She was relieved, she said. She had known something was wrong. She was reproachful of herself for having allowed him to leave earlier.

'Something unforeseen must have happened to make them move this quickly,' she told him. 'They seem suddenly desperate.'

She was apprehensive that he might have been followed to her apartment, but he put her mind at ease. He had come by a far from direct route. He had back-tracked and double-tracked and sown numerous false leads to confound any would-be pursuers. Outside the apartment block he had lain hidden for more than an hour, observing and settling his own suspicions. For it was true, she had told him that morning that she had had more than ample opportunity to subdue him, had she wished. And he had conceded that four thugs in an alley was not her style.

Now, as he stared at the small city emblem on which her pale finger rested, she said, 'You have been there before on more than one occasion. Do you not recall?'

He shook his head.

'Perhaps that's not unexpected. After all, you believed then that you were there with another purpose. And you didn't find what you sought. Or perhaps you found it but failed to recognize it. Anyway, you are here now, and better equipped.'

He was back amongst her mysteries and ellipses, and under her spell. Whether it was madness she wielded with such dextrously ambivalent charm, or some other subtle and indefinable quality of illusion and enchantment mattered little. He was consciously held captive. Held by her promise of the possibility of escape. And additionally, the anticipation of the encounter her route out made possible. Her companion, she insisted, the man whom Adam had come so far to find, was ready to talk to him now. He would tell him what she could not, and bring this mystery to an end. Everything was set. It was merely for Adam to make the final run.

'You've brought no baggage,' she said, 'and there's nothing you need to take bar money and the papers I'll provide. Sleep here tonight. I must go out quickly and make arrangements. If we leave early tomorrow you'll be there by evening.'

During the hour she was gone Adam, tired as he was, kept a

tense vigil between windows and door, his senses alert to every sound in the corridor outside, every movement or lack of it on the streets below. When she returned he slept. It seemed only minutes had passed before she was shaking him gently awake, telling him it was time to leave.

Weltsterben

There was a feeling of having stepped back in time, entirely appropriate under the circumstances. The few cars that rolled over the frozen, half-cleared streets were of outdated design and generally in less than good repair. The trams that trundled noisily by, from the windows of which occasional muffled faces peered out at a twilit world, bore traces of rust and paintwork that should long ago have been renewed. The buildings were brown and grey and lifeless. They were cracked and aged, in need of renovation or, in many cases, complete demolition and reconstruction. Vast identical apartment blocks loomed in rank after endless rank, purely functional, built to demand since the war. The only indications of affluence, the only new designs, applied to government offices and huge hotels built to accommodate wealthy tourists, businessmen and official functionaries from East and West. The people, those who were out at such an hour, were wrapped in well-worn coats, boots and headgear. Style, in its rare instances of discernibility, was reminiscent of the fashions of thirty years ago or more, the occasional exception taking the form of one or two self-consciously overdressed punks.

The further Adam drove from the city the more pronounced these impressions became. Steam locomotives in railway sidings, little shuttered-up houses on the sadder side of quaint. Items of agricultural equipment long obsolete in the West littered fields and farm precincts like the rusting hulks of long-abandoned war machines.

He was alone now in the old grey Travant Ruth had picked up outside a disused warehouse after they had crossed from the West. The control point had proved no obstacle, though he had passed through unaccompanied. Ruth, as a resident, was subject to a separate procedure. He had suffered the formalities in a condition of nervous suspension, convinced that the young blond starched-uniformed customs officer would declare some irregularity in his papers and that he would be marched away under this or some other trumped-up discrepancy. But he had emerged with cursory delay into the creeping Eastern dawn, and moments later rendezvous'd with Ruth. True to her word she had delivered him as far as the East Berlin boundary and then handed over the wheel and climbed from the car.

'Take this route,' she had said, passing him a map on which she had overscored certain provincial roads in red. 'Avoid the main auto-routes. It's important.' She had not explained why.

It was cold in the car. The heating system worked intermittently, and then inadequately, and the bodywork was peppered with unseen openings through which blasts of icy air penetrated relentlessly. The engine was loud and had a tendency to chug and wheeze. His skin was causing him mild discomfort; possibly, he thought, in response to the extreme conditions.

Making their way through East Berlin they had talked, he and Ruth. He had been questioning her, probing for concrete information, for facts, and she, characteristically, had avoided them, preferring to address subjects of, to her mind, far more embracing significance than his individual plight.

'Do you see evil in the world?' she had asked as they drove towards Oberschöneweide. 'What do you think constitutes evil?'

The question was one he had found himself contemplating only the day before, sometime after leaving her flat. He studied her features before answering for some clue as to why she had sprung it on him now, but her expression gave nothing away. She was intent on driving.

The notion had come to him, he replied, that the only evil that exists comes from Man, that the nature of evil as an entity was little understood. The one true evil, he said, must be ignorance. Hardly original, but vitally important. All negative conditions in the world – greed, intolerance, jealousy, superstition, and the material conditions that follow as a consequence, such as war, famine, even disease, can be seen as stemming from that one central state. The greatest crime a person is capable of, he told her, had to be the controlled perpetuation for self-gain of ignorance in others. Such an act revealed the greater ignorance on the part of its perpetrator, and constituted a crime against self, against humanity and against God.

He wanted to continue but she interrupted him with another question. 'Can those who don't know be punished for crimes they are unaware of having committed? You would seem to be accusing humanity of a mass psychopathy. Do you advocate psychiatric rehabilitation as a species?'

'The crime is not-knowing,' Adam said, prodded into earnestness by her apparent sarcasm. 'Therefore the punishment is not a punishment. Knowledge is a reward, is freedom.'

'Ah, instantaneous, global enlightenment. An ideal world,' Ruth said, then added, 'I'm not belittling you. I'm asking the same questions and finding similar answers, as have others before – and always coming up against the same wall of impracticability that separates the now from the would-be. Of course you are right. If we as human beings have a single moral duty in this life it is to rid ourselves of ignorance. And undeniably we exist in a time where our future and that of our planet depend on it. But ...' She allowed the silence to speak, waiting on an otherwise empty road for a red light to change. 'Has your view of your own situation altered?' she asked as they moved forward again.

'I can no longer consider those I am running from as enemies. That would appear to be a natural consequence. But it is isolating, and makes me afraid. If I consider them now as blind, misguided, as victims, by extension I set myself apart, in a position of superiority. That is a dangerous, lonely and fragile position to occupy.'

'It needn't be,' was her reply. 'It depends upon its application. Like all things it can go either way. Used wisely it's an expansion of view. It allows you to become part rather than setting you apart.'

'It has the aspect of a last refuge for misfits and failures, people whose only recourse is to convince themselves they are superior,' he said.

'With the difference that you can see where you stand, and the consequences of being there. They cannot. And God knows, you are not alone. Believe me.'

Adam fell into introspection. They followed the course of the Spree, entering the tunnel beneath the river and emerging into the forests and hills that surround the Grosser Muggelsee, and Ruth began talking about symbolism and meaning. It was a topic which held a fascination for her that she seemed anxious to share – the tendency of the psyche to transmute into symbolic form, in both the material and the psychic world, those things that the self cannot or will not acknowledge.

'Everything was thought before it was anything else,' she said. 'Whether conscious or unconscious. Everything you see, hear, feel, touch. The world. Everything.'

And as she pursued her subject she eventually touched, with an air of flippancy he at first thought, on his name. 'Have you ever given thought to its etymology? Adam, of course, was the first human being, but the word has other meanings. Red earth is one. The dust from which God created the first man. And Adam is the Hebrew word for man, signifying man in general rather than a particular individual. Jewish writings of the New Testament period use the name to typify man in his limitation – Adam was the means by which sin and wrong-doing entered the world. And St Paul contrasted the old Adam – the evil of mankind – with the new, or last Adam, which is Christ. So the name is not used simply in reference to an individual, the mythical "first man", but more broadly, describing mankind and everything it embodies.'

'And your surname, it's very unusual.'

'I'm the only Shatt in the book,' Adam commented drily.

She smiled. 'Its roots lie in an ancient Middle Eastern language of obscure origins, though there are correspondences with both pre-dynastic Egyptian and Sanskrit. The name takes several forms but its most consistent reference is to movement or change. A flowing, a state of flux. As it evolved it came to acquire, as far as can be ascertained, a more specific reference and was used as a noun to describe a river or stream. So there you are!' she concluded brightly. 'Quite literally, "the river of mankind". Intriguing, isn't it.'

She pulled the car into the roadside, braking and neutralizing the gears; this was as far as she could go. The wind whipped along the empty street, flurrying the thinly falling snow, and once outside the vehicle she hugged her coat protectively about her.

'By the way,' she said, just before she closed the door, 'it's

Elizabeth, not Ruth. Your friend got it wrong, but no matter. It's sad, he tried so hard.' She pushed the door shut. 'Good luck!'

Adam drove away, not knowing if he would see her again. In the rear-view mirror she had her back to him, her hands in her coat pockets, making her way back into the city. As he turned a corner and she was obscured from sight it came to him that, beyond that parting scrap of information, he knew nothing more about her now than when he had arrived.

He drove steadily for some hours as the morning drew on a sullen light, and stopped for lunch at a small village inn. He was the sole customer. He sat at a table beside a fading Christmas tree decked with coloured paper strips and a string of miniature lamps. There was no official recognition of Christianity here but he had several times spotted lights and trees in windows along the way. Enquiring of the landlord he learned that Christmas Day, the celebration of Christ's birth, was only two days hence.

He ate broth with dark ryebread followed by cold meat, potatoes and fruit, and felt better for it.

He drove on between wide, empty fields of dark tilled soil or sparse turf. The landscape was bleak and for a time unvarying. Trees stood out leafless and black against a low skyline. There had been no snow here, or very little.

Gradually the terrain began to change. The flatness gave way to gently rolling hills, which grew steeper, the monotonously straight roads conceding to curves and twists. The hills became wooded and were carrying him circuitously towards a range of mountains crouched in the distance. It was early afternoon; he estimated he was no more than a couple of hours, perhaps three, from his destination.

As the day progressed he had been suffering increasing irritation from the strange red blotches on the skin of his arms and body. It was no longer possible to push it from his thoughts. A maddening inaccessible burning scoured his skin and leached deep into the flesh beneath. Glancing frequently at his forearms he saw their redness growing hotter and more angry as he drove. It was like nothing he knew. Either he had contracted some disabling nervous disease or this was a consequence, direct or indirect, of Gospel. Whichever it was he lacked any form of relief and the pain was intensifying beyond anything he had previously suffered.

A point came where he could no longer concentrate on driving. He stopped the car, sitting rigidly still, afraid to move for the penalty it would cost him as clothing shifted against skin. He centred on his breathing but after several minutes began weeping, unable to reclaim his mind from the agony. Then, on an impulse that activity of some kind might at least provide a distraction, he forced himself to leave the car.

Gritting his teeth in the cold sharp air he became aware of the landscape that surrounded him. He had entered a forest of saplings. Young ash, silver birch, beech, oak and conifers, all stripped by winter, covered the steep and craggy hill slopes. It was a remote and silent place but signs of human passage were evident in the form of sundry litter – scraps of paper, bottles, cans. Nearby, within the trees, a mound of bulging plastic sacks had been dumped, and the only sound that reached his ears was that of the torn strips of plastic that had caught in the branches of trees and were flapping in the piercing breeze.

He entered the forest, aware of a strangeness that clung about this place, but too distracted to perceive what it was. The ground was uneven and he stumbled as he walked, crying out with each new seizure of pain. There was a large amount of deadwood on the forest floor, and a profusion of small shrubs, the twigs and branches of which snapped and fell away as he brushed against them. Underfoot the thin turf was brown-tinged and papery. A dark moss proliferated, but this when he touched it was brittle and disintegrated between his fingers.

It was the conifers that finally gave him the secret of this place. Evergreens that had shed their needles or scale-leaves. Shreds of discoloured foliage were all that remained on the overhanging branches. Perceiving this he saw it all. He advanced further, caught between his own pain which, impossibly, still grew, and an increasing horror at what he was witnessing.

The trees now were more mature, towering, and cutting out much of the already weak winter light, but they told the same tale. He touched the bark of a huge beech; it fell away like old parchment. The wood underneath was in an advanced state of petrification. He raked his fingernails down its surface and left deep furrows as its dust fell pattering down the trunk to the floor.

With difficulty, gasping with pain, Adam lowered himself onto hands and knees. He tugged at a clump of fescue and it came away from the soil without resistance. A small bush came out wholesale, its roots destroyed.

He struggled back to his feet ready to retrace his steps to the car, but up ahead something glittered. A quick silver flash not far off between the trees. He moved towards it, verbally urging his protesting body on. His legs, trapped in the ceaseless shock of pain, rebelled against supporting his weight. But he broke free of the trees after some yards and found himself on the narrow strand of a lake.

Waterlilies rested on the rippled surface and the water was unusually clear. It deepened rapidly but from where he stood he could see well into the undisturbed depths. No fish moved there and it came to him now that there was no sound in this place except the occasional weary creak of a branch of a tree in the breeze. There were no birds, no insects. The lake and the forest around it had a peaceful, picture-postcard quality, but it was not the quietude of natural life, not the temporary dormancy of winter that he had at first supposed unquestioningly. It was the peacefulness of death. He looked about him and as far as he could see the pattern was the same. Countless acres of land that supported no living thing.

He shivered, and a sudden surge of pain more excruciating than anything that had come before clawed into his flesh. He cried out, clutching himself, knocked backwards by the shock of it, and his legs gave way. He could barely breathe. His limbs began to shake and he was aware of his whole body going into convulsions. And the pitch of pain grew. His tears had given way as all his senses became overloaded, blotting out everything but the agony. Out of this came the only conscious response available to him, an unreasoning, violent madness, an all-consuming, futile rage.

On his knees on the shore of the dead lake he twisted his tortured features to the pale sky and screamed.

And screamed.

And screamed.

*　*　*

'Catastrophic!' Asprey declared, not bothering to sit.

'And how would you have gone about it?' demanded Mackelvoye.

'Well, Good Lord, I would have employed a little less of the thuggery. I thought the intention was to pick him up, after all, not knock the living daylights out of him.'

'The order the team was given was to take him off the street to a safe-house for subsequent de-briefing. They may have been over-enthusiastic but their logic was faultless. The chances of his going with them voluntarily were virtually nil. Expedience demanded the minimum delay in getting him into safe-keeping.'

'Well, he rather hoisted them by their own bloody petards, didn't he. Who on Earth did you put onto him? A team of hairdressers?'

'Two of those men were former Artists,' replied Mackelvoye coolly. 'Indeed, one was an officer, long-serving.'

Asprey shook his head blankly.

'The Twenty-Second Artists' Rifles,' Mackelvoye explained. 'SAS. The other two have similar training.'

'And the Apostle swatted them away like gnats, single-handed? My God, let's hope the Russkies don't decide to invade tomorrow. If that's the best we can offer it would be like storming a kindergarten!'

'It's not a reflection on their talents,' Mackelvoye began, and Doctor Geld completed the thought:

'It is what I had feared,' he said with a sidelong glance at Judith, who was silent. 'He has regained his old skills.'

'And his memory?'

Geld shrugged. 'It is not possible to say.'

'So what's being done about it? Are you still with him? I can't stall the Heads any longer, you know.'

'We've not lost him,' Mackelvoye said. 'But he's on the move again. We're in control, Geoffrey, and we'll bring him back or terminate.'

'And what about Six? Any progress there? And your device – I assume none of your fellows succeeded in planting it?'

Mackelvoye shook his head. 'Six is ready to make contact, and the device will be planted.'

Asprey grunted. 'Well, I have bad news for you.' He pulled a piece of paper from his inside pocket. 'This is a directive. Its origins are disguised but it's from Downing Street. You have been ordered to terminate. Immediately. We no longer want him back.'

The engine of the car ticked over in neutral. The heater was on maximum, noisily pumping warmer air into the interior. Adam had kept the vehicle stationary, waiting for the circulation to bring life back to his frozen limbs. He was not yet able to control the car, or willing to endure the freezing draughts that would enter as he drove.

The pain had abated to a tolerable level, but as if in warning still held dully to his frame, gathering for a renewed assault. His nerves were shattered and raw, tremblingly fearful of its return. He was unsure how long he had lain unconscious, though the afternoon light told him it could only have been minutes. He dozed now, and was shocked into wakefulness again and again by the violence of the dream images that swept across his consciousness. Eventually, as the warmth crept back into him, he slipped the engine into gear and moved away.

The forest continued unchanging for some kilometres as he climbed higher into the mountains he had spied earlier. On the steep hills and bends the old Travant made heavy weather of the journey. Its engine roared but at times it barely crawled. According to his map he was close to his destination and he murmured words of encouragement at each new hill crest or each new hairpin the old car struggled to get the better of.

Eventually the ruined trees came to an end, quite abruptly. He climbed for some minutes more then crested a last ridge and began his descent. And it was then, coming around a sharp bend cut through a projecting rocky spur, that the panorama opened before him.

He stopped the car. He was looking down on a broad flat plain completely encircled by mountains. Near its centre two rivers joined and it was here that the city had sprung up. Adam could make out the red-tiled roofs of the old city clustered around the river junction, and radiating out from that central hub, perfectly straight highways, like spokes. The city environs had expanded over centuries, the modern replacing much of the old, until now it covered almost the entire plain. A blanket of cloud hung above it all, hiding the mountain peaks.

Adam sat for some minutes, his chin resting on his hands which were supported by the steering wheel. He was nervous. Nothing was unfamiliar. The sight haunted the back of his mind, lying there in a way he did not yet want to acknowledge, like an aspect of a dream. It mesmerized him, it beckoned. A deep fear was opening within him, a terror, suddenly, that the dream would spring from its lair and overwhelm him. It was the unknown, and the inevitable. It was himself he would be seeking when he entered this place.

When his hand went back to the ignition and turned the key the engine refused to spark. He tried several times but it choked and coughed and would not start. Facing downhill he was able to let the car roll, jumping the clutch to no avail. He coasted the remaining distance down the mountain road. On level ground the vehicle rolled eventually to a halt, and he had no choice but to abandon it and cover the remaining distance into the city on foot.

Terra (In)cognita

It seemed a desolate place. He made his way directly to the old quarter where narrow twisting sett and asphalt streets linked with alleyways and occasional tiny squares to form a dense maze between the high, unending, uneven mortar and part-timbered walls of homes, shops and business premises. A light fall of snow rose around his feet like powder. The sky overhead was a sombre pall and occasionally, between buildings, he would glimpse the nearby mountains, mist-shrouded and uncomfortably close.

Evening was only just approaching but almost everywhere was closed. Shops, cafeterias, bars; the city had a sense of expectation, its inhabitants mostly shut away, safe from the cold, waiting. He checked into a hotel and was given a room on the fourth, top, floor. It was clean and quite adequate. A window in the wall at the foot of his bed gave a view across the crowding red rooftops to the mountains, and for some time he stood there in introspection, watching the cloud, at first virtually still, begin to shift and weave, its great body slowly lifting from the high slopes.

What should he do now? Ruth/Elizabeth had given him no address, no instruction to follow. He had nothing other than her word that the person he was looking for would be here. Here, but where? Would he come to him, in this room? How would he know which hotel? Should Adam go out and look? But where in a strange city should he begin?

The passivity with which he had come here, acting only on the word of a stranger, now became a disquieting and undermining force. What state of mind was this that would cause him to act with such an absence of judgement or thought?

He was tired, but too restless, too wound up for sleep. His skin irritated him but it was at least bearable. He thought back over the journey, over recent weeks. He felt like weeping.

Beyond him the rapidly dispersing cloud and mist gave veiled glimpses of snow-covered peaks. The great chain of encircling black mountains began to loom in a full, harsh grandeur. And as he watched, his mind borne down by betrayals, by disorder, by loss, by uncertainty, by physical and mental angst, he witnessed a transformation.

From somewhere hidden the late sun was throwing dying rays almost horizontally over the rooftops onto the peaks. The snowy crests and ridges suspended above deep shadow were tinged a roseate pink. They had begun to glow softly, some forming islands that soared out of the grey-white cloud clinging to the lower slopes. At their back the sky was a luminous turquoise, merging as the minutes passed through green to yellow-gold, to bright sapphire, to blue violet, to a deepening velvet expanse of impenetrable indigo. Wraiths of dissolving cloud stretched and wound in dazzling formations, changing as he watched, reflecting the sinking sun in molten gold and purple, orange, carmine, crimson and pearl black. He was transfixed, transported and emptied of all thought, until too quickly the moments passed and the light was gone, the mountains turned a uniform grey-black, a ragged hulk not easily distinguished from the darkening heavens where, high above, the first stars were now visible. He sat on the end of the bed until there was nothing before his eyes but a double black rectangle that was the window.

When he left the hotel he was directed by the reception-clerk to a nearby square. In the streets around it he found a choice of bars and places to eat that had stayed open for business. He ate in a small tavern, taking a window seat and distractedly observing the few huddled figures that passed in the street. As he ate the snow began to fall again, and by the time he had finished it was falling heavily, big soft flakes that quickly covered the surface of the street and pavement outside. There were few other customers. A faulty cassette player behind the bar played folk songs and instrumentals slippingly, and a bloodhound snoozed in front of an open fire. When his meal was over he resigned himself to returning to the hotel, at a loss for anything else he might purposefully do.

A group passed in the street, close to his window. Three men and a woman, laughing and talking loudly, a little merry with drink. His eyes followed them until the partition wall of the next building blocked them from sight. He almost failed to notice the darkly hooded figure that trailed unobtrusively a few yards behind them on the other side of the little street. It was a man, by build, though the face was obscured. He wore a duffel-coat, untoggled, his hands in its pockets, seemingly deep in thought as he passed, head slightly bowed, looking neither to left nor right, walking in a manner that suggested no sense of going anywhere in particular.

There was no streetlamp outside and it was difficult to see clearly, but Adam's heart gave a leap. Already the man's back was to him, and there had been no opportunity to define any features. But Adam slapped down a bundle of notes and weaved quickly between tables and chairs to the exit, under the eye of the landlord who, roused by the hasty departure, darted a frown towards his table before relaxing.

Outside the figure had advanced twenty yards. Adam hesitated at the door and watched, fearful. Could he have made an error? Surely not? The way the man held himself, the wide, sloping shoulders, short legs and slightly tripping gait, the air of deep absorption; he knew it all well.

He started off after him and then, catching up, a yard or so behind, began again to doubt. There was a sense of dislocation, a vertiginous sensation of being sucked backwards too quickly down a long tunnel, of stepping into a moment he had experienced too many times before. The figure in front remained oblivious to his presence. It entered a field of shallow orange sodium lamplight. Adam took a breath and quickly moved up to bring himself alongside, turning for a view of the face. He saw only the nose, the roundness of a cheek in shadow, a clean-shaven chin and faintly smiling lips, wisps of long pale hair flying free of the grey hood. He reached out and placed his hand on the man's arm.

'Helm?'

They both stopped walking.

'Helmut?'

The expression was at first that of a man roused suddenly from a comfortable sleep. Then Helmut's rounded features crinkled and were lit by a broad smile. 'Adam! My friend!'

He opened his arms.

'Helmut, what are you doing here?' They embraced warmly. 'It's so good to see you! I can't believe it!'

The scent of Helmut's French perfume, the familiar, faintly unwashed essence of his clothing, the warmth of his body, the sound of his voice, the sight of his face . . . Adam was returned to London, to something he had left, and lost. It seemed long ago, a distant memory. He was overwhelmed, overjoyed, and at the same time disturbed. He clung to his old friend tightly, afraid to let him go.

Helmut was laughing, a high-pitched laugh. 'My friend, the feeling is entirely reciprocated, in all respects. This is a happy coincidence!'

'I've been so worried. I thought . . . I thought . . .' Adam released him, but kept his hands on Helmut's shoulders. 'What are you doing here?'

'I came for escape, and for inspiration!' Helmut took out from his coat pocket an old exercise book and a pen. His cheeks were flushed. 'This region is my home, my ancestral home. I have never visited but all my life I have felt its call. I always resisted for I felt it could serve no purpose to come here. After all, I know nobody. There are relations, no doubt, but they are unaware of me, and I have no wish to strike up any acquaintance. But nevertheless it is part of me and its influence is undeniable. So the opportunity arose and I came. Like you, my friend, I am looking for my past.'

He grinned and clasped Adam's arms, but there was something guarded in his manner. He had left something unsaid. His eyes, from studying Adam's face, glanced quickly down the street then back again. Adam tacitly acknowledged his implication; now was perhaps not the time to make all things clear.

The ends of Helmut's long fair hair collected large crystal snowflakes as they shifted restlessly about his hood. His breath, like Adam's, made brief clouds of white vapour in the night air. Beneath the open duffel-coat he wore a red sweatshirt over at least one other layer of clothing. On its front there was an emblem which Adam could not make out for the woollen scarf that hung over it. Adam lifted the scarf aside. 'ANYTHING GOES', he read in meniscus form in white lettering. He smiled and hugged his friend again.

'But you, my friend,' Helmut said in a graver voice. 'What is it that brings you to such a distant place? I have to say, I have been concerned about you also.'

He took Adam's arm and they resumed walking. Adam watched his shoes pushing furrows through the pure white snow. So much needed saying, so much discovering. The meeting had thrown him into a whirl of elation bordering on the manic. He could not order his thoughts and did not know where to begin. His joy at meeting Helmut was tempered by Helmut's caution, and by the almost certain knowledge that it could not be pure coincidence. He was aware of phantoms, of dangers both within him and without, and of intelligences at work behind the scenes, ordering events over which he had no control. And he knew nothing. Nothing at all.

Where to begin?

'Helm?' he said eventually, lowering his voice. 'Do you know about Dennis?'

There was the slightest pause in Helmut's forward motion, then his footsteps continued. 'I do,' he said quietly. 'In truth it was the spur that drove me here at this time. It drew me to the conviction that my own environment was no safe haven.'

'Do you know what they are doing? I tried to contact you. I thought they had got you too.'

'They? Do you know who was responsible?'

With relief Adam began to pour out what he had learned about

Geld and Gospel. As briefly as possible he told Helmut of the events that had befallen him since they had last spoken. He told him of his meetings with Simon Partridge, and of Partridge's death on the steps of St Paul's. He included the young woman in Kensington who, like Dennis, had died with her throat cut. 'For no reason other than that she'd had contact with me. That has to be the reason.' He had speculated that perhaps she possessed more information, but he doubted that. 'It was so senseless. All she did was pass on a neighbour's address.' He shook his head. He had abandoned attempts to find sense in what was happening.

Bitterly he went on to tell of his discovery of Judith's involvement, her longstanding collusion with Geld, her participation in Gospel. 'It was not true betrayal, I accept that. We were in it together. But why the cover-up? To maintain such a grand and intricate deception for so long – it can only have hindered my progress. And for what?' He could not keep the emotion from his voice. 'For *what*?'

'Then you still have no memory of it all?' Helmut enquired.

'Snatches. The briefest hints, vaguest impressions. It's coming, bit by tiny bit, but there's nothing truly cohesive, no clear picture or unbroken stream.'

They had entered a small square. At its centre stood a fountain and pool with a baroque stone statue. Water that normally spouted from the genitalia of cherubs and the throats of dolphins was stilled, frozen into fantastical forms.

Adam turned to Helmut. 'You must have known something, Helm. You must have had some idea. Why didn't you tell me? Why didn't somebody tell me *something*?'

Helmut left his side and crossed to the fountain. He brushed snow from the rim and sat. As Adam approached he surveyed his features for some seconds with a slight rhythmic rocking of his head and shoulders. 'My friend, more like an evacuee from Poe than ever.' He looked at the disturbed snow around his feet, at their tracks across the square. He said, 'All I had was suspicion. Something – with you at its core – was not as it was set out to be. But what, or who, or how, or why . . . these things eluded me. And whilst I gently probed, anxious as I was for you to regain the details of your life, I could not dare push you. There were times when I doubted myself, my suspicions as they gained ground would have stretched the threshold of credulity of the most imaginative of men. To have attempted to present them to you in your condition would have been to invite catastrophe. I could only sit and wait and observe and, as far as possible, encourage. The process was intolerably slow but I could not subject you to anything more rigorous. And of course, I had my own hide to consider. I dared not risk being anything to you, in their eyes, other than a friend, a concerned but unknowing friend.'

Adam listened agitatedly. Drawing his coat about him, he sat down on the rim of the fountain beside his friend. The falling snow was tossed on breaths of cold wind about the square. Over their heads the phones and leads of an old tannoy system had been strung across the square from buildings and lamp-posts, oscillating with occasional barely heard rasps and creaks.

'So of course, it is not a coincidence that we should meet in this place,' Helmut went on. 'Though it is sheer coincidence that we should meet here just now. I, like you, have just arrived, just checked into a hotel and eaten. I had anticipated a lengthy and perhaps fruitless search – I came here to find you; I have been following your movements as best I could. With Dennis's death things took a new and menacing turn, and I could only assume that the danger extended directly to myself. I wanted to contact you but security around you would obviously have been stepped up. So I got away, at least temporarily, while I still could. That we should find each other like this . . .' he lifted his hands and let them fall back onto his thighs, 'is sheer good fortune. Perhaps the gods are smiling on us.'

'I thought you eschewed superstition,' Adam said with a wry attempt at humour he did not feel. Helmut gave a throaty chuckle but made no comment.

'Do you know Ruth, then? Or Elizabeth, or whatever her name is?' Adam said with a rising fervour. He felt suddenly that he was about to be crushed, washed away, drowned. The nightmare of preceding weeks was threatening to spill through, distorting his perception, his judgement, his ability to reason. He wanted to come out with everything, pass it all over and have done. No more questions. No more mysteries. 'Do you know her friend? The man who was with her at the party when you gave your reading? I came here to find him. He knows something. She told me he would be here, waiting for me. Do you have a connection with them, Helm? They know about Gospel. About me. But they're apart from it.'

Helmut shook his head. He had removed his exercise book from his pocket again and was staring at the blue, dog-eared cover. He held a silver pen in the fingers of his other hand. Adam wondered for a moment whether he was listening. 'I know very little, my friend. I am almost as baffled by this business as you are. I can only suggest that you take great care. Remember, you are in great danger, we both are, and nothing is ever quite what it seems. Should you encounter this person, by all means try and get any information you can out of him, but do not take undue risks. It might be preferable if we can confront him together, though I suspect the opportunity will not arise. Perhaps we can arrange some deception that will draw him to us.'

But now it was Adam who was not listening. With little heed of what Helmut had said he blurted out, not thinking of his words but more to hear himself speak, to reassure himself that he was speaking to someone, a willing ear, a real person who could respond, who was there, who knew: 'Helm, there are so many things, not just Gospel. What's it all about? It's madness. I've been healing people, do you know that? Curing incurable illnesses. I have visions, experiences that turn out to have been premonitions. Because of me people die, and others are given a new life. What does it mean? My past comes back in flashes that I can barely distinguish from dreams, and every element reveals something more fantastic, more incredible than I could ever have imagined. I know I'm crazy. I can't depend on my perception. I stagger through a nightmare and the truth becomes wilder and seemingly more irrational. But there's a thread. There has to be. Something that connects, that means something. I can't fully grasp it but I keep trying. I'm convinced of it, though everything conspires to persuade me otherwise.'

He pushed himself up off the cold stone rim, his fists bunched at his sides, and took a couple of steps away, then turned. 'Helm, do you remember when you brought me home after that party?' He returned. There was a strained look on Helmut's face and an accompanying cautioning gesture with one hand. But Adam did not sit. 'You told Jude I had assumed this personality, this empathic identification with the planet. I was in pain and raving, that I was going to die, pleading with people to stop hurting me. Do you remember that? You mentioned it again when you visited later.'

Helmut nodded. 'I remember.'

'Well, this sounds more fantastic than anything, but I've been forced to think hard about it. I think there's something in it.'

Helmut shifted his gaze to the guttering of a nearby building. He had resumed a sleepy look, as though a large part of him was engaged in business elsewhere. 'Go on,' he said, though it was hardly necessary.

'Today, driving here, I came through a forest, a huge area that had been killed. The trees were all dead, the grass, the lakes, everything. The soil ruined, poisoned. And as I was approaching it, before I had even become aware of it, my skin erupted. It was so bad I had to stop the car. I went into the forest and I felt it, Helm. That same poison, that same death, burning into me. I felt what was happening and it was unbearable. And there was nothing I could do, no one I could get through to. I felt I was at the end. Things had been done to me and it had gone too far, got out of control. It no longer served a purpose and it was killing me.' He stopped, his breathing had grown rapid. His arms and hands had unconsciously wrapped themselves around his upper body. 'All I had left was rage. A blind, maddened, helpless fury directed at everyone who had put me through this. I no longer cared about answers or reasons, I just wanted to stop it all by any means. In that rage I saw, I thought I saw, so clearly. I was *driven* to see, but it was too late.'

'See what, my friend?' Helmut enquired gently after a pause. Adam was suddenly deflated. He stared at Helmut and shook his head, dazed, all animation gone. Slumping, he sat down beside him again.

'Our death,' he said. 'Contained within the attitude that engenders this kind of thoughtlessness and permits such a legacy to grow unchecked. It isn't just here, it's everywhere. In everything. We are killing ourselves and taking everything with us. God!' He covered his face with his hands. 'I can't see any more. There isn't any order, there isn't any meaning. It's just chaos. I don't know what I'm doing now. I'm just one man. I've been through all this and still there's no meaning, I just go deeper into misunderstanding. Everything turns to dust. Oh God, I don't know. What are we?' He looked up at the black sky. 'What are we in this vastness, this monstrous treacherous void? Where is there something to hold on to?'

Helmut at first made no comment. He sat at Adam's side, deep in thought, then he wrote something briefly in the exercise book on his thigh. Then in a soft voice he said, 'My friend, you are overwrought. You know the world's pain and wish to put things to rights, but, as you say, you are only one man. You cannot change the world, nor, I believe, can you make sense of it.'

'Then what is there, Helm? What are we here for?'

Helmut shook his head. 'I have no solace to offer you. If, as you indicate, you expect to find meaning, or evidence of some divine intelligence that will hold all this together, I fear you are bound for even further disappointment. The only comfort, the only binding force that exists is the very fact that there is none – at least, not of the kind that you would hope to believe in. Greater minds than yours or mine have wrestled with the same essential problem, the concept of a world that is fundamentally lawless, where events are measured in terms of probabilities and uncertainties rather than measurable and predictable determinants. Even Einstein, clinging to his conviction that God does not play dice with the cosmos, found himself eventually staring into chaos.'

Adam lowered his hands. 'That does not mean there is no God, merely that we are unable to understand it.'

Helmut sighed. 'So do you believe you are close to understanding God?'

'I don't know anything but my own experience, Helm. I've told you.'

'And your experience tells you there is only chaos and meaninglessness.'

Helmut waited but Adam did not reply, and eventually he gave a grin. 'It is my own belief that in the face of such immensities there can be but one rational response if we are to retain any vestige of sanity.' He twisted his body towards Adam, opening the flaps of his duffel-coat to expose once again the large white lettering on the chest of his sweatshirt.

Adam half-smiled, but he wanted to entreat him, No! That is not the way. It engenders purposelessness, it negates responsibility. It dissociates, it dehumanizes. It creates a moral and spiritual desert. It degenerates, it represses, it degrades. It passes everything into the hands of ego, it permits our beasts and demons to roam free. It is responsible for all this.

But he said nothing, for he knew that Helmut would not deny these things, any of them, but would merely claim in his own defence that 'Anything Goes' is a response to, not a creator of, an already existing condition. The conversation could proceed in no fruitful direction. It was directed, after all, at meaninglessness.

Helmut too seemed to acknowledge this. He had closed his coat and was brushing at the snow that had settled on his shoulders and hood. 'Where are you staying, my friend?' he said abruptly.

Adam told him.

'It isn't advisable for us to spend too much time in each other's company just now. We must assume that you are being watched, and whilst they are unlikely to attempt another direct assault, they do have other means. And knowing that you have regained some of your former skills will have increased their nervousness. I think you should go back to your hotel. I want to give some thought to our next move. Later, if I judge it clear, I shall come to your room, but alternatively we should meet early tomorrow. It is Sunday and there will be few people about. Can you find this square again?'

Adam nodded and Helmut pointed to a narrow gap between two buildings. 'Through there you will find a small park. It is quite private. The river runs alongside. There are benches on the right, with trees covering three sides. Meet me there at eight if I don't come tonight.'

He had risen to his feet, he seemed hurried, as if just re-alerted to the dangers of their situation. Adam followed suit and they embraced. Again Helmut's scent, the aura that was him, penetrating Adam's nostrils and whisking him vividly back to the world he had fled from, which he desired so much to return to but could not for fear of what it, and he, had become. And his impressions went beyond, deep into his past, stirring up much but revealing little. He shuddered as he loosed his grip on his friend, a brief dizziness overcoming him.

'You are all right, my friend?'

Adam nodded. 'I'm glad you're here, Helm.'

'It's been a fortuitous evening,' Helmut agreed. 'Now let us look to your future.'

They parted, and when Helmut had gone from the square Adam left the fountain and made his way back to his hotel.

Confrontation

Sleep did not come easily. He would have sworn that he slept for no more than two or three minutes at a time.

He climbed those stairs to his room and lay on his back on the bed. The black double-rectangle that was the window revealed nothing of the world other than the tumbling flakes of snow that were blown against its surface or dropped past it towards the earth below. He listened to the scuffling of pigeons beneath the eaves.

He climbed the stairs. He was deeply afraid. The sounds and smells of the old house filled him with foreboding. He was wet and shivering. Foolishly he had come without anything. There was no light, nothing living. A shift of an unseen something nearby. He had to feel his way, groping in darkness. The rain beat in gusts on the window panes, the wind came in under doors, rattling latches and lifting untacked carpet. He was on the last flight of stairs, picking his steps over discarded junk. The odours of dampness and decay had an almost physical touch, mingling with other smells, containing histories that would never be known, of estrangement and want, neglect and despair. Poached fish sickened him, a waft of curried air, a stale tang of alcohol, an unhealthy warmth that he was reluctant to allow into his lungs, a faint, barely registered scent that had no place here and yet belonged. It came to him and passed him by. He was at the top. He faced the yellow door.

He knew what was behind it, but when he pushed, expecting resistance, the door swung open freely and he stepped through into a circle. He was surrounded by faces. Directly in front of him the woman, near-naked, cooed lullabies to a loaf of bread. He healed her. He turned to the encircling watchers who grinned or gaped or stared in curious silence, to the men at the brasserie door who made jokes. At his shoulder a voice: '*We all need help, Mr Shatt. Every single one of us.*'

But who most? he asked. There was no reply.

He stepped over to the men at the door. He healed them, one by one. Then he healed the women, then the children. He healed them all and he stood at their centre, and when they understood what he had done to them they turned to him, their faces twisted with malice. '*God is without mercy,*' the voice hissed. '*That's all there is.*'

'*No!*' he shouted as he fell beneath them, as their nails ripped his flesh, as they kicked and trampled his body. 'No! There is more!'

But that was not what they wanted to hear.

He had woken. Nothing had changed. The light was on, as he had left it, and the black rectangle still hovered over the foot of his bed. He was fully clothed, alert and tensed. What had woken him? He sat up and shook the sleep from his head. A sound, some alien disturbance had entered his room and his consciousness. The door. There had been a knock at the door.

It was Helmut!

He left the bed and listened at the door, then opened it. The corridor outside was empty. He returned to sit on the edge of the bed, and some moments later caught sight of the slip of white paper, folded, lying on the carpet some inches inside the room. He picked it up, opened it, and read: 'I am outside'.

It had been written in blue ink, by hand, in an unnatural jerky script, as though on an uneven surface. He took his coat and left.

The street appeared deserted. He advanced some steps through the tumbling snow, peering about him into the half-darkness, looking for his friend in doorways or recesses, but there seemed to be no one. He went further, then paused and looked back to the hotel entrance. The night was bitter; he clenched his jaw, shivering.

A few more yards, then he would turn back the other way. But three paces on he saw him, just a movement, a figure, recognizably human, that seemed to step out of a wall some yards ahead, beckon hurriedly, then disappear again. Adam, a new apprehension in his heart, moved up.

When he reached the place he found a passage squeezed between two tall houses. Ahead he saw him again, a shadow, waiting, gesturing, dematerializing.

Adam followed. In this manner he was led through a maze of passageways and alleys, barely lit except for an occasional solitary bulb hanging over an anonymous door. He slipped several times. His breath burned in his chest. Always the figure was just a few yards ahead, at the next corner, the next twist. His white clothing was a ghostly blur; a fading cynosure in an enclosing darkness.

He was led through a gateless entrance beneath a low stone arch into a small courtyard enclosed by high walls. He stood for a moment, short of breath. Across from him the man stood framed in the doorway of a house, silhouetted against yellow light from the interior. On the walls ivy or some other clinging plant crept. Adam took a step forward and the man withdrew into the house, leaving the door wide.

Following, Adam found himself in a lobby. It was uncarpeted and bare but for a single radiator and water pipes which gave out a welcome heat in contrast to the freezing temperature outside. A narrow, spiralling stone staircase led up to his left, and ahead another door stood partially open. Beyond it a dimness, a fuzzy flickering of orange and shadow. He walked up to it. His legs were trembling and he had broken into a sudden drenching sweat. His heart and temples pounded, his throat was parched and he could barely swallow. He pressed his fingers to the door and stepped through.

The room, like the lobby, was almost bare. A log fire burned heartily in an open hearth, and it was this that threw the shadow and colour onto the undraped walls. There was no other light source, a single small window was covered with a blank blue curtain. The only furniture was an antique writing desk and two chairs. A crystal decanter stood on the desk with two tumblers, and behind it, seated facing Adam, was the man he had followed, who had followed him, whom he had come this far to find.

Adam supported himself with one hand on the door. For some moments neither spoke or made any move. Each took the measure of the other, then the man, rising from his seat, gestured to the empty chair in front of the desk. 'Please, sit down. You look as if you might collapse.'

He had an affable smile. He walked around the desk and crossed the room to close the door behind Adam, who moved to sink wearily onto the chair offered. In such light it was not easy to make out his features. He moved with a relaxed, assured manner. He was not old but had an ageless quality about him, and there was something vaguely familiar in his look, as though Adam had known him before, though he could not place him. Returning and sitting he poured a tumbler full of clear liquid from the decanter and placed it on the desktop before Adam. 'I'm sorry I have no other refreshment. As you can see, this is not a permanent arrangement.'

Adam accepted the glass and tested the contents. Water. He gulped it down and the man smiled again. There was something in him that brought to mind Ruth, or Elizabeth, or whatever she chose to call herself. He placed his fingertips on the desk; beside one hand was a notepad, and on the other side of the desk a small booklet or pamphlet of some kind, which as far as Adam could make out had no title on its cover.

'No doubt you have a lot of questions,' the man began, but Adam for the moment could find nothing to say. Perhaps it was the warmth of the room, combined with his exhaustion, countering his wariness, but he no longer felt any urgency. He felt detached and somewhat entranced, as though nothing particularly mattered. He could only stare blankly and the man, observing him, seemed to understand. 'I can give you answers,' he went on unhurriedly, 'though in fact none of them, in a real sense, will be new to you.' At his back the shadows and shapes thrown from the flames of the open fire played in blurred and restless motion over the red-hued wall. He linked his fingers on the desktop. 'Let's begin at the beginning. Why did I follow you? The answer to that is simple and anticipates the next question, Why have I led you here? I had to gain your attention, that is all. And having done that I had to ensure I did not lose it again. I knew you, and I knew more about you than you possibly could in the state you were in.'

'You knew me?' Adam said, roused slightly. 'In my past?'

The man went on as if he had not heard. 'No matter by what

means, I had to make you come after me. I had to get you away from the situation you were in. You were already looking for me, you see, though you did not know it. The chaos in which you floundered so pathetically obscured everything. You wanted to escape but you couldn't see. You didn't know, and if I had not acted you would have been lost.'

He paused, either to allow this to sink in or to gather his next words. His eyes did not leave Adam's face. 'The next questions – Why? What is happening? What *has* happened? – are not as simply answered. To fully appreciate everything behind your recent experiences, and in fact your whole life, demands an adjusting of consciousness, a way of seeing and assimilating that normal perception does not embrace. It is a natural process and it takes time, and is not always easy. You have begun to make that adjustment and have experienced some of the rewards, and the penalties as you at present perceive them, that such adjustment entails. It is not easily put into words. At present you still know little more than confusion and it is not my wish or role to heighten that confusion. Unavoidably though, things cannot all become clear until the full process is complete.'

He withdrew his hands from the desk and sat back, swinging around in his chair to watch for some moments the shadows on the wall. Presently, without turning back, he said, 'Imagine yourself the prisoner in Plato's cave who has just slipped his bonds and who, whilst realizing, yes, these things I see before me are real, is also just beginning to see that they do not actually constitute the totality of the world as he had previously believed unquestioningly. Imagine that you, a prisoner since childhood, are for the first time beginning to see more than mere shadows. You are startled and bewildered. Your new freedom, far from liberating, appears to bind, to obfuscate rather than illuminate. It is alien, it is madness, for it can't be true, it defies all previous experience and belief, all learning. It dazzles and blinds, it terrifies and confounds, it debilitates and it isolates. And yet, despite all this, it is freedom, and once grasped it can never be released. At times you will beg and pray to be delivered from it, even to return to your previous state, but you know within yourself that even were the choice offered you would not take it. Burdensome as it seems it is infinitely preferable to the confinement of what went before.'

He rotated back in his chair to face Adam again, scrutinizing him closely to be sure he had not lost him. Again he waited before continuing: 'Perhaps you can see, then, that the loss of your past was necessary. It was a hindrance, keeping you from those first essential steps. Now it will no longer exert the same influence. Everything needs to be perceived in its rightful context, and as you, to remain with the simile, are able now to see more than shadows, it can return. Be careful, though. It still has the power to destroy you.

'I can hardly explain further. Suffice to say that your knowledge is not lost, and once you can learn to accept that you will see more clearly. The dark night of your soul is almost at an end, but only because it is not yours alone and you have begun to see that. You *know* that what you have experienced is true: this is the obscure night, the dark night of the world's soul. We are near its end. This is the turning point, the joining of rivers, the birth of the future, or it is the death of everything. You are becoming aware that you have a part to play, and that it is not a delusion. You have been offered a choice which is no choice, for you know what it will mean to disregard it. There is a child waiting to be born, and you, who no longer gaze at shadows in a cave, are here to help.'

The man's eyes held Adam's now as he spoke. His distantly familiar features were licked by the glow and flickering shadow of the flames. His expression was one of penetrating, questioning benignity. Adam stretched the muscles of his back and legs. His arms and legs burned. He smoothed his hands together – the palms were liquid – and let his gaze wander quickly about the room. He was searching for a focus, something that he could fasten on, that would establish reason in this unreason. He came to rest on the glass decanter, for there was little else. In the still water the fire was reflected in miniature. Just beyond it, beside the man's pale hand, was the notepad, and Adam, groping for something to say, latched onto this and spoke. 'You were writing about me.'

The man nodded.

'Why? What did you write?'

He gathered his hands beneath his chin and gazed thoughtfully at the desktop for some moments. Then he took the notepad and pushed it across the surface towards Adam.

With fingers that hardly belonged to him Adam lifted the cover of the pad. He turned it around to read what was written on the first lined page: 'He failed to hear the furied gunning of the engine, or see the cherry red Fiat that tore around a corner a little way off. In a daze he had stepped back from the pavement'.

Adam frowned. 'Is that it? All you wrote?'

'Almost.' The man leaned across and lifted the sheet.

On the next page Adam saw: 'Like a charging bull, with its head lowered, it caught him mid-thigh and tossed him high over its bonnet, bouncing him off the reinforced windshield as though he were no more than a rag doll. In that second, as he flew, as the earth waited to receive his body, there was a loud but muffled sound. An ugly sound of anger and awful finality, that sent a shockwave through the narrow confine of the street. He was blown apart before he touched the ground, fragments of blood, bone and gristle scattering wide and spattering the walls and windows of the nearest buildings'.

Adam stiffened. 'What's this? It makes no sense.'

The man lifted his hands. 'Perhaps not. I had written the first when you saw me at the party where your friend was reading. The second I did in an Islington street. The last one was at the meeting in the infants' school.'

Adam turned one more page. Written there was a single sentence: 'And his blood and guts mingled with the red, red snow'.

This caused him a greater dismay than the other two entries combined. 'What the hell — ' he began.

'I have told you,' the man said evenly, 'your past still has the power to destroy you. You have to be aware of that. But there are many deaths, in many forms, and it need not be what it seems. We write our own stories, you see, whether we are aware of it or not. What you have just read may have no bearing now, perhaps not ever. But just remember, the past is never behind us. It is with us and before us, and we stand in its path.'

'Enough!' Adam pushed the pad away with a force that sent it over the desk's edge and onto the floor with a loud slap. 'Just tell me!' He rose from the chair, shaking, supporting himself with his hands on the desk. The one question that had been burning in his mind for so many weeks, that he had asked again and again and discovered no answer to, that he had wanted but found himself unable to ask when he had entered this room, now rose and fell from his tongue. 'Who are you? You say you are from my past. Who the *hell* are you?'

The man had risen too, mirroring his movement, not in a threatening manner, but as if in anticipation of something. The smile did not leave his lips. 'You don't know?' He was unruffled. 'You have come so far, suffered so much to find me, and after all this you still don't know?'

'*Tell me!*'

The voice was calm and even. It seemed to float as though borne on the shadows of the flames that gave life to the room. As it spoke there was nothing else. The room, the speaker, the fire, the chairs and desk, all were removed. There was Adam, the void, and the voice that filled it. The voice was Adam, and he was the void; he both created and received it, he contained it and was contained within it, and everything that was belonged in this moment. He said, 'I am what you have been searching for all this time. I am your past. I am your present, and your future too. I have brought you to this because that is what you demanded, because you were prepared to come. I am everything, you see. I am you.'

So he was insane. After all this, to come, or believe he had come, so far; to go through, or believe he had gone through, so much, only to discover that it was, after all, nothing but delusion and nightmare. He raised his head and looked around him. Was he here, where he believed himself to be? Was he not at home? Would he not wake once again to find himself in his own bed, Judith curled beside him? Or was he in a hospital somewhere, a still body on a bed, surrounded by monitors, drips, scanners, irretrievably lost within a nightmare world a degenerating consciousness had conjured up? Was this the truth, that everything was his own created chaos, that nothing existed beyond himself and the disease that had taken his mind? How could he know? How could he know anything? Was he mad? Was there nothing more to it? Or was he simply a man dreaming he was mad? Or a madman about to wake to find he was a butterfly? He screamed and fell away from the desk he believed to be there.

And the voice was relentless. Even now, as he tried to get away, it would not leave him. 'It is the hardest thing, to face yourself. You are bound to try to run, but there is nowhere to go.'

'No!'

'You have brought yourself here. It was your decision.'

'No!'

There was a sensation as of hands touching him, on his chest, then lower, at his side, not restraining. 'Take this. It will help.'

He lashed out, pushing away. *What were they giving him? They were keeping him under!*

'No! No more! Please!'

There was no resistance. Had they gone? He ran. He had seen nothing. What had they given him? What had they done to him?

'It will come back.'

He was back outside, or still inside, stumbling across the snow-filled courtyard or the landscape of his nightmare, out into the labyrinth of passageways where no light fell.

Revelation

He lay sprawled, face down. The lamp was on over the bedside cabinet, as he had left it. He stared for some time at a pattern, pale floral stripes, before awareness came that he was awake. He twisted his head. The twin-rectangle that hung above the foot of the bed told him morning had not yet come. He heaved himself up to a sitting position. He was fully clothed. He wondered how long he had slept.

For a time he sat and gradually orientated himself to the world of touch, sight, smell and hearing his senses conveyed. He was shaking. He pulled his coat about him; whilst he believed the air in the room was warm he felt both hot and cold. He remembered Helmut with a start. Was it his knock that had awoken him?

In a daze he went to the door, listened, opened it. There was no one there. From a room across the hall came the muted sound of snoring. He closed the door and leaned against it, returned to the bed and sat for another minute in thought, then phoned downstairs. The reception-clerk assured him he had made no call to his room. Adam enquired the time. He ordered an early breakfast of coffee, eggs and bread rolls in his room. It seemed unlikely that Helmut would come now, they would have to meet instead at the agreed-upon rendezvous.

He ate hungrily when the meal arrived, then permitted himself to go over the night's occurrences. Memory unfolded and reason denied it, arguing that it could not be correct, at least not detail for detail. He concluded unhappily, as the two rectangles were suffused a luminescent grey, on the side of reason: he had not left the room. He was grateful that time pressed, that the great dark ring of mountains had risen beyond the rooftops through the heavily descending snow, that Helmut would soon be waiting.

He walked quickly towards the tiny square where they had talked last night. Ahead of and above him the first light had touched the mountain peaks with a tinge of soft colour, a pinkish glow that had none of the spectacular violence of the previous evening's sunset, standing out in a field of unrelieved grey. He noticed starlings roosting beneath eaves and on scaffolding and the branches of trees at the side of the streets.

The square was empty as he passed through. He entered the passageway Helmut had pointed out and slipped his hands into his coat pockets, psychologically as much as physically cold. He had emerged from the passage into a clearing bounded on two sides by buildings, and ahead and to his right by woodland, when he became aware that what his fingertips had made contact with should not be there. He withdrew one hand from its pocket and stared at the small, floppy, paperbound booklet it held. The plain grey cover contained no title, nor a publisher's impress. He opened it and saw printed inside: *The Simile Of The Cave*. The following pages, about a dozen or so, contained Plato's full text. In his other hand he had a crumpled scrap of notepaper on which was scribbled a single sentence: 'I am outside'.

He moved on with an uncertain gait, following a narrow path that circumvented the trees, and found himself facing a river. The river was dangerously swollen. In front of him stood a low stone wall which, when he looked over, he saw fell some six feet to the water. On the other side of the river were more buildings of the old town, and immediately behind them, it appeared, the first of the mountains suddenly rose.

It seemed to Adam that he was experiencing a slight distortion or fallacy of vision. The snow was disorienting, blurring details, but the light that fell across the looming black rock as he gazed seemed to have undergone a change. The rosiness of minutes before had acquired a fuller hue, a deeper, earthier tone that was not ascribable to the distortion of sunlight. And this redness extended further down the crags and slopes than the light, in these conditions, should have permitted. It was perhaps an optical illusion, but it was an unsettling one. He fingered the slim booklet in his pocket and looked around for Helmut.

The wall ended a few yards to his right and was replaced by a green iron fence. Here was an open area set back from the river and sheltered on three sides by woodland. As described, two wooden benches stood at its centre, facing the river and the city and mountains beyond. On one of the two benches a hooded figure in a grey duffel-coat was seated.

'My friend!' Helmut, who had been staring at his feet, his short legs extended, heels and trouser hems in the snow, greeted him with a heavy-lidded smile. His exercise book lay open on his lap. 'I was growing concerned. You were not in your room when I called.'

'You came to my room?'

'I knocked and got no reply. I woke the night clerk and had him ring you. Did you go out in the night?'

Adam shifted his gaze to the river. The water swept by, yellow-brown, churning, straining to burst its banks. It carried with it pieces of driftwood, broken branches, paper, plastic, polystyrene cups and other pieces of unidentifiable refuse. It was a living thing roused to wrath. He became mesmerized by the motion.

'How's Boadicea, Helm?' he asked, without knowing why.

'Boadicea?'

'Your wheels. That's the name, isn't it?'

'Ah. Yes. No. I renamed her. Enola Gay.'

Something almost latched into place. Adam looked across at the mountains. He was on the verge of something. He turned and looked into Helmut's puzzled eyes, as if the answer might be found there.

'Something happened,' he muttered. 'Last night, something happened.'

Helmut squinted at him and lifted an arm to push back his hood. He shook his long hair free and smoothed the hand over his broad dome. A faint breath of scent escaped his clothing. Adam turned away quickly, gagging on the breakfast he had eaten.

'Adam, are you all right?'

He leaned back, afraid now to look at Helmut. Pieces of a jigsaw were falling into place. A snake had pushed out its snout from beneath a rock; still hidden from daylight a sinuous body was preparing to uncoil.

'Helmut, can you see that?'

'Yes, I see.'

'What do you see?'

'The same as you, my friend. The mountains are turning red.'

'How, then? It's not the light, is it?'

The daylight was strong enough now to show the mountains almost without shadow. And the redness of moments before had indeed extended to the lower slopes, as far as the town across the river. The buildings, with their red roofs, were growing vague and difficult to distinguish against the uncanny red haze all around. Above, even the pregnant snowclouds were heavy with the same unearthly colour.

'It is not the light,' Helmut agreed. He extended a hand, palm up. 'It is not the light.'

'Then what is it?'

'Perhaps a dream.' He withdrew the hand and gazed at his palm. 'Look, the first flakes.'

Adam was mute. Interspersed amongst the crystal white flakes that Helmut had trapped were several of a different hue, glistening then quickly melting on the warmth of his hand, running to the centre to form a tiny pool of reddish water. More were falling as the seconds passed, the white turning to red.

The Nuclear Age Thinker looked at him in the eye and grinned. 'The blood of the slain, my friend? Or those who have yet to die?'

Adam let his lids close for a second; the serpent had withdrawn again into its hidden place. 'Don't be alarmed, my friend,' he heard Helmut say. 'It is readily explained.'

He opened his eyes. 'Is it?'

'Quite simple. It's an uncommon occurrence, and in this

instance a quite extraordinary coincidence, but it is a well-known meteorological phenomenon.'

Adam lifted his face. Blown on the breeze, light cold flakes pricked his skin. He was unutterably tired.

'Under unusual atmospheric conditions minute particles of sand and dust can be carried on prevailing air currents,' Helmut went on. 'In this instance, judging from the coloration, from the Holy Land or somewhere in the region, I would imagine. The change in temperature, or pressure, or whatever the case may be, accounts for their precipitation at this particular point. It could have been almost anywhere.'

'And that's all there is to it?' Adam said. He was still aware of something else taking place here, something he could not yet quite grasp. The hairs on the back of his neck had begun to crawl.

'What else do you propose? Synchronicity? Some other form of psychic phenomenon? No. I am no subscriber to such views, not when we have the rational explanation to hand. Years ago that would have been the natural recourse, before things were understood. Now it would be a regression into superstitious ignorance. This has been recorded elsewhere, many times, in many variations. Green rain in Russia — subsequently discovered to be tons and tons of pollen transported from God knows where. Elsewhere it has rained froglets or fish! You name it, it has probably rained or snowed it!'

'Helm, this is what I've been seeing all this time. I've been drawn here. Do you honestly believe you can dismiss it as coincidence?'

'My friend, the path you are treading is a most unstable one, believe me. The facts are before us. I have already expressed to you my sentiments regarding a search for any deeper, hidden meaning or significance.'

'And last night, Helm? Was that only a coincidence, that we met like we did?'

Helmut shrugged. 'It was hardly remarkable, all things considered.'

Adam turned back to the snow, huge red flakes, falling, pieces of a great puzzle, almost fitting into place. He saw the coiled body flexing again as the head, mistrustful, re-emerged.

'It can't be,' he said. 'Yes, it is a natural phenomenon, I'm not denying that, but it's part of a process, something much, much bigger. There are connections. I know it.'

'You know it?' There was a hint of mockery in Helmut's voice, which took him slightly aback. 'Pray, then, enlighten me.'

'Helm, I told you last night about the forest, and the other experiences I've had. And look, my hands, my arms. See? There is something going on and we are part of it, not merely observers of unconnected isolated events. I believe I feel it, Helm. I feel what is happening.'

'Ah yes, the world's pain.' Helmut smiled at his shoes.

'Do you remember the things I used to write? I didn't show you all of them, they used to pour out of me. I didn't understand them.' Disconcerted by Helmut's attitude Adam grew impatient. This was unlike Helmut; he felt he had to drum something into his head. 'But I'm beginning to see now what they referred to. It's becoming obvious, don't you see, Helm. I believed – I was *made* to believe – that it was me, but it isn't. Not all of it. There's a process, a natural, evolutionary process. It's a next stage, a moving forward. I know it.'

'You know it? You alone?'

'How do we know anything, Helm? How can we know? Our senses convey to us certain information about the world – they tell me, for instance, that I am sitting here talking to you. But how can I *know* that? I could be dreaming, hallucinating, inventing. How do we distinguish what is realized – that is, what is made real to us by our senses – from what is actual, what is actually there?'

'The question has engaged philosophical minds for centuries,' said Helmut, brightening a little. 'And the short answer is that we can't.'

'We can't? Why? Why can't we?'

'We are reliant upon our objective and subjective faculties for our experience of the world. They make it a generally manageable if not wholly comprehensible place. By agreeing between ourselves upon certain aspects of our experience we build a fairly dependable model, but even so, individual experience is highly personalized. And there are many factors to be considered – our equipment may be faulty, for instance. The *noumenon*, the actuality itself, cannot be known. We fall back at all times on a certain degree of faith.'

'But is that all, Helm? Are there not other ways of knowing, of seeing? Are there not other modes of experience beyond those we take for granted? Ways of perceiving, senses not fully developed that would open up a new world to us?'

Helmut stretched his jaw and looked at the blank open pages of his exercise book, which had grown damp and blotchy. 'All modes of experience are subject to breakdown, as you well know, my friend.'

'Helm, all I'm trying to say is that I've been told all along that I'm insane. I have believed it myself more than once, but something inside me has kept me pushing through it. Something said there is more to it. And every time, when I've been about to give up, something has happened. Inexplicable things. Healing people, having visions, things that made me keep going. It wasn't faith, it wasn't belief, it was actual, measurable, physical events. Even the negative − Gospel, my past, the betrayals and deceit, the murders − everything combined to bring me here. Why? There has to be a purpose.'

Helmut surveyed him loftily. 'My friend, do you know what you are saying?'

'I do, Helm. But I don't know what comes next.'

After a moment's contemplation Helmut stood up. He put the exercise book and his pen into his coat pocket, then stamped his feet and rubbed his hands.

Again a waft of his perfume, and with it the snake uncoiled. The long black body writhed and poured from its hiding place. The pieces dropped suddenly and landed in their place. The river burst its banks. At a rate that he was unable to order or arrest something flooded into Adam's consciousness, and with it, with brutal suddenness, the futility of continuing the conversation they were engaged in became known to him. He looked up in final dismay at his old friend's broad grey back.

Helmut was looking towards the mountains, still shifting his feet in the snow. He pulled the hood of his duffel-coat up again.

'It seems to me, my friend, that what − ' he began, turning, then interrupted himself. 'What on Earth is the matter? You look as though you have seen a ghost!'

Shock after shock. Adam reeled under the emotional blow. 'You were there,' he said.

Beneath the hood Helmut's eyebrows lifted infinitesimally. Behind him the river raced by, the muddied water reflecting now a deep dark redness beneath the changing sky. 'I was where, my friend?'

For the moment Adam could say nothing more, stupefied as the body continued to flow out, long lost fragments like individual scales emerging into view. Still some were obscured, or flashed by too quickly for him to particularize. There was so much: not everything was yet clear. He murmured, 'At the house, that night. In Notting Hill.'

Helmut appeared nonplussed. He slipped his hands into his coat pockets.

'It was you,' Adam said, still barely able to believe himself.

'What was me, my friend? You are not making yourself clear.'

'You did it.'

'Did what?'

'You killed him. You killed Dennis.'

A flight of starlings lifted raucously from behind nearby bushes, making them both start. They rose over the tops of the trees, a milling, undecided dark cloud, then wheeled away in a single body over the river towards the glowering red mountains. Helmut, turning to observe them with seeming especial interest, smiled distantly into the low sky.

'What an extraordinary accusation. By what means have you come to such a conclusion?'

Adam looked down at his feet in the eldritch snow. He could not bring himself to say any more. Possibly his expression conveyed more than words would have, for Helmut glanced at him then turned away with a flickeringly rueful twisting of the features, which then became set into something entirely different. He wandered slowly across to the low iron fence and gazed into the river. When he turned back there was a gun in his hand.

Entering the room with curt nods to his two colleagues Mackelvoye, unshaven, had with him a small slim black case which he held flat with both hands. He set it down on a worktop, alongside a computer terminal, and unlocked it with a key on a chain attached to his wrist. He flipped up its catches with his thumbs and the case lid sprang open.

'Six made contact last night.'

'I gathered.' Asprey watched him keenly.

'You mean you actually read a dispatch?'

Inside the case, flush with three sides and the rim was a small keyboard surmounted by a single-line thirty-character monitor display screen. Along the fourth side was a peripheral black cuboid with several leads attached. On the base of its facing edge ran a row of metal teeth, protected within the same hard black casing.

Mackelvoye removed the keyboard, unwound the leads and slotted the teeth into a receptor port on the rear of the larger computer on the worktop. He took two of the leads, which terminated in identical nine-pin jacks, and connected them to a complementary external socket on the spine of his little case. The third and last lead he connected to the mains.

'Where is Judith this morning?' he enquired as he concentrated on his task.

'Unwell,' said Geld. 'The strain. I thought her presence inadvisable today.'

Asprey, hiding a yawn, said, 'Is she secure?'

'She is sedated. I had her removed – I felt it wise – to keep her under observation. She has been exhibiting certain, ah, symptoms.'

'Done!' announced Mackelvoye, and straightened. He turned to the psychiatrist with an expectant look.

'What are you doing?' Asprey enquired, and fished for a cigar. 'What is that gizmo?'

'It's the transmitter, to pass the detonation code to Six.'

'Detonation? I thought we were activating the device here.'

'Not exactly. We are too far removed. That was an item of disinformation supplied for Judith's benefit. We thought it might calm her fears. She was never happy with the idea of ultimate responsibility residing with Six. In fact, it's as good as the case, though. The destruct and termination code was originally Gard's alone, but he passed it down as one of his last acts before removing himself. To prevent mishap it is in three portions. Six currently has one, and Theodore and myself the other two. None of us know the other sections, and the device is harmless until it has an input of all three.'

'It's emplaced, then?'

'I'm awaiting confirmation on that.'

Asprey grunted, lit his cigar and billowed smoke into the atmosphere. 'May as well send your bits, though. Eh?'

'That is what we were about to do, Geoffrey. Theodore?'

Doctor Geld stepped forward, a small diary rimmed in gold plate in his hands. He was far from happy, but finally resigned to the inescapable. Gospel was over, and with it his dreams. There was nothing more he could do to save them. He had to bow to a higher authority. Self-preservation had become the key now. He had to look to the future, and hope. For all its cost termination now would at least ensure that his secret was never exposed. There was Judith, of course. He cursed himself for his foolishness – the strain was showing on him, too. She would have to be dealt with presently, but at least the others were aware to a manipulable degree of her instability.

'You are not waiting for confirmation, then?' Geld asked Mackelvoye.

Asprey answered. 'What for? Give Six the full code now and he can terminate at his leisure – at the first opportunity, I mean. Far more efficient than having him wait for authorization. He might miss his chance. I want to see this business done and out of the way. Good Lord, we've been dragged from our beds at an ungodly enough hour, let's make sure we have something to show for it. And I might remind you that it's almost Christmas. I'd like to be off home sometime today.'

Geld grinned palely and Mackelvoye tapped a sequence of keys on his micro. The little monitor display lit up with a scrolling message: TRANSMISSION DIRECTIVE. DEST. AND TERM. CODE ENTRY. PLEASE CONFIRM.

He pressed more keys.

DIRECTIVE CONFIRMED, the screen displayed. PASS REQUIRED. WHAT IS THE WORD?

Mackelvoye meticulously entered the next sequence: I – N – T – E – R – V – E – N – T – I – O – N.

There was a pause as the central processor compared this,

then it came back with: CORRECT. PLEASE INPUT FIRST
DATUM.

He punched another set, and received: THANK YOU. FIRST
DATUM RECEIVED. PLEASE INPUT SECOND DATUM.

Mackelvoye now took the diary from Geld and entered the
code sequence that was printed on the page he had open.

THANK YOU. SECOND DATUM RECEIVED. PREPARING TO
CONVEY. PLEASE CONFIRM.

There was a single red key at the bottom of the little console.
This he now pressed. The message faded, came up with:
CONFIRMED. DATA NOW CONVEYING. THANK YOU, then
faded for the last time.

Mackelvoye exhaled a long sigh and sat down on the nearest
chair.

'What now?' asked Asprey.

'We wait.' Unwilling to meet anyone's eye Mackelvoye had
folded his arms and fixed his gaze on the ceiling. 'When the third
sequence is entered and destruct imminent the computer will set
off an alarm. There will be a delay of sixty seconds before actual
detonation. A vacillation period.'

'So we could still instigate a last-minute reprieve?'

'*We* couldn't, no. The code is passed. The only person who
can save the Apostle now is Six. And all things considered I don't
think we can view that as a likely prospect, do you?'

Apocalypse

'Why, Helm? Why Dennis? He was no threat.'

Adam watched his old friend through the reddish veil of falling
snow. Helmut showed little emotion. He rested his buttocks
casually against the iron railing and asked, 'How on Earth have
you arrived at such a conclusion? It's outlandish, don't you think?'

'I told you, something happened last night. Something is
happening now. I know, Helmut. That's all.'

'My impression, my friend, is that you "know" many things, but
it seems you build your evidence on the flimsiest foundations.
Think about what you are saying for a moment. Take everything
into consideration and then tell me, can you really be so sure of
yourself?'

Adam was not swayed. The body of the snake uncoiled remorselessly. Its hidden length stretched back, far back, and with each flex of its muscles his inner world was rocked a little more. But he no longer doubted. Not now.

He sensed that this cool bluff, this attempt to undermine him, concealed a loaded curiosity. More than curiosity. Helmut was feeling his way in partial darkness. He needed to discover just what Adam knew, how much was genuine returning memory. He held the gun but, for a time, it represented no real danger. As things stood it was of little more than symbolic value. It held them in a bubble, a state of timeless suspense and concentration, a 'safe zone'. It laid a specific grave emphasis on everything that passed between them and accentuated the focus from which their thoughts could not stray. But it would not fire. Helmut's response in the face of Adam's accusation was unsettling and mystifying, but he would not at present commit himself to any action unless compelled. Adam recognized this, and knowing why, what it was that Helmut wished above all to be certain of, felt at liberty to proceed without fear. Caution, yes: the situation could change with little warning. Everything depended on how much each was willing to reveal.

'You gave yourself away,' he said.

Helmut cocked his head slightly and adjusted the weight of the gun in his hand. It was a Smith and Wesson .45 revolver. Standard issue, Adam recalled. 'I'm intrigued. By what means did I "give myself away"?'

'I had no reason to suspect anything at the time, so I missed it, but it has nagged at me since. It was your scent.'

'My scent?'

'It was there in the house, so faint I barely noticed it.'

'And on that you rest your case for the hangman's noose? My friend, you must be out of your mind! I'm sure I don't need to tell you that the perfume I wear is quite a popular brand. It's widely available. I would guess there are dozens if not scores of men exuding it at this very moment in London alone.' He surveyed Adam for a moment with cold amusement, then said, 'And let's say that it was mine that your sensitive nostrils detected. What does that prove? That I visited the house of a friend, that is all.'

'There are other factors, Helmut,' Adam said tiredly. He had no desire to participate in this game. Helmut's charade needled, and the "safe" wall of the bubble was confining. He wanted to step out.

'Ah. Go on,' said Helmut.

'Partridge – ' he began.

'Mr Partridge?' Helmut interrupted him, his posture tightening infinitesimally. 'The little bird from Judith's section? He knew about Dennis?'

'Not Dennis, no. He knew nothing about him. But he alerted me to other possibilities, not immediately apparent. I didn't know what he was telling me at the time, about Jude, but I can see things now. And there's more than that. Last night, for instance. You were taken aback when we met. I mistook your unease for caution and accepted your story. But something wasn't right. It was all too . . . convenient. But like a fool I did all the talking and told you what you wanted to know, how much I had discovered, or rather, how much I had not. I gave you all you needed to manufacture a cover on the spot. And I was in no condition to look for holes, but . . .' He bowed his head, shaking it slowly. 'There's so much. It all goes back a long way. It's so obvious now.'

'My friend, this is still not proof of anything. It is supposition. These are the deductions of a severely overtaxed psyche.'

'Helmut, cut it, will you!' Adam flared. 'I know, do you understand? It has come back to me. It's coming back now, as we speak. So let's dispense with this pretence. For God's sake, you've got a gun on me. What else is there?'

The bubble burst; the revolver was stripped of its symbolism with these words and re-endowed with the purpose of its creation. It would not be quite enough for Helmut – prior to squeezing the trigger he would still demand total certainty – but it brought the moment closer. Adam, just then, felt he had passed the point of caring. He looked back into his past and what he saw there made him recoil. He realized the ineluctability of this moment and felt his remaining spirit being sucked from him. He had followed a dream, been through so much to arrive here. Everything had combined to bring this about. Had it all been so that he might die here, on the bank of a swollen river, shot by his closest friend as the red snow swirled about them? If so, then let it be. He would not fight it, not any more. But first let there be truth. Let it come out, here and now, and let the consequences be what they may. But let it end. Just let it end.

Helmut eased his weight from the railing and approached a couple of paces, scrutinizing Adam loftily but closely. His grey-blue eyes were narrowed and glittering and they held a look that Adam had not seen before. It was a look of fierce and chilling intensity; a kind of exultation. There was an intelligence that seemed detached and almost predatory. Adam averted his gaze, unnerved by what was lacking.

With his next words Helmut affirmed a willingness to be done with the pretence. 'You understand why he had to be removed – '

'I understand nothing!' Adam snapped. Then, in a more controlled tone, 'Nothing and everything.'

'My friend, do not look upon this as a betrayal. It transcends that.'

The sentiment had a familiar ring. Adam closed his eyes. 'Transcends?' He forced a grim smile. 'Oh, Helmut. Helmut.'

'Gospel was jeopardized.'

'Just a minute, Helm.' He held up a hand. 'One thing I don't understand. Why? Not your why, I know that well enough now, but Gospel's. That's still a mystery. Such lengths to safeguard me, to cover me, to pursue me, and then to have you kill me at the end. I know that you are following a dream like me, but I assume you are also acting on orders. So what changed? What went wrong?'

'You did. But you are jumping the gun. I have to tell you about Dennis.' He had become quite animated. He came forward and stepped up onto the end of the bench furthest from Adam, and perched himself on the arm support, his feet on the thick slats. He kept the gun levelled at Adam's chest.

'What is there to tell, other than that you murdered your friend in cold blood?' Adam said. 'He wasn't a threat and you know it. His death can have gained you nothing.'

'He had declared himself an enemy,' Helmut said. 'Of Gospel. Unwittingly, it is true, but no less a danger because of that. He was meddling, and with that insipid, unreasonable idealism of his he placed everything in jeopardy. Fortunately he gave us wind of it – or rather, you did – but that was not before he had placed notions in your head that we would have preferred you to have been without. You see, until you revealed it to me when I visited you at home after the party, we had no idea that he was acquainted with Doctor Geld. Much less that he had declared himself an active opponent. But there is another point I want to make: something happened that night – a series of things really. The evening was fraught with hazards, but overall something became very clear to me.'

The words tumbled forth now. The criminal's psychological need to confess, perhaps; but there was an implication of something more. Helmut seemed quite elevated by what he was recalling.

'I went to see him,' he said, 'to determine, without arousing his suspicions, just what his motives and possible intentions might be. When I arrived Dennis was most excited about some Eastern doctrine he had been reading. As was his wont, he was in a state of semi-narcosis and had persuaded himself that some kind of enlightening experience was imminent. He wanted to draw my attention to the subject, and try as I might I could not divert him sufficiently to gain much information. Still, that was not of great consequence. His future was already spoken for, I'm afraid, though it might have been instructive to have learned the full extent of his involvements, and connections if he had any. My feeling from the outset, though, was that he was an independent operator, and I became more convinced of that as the minutes passed. What became obvious was his hope of seeing you again. He considered you a kindred spirit, I think. And more, perhaps, an ally.

'Well, it was not without regret, I can assure you, that I resolved that nothing further was to be gained from this idle *conversazione* and that the hour was at hand for the culmination of my visit. Dennis, at a certain point, slipped obligingly into unconsciousness so I seized the opportunity and left my seat and took a large knife from the kitchen. But as I bent over him he took it into his head to revive. He failed to spot the knife as I quickly slipped it behind my back, but he got up and announced, in a manner which suggested that the business he was about to undertake might fundamentally alter the course his life was taking, that nature called with a degree of urgency. He took a magazine with

337

him, the one containing the article that had so inspired him prior to my arrival, so evidently I could not expect his swift return.

'I allowed him time to settle then went down taking a blanket and a large sheet of polythene from his room. He is one of those persons who never bolts a toilet door, and when I pushed it and entered, knife in hand, he simply looked up and grinned.' Helmut pressed his weight down on the wooden arm support. A bright flush had ascended to his cheeks and he seemed taken over, impassioned. His eyes shone with mirth. 'You see, my friend, here was something I could never have dreamed of. He thought it was a joke! He saw the knife but he took it for his own trick knife! He thought my entrance supremely humorous. Can you imagine it? He actually tipped back his head, lifted his beard and offered me his throat. He was still giggling when I slit his larynx.'

Briefly Helmut looked skywards, then quickly focussed back on Adam, who stared up at him in horror, scarcely believing what he heard.

'I must say,' Helmut went on, oblivious, 'that he showed surprise at the discovery that he could no longer breathe, but he took it well. You see, here is the crucial point, this is what I mean when I say that something became clear: he made no struggle. Even when he realized, even as the life was exiting his body, he made no more than reflexive efforts to seal the wound. I was able to hold him virtually still with minimal effort, and this threw a very new light on things.' Helmut had grown a little breathless now, and his eyes were glazed. Still glittering they took in something no other person could have seen, and his speech had sunk to barely more than a passionate whisper. 'You see, he was grateful. Caught by surprise, yes. Who wouldn't have been? But beyond and above everything else he was grateful. I had done him a favour. I had done what he had long wanted but never been able to do. Do you understand, my friend? It was not murder. It is important you disabuse yourself of any such notion. It was not murder, it was disburdenment. The act of a friend, a true friend, and Dennis recognized it as such. I had done what he could not, what he could not even give voice to. I had committed his suicide.

'Everything in his life points to this being his most heartfelt wish. He did not belong here. He could not confront the harshness of reality. He took drugs to the point of oblivion rather than face up to life. He threw himself into studies of the kinds of occult, religious and psychological thought which demand little real contact with the outside world. He was a painfully oversensitive and guilt-ridden soul, you know that yourself. Witness his distress over the mice and his kittens. He supported so-called "benevolent" groups. My God, do you know that he once broke down in tears when he was told that even vegetables scream when pulled from the ground! Oh, if you knew him as I have done you would understand more fully. He was a pathological case, a lonely, pathetic, compulsive hoarder, unhappy and confused, a victim of life, a complete and utter misfit. What I did was what he desired. Everything indicated it, right down to the last conversation we had. Why, even the article he was reading at the end!'

Adam saw again the bloodied periodical open on Dennis's white knees. He swallowed and turned his face to the mountains.

'Flippancy doesn't become you, Helmut.'

'Flippancy? I assure you I intend nothing of the kind. He sought annihilation, by one means or another. I granted it him.'

'And you seek annihilation of any poor bastard who happens not to think in quite the same way as you?' He stood up angrily. 'Damn you, Helmut! Damn you!'

Helmut had tensed. 'My friend, no sudden moves, please.' He gestured with the gun. 'This is no theatrical prop, believe me.'

Adam calculated the distance that separated them. He could disarm Helmut. A feint with arms, body and disguised intention to draw the first bullet, and a spin in the opposite direction to bring him alongside, centre low and knees bent to cancel the relative height discrepancy. Hug the pistol arm to his ribs whilst steadying the hand and forearm with his own. Lever up from the elbow with his right, bending the wrist in, easing the grip with pressure to the knuckle of the trigger finger. All done in less than a second. Helmut would find himself staring down his own barrel. Shock would do the rest.

But he let the moment go: truth under coercion might not match that of a man who believed himself in control.

Helmut had evidently been thinking along similar lines for he gestured again with the gun and said, 'On the whole I would be happier if you sat.'

He obliged. Still angry he said, 'Dennis was trying to find himself, to make some sense of the world. You know that. He was like us all, he did not know why he was here, he was overwhelmed by it all. But in his own way he wanted to do some good.'

Helmut, unmoved, was impatient to get on. 'There is more to tell you. Perhaps then you will begin to see without the hindrance of your preconceived values. You see, further events unfolded. It was as though my action had set something in motion, as though something held in stasis had been released.'

Adam shook his head. What was missing here in all this grotesque paralogism (for he did not doubt Helmut's sincerity), this twisted rationalization, was that very quality, the rational, the logical. Helmut was conjuring the untenable to support his actions. Helmut, whose pride was in having freed himself of superstition, was now teetering on the edge of that very thing he had just minutes earlier been deriding Adam for.

He was making himself a mirror. Was it deliberate? Its most frightening aspect in Adam's mind was that its distortion was so slight. Helmut's truth, like Adam's, was built on inner certainty. The difference had to lie in the bedrock from which that certainty had grown. Helmut's rationale, surely, could be sustained only by a careful skimming of the surface, a refusal to investigate what lay beneath. That it could be nonetheless unshakeable was a further undermining force that threw Adam back in search of his own defences.

He now knew, of course, how it was that Helmut could construct such an edifice without due consideration of the depths that swirled beneath it. It was in contradiction to his propounded beliefs, but under these circumstances that was inescapable, and Adam could empathize. He himself had unwittingly provided the cornerstone to its construction.

The writhing body of the snake gave a shudder, and he flinched. Helmut was possessed, but was he also playing a game? Was this mirroring of Adam a purposeful ploy or was he innocent and serious in what he said? The past continued to flow forth, and Adam put his arms about himself. *My God*, he asked again, *what are we? What are we? What is it all for?*

'My intention was to take the body upstairs,' said Helmut,

'hence the blanket and polythene. Once back in the room he was unlikely to be discovered for some days, if not weeks. But as I unfolded the sheet I received a sudden breathtaking shove from behind. I was almost propelled into Dennis's lap, and you can imagine my disquiet – someone wanted to get in.

'I quickly put my weight to the door and called out, and naturally enough they withdrew. Fortunately it had not been opened very far. So I waited, and after some moments eased it open a crack and peered out. But who should I see seated just feet away at the bottom of the stairs leading up to Dennis's floor than the big Scottish fellow – you remember, he who usually loafs in a stupor on the stairs.

'Now I faced a dilemma. I had assumed that whoever it was would not wait – there is another washroom in the house. But this great buffoon seemed intent on using the one I occupied. I gave him another minute or two but he gave no signs of budging, so eventually I had little option but to go out and confront him. Some clever talking was demanded, but I did have one card up my sleeve. That is, he had been unconscious on the stairs when I entered the house and I had passed by without disturbing him, thus I was now able to offer him refreshment.

'In the event he turned out to be quite amenable. In fact he initiated the conversation with a request for the very thing I was intending giving him. Now, my primary objective being to draw him away, I let him have the drink whilst giving the impression that I had more. And with this and the medium of sympathetic conversation I was able to divert his attention from his bladder and secure an invitation to his room.

'Doubtless it will not surprise you to hear that he talked solely of his lost wife. It seems he truly loved that woman, in his own way.' Helmut ceased recounting to contemplate Adam ruefully. 'You know, I had to agree with him, they can certainly make you suffer, can't they, my friend. I had advised him long ago that it is better to avoid the drink. It just stirs up the memories, but I suppose that was what he wanted as a temporary solace, with further drinking to obliterate them. It's a common enough pattern.

'But ... I couldn't stay all night. Every second I spent in the company of this maudlin fellow lamenting the departure of his hog of a wife (and she was a hog, my friend. I met her once) increased the chances of somebody stumbling upon poor Dennis. And, of course, I had set myself a new and very grave problem: this fellow was now a witness to my passage.'

Helmut made a strange clucking sound with his tongue and lapsed into silence. Slowly the full implications of his last statement filtered through to Adam and he turned again with renewed disbelief.

'There was always the possibility of his not remembering,' Helmut said matter-of-factly, 'but I could hardly let everything hang on something so tenuous, could I?'

'You killed him?'

'I disburdened him, my friend. Of his pain. As I had Dennis. It was what he wanted, you can see that, surely? You know how he suffered. What use is a life like that? It is a mistake, a travesty. But listen, there is a footnote to this story. I think this will help you understand. It caused me much dismay and self-examination, I must admit, until I saw its full connotations. In fact it brings to mind questions you raised last night, when you spoke about how people have died because of you whilst others have been given a new life. You see, a most extraordinary "coincidence" occurred the very day following all this. Would you believe it, the most unlikely of events: his wife came home!

'Adam, when this news was passed to me a week or so later it gave me a deep shock. I questioned myself. Was I mistaken? Had I acted wrongly? What else could I, *should I*, have done in the circumstances? Was there something happening here that I simply did not understand?

'But it came to me eventually, after much soul-searching. I had not acted wrongly. On the contrary, by my actions I had saved her, for I have no doubt she would have died miserably at his hands within seconds of his setting eyes on her. Notwithstanding his professed love for her, there was a rage within him. He was not a man to sit down and discuss past wrongs. He would have acted before he thought, I'm sure of it.' He paused, then added, chillingly, 'Mysterious ways, my friend. Mysterious ways indeed.'

If this was sham then Helmut was a master; his expression gave no indication. But if not it constituted a total *volte face*, an almost hysterical avoidance of any form of acknowledgement of the enormity of what he had done and what he was saying. His implication now was that he acted as an agent, of God, or of the devil – the distinction hardly mattered. He spoke with the voice of the criminally insane, and yet there was something . . .

'I did not take it upon myself to play God,' Adam said, responding initially to Helmut's veiled insinuation of complicity.

Helmut arched an eyebrow. 'Did you not? You acted, my friend, and by your actions the world became a different place. You believe you acted for good, but by what criteria do you make that judgement? What do you know of the persons you helped? How do you know what they will do with their new lives? What if I tell you now that the man you helped on his way in the Berlin cafe is a murderer, a known terrorist responsible for the deaths and maiming of many innocent persons? Do you still claim that you acted for good?'

'That's ridiculous.'

'Is it? What about the woman in London who, thanks to your intervention, will next year give birth to the next Hitler? You changed the natural order of things, that is all I am saying to you. You played God, or at least acted as if believing yourself imbued with His authority, without giving thought to later consequences. You, in your own way, performed the same function that I have done in mine.'

Yes, there was something. Adam turned back to the river. Madness or not, Helmut's words contained a truth that was irrefutable. One's actions changed the world. For good or evil – both, after all, being relative concepts, polarities devised to give substance to something not understood – every action, and every thought that preceded it, had its consequence, effects that could never be conceived of in its institution. They set things in motion, rearranging the natural order of things. They made history. No matter what is done, or equally not done, it will have its effect, establish its mark, its unending chain of consequence.

We are never our own masters, Adam thought. He took a breath. He had gazed for too long into the abyss, now the abyss gazed back.

'But I digress,' said Helmut. 'There is something else still, something which concerns you directly. It may amuse you. You see, when I left the big Scot's room to go back up and collect

Dennis, I heard a noise on the floor below. I peered over the banister and who do you think I saw making his way in the weak light, with some trepidation I think, up the stairs towards me, but yourself! Now this again threw me into a dilemma, but fortunately I was able to retreat into darkness and wait in a doorway until you had passed. Good Lord, my friend, it was a tense moment! I actually felt your breath on my cheek. I was sure your hand would find me as you felt your way forward. But you didn't. Fate was on my side, I think, and once you had passed, well, there was little I could do but abandon my plans and leave. But you can appreciate it was an extraordinary adventure.'

It seemed that the world teetered, balanced on the whims of the insane. Adam's mind span, and he could no longer contemplate everything that was presented to him. He thought to question Helmut: What if I had found you? What then? How would that have changed things? But he sensed that was a fruitless trail to follow. He needed to bring things down closer to earth, to find a manageable perspective. And there was something more personal, more immediate, that had to be resolved.

He thought carefully about what he was going to ask, then said, 'What about the woman in Kensington? She had no connection. She knew nothing. She merely passed on a neighbour's address. Didn't you know that?'

Here, now, he was closing in on the real reason for their both being here. And he knew that by confronting it he was confronting his own death. He watched the transformation in Helmut's features. He had hit home. Helmut came down off his cloud.

'She was a *whore*!' The emotion in his voice, irrationally charged but undisguisably genuine and irrepressible, effectively gave the lie to his entire argument. But if he was aware of it he showed no concern. He glared hotly into near-space.

'A whore?' Adam led him on with calculated ingenuousness. 'Is that all? All she was?' He allowed a few seconds of silence, then added, 'But they all are, aren't they?'

Helmut glanced sharply his way.

'Isn't that what you think?' Adam pressed him. 'All cheap? Worthless? Or is it just one of them?'

'One of them?'

'Judith, for instance.'

'Judith?' Helmut said with surprise. 'You call your own wife a worthless whore?'

'Not me, Helm. Not me.' Adam drew another long, shaking breath. 'Let me ask you something. Who was it you really killed when you took that woman's life, when you mutilated and tortured her before slitting her throat? Whose face looked back at you? Who begged you for mercy?'

For a long time Helmut appraised him. His agitation appeared to have passed and in its place was a cold and calculating calmness. Eventually, quietly, he said, 'So you were telling the truth. It has all come back.'

'Not all, but enough.' He flexed the tight muscles of his back. 'Do you mind now if I stand?'

Helmut shrugged. 'As you please. But . . . move away a little.'

Adam rose with stiff limbs and walked to the riverside, placing his feet, at the railing, in the depressions Helmut's own had left in the reddening snow. Towards the other side of the river, some yards upstream, a great log, the bole of some uprooted tree, was being borne towards him, its limbs splayed like a corpse.

'So is that it, Helm?' he asked without turning. 'Now you have what you needed to be sure of. Do you kill me and go home a happy man?'

Again Helmut's reply was slow in coming. When he did speak it was in a subdued and distant tone, not answering Adam's question.

'You believe she loved you,' he said, 'but she never did. It was duty, all along the line. She loved me but she made the sacrifice for a greater cause.'

The log, as Adam watched, vanished suddenly beneath the turbulent surface, drawn down by an unseen vortex. He stared at the muddy water. It wasn't true. Helmut was inventing. Perhaps, for survival's sake, he had convinced himself. Perhaps by burying everything that was too painful to bear and substituting it with something more manageable he had created a surface reality of his own, that held up as long as he did not peer beneath its gloss.

Adam closed his eyes. *All these years!* He gripped the icy rail with both hands. When he looked again the log had not reappeared. He turned from the river. Helmut had left the bench and was standing, facing him now, ten feet away.

'If there's any truth in that,' Adam said, 'then tell me why.'

'She was an inducement, that's all. We needed you. Your skills, your personality. We had been watching you, at Oxford and earlier, before we recruited you. You were perfect for us. Invaluable. Or so we thought. But we had to ice the cake to be sure.'

Could this be true? How could he know? His returning memory was patchy, but even with full command, how could he know? How could he ever be sure that Judith, from the very beginning, had not been pretending, deceiving him? He tried to dismiss the thought but it was too important. Helmut had scored; and was this his aim, then, his revenge, to send him spinning out of this world in confusion, bewildered, never knowing – for Adam accepted now that he was not going to walk away from this place. His mind rebelled and would not grasp thoughts. And then, quite suddenly, she was there. Judith. In front of him.

She lay beneath a sheet, on a bed. Her eyes were closed. Her face was terribly pale.

'Judith,' he said, but she was still. Involuntarily he took a step forward. 'Helmut. She's dying.'

Helmut tensed. 'No tricks.'

'She's dying.' The image was fading. 'I don't know what is happening but I can see her. She's in a room somewhere. She's dying.'

Blinking, he focussed on Helmut, who returned his look with scorn.

'Helm, there's a lot more going on here than either you or I can hope to know. Listen to me a minute.'

But Helmut was not prepared to listen. This was his moment and he was closed to anything that might interfere with his design. He had waited, sustaining himself on his conviction that this day would come. He was its servant and could not release himself from its bond.

Adam relented, seeing this. He said, 'Tell me this, then. Are you acting in defiance of Gospel, on your own initiative? Or are you still following orders?'

'Both,' Helmut smiled. 'Gospel is over. The puppet cut its own strings. Now the decision has been made that it must be allowed its total freedom.'

'A happy coincidence, then.'

'Coincidence? Do you think so?'

'Would you have carried out your orders if I had not remembered? You could have done it last night.'

Helmut chuckled throatily. 'Last night may well have been coincidence. As it happened I had not received my final directive. Nor, by a curious oversight, was I carrying my gun. But more significantly, yes, you are right, I would not have wished to execute an innocent man.'

'Not even to relieve me of my pain?'

Helmut smiled again but did not rise to the taunt.

'Well, now everything is complete,' Adam said. 'Here I am. You can have your revenge at last.'

'Oh, tsk, tsk. Nothing so trite. Nothing so petty. Revenge, rancour, bitterness . . . I am beyond such motivations. I was their victim once, it's true, but I fought and vanquished them. That is, I gave myself over to philosophical enquiry and analysis, and as my understanding of the world grew they diminished, naturally. Now . . . well, it is a matter of justice, not revenge. And in relation to present circumstance, your demise has simply become expedient. We must bow to higher authority.'

'Justice?' Adam picked him up. 'Justice for what? You are contradicting yourself. You say she left you for duty's sake, that she never loved me – '

'You stole her from me,' Helmut said fiercely, 'and on that day *I* died.'

There was no reaching him. His defences were too many and too tricky. They held him in the past, trapped him there, scarred and beaten, and blind to any mode of escape.

In truth it was Helmut over whom the past exercised the greater power. He had become its victim by partial consent. Seen through his eyes his life was a catalogue of losses and disappointments and, as he had colluded with himself to view them, betrayals. On the opening pages stood his father, a man he had never known and who had not wanted to know him, a coward, a thief, a faceless, formless entity who had come and seen and then run, leaving a child to deal with the suffering and eventual death of its mother. Nearby skulked his maternal grandparents, mean-spirited and pompous, heartless creatures who had

347

rejected him, disinheriting his mother and denying them both the comfort, the support, the love that was rightfully theirs.

In the next chapter his mother, who had tried so hard, was finally herself unable to cope. She too had abandoned him, giving herself up to disease, forcing him to live through her terrible, endless death. She had punished him with her agony, the days and nights of interminable pain, the screaming and delirium, the rages he could not understand. Punishing him, punishing him, merely for being there with her, torturing him as she herself was tortured, until the men came and wrapped her in a red blanket and carried her away, telling him nothing, and he had not seen her again.

Then followed the aunt who hid him from the world and sheltered him beneath a stifling wing, only to thrust him out when he came to believe himself secure, into a world he had no experience to deal with. In a short life, so much. Small wonder that he should be attracted to an organization in which trust, benevolence, constancy, stability or sympathy found no place.

In the hidden regions of Helmut's psyche all this and more had been held down so that he might seem to live a normal life. And gradually it had appeared to lose its potency, life had begun to reveal riches, he had found friendship and had fallen in love. The pent-up energies within him could be dispersed harmlessly and even productively.

And then the final blow. The truth as Adam now recalled it, and as Helmut struggled to deny, was that the woman who had given him renewed life and for whom he would have given the same, had renounced him for his closest friend.

Someone should have suspected earlier the depths of emotion that his calmly accepting manner concealed. Someone should have seen that the cheerful mask disguised something dark and dangerous. And of course there were those who did, but who kept it to themselves.

And Helmut, accustomed by life to pushing it all back, holding it all in, maintained a bright front whilst, like the little car he drove, encasing himself in hidden armour. He had not unleashed his hatred or wreaked his revenge but rather had immersed himself in work and, as he now put it, given himself over to philosophical enquiry and analysis. Quite quietly he had gone insane.

Out of this had come his *carte blanche*. The nihilistic survivalist philosophy of 'Anything Goes', apparently reasonable and defensible, if pessimistic. It presented itself as the product of a wry but harmlessly eccentric mind. In itself it gave no real indication of the misery that had spawned it, or of the terrible underlying force that Helmut, given full rein, would unconcernedly vent against his fellow men. For it was true that it was not Adam who stood now staring down the barrel of his gun. Whilst there was a sense in which Helmut *was* the past Adam had lost; whilst Helmut had waited patiently, retaining the guise of friend and advisor and lurking simultaneously at the edges of their life with opposing intentions, it was not Adam who was the enemy, nor any other single person. It was mankind. More, it was life. The world. Everyone and every*thing*.

Armed with his justification he needed never question himself. He was an innocent, a pure soul, cast into a world that had abused him. It offered him no place, snatched away anything it gave, crushed every morsel that he might reach to for succour, denied hope or happiness. To be born without reason and tossed into the storm was all it took. And in his maddened state he might actually be capable of believing that what he did now he did out of kindness, but that was of no consequence. He had his justification and had constructed his life upon it. By his decree this was the Age of Unreason, the Time of the Psychopath. There was no meaning. Conscience was dead, or at best a moribund thing. No law existed but No-Law. There was no trust, no truth, no beauty, no love. Life was chaos: *expunge it!* Anything Goes.

'It was duty, my friend. Remember that.' Helmut's face showed no triumph now. The skin was taut, the eyes misted and for a moment downcast. 'She never loved you.'

Simon Partridge's words at their first meeting in the cellar bar in London whispered in Adam's ear: 'Love – you will see the carnage it inspires. It is the opposite of itself. Out of it all other destructive forces are born.'

At the time he had dismissed it, he had not understood. But now he saw. What was it to love and not be loved in return? To love and to lose? To love and have it stolen from you? Was it better never to have loved? He saw how, under innumerable guises, all destructive forces might be born from that source.

'Helm – ' he began, but Helmut stopped him.

'I want you to think about that. It is important that you do. It is important that you understand how it is that you and I are here today. It is important that you know what you have done.'

'Helmut, you are wrong. The way you are looking at it, you are blinding yourself.'

Helmut, for a second, looked lost, as though something in the past he had concocted and the past that was had come face to face. The barrel of the revolver dipped slightly earthwards. 'You'll never know,' he said. 'You'll never know how much I loved her.'

It had seemed for the briefest of moments as though something might have broken through, something Adam could have taken and made advantage of. Then his defences were up again; he was alert, and cold. Whatever he had just seen, he had successfully pushed it back from sight.

'The time is perfect, my friend. You can see that. Here we are in this city of dreams and revelations, of towering mountains and tumbling red snow. Everything has converged to reveal to us the perfection of this moment. It has a beauty, a poetry, does it not? I can't profess to understanding it in its totality but it brings a tear and a thrill. You must feel it?'

'Helmut,' Adam entreated him. 'There is much more going on. Don't you see that?'

But if anything there was mockery now in Helmut's eyes. Nothing could pierce his armour.

'You and I are fortunate,' he said. 'I know that. Many people live out their entire lives without ever understanding anything, without the slightest inkling of the reasons for their being here. I think that is tragedy. But you and I, we are privileged. We know.'

From somewhere at his back came music. A tinny, distanced sound fluctuating on the shifting currents of air. Adam thought of the tannoy strung over the square. A choir sang, in English, he noted, a carol: 'Unto Us A Child'. It brought to mind the day.

'I hope you will accept what is happening,' Helmut said. He straightened his back, his feet separating in the snow to take a firmer stance. He bent his knees, lowering his body an inch, and bringing his free hand up to support the heel of his right, steadying his grip on the revolver stock. The weapon was raised, levelled directly into Adam's face. 'Don't look for a way around it, there isn't one. You know that you are quite mad, my friend, and you have done too much harm. Judith is not dying. This,' he nodded his wide forehead at the snow, 'is no prefiguration of the world's end. You do not feel the world's pain, just your own. What is happening is meant to happen, and you ...' the mockery was blatant now, in his eyes, the thin smile that played on his lips, even his exaggeratedly precise posture, '... will not save the Earth. It is too late.'

'It isn't the Earth that will die, Helm,' Adam said quietly. 'It's us. We can take everything with us but the planet will survive. It will merely become dormant, and when it has recovered from our passing, begin again. Nature anticipates us, always. Do you see? It gives us every chance but in the end, if we don't heed it, it can turn us against ourselves to ensure we perish. We are not our own masters, Helm. We are part of something, some vast and incomprehensible intelligence. We can't hope to know it fully, and it will continue its work with or without us. But we have the chance to move with it, to enter the next stage, and we don't know. We refuse to see. That is the tragedy.'

He thought, *the child does not have to be born.*

Helmut gave an emotionless smile. He eased back the hammer with his thumb, and his forefinger curled around the trigger. His grey-blue eyes bored intently down the barrel, directly into Adam's. Helmut the Avenger, the Sixth Angel, the Bringer of Destiny, waited one last moment, and watched. Then he squeezed the trigger.

There was a dead metallic click exactly coincident with Adam's spotting the empty cylinder.

'Bang,' Helmut said.

He remained gazing expressionlessly along the length of the barrel, then his hands and the revolver dropped to his sides and he lifted himself to his full height. He said nothing. It was a surprise when he turned, giving Adam his back, and walked slowly away to the bench.

He stooped and placed the gun there.

'One bullet,' he said, turning again and facing Adam. A strand of pale hair had fallen across his mouth and he brushed it away as though it were a cobweb. 'It is yours, my friend. There is one thing left for you to do. You have nothing now, nothing but a past you have spent too much time looking for, and a vision that is too much to bear. Was it worth it? It gained you nothing. You could have saved yourself, avoided all this, but you chose to persist. Now you have to face what you have brought upon yourself. You now know that nothing is true. You *are* of unsound mind and have been all along. Your life's quest merely reveals the depths of that insanity. And I know you, and I know that I don't have to pull the trigger. I have confidence in you.' He brought his hands together, rubbing them then holding them still for a moment in contemplation. Then he looked up afresh. 'I must go. I leave it with you, then. *Adieu*, my friend. We won't meet again.'

He walked away, his broad back diminishing as Adam watched until he was lost to sight around the curve of the path behind the trees. A trail of footsteps in the redness along the riverside path was all that remained.

A minute passed and then Adam slowly crossed to the bench and picked up the gun. It was still warm from Helmut's grip. He weighed it in his hand; it felt snug and comfortably balanced.

Alone again he had time now to be oppressed by the fear. The fear that Helmut might not have been entirely lying. How could he know that Judith had loved him, that everything had not been for 'duty', or some other call? Was it possible that love had never had a part to play, other than the part he was fooled into giving? In the light of all else he had to accept that what his memory told him now might be no more reliable than before. And if it did not deceive him it still gave him only what he had been made to believe was truth. How could he be sure that the life they had shared had not been sham from the beginning? It seemed impossible, but how, *how* could he ever know?

He looked up at the red laden sky. All this way, through madness, through deceit, through violence and betrayal, to discover at the end that he knew everything and nothing. Everything had changed and yet all was the same, and there was no end. No resolution. No peace, no meaning, no love. He was apart, had placed himself there, and now must face what that entailed.

He turned his face across the river. The mountains were a

vague form in the slowly descending snow. Reddening everything it compounded his inability to perceive or reason. It was a dream. He had followed, or been led by it, to this place, searching, and had entered a void, an infinite and expanding emptiness. He had found nothing.

He pocketed the gun. One thing left to do.

He made to move away but as he did so his foot came to rest on something, some firm though not hard object that lay partially buried in the snow in front of the bench. Curiously, half-recognizing what he saw there and not fully acknowledging it in this alien location, he bent and picked it up. A small teddy bear. He knew it. It was Helmut's favourite, Bruno. He gently brushed away the flakes of snow that fell across its face and gazed into the black and amber eyes.

All children, he thought, who can't grow up. Held in our past, victims of our ignorance. Always searching for the lost and irrecoverable, and held in it and without it by experiences which mould and shape us far earlier and far more thoroughly than we know. We believe we can shape a future when it is in fact predetermined. It is not what happens now that will change it, as much as what has gone before. We have to go back to free ourselves.

He looked at the river racing past, the mountains, the trees, at the Earth which seemed to him to be shedding its very lifeblood in its last attempt to break through. A child is waiting to be born, he thought, and we are preventing it. But how do we break the pattern to allow the future to unfold unhindered? How do we free ourselves if we are not even aware that we are prisoners?

He slipped the little bear into his pocket alongside the Smith and Wesson and walked away from the park. He returned by the route that had brought him here, in the opposite direction to that which Helmut had taken. With no one thought uppermost in his mind he made his way back towards the old city from which the peal of cathedral bells now rang out, drowning the sound of the tannoy in the square.

Ecce Homo

They had waited tensely all day.

An earlier printout on the mainframe computer, that the device was successfully emplaced, had convinced all three that termination was imminent. But it was afternoon before the shrill electronic alarm with its alternating dual-pitched computerized tones had split the air in their stuffy underground room.

Mackelvoye had sprung from his chair to the micro, hovering over it as though his intent might somehow influence the message it was to transmit. Tiny beads of perspiration broke out on his brow and above his lip. His hair was dishevelled, his tie and collar loose. He was suddenly breathing heavily.

'He's done it!' His eyes were on the digits counting down on the monitor display. 54 ... 53 ... 52 ... 51 ... 'He's activated the device!'

Asprey, who had spent the day fussing and complaining while making the air nigh-unbreathable, was in a cantankerous mood. He left his seat. He was similarly dishevelled and had gone so far as to remove both jacket and shoes. To the relief of the other two he had now used up his stock of Havanas. In stockinged feet he joined the Deputy D-G and the two of them watched the seconds. 50 ... 49 ... 48 ... 47 ...

Doctor Geld did not stir from his position. He was perched on the edge of a nearby table, his thin legs dangling free. His eyes were on his two colleagues but his brain worked busily, his thoughts on the future.

... 46 ... 45 ... 44 ... 43 ...

Asprey scowled at the computer. 'Infernal racket! Can't you do something?'

Mackelvoye, raising his head, answered with deliberate irony, 'Hold tight, Geoffrey. It will all be over in a little more than half a minute. Then I suggest we have a nice cup of tea, and following that, once you have made out your report, you can go off home and enjoy the holiday.'

He turned back to the changing digits.

... 42 ... 41 ... 40 ...

It had been a day of searching. For hours he had been wandering in that warren, that complex maze within a maze within the city. He had scoured the passageways and alleys, but no matter how many times he retraced his steps, no matter the checks and double checks at each twist, each corner, each intersection of passages, he could not find again that low-arched entrance and the small courtyard within with the high walls and the house with the creeping ivy on its facing wall.

He was about to give up. Emerging from yet another alley into another street, and following this then taking the first turning he came to, he had found himself back in the street in which his hotel was situated. He could do no more. This was the fourth, or was it fifth? time he had arrived back here, and each time he had plunged back into the labyrinth via the entrance by which he had first been led last night. Each time he had chased a little more wildly through, to find himself, eventually, emerging at some new or perhaps familiar location.

He would return to the hotel, for what else was there to do? It seemed he was to be denied even this one last act.

In a dream, a slow delirium, he made his way along the pavement. It no longer snowed, though it had hardly ceased all day. It lay thickly and strangely over the street, largely undisturbed. In his pocket, with one hand, Adam fingered the gun. In the other he held the bear and the mysterious booklet and crumpled note, his only evidence that last night's phenomena had at least been not wholly a dream. He might have passed without noticing the figure approaching from the opposite direction had he not raised his head to glance one last time into the narrow passage as he walked by. The man also glanced up as they met, not with surprise but with recognition, and stepped back a pace. They faced each other at the entrance to the labyrinth.

'You!' Adam was at first too surprised for coherent response. This that he had been searching for had become the last thing he had expected to find. Now with his resignation, his ceasing to search, it was present. He faltered, then, recollecting his purpose, drew the revolver from his coat.

The man showed no alarm. He smiled, but a certain reproach came into his eyes and he shook his head slightly as Adam, trembling, levelled the gun at him. 'No,' he said gently. 'That's not the way. That's never the way. You know that.'

He raised an open hand as if to take the weapon. 'This is not the answer.'

'Back!' Adam warned.

'You have the future,' the man said.

'There is no future.'

'There is a future, and you are part of it. You *know*. You make it.'

Adam shook his head. The man had lowered his hand. He was no longer smiling, and though there was a sternness in his voice and expression, there was also calm reassurance. He showed no fear. He seemed to be waiting as Adam, torn between conflicting impulses, felt the tension gradually discharge itself from his body. His arms relaxed. The gun slipped, then fell to the ground.

From behind him came a sound that made him freeze. A snuffling sound, barely heard at first, then something louder. He spun around. At the corner of the street from which he had just come stood a figure. More precisely, two figures, moulded as he had come to associate them, into one. They stood out against the blank wall of a building behind: the compact muscular figure of his former neighbour, and heaving on the chain he held, the great hound that was his pet.

It was the animal he had heard. Now it whined excitedly, and then abruptly began baying, a deep sound of mournful triumph that was intermittently strangled as it strained the harder against its constricting chain.

They stared at each other along the length of the reddened pavement. Then the Slav, in a movement that was brief and terrifying, slipped a hand to the dog's neck, staggering a little as the animal lunged again, and unhasped the steel chain from the collar.

The dog leapt free. It skidded wildly as its forepaws came down in the snow, and twisted its head in all directions, confused by its liberty. It gave a last glance back at its master, then focussed on Adam, hesitating for a moment and raising its ears. Then with a renewed baying, as if suddenly cognizant of something, it bounded forward.

Its motion seemed slowed and clumsy through the thick snow, yet it took no time to reach him. Only feet separated them when it leapt, gobbets of foam flying from its jaws.

Its flight lasted less than a second, but in that time Adam stared again into its eyes and into its history, into its madness and the long, painful unfolding of its existence. And he saw, with a shock that thrilled and numbed him, something he had not seen before. Perhaps it had not been there to see, or perhaps he had been blind to it. Something had changed now, within him or within the animal, or both. It gave him an access, an overwhelming impression of the sheer necessity and inescapability of it all, as if everything had been made for, brought towards, driven to, this moment. He understood suddenly that nothing was lost and nothing destroyed; there was the possibility of beauty, but always there would be perceived its opposite, ugliness and pain; there could be trust, and with it hope, balanced against uncertainty; there could be meaning, extracted from chaos only through the striving to know that chaos; there could be love, but there must be conflict. And there was God, in and throughout an infinity that was not yet ours to understand.

He saw this, and he saw that there had been a choice which he had been on the verge of denying. He had searched and found and not recognized. All things had changed and yet the world remained the same until he perceived it. It was within him to see, and he had preferred abandonment. He had turned around to re-enter the cave rather than accept the responsibility that such perception conferred.

Now the beast was upon him.

It hit him with its full weight, bowling him over into the snow. As he fell something glinted at its neck, and grasping the great head he glimpsed the steel plaque on the collar, and engraved upon it the name, *Kali-yuga*. He rolled with it as he hit the ground and came up into a kneeling position. The dog was all over him, its paws bearing down on his shoulders, its great muzzle at his face, slobbering and whimpering. He wrestled it and hugged it and laughed, 'I told you! I told you!'

He glanced back over the animal's shoulder to where its former master still stood, his hands on his wide hips, watching. The Slav nodded in acknowledgement. He raised a hand in a brief salute and turned and walked away, was quickly obscured by the wall of the corner building.

Now Adam climbed to his feet as the dog's initial excitement abated. Still clutching its head and stroking the coarse hair he turned to face the man in the white suit. But there was no longer anyone standing there. In the place he had occupied, as Adam stared, there now appeared something else, indistinct and without form, a haze, a whiteness that hung in the air in front of him. He blinked to clear his vision but the whiteness persisted, and as he watched began to shimmer, growing brighter. Then he thought he saw something shift within it.

Gradually he began to discern a form within the brilliance. It was that of a child, an infant, newborn, that gazed at him in silence with wide, questioning, innocent eyes. Tiny fingers flexed and stretched, tiny toes curled. Adam was mesmerized. The infant grew before him to become a child, watching him, alert and hopeful, looking to him for encouragement, for support, and in its features he began to discern something familiar. Before he could grasp it the child too had grown and was now a youth, a new being preparing for adulthood. And with a jolt Adam recognized his own features. He gazed in wonder at himself and saw himself gaze back.

He could hear his breathing, felt his legs growing weak. And with a further shock he saw the stark accusation in the eyes that surveyed him. Then the youth had gained adulthood and maturity. The haze, which had come to its fullest brilliance, began now slowly, barely perceptibly, to diminish. Correspondingly the figure within it continued to age. The firm straight shoulders started to sag. The hair on its head slowly thinned and greyed. The body succumbed to a stoop. Still the eyes stared back, but now with a haunting look, of warning. It dwindled. Adam faced a shrunken, enfeebled, ancient figure, its body past use though a strong light, an ageless wisdom still burned in its eyes. And it looked out and mouthed something that he did not catch before it was gone. The whiteness dissolved; he was looking through where it had been and seeing only the grey mortar of the nearest building and the soft fantastic snow around its base.

The dog's warm tongue licked his fingers and he looked down. So stunned was he by what he had witnessed that he saw nothing. He failed to hear the furied gunning of the engine, or see the cherry red Fiat that tore around a corner a little way off. In a daze he had stepped back from the pavement.

The dog, on its haunches, cocked its ears, then rose onto all fours and barked. Adam stared at it and extended a hand.

Like a charging bull with its head lowered the car caught him mid-thigh and tossed him high over its bonnet, bouncing him off the reinforced windshield as though he were no more than a rag doll. In that second, as he flew, as the earth waited to receive his body, there was a loud but muffled sound. An ugly sound, of anger and awful finality that sent a shockwave through the narrow confines of the street. He was blown apart before he touched the ground, fragments of blood, bone and gristle scattering wide and spattering the walls and windows of the nearest buildings.

Yes.

And his blood and guts mingled with the red, red snow.

Aftermath

'"And what of 'I'?", you may ask.
'"What part does 'I' play in all of this?"
'Ah, well that is something that still remains
to be seen.'

Iddio E. Scompiglio.

With a sigh the Deputy D-G slumped back on his seat and cast a haggard look at his colleagues.

'It's over.'

The day, unquestionably, had been fraught for all three. Asprey chewed his lip in cigarless agitation and gazed for some time at the silently flashing message on the terminal display: TERM. AND DEST. EFFECTED. CONFIRMED. NO SUBSEQUENT DATA. THANK YOU.

He heaved himself erect and moved away to his seat. 'Thanks be,' he muttered. Then, 'But what on Earth was the last-minute panic about? Did Six really have to intervene? He could have killed himself. In fact, for all we know he may have done just that.'

'He didn't know,' Mackelvoye said, shaking his head. 'I've only just realized it myself. Nobody told him – about the sixty-second delay. He thought the device had failed so he tried to run him down with the car.'

His eyes were on the printout of the penultimate message which had come through in the last twenty-five seconds of the countdown. NON-OPERATIONAL, it read. EMPLOYING MANUAL.

'Well, I hope he's all right. He gave me a bit of a turn.' He buttoned his collar and tightened his tie, then pushed his feet back into their soft pigskins. 'Anyway, all's well that ends well, eh? At least we've got it out of the way. Well, it's the country for me now. I wish you both a jolly good evening.'

He rose, gathered his papers and strode to the electronically sealed door. 'Oh,' he called back over his shoulder as he punched his code and the door slid open, 'and a Merry Christmas.'

*　*　*

Mackelvoye began disconnecting his terminals and packing them with the micro back into its case. 'You're quiet, Theodore. Anything the matter?'

The psychiatrist twitched slightly and behind his thick glasses he raised his enlarged melancholy orbs. 'No, nothing in particular,' he said, with a feeble attempt at irony, adding, 'I have just witnessed the death of my child, that is all.'

Mackelvoye nodded. He closed the lid of his case and snapped shut the catches. He locked it, then re-attached the chain to his wrist. 'Anything lined up? For the holiday, I mean?'

'Oh, yes. I have a little diversion arranged.'

'Good. Good. Well, I'd best be away.' He hesitated. 'Don't brood too deeply, Theodore. I understand how you must feel. It's a bitter blow for us all, but there really was no other way. You know that.'

'Yes, I do know that,' the doctor said. 'I know it perfectly well. There was really nothing else that anyone could have done. Nevertheless, it is painful to contemplate what I have lost.'

It was late that evening, following the midnight carol service at the Abbey, that Doctor Geld, his head abrim with the day's events and aburst with the news he had been in receipt of only minutes after parting with Mackelvoye, made his way thoughtfully through the cold streets in the general direction of Victoria. Of course, what had happened was really to his advantage. It obviated a major difficulty. But his thoughts were converging upon a decisive conclusion: that Fate had somehow intervened this afternoon; that something other than his own cerebral machinations had played a definitive role.

The report that had reached him on his return to his office detailed an incident at his private hospital that afternoon. A female patient, recently admitted, had exhibited sudden violent tendencies towards another inmate, a former artist named Rogelio Ramon Reyero. When staff had intervened she had turned on them and as a result had been transferred upstairs under sedation to the security wing. The attendant who had escorted her there had, after handing her over, for some reason taken it into his head to explore the wing. In doing so he had discovered, in an isolation ward quite remote from the others, a patient for whom he knew of no admittance papers or diagnostic charts.

The facts were that such papers did exist, but more importantly this member of staff should not have had access to that particular area of the hospital. Nor did he have the authority to be in possession of the keys which permitted him to enter the isolation ward. No doubt the blame lay legitimately on severe short-staffing and overwork, but the consequences laid the ground for a dramatic overhaul of staffing procedures.

In a show of diligence the attendant had taken himself off to Registry with the aim of identifying the patient. Unhappily, in doing so he had neglected to lock not only the door of the isolation ward, but that of the security wing itself. The result, within minutes, was pandemonium. And within that moment, as the criminally insane ran free in the grounds, the inmate of the isolation ward, a Mr Ernest Turner, had escaped.

That he was conscious of what he did was improbable. That he was even capable of walking came as a surprise to Geld. But that in his stupefied state he should have successfully navigated his way through the hospital maze, through the grounds and out into the surrounding countryside, was nothing short of a minor miracle. Nevertheless, he had. He had covered a distance of some two miles and reached the outskirts of a nearby village before wandering into the path of an oncoming international transporter.

The distraught driver, a Belgian, insisted that the man had stepped into the road without warning. Witnesses backed up his statement, and others had since reported seeing the old gentleman wambling along nearby lanes before the accident. So it was unlikely anyone would be held personally to account, but the hospital would be obliged to furnish a full report.

'But what does it mean?' Doctor Geld muttered to himself. 'What does it all mean?'

His steps had not been aimless. Turning away from the better-populated areas he had, after a few minutes, arrived at a narrow slanting street, half-dark and brick-paved. About midway along this he halted at a doorway of varnished oak. Pressing the entrance buzzer he self-consciously raised and rotated his head a few degrees, the better to present himself to the overhead video-scanner. He jumped slightly at the answering buzz, nervously smoothed his coat, then put his hand to the door and pushed.

He passed through the tiny vestibule within and stepped into the reception area. Behind her desk the pretty young thing – the very same pretty young thing that had greeted him on his first visit – looked up from her telephones and screen and smiled. 'Good evening, Mr Fowler. How are you?'

With a grin he approached her.

'Everything has been arranged.' She gave a discreet glance to his membership credentials and handed him a golden key. 'As you requested. Here is the key to your room. William will show you the way. We hope everything is to your satisfaction. Should you need anything at all don't hesitate to use the intercom. *William!*'

From nowhere William glided to his side. Doctor Geld accepted the proffered key and followed the tall figure up the wide staircase.

Thank God for Society!

He mounted the soft carpeted stairs.

With time all is forgotten, all forgiven. Anything is possible. There are no grudges, and no one to judge you. It is a veritable Earthly paradise – for those who have the means. Here in Society, and now in his hour of need, Doctor Geld was guaranteed that which he so craved to soothe his savaged breast. It gave him heart.

At the head of the staircase William led right, and the psychiatrist was tempted for a second to go left, to view again those fleshly delights that had teased his vision so fleetingly on the night of his first call. But all in good time. Later would do. It would provide a relaxing *après-diner* to his prearranged first course. The night was his, he reminded himself, and tagged along with William.

Revellers passed in varying states of intoxication and undress. A couple crawled in pursuit of a rolling magnum of Möet towards an open door. The establishment had been lavishly decorated in keeping with the season. The doctor passed his eyes briefly about the walls; he recalled the magnificent tree positioned at the bottom of the stairs.

William halted at a closed door. 'Here we are, sir. I'll leave you. If you need anything, please call.'

'Thank you, William,' Geld said, and William glided away.

The doctor toyed abstractedly with the key in his hand, weighing over all he had learned, considering its implications. It seemed extraordinary. It *was* extraordinary.

'Gard is dead,' he murmured beneath his breath. He shook his large head. It was a profound and moving statement, precluding antiphony by its sweeping nature, so he said it again, 'Gard is dead.'

He stretched his lips across his teeth. Judith remained to be dealt with, of course. And Nevus, though his disposal would create minimal inconvenience, if any. All in all the doctor was optimistic, but saddened. It was a tragedy, an immense loss. And such a blow, to have ... *but no*! This was not the time to immerse himself in pity or regret. This was a time to dismiss dilemmas, the drudgeries and disappointments of the working day, in favour of leisurely pursuit! He was here for distraction, for the delights Society afforded its members. Without another thought he inserted the golden key in the lock and pushed open his door.

The room he entered was spacious and plushly furnished with twin chaises-longues, drapes, a dressing table, mirrored walls and ceiling, and the crowning glory, a luxurious king-sized bed. A drinks cabinet occupied a niche nearby, and he had been discreetly informed that other intoxicants, unavailable for open display, were his upon request. He only had to call.

Soft music played. There was a wide-screen television at the foot of the bed, with video and camcorder, plus a selection of blank and pre-recorded video cassettes.

The room had two occupants, one of each gender. They reclined on the bed. Doctor Geld quickly ran his eyes over their slender bodies. They were delightfully attired, he noted. Quite according to his specifications. They watched him in silence as he unwound his scarf and removed his coat and hung them up.

He turned, donning his most endearing and avuncular grin as he approached the couple on the bed. Tomorrow there would be time to attend to life's problems. Tomorrow the world would be a different place. But tonight, tonight was for dreams, for fulfilment, the forgetting of all else in the name of pleasure. Tonight was his. His alone.

'Hello, children,' he said.

* * *

The little red car sped like a devil between Europe's barren fields. Helmut Wasser, secure in himself, sang loudly with the 'Dies Irae' from Verdi's great Requiem. The sound filled the armoured bubble he drove, drowning all aural intrusion from the world outside.

He was a changed man, a new man, and he was on his way home. He, like his old friend, the late Adam Shatt, had found something he had long been searching for in the city that now fell away at his back. He had found fulfilment in an end of something – and more, in a series of endings – and everything had become very clear. Everything had converged to reveal to him the reasons for his being where he was. He was free of conscience or guilt; reassured in his convictions; elected to pursue a chosen course. He had no doubt. Everything was just hunky-dory. He was a man of the future, bent on his mission. It was all quite plain, quite self-evident.

In The Age of Unreason, The Time of the Psychopath, Anything Goes – for those who can keep themselves at bay.

World (with end)

Almost darkness,
I, alone in this doomed room,
Stare out
Through transparent wall fixture,
At endless empty grey no matter world,
Wondering.

And wait,
Like forgotten pet in glass jam-jar,
Dreaming that destiny, yours and mine,
May meet.
One day.

I question,
Eyes raised to sky.
Being seeking,
And jagged soul beseeching.
While the question, spoken or unuttered,
Is unanswered:

'Oh God, what are we in this vastness, this treacherous void?
Where is there something to hold onto?'

. . .

Helmut Wasser

Winter 19--
(DARK NIGHT is a UNIVERSITY OF LIFE novel.
Also published: THE GREAT PERVADER.
To come: THE SEARCH FOR IDDIO, in which
questions are answered and secrets revealed.)

APPENDIX
The Simile of the Cave

This is a more graphic presentation of the truths presented in the analogy of the Line; in particular, it tells us more about the two states of mind called in the Line analogy Belief and Illusion. We are shown the ascent of the mind from illusion to pure philosophy, and the difficulties which accompany its progress. And the philosopher, when he has achieved the supreme vision, is required to return to the cave and serve his fellows, his very unwillingness to do so being his chief qualification.

As Cornford pointed out, the best way to understand the simile is to replace 'the clumsier apparatus' of the cave by the cinema, though today television is an even better comparison. It is the moral and intellectual condition of the average man from which Plato starts; and though clearly the ordinary man knows the difference between substance and shadow in the physical world, the simile suggests that his moral and intellectual opinions often bear as little relation to the truth as the average film or television programme does to real life.

'I want you to go on to picture the enlightenment or ignorance of our human condition somewhat as follows. Imagine an underground chamber like a cave, with a long entrance open to the daylight and as wide as the cave. In this chamber are men who have been prisoners there since they were children, their legs and necks being so fastened that they can only look straight ahead of them and cannot turn their heads. Some way off, behind and higher up, a fire is burning, and between the fire and the prisoners and above them runs a road, in front of which a curtain-wall has been built, like the screen at puppet shows between the operators and their audience, above which they show their puppets.'

'I see.'

'Imagine further that there are men carrying all sorts of gear along behind the curtain-wall, projecting above it and including figures of men and animals made of wood and stone and all sorts of other materials, and that some of these men, as you would expect, are talking and some not.'

'An odd picture and an odd sort of prisoner.'

'They are drawn from life,'[1] I replied. 'For, tell me, do you think our prisoners could see anything of themselves or their fellows except the shadows thrown by the fire on the wall of the cave opposite them?'

'How could they see anything else if they were prevented from moving their heads all their lives?'

'And would they see anything more of the objects carried along the road?'

'Of course not.'

'Then if they were able to talk to each other, would they not assume that the shadows they saw were the real things?'

'Inevitably.'

'And if the wall of their prison opposite them reflected sound, don't you think that they would suppose, whenever one of the passers-by on the road spoke, that the voice belonged to the shadow passing before them?'

'They would be bound to think so.'

'And so in every way they would believe that the shadows of the objects we mentioned were the whole truth.'[2]

'Yes, inevitably.'

'Then think what would naturally happen to them if they were released from their bonds and cured of their delusions. Suppose one of them were let loose, and suddenly compelled to stand up and turn his head and look and walk towards the fire; all these actions would be painful and he would be too dazzled to see properly the objects of which he used to see the shadows. What

[1] Lit: 'like us'. How 'like' has been a matter of controversy. Plato can hardly have meant that the ordinary man cannot distinguish between shadows and real things. But he does seem to be saying, with a touch of caricature (we must not take him too solemnly), that the ordinary man is often very uncritical in his beliefs, which are little more than a 'careless acceptance of appearances' (Crombie).

[2] Lit: 'regard nothing else as true but the shadows'. The Greek word *alēthēs* (true) carries an implication of genuineness, and some translators render it here as 'real'.

do you think he would say if he was told that what he used to see was so much empty nonsense and that he was now nearer reality and seeing more correctly, because he was turned towards objects that were more real, and if on top of that he were compelled to say what each of the passing objects was when it was pointed out to him? Don't you think he would be at a loss, and think that what he used to see was far truer[3] than the objects now being pointed out to him?'

'Yes, far truer.'

'And if he were made to look directly at the light of the fire, it would hurt his eyes and he would turn back and retreat to the things which he could see properly, which he would think really clearer than the things being shown him.'

'Yes.'

'And if,' I went on, 'he were forcibly dragged up the steep and rugged ascent and not let go till he had been dragged out into the sunlight, the process would be a painful one, to which he would much object, and when he emerged into the light his eyes would be so dazzled by the glare of it that he wouldn't be able to see a single one of the things he was now told were real.'[4]

'Certainly not at first,' he agreed.

'Because, of course, he would need to grow accustomed to the light before he could see things in the upper world outside the cave. First he would find it easiest to look at shadows, next at the reflections of men and other objects in water, and later on at the objects themselves. After that he would find it easier to observe the heavenly bodies and the sky itself at night, and to look at the light of the moon and stars rather than at the sun and its light by day.'

'Of course.'

'The thing he would be able to do last would be to look directly at the sun itself, and gaze at it without using reflections in water or any other medium, but as it is in itself.'

'That must come last.'

'Later on he would come to the conclusion that it is the sun that produces the changing seasons and years and controls

[3] Or 'more real'.
[4] Or 'true', 'genuine'.

everything in the visible world, and is in a sense responsible for everything that he and his fellow-prisoners used to see.'

'That is the conclusion which he would obviously reach.'

'And when he thought of his first home and what passed for wisdom there, and of his fellow-prisoners, don't you think he would congratulate himself on his good fortune and be sorry for them?'

'Very much so.'

'There was probably a certain amount of honour and glory to be won among the prisoners, and prizes for keensightedness for those best able to remember the order of sequence among the passing shadows and so be best able to divine their future appearances. Will our released prisoner hanker after these prizes or envy this power or honour? Won't he be more likely to feel, as Homer says, that he would far rather be "a serf in the house of some landless man",[5] or indeed anything else in the world, than hold the opinions and live the life that they do?'

'Yes,' he replied, 'he would prefer anything to a life like theirs.'

'Then what do you think would happen,' I asked, 'if he went back to sit in his old seat in the cave? Wouldn't his eyes be blinded by the darkness, because he had come in suddenly out of the sunlight?'

'Certainly.'

'And if he had to discriminate between the shadows, in competition with the other prisoners, while he was still blinded and before his eyes got used to the darkness – a process that would take some time – wouldn't he be likely to make a fool of himself? And they would say that his visit to the upper world had ruined his sight, and that the ascent was not worth even attempting. And if anyone tried to release them and lead them up, they would kill him if they could lay hands on him.'

'They certainly would.'

'Now, my dear Glaucon,' I went on, 'this simile must be connected throughout with what preceded it.[6] The realm revealed

---

[5] *Odyssey*, XI, 489.

[6] I.e. The similes of the Sun and the Line (though pp. 267-76 must surely also be referred to). The detailed relations between the three similes have been much disputed, as has the meaning of the word here translated 'connected'. Some interpret it to mean a detailed correspondence ('every feature . . . is meant to fit' –

by sight corresponds to the prison, and the light of the fire in the prison to the power of the sun. And you won't go wrong if you connect the ascent into the upper world and the sight of the objects there with the upward progress of the mind into the intelligible region. That at any rate is my interpretation, which is what you are anxious to hear; the truth of the matter is, after all, known only to God. But in my opinion, for what it is worth, the final thing to be perceived in the intelligible region, and perceived only with difficulty, is the form of the good; once seen, it is inferred to be responsible for whatever is right and valuable in anything, producing in the visible region light and the source of light, and being in the intelligible region itself controlling source of truth and intelligence. And anyone who is going to act rationally either in public or private life must have sight of it.'

'I agree,' he said, 'so far as I am able to understand you.'

'Then you will perhaps also agree with me that it won't be surprising if those who get so far are unwilling to involve themselves in human affairs, and if their minds long to remain in the realm above. That's what we should expect if our simile holds good again.'

'Yes, that's to be expected.'

'Nor will you think it strange that anyone who descends from contemplation of the divine to human life and its ills should blunder and make a fool of himself, if, while still blinded and

---

Cornford), others to mean, more loosely, 'attached' or 'linked to'. That Plato intended some degree of 'connection' between the three similes cannot be in doubt in view of the sentences which follow. But we should remember that they are similes, not scientific descriptions, and it would be a mistake to try to find too much detailed precision. Plato has just spoken of the prisoners 'getting their hands' on their returned fellow and killing him. How could they do that if fettered as described at the opening of the simile (p. 317)? But Socrates was executed, so of course they must.

This translation assumes the following main correspondences:

Tied prisoner in the cave	Illusion
Freed prisoner in the cave	Belief
Looking at shadows and reflections in the world outside the cave and the ascent thereto	Reason
Looking at real things in the world outside the cave	Intelligence
Looking at the sun	Vision of the form of the good.

unaccustomed to the surrounding darkness, he's forcibly put on trial in the law-courts or elsewhere about the shadows of justice or the figures of which they are shadows, and made to dispute about the notions of them held by men who have never seen justice itself.'

'There's nothing strange in that.'

'But anyone with any sense,' I said, 'will remember that the eyes may be unsighted in two ways, by a transition either from light to darkness or from darkness to light, and will recognize that the same thing applies to the mind. So when he sees a mind confused and unable to see clearly he will not laugh without thinking, but will ask himself whether it has come from a clearer world and is confused by the unaccustomed darkness, or whether it is dazzled by the stronger light of the clearer world to which it has escaped from its previous ignorance. The first condition of life is a reason for congratulation, the second for sympathy, though if one wants to laugh at it one can do so with less absurdity than at the mind that has descended from the daylight of the upper world.'

'You put it very reasonably.'

'If this is true,' I continued, 'we must reject the conception of education professed by those who say that they can put into the mind knowledge that was not there before – rather as if they could put sight into blind eyes.'

'It is a claim that is certainly made,' he said.

'But our argument indicates that the capacity for knowledge is innate in each man's mind, and that the organ by which he learns is like an eye which cannot be turned from darkness to light unless the whole body is turned; in the same way the mind as a whole must be turned away from the world of change until its eye can bear to look straight at reality, and at the brightest of all realities which is what we call the good. Isn't that so?'

'Yes.'

'Then this turning around of the mind itself might be made a subject of professional skill,[7] which would effect the conversion as easily and effectively as possible. It would not be concerned to implant sight, but to ensure that someone who had it already was

[7] *Technē.*

not either turned in the wrong direction or looking the wrong way.'

'That may well be so.'

'The rest, therefore, of what are commonly called excellences[8] of the mind perhaps resemble those of the body, in that they are not in fact innate, but are implanted by subsequent training and practice; but knowledge, it seems, must surely have a diviner quality, something which never loses its power, but whose effects are useful and salutary or again useless and harmful according to the direction in which it is turned. Have you never noticed how shrewd is the glance of the type of men commonly called bad but clever? They have small minds, but their sight is sharp and piercing enough in matters that concern them; it's not that their sight is weak, but that they are forced to serve evil, so that the keener their sight the more effective that evil is.'

'That's true.'

'But suppose,' I said, 'that such natures were cut loose, when they were still children, from all the dead weights natural to this world of change and fastened on them by sensual indulgences like gluttony, which twist their minds' vision to lower things, and suppose that when so freed they were turned towards the truth, then this same part of these same individuals would have as keen a vision of truth as it has of the objects on which it is at present turned.'

'Very likely.'

'And is it not also likely, and indeed a necessary consequence of what we have said, that society will never be properly governed either by the uneducated, who have no knowledge of the truth, or by those who are allowed to spend all their lives in purely intellectual pursuits? The uneducated have no single aim in life to which all their actions, public and private, are to be directed; the intellectuals will take no practical action of their own accord, fancying themselves to be out of this world in some kind of earthly paradise.'

'True.'

'Then our job as lawgivers is to compel the best minds to attain what we have called the highest form of knowledge, and to

8 *Aretē.*

ascend to the vision of the good as we have described, and when they have achieved this and see well enough, prevent them behaving as they are now allowed to.'

'What do you mean by that?'

'Remaining in the upper world, and refusing to return again to the prisoners in the cave below and share their labours and rewards, whether trivial or serious.'

'But surely,' he protested, 'that will not be fair. We shall be compelling them to live a poorer life than they might live.'

'The object of our legislation,' I reminded him again, 'is not the special welfare of any particular class in our society, but of the society as a whole; and it uses persuasion or compulsion to unite all citizens and make them share together the benefits which each individually can confer on the community; and its purpose in fostering this attitude is not to leave everyone to please himself, but to make each man a link in the unity of the whole.'

'You are right; I had forgotten,' he said.

'You see, then, Glaucon,' I went on, 'we shan't be unfair to our philosophers, but shall be quite fair in what we say when we compel them to have some care and responsibility for others. We shall tell them that philosophers born in other states can reasonably refuse to take part in the hard work of politics; for society produces them quite involuntarily and unintentionally, and it is only just that anything that grows up on its own should feel it has nothing to repay for an upbringing which it owes to no one. "But," we shall say, "we have bred you both for your own sake and that of the whole community to act as leaders and king-bees in a hive; you are better and more fully educated than the rest and better qualified to combine the practice of philosophy and politics. You must therefore each descend in turn and live with your fellows in the cave and get used to seeing in the dark; once you get used to it you will see a thousand times better than they do and will distinguish the various shadows, and know what they are shadows of, because you have seen the truth about things admirable and just and good. And so our state and yours will be really awake, and not merely dreaming like most societies today, with their shadow battles and their struggles for political power, which they treat as some great prize. The truth is quite different: the state whose prospective rulers come to their duties with least enthusiasm is bound to have the best and most tranquil government, and the state whose rulers are eager to rule the worst."'

'I quite agree.'

'Then will our pupils, when they hear what we say, dissent and refuse to take their share of the hard work of government, even though spending the greater part of their time together in the pure air above?'

'They cannot refuse, for we are making a just demand of just men. But of course, unlike present rulers, they will approach the business of government as an unavoidable necessity.'

'Yes, of course,' I agreed. 'The truth is that if you want a well-governed state to be possible, you must find for your future rulers some way of life they like better than government; for only then will you have government by the truly rich, those, that is, whose riches consist not of gold, but of the true happiness of a good and rational life. If you get, in public affairs, men whose life is impoverished and destitute of personal satisfactions, but who hope to snatch some compensation for their own inadequacy from a political career, there can never be good government. They start fighting for power, and the consequent internal and domestic conflicts ruin both them and society.'

'True indeed.'

'Is there any life except that of true philosophy which looks down on positions of political power?'

'None whatever.'

'But what we need is that the only men to get power should be men who do not love it, otherwise we shall have rivals' quarrels.'

'That is certain.'

'Who else, then, will you compel to undertake the responsibilities of Guardians of our state, if it is not to be those who know most about the principles of good government and who have other rewards and a better life than the politician's?'

'There is no one else.'

From PLATO: THE REPUBLIC, translated by Desmond Lee (Penguin Classics, 1955, 1974, 1987.) Copyright © H.D.P. Lee 1955, 1974, 1987.